A CUT ABOVE

Lam moved cautiously through a patch of grass and weeds toward the guard. The soldier had his rifle across his chest, his arms folded over it and his head lolled back against the side of the house. He was sleeping. Lam drew his KA-BAR knife, with its six-inch honed sharp blade, and slid forward on his belly another five feet, then lifted up and with silent steps rushed the guard.

Lam held the knife straight out in front of him like a sword, driving it into the guard's chest between his ribs and through the side of his heart. The guard came awake, his eyes went wide, he tried to call out, but Lam's hand had clamped over his mouth. Lam stared at the soldier as his body's vital functions began shutting down, then his head slumped to one side and he slid to the ground, dead . . .

Titles by Keith Douglass

THE SEAL TEAM SERIES

THE CARRIER SERIES

SEAL TEAM SEVEN
UNDER SIEGE

KEITH DOUGLASS

BERKLEY BOOKS, NEW YORK

THE BERKLEY PUBLISHING GROUP
Published by the Penguin Group
Penguin Group (USA) Inc.
375 Hudson Street, New York, New York 10014, USA
Penguin Group (Canada), 10 Alcorn Avenue, Toronto, Ontario M4V 3B2, Canada
(a division of Pearson Penguin Canada Inc.)
Penguin Books Ltd., 80 Strand, London WC2R 0RL, England
Penguin Group Ireland, 25 St. Stephen's Green, Dublin 2, Ireland (a division of Penguin Books Ltd.)
Penguin Group (Australia), 250 Camberwell Road, Camberwell, Victoria 3124, Australia
(a division of Pearson Australia Group Pty. Ltd.)
Penguin Books India Pvt. Ltd., 11 Community Centre, Panchsheel Park, New Delhi—110 017, India
Penguin Group (NZ), Cnr. Airborne and Rosedale Roads, Albany, Auckland 1310, New Zealand
(a division of Pearson New Zealand Ltd.)
Penguin Books (South Africa) (Pty.) Ltd., 24 Sturdee Avenue, Rosebank, Johannesburg 2196, South Africa

Penguin Books Ltd., Registered Offices: 80 Strand, London WC2R 0RL, England

Special thanks to Chet Cunningham for his contributions to this book.
www.chetcunningham.com

This is a work of fiction. Names, characters, places, and incidents either are the product of the author's imagination or are used fictitiously, and any resemblance to actual persons, living or dead, business establishments, events, or locales is entirely coincidental.

SEAL TEAM SEVEN: UNDER SIEGE

A Berkley Book / published by arrangement with the author

PRINTING HISTORY
Berkley mass-market edition / May 2005

Copyright © 2005 by The Berkley Publishing Group.
SEAL TEAM SEVEN logo illustration by Michael Racz.

ISBN: 0-425-20287-9

BERKLEY®
Berkley Books are published by The Berkley Publishing Group,
a division of Penguin Group (USA) Inc.,
375 Hudson Street, New York, New York 10014.
BERKLEY is a registered trademark of Penguin Group (USA) Inc.
The "B" design is a trademark belonging to Penguin Group (USA) Inc.

PRINTED IN THE UNITED STATES OF AMERICA

10 9 8 7 6 5 4 3 2 1

Dedicated
to the real members of
SEAL Team Seven based
at NAVSPECWARGRUP-ONE
in Coronado, California.
The fictional SEALs in these books
get to do everything the real SEAL Team Seven
wished that it could.

SEAL TEAM SEVEN

Rear Admiral (L) Richard Kenner. Commander of All SEALs. Based in Little Creek, Virginia.

Captain Harry L. Arjarack. Commanding Officer of NAVSPECWARGRUP-ONE, in Coronado, California. 51.

Commander Dean Masciareli. Commanding Officer of NAVY SPECIAL WARFARE GROUP ONE's SEAL Team Seven in Coronado, California. 47, 5' 11", 220 pounds. Annapolis graduate.

Master Chief Petty Officer Gordon MacKenzie. Administrator and head enlisted man of all of SEAL Teams in Coronado. 47, 5' 10", 180 pounds.

Lieutenant Commander Blake Murdock. Platoon Leader, Third Platoon. 32, 6' 2", 210 pounds. Annapolis graduate. Six years in SEALs. Father an important Congressman from Virginia. Murdock has a condo in La Jolla. Owns a car and a motorcycle. Loves to fish. Weapon: Alliant Bull Pup duo 5.56mm & 20mm. Speaks Arabic.

ALPHA SQUAD

Elmer Neal. Senior Chief Petty Officer. Top EM in platoon and third in command. 34, 6' 1", 200 pounds. Divorced. Fifteen years in Navy, four in SEALs. Expert chess player and good bowler. A buzz cut on his hair. Weapon: Alliant Bull Pup duo 5.56mm & 20mm with air-burst round. Speaks German and French.

---

*Third Platoon assigned exclusively to the Central Intelligence Agency to perform any needed tasks on a covert basis anywhere in the world. All are top-secret assignments. Goes around Navy chain of command. Direct orders from the CIA and the CNO.

David "Jaybird" Sterling. Machinist Mate First Class. Lead petty officer. 24, 5' 10", 170 pounds. Quick mind, fine tactician. Single. Drinks too much sometimes. Crack shot with all arms. Grew up in Oregon. Helps plan attack operations. Weapon: H & K MP-5SD submachine gun.

Luke "Mountain" Howard. Gunner's Mate Second Class. 28, 6' 4", 250 pounds. Black man. Football at Oregon State. Tryout with Oakland Raiders six years ago. In Navy six years, SEAL for four. Single. Rides a motorcycle. A skiing and wind surfing nut. Squad sniper. Weapon H & K PSG1 7.62 NATO sniper rifle.

Bill Bradford. Quartermaster First Class. 24, 6' 2", 215 pounds. An artist in spare time. Paints oils. He sells his marine paintings. Single. Quiet. Reads a lot. Has two years of college. Platoon radio operator. Carries a SATCOM on most missions. Weapon: Alliant Bull Pup duo 5.56mm & 20mm explosive round. Speaks Italian and some Arabic.

Joe "Ricochet" Lampedusa. Operations Specialist First Class. 21, 5' 11", 175 pounds. Good tracker, quick thinker. Had a year of college. Loves motorcycles. Wants a Hog. Pot smoker on the sly. Picks up plain girls. Platoon scout. Weapon: Colt M-4A1 with grenade launcher, alternate Bull Pup duo 5.56mm & 20mm explosive round.

Kenneth Ching. Quartermaster First Class. 25, 6' even, 180 pounds. Full blooded Chinese. Platoon translator. Speaks Mandarin Chinese, Japanese, Russian, and Spanish. Bicycling nut. Paid $1,200 for off-road bike. Is trying for Officer Candidate School. Weapon: H & K MP-5SD submachine gun.

Vincent "Vinnie" Van Dyke. Electrician's Mate Second Class. 24, 6' 2", 220 pounds. Enlisted out of high school. Played varsity basketball. Wants to be a commercial fisherman after his current hitch. Good with his hands. Squad machine gunner. Weapon: H & K 21-E 7.62 NATO round machine gun. Speaks Dutch, German, and some Arabic.

Bravo Squad

Lieutenant (J.G.) Christopher "Chris" Gardner. Squad Leader Bravo Squad. Second in Command of the platoon. 28, 6' 4", 240 pounds. From Seattle. Four years in SEALs. Hang glider nut. Married to Wanda, a clothing designer. No kids. Annapolis graduate. Father is a Navy rear admiral. Grew up in ten different states. Weapon: Alliant Bull Pup duo 5.56mm & 20mm explosive round. Alternate: H & K G-11 submachine gun.

George "Petard" Canzoneri. Torpedoman's Mate First class, 27, 5' 11", 190 pounds. Married to Navy wife Phyllis. No kids. Nine years in Navy. Expert on explosives. Nicknamed "Petard" for almost hoisting himself one time. Top pick in platoon for explosives work. Weapon: Alliant Bull Pup duo 5.56mm & 20mm explosive round.

Miguel Fernandez. Gunner's Mate First Class. 26, 6' 1", 180 pounds. Wife, Maria; daughter, Linda, 7, in Coronado. Spends his off time with them. Highly family oriented. He has family in San Diego. Speaks Spanish and Portuguese. Squad sniper. Weapon: H & K PSG1 7.62 NATO sniper rifle.

Omar "Ollie" Rafii. Yeoman Second Class. 24, 6' even, 180 pounds. Saudi Arabian. In U.S. since he was four. Loves horses, has two. Married, two children. Speaks perfect Farsi and Arabic. Expert with all knives. Throws killing knives with deadly accuracy. Weapon: H & K MP-5SD submachine gun.

Derek Prescott. Radioman Second Class. 23, 6' 3". Comes from a small town in Idaho. Expert marksman. On the Navy rifle team before SEALs. Played college football at University of Idaho as a tight end. Is an expert kayak man who does ocean runs when he has a chance. Unmarried. Speaks good Japanese. Weapon: H & K G-11, which fires caseless rounds.

Jack Mahanani. Hospital Corpsman First Class. 25, 6' 4", 240 pounds. Platoon medic. Tahitian/Hawaiian. Expert swimmer.

Bench-presses four hundred pounds. Divorced. Top surfer. Weapon: Alliant Bull Pup duo 5.56mm & 20mm explosive round. Alternate: Colt M-4A1 with grenade launcher.

Robert Doyle. Gunner's Mate Second Class. 23, 6' 2", 210 pounds. Single, flies fighting kites, played football in high school, is an opera buff, lives with a girl in Coronado. Went to Navy language school to learn Farsi and Arabic. Weapon: Alliant Bull Pup duo with 20mm & 5.56mm rounds.

Dexter M. Tate. Second Class Electrician's Mate. 23, 5' 11", 190 pounds. An African-American. Computer literate, loves to dive on old shipwrecks. Rides a motorcycle. Weapon: Alliant Bull Pup duo 5.56mm & 20mm lasered air-burst round.

1

North Korea

Angry black waves and nasty currents tore at the sixteen men as they swam through the frigid dark waters just off the coast of North Korea. Lieutenant Commander Blake Murdock took his turn towing the deflated IBS—Inflatable Boat Small—as they eyed the crashing waves breaking against the deserted shoreline. At least it was supposed to be deserted. He knew you could never tell about the North Koreans.

Most of the Third Platoon, SEAL Team Seven, swam underwater, where forward movement was easier. Only three SEALs were on the surface to keep the cumbersome deflated Rubber Duck angling in to the beach. The SEALs wore their cammies and combat vests. Rubber suits would have kept them warmer, but they slowed down and hampered their mission on land. They were used to going on missions in their cammies. Usually they dried out before the work was done.

"Beach patrol."

The words jolted into Murdock's earpiece and the SEALs came to a stop just outside of the breakers.

"Looks like a Jeep and two men," Lam said. Joe Lampedusa, Operations Specialist First Class, reported from his position on the surface twenty yards ahead of the others. The signal came through the SEALs' underwater/dry land Motorola personal communications radios with a range of five miles. The men below the water heard the warning and one by one came to the surface showing only their faces as they gathered around the Duck.

"Moving past," Lam said. "The driver and the one guard look bored as hell. Should be clear here in five. Suggest we charge in quickly now before he makes a return swing."

"Move it," Murdock ordered, and the SEALs surged ahead into the breakers, letting the four-foot walls of water catch them and drive them forward like water-soaked logs. One by one they washed up on the wet sand and lay there without moving. The next few waves rushed over them and receded.

Murdock; Luke Howard, Gunner's Mate Second Class; and David "Jaybird" Sterling, Machinist's Mate Second Class, shepherded the bulky Rubber Duck through the breakers and then ran with it up the open beach to a smattering of trees and brush twenty yards inland. They pushed the black bulk into the trees and broke off branches to hide it from the roving beach patrol.

By then Lieutenant (J.G.) Christopher Gardner, leader of Bravo Squad, had the rest of the SEALs prone on the beach, forming a defensive formation aimed at a small road fifty yards farther from the surf.

"Lam, is this the right beach?" Murdock asked on his mike.

"Right as rain, Commander. I have both landmarks: that small shack to the north and a pair of tall, scraggly trees to the south. A one hundred percent affirmative on the right op landing. Hold it, Commander. That Jeep rig is returning. No way they can miss us. Be here in two."

"We have to take them out," Murdock said. "How many silenced weapons do we have?"

"Four in Alpha," Jaybird said.

"Three in Bravo," Gardner reported.

"Bravo take the driver, Alpha gunners get the guard. Get ready."

They all could then hear the Jeep coming over the crash and roar of the surf. It powered down the hard wet sand just out of reach of the foaming breakers in their rush up the beach. The Jeep materialized out of the soft night air when it was fifty feet away.

"Now," Murdock said. Seven silenced weapons seemed to fire all at once with their soft chugging sounds, and then more rounds came. The first volley blasted the driver off the rig into the sand and nailed the passenger in his seat with four shots to his chest. He dropped his rifle and it spilled out of the rig onto the wet sand.

The vehicle continued on its way for twenty feet, then the softer sand on the driver's side of the rig pulled it to the side and it headed straight at the oncoming waves.

"Make sure, Jaybird," Murdock said into his mike.

Jaybird lifted up and ran to the North Korean soldier who had been driving. He kicked the silent form twice, then hurried to where the second man had fallen from the rig into the water. A moment later Jaybird ran back to the group lying in the sand.

"Splash two," he said.

"As you know, the op plans for us to move a little over two kilometers to the package," Murdock said. "Not supposed to be any NK army units in the area. So let's choggie. Bravo will take the lead in a column of ducks ten yards apart. Lam out front by a hundred. Alpha to follow in the same pattern. Howard and Jaybird are rear guard. Move it, now."

Lam jogged out to the road, turned north, and put a hundred yards between him and the lead man from Bravo. Then they settled into a short-hike mode. Murdock nodded. The men were responding well. They'd had a two-month training schedule after the last mission, and had integrated one new man into Bravo and kept the rest of the men sharp. All of their slices, burns, cuts, and bullet holes from the last mission had healed.

Murdock led out the Alpha squad behind Bravo's last

man by twenty yards. He was six-feet-two and a solid 210 pounds, with dark black hair that he had let grow longer to a businessman's cut. Half of his men had longer hair than the Navy liked, but it was tactical. If he and four men had to go undercover into some enemy land, they couldn't all have shaved heads or close-clipped "whiteside" haircuts that would pinpoint them in an instant as military men. Murdock's dark green eyes showed flecks of brown, and his rugged face held more than one scar from his work on the live-or-die missions in the SEALs. He had nearly seven years with the SEALs and no thoughts of getting into politics as his congressman father often urged him to do.

Now this small task that Don Stroh had called Quick and Easy. A typical Q&E operation. Stroh was their handler from the CIA and worked closely with the head of the CIA, Wally Covington, and the Chief of Naval Operations. Most of their assignments came directly from Stroh with the orders from the president and the CNO, which made the local NAVSPECWARGRUP-ONE big brass mad. The orders did not come through regular Navy channels.

The package they went for was code named Kimchee. He was a CIA spy who had worked North Korea for two years, but now was compromised and had to be brought out with some important information that he obtained about the production progress of the North's nuclear weapons program. He had no way to communicate the data. For two days the North Koreans knew about him and had started a search. Murdock's orders were to bring out Kimchee and his wife and two daughters. That's why they brought the rubber boat into shore.

Lam moved ahead of the SEALs like a shadow's ghost, always watching, working forward so silently not even the chirping crickets could hear him. He paused and studied the area ahead. The coastal plain had fields covered with rice stubble less than an inch off the ground. With the famine in North Korea, they were eating everything they could grow and sometimes even the leaves and bark off the trees. Two houses showed two hundred yards inland. Neither had lights on. It was just past 2200. Time for most farmers to be in bed. Lam had positioned himself near a tree at the side of the road.

"Hold it," he whispered into his mike. Ahead on the road he could just make out a military checkpoint. There were two large trucks blocking the road. He couldn't see any men until he lifted his thermal imager and scanned the area. Six white blobs showed on the black screen as the imager picked up the body heat of the soldiers. He radioed Murdock about the NK troops.

"Suggest a half mile to the left before we work on north," Lam said.

"Agreed," Murdock said. "We're moving now. Stay out of trouble up there. They must have radios. We need surprise to get the package out."

"Roger that, LC. I'm moving now. I'll wait for you to hook up with me out a half."

In his spot right behind Murdock with Alpha squad, Jaybird swore softly for two minutes. "What in hell did Stroh mean 'Quick and Easy'? This his idea? No army units in this remote area, he said. He sure as hell hit that one right in the balls. Stroh owes us another one."

Murdock chuckled as he led the men ninety degrees away from the road into the harvested rice paddies. "Charging Stroh with it is one thing, collecting is something else entirely."

Five minutes later, Lam stepped out from behind a tree and surprised J.G. Gardner. The officer lowered his weapon and shook his head.

"Damnit, Lam. I almost drilled you that time. Give me some warning before you do that."

"Sorry, J.G. From here we go directly north. I saw some flankers they had out about a hundred, so we should be okay. Still keep it as silent as yesterday's obituary."

Lam worked north, watching everything, taking nothing for granted. He paused at a road for five minutes watching it. He'd stopped the men behind him. Now he grinned and spoke into his radio mike. "Yeah, LC. We've got some heavy trucks coming this way. Hold another five and they should be here and past. They don't know we're here, so we're safe and sexy."

"Holding, Lam," Murdock said.

"Lam, that blonde you had out last week didn't mention a word about your being sexy," Jaybird said. "You putting us on?"

"Everyway but loose, oh nude one. How many buildings have you climbed drunk and naked now?"

"At ease, you two," Murdock said, his voice tone just short of a laugh. "How many trucks, Lam, and do they have troops in them?"

"Here they come: six transporters, each with about twenty men. Going, going, gone. Take five and then follow me."

Lam led them slowly over the rice paddies, down foot paths, and past a small house or two. Once they strayed too close to a building and a dog barked at them. Omar Rafii Yozman Second Class, an expert with knives, faded into the soft night air and found the dog. He used one of his throwing knives and hit the barking animal in the throat from twenty feet. The barking stopped. They continued to move and five minutes later came into the target area. It was a settlement of ten houses along the main road. All were dark except one. The small structures had roofs made of rice straw thatched a foot thick. Most of the houses were built of cheap bricks with white stucco on the outside. They had doors but no windows. Eight feet off the ground the sides had rectangular panels a foot high and two feet long. Rice paper covered the frames that could be slid open to let out the charcoal fumes.

"That one with the lights on, third one from the edge of town to the north, is our target," Lam said.

"Check it for outside guards," Murdock said.

Lam faded into the night. Murdock tried to watch him but soon gave up. The man moved like a ghost on an air cushion.

Lam came back five minutes later. "Didn't see any guards, but my guess is there are some there."

Murdock frowned. "Let's move up so we can throw rocks at the side door. We might get a reaction."

They did. Luke Howard had the best arm in the platoon. He threw egg-sized rocks at the door hitting it four times. Nothing happened. Howard threw rocks again, this time breaking one of the rice-paper windows. The side door jolted open. A Korean civilian bellowed something at them, made some angry gestures, and fired an automatic rifle haphazardly into the night. He missed everyone. He shouted again and slammed the door.

"Gotcha," Lam said. "In the splash of light from inside, I spotted a guard to the right. If there's one, there may be more. Rafii and I can take them out. Okay, LC?"

"That's a go, Lam. We're getting short on time. So any speed . . ."

Lam and Rafii vanished into the gloom. They crawled up to within twenty feet of the house and watched. Lam saw the guard again, and pointed to himself. He motioned for Rafii to go around the house the other way.

Lam moved cautiously through a patch of grass and weeds toward the guard. At fifteen feet, Lam paused near a small shrub and stared around it. The guard had his rifle across his chest, his arms folded over it, and his head lolled back against the side of the house. He was sleeping. Lam drew his KA-BAR knife, with its six-inch honed, sharp blade, and slid forward on his belly another five feet, then lifted up and with silent steps rushed the guard.

Lam held the knife straight out in front of him like a sword, driving it into the guard's chest between his ribs and through the side of his heart. The guard came awake, his eyes went wide, and he tried to call out, but Lam's hand had clamped over his mouth. Lam stared at the soldier as his body's vital functions began shutting down, then his head slumped to one side and he slid to the ground.

Rafii came around the building shaking his head. Lam looked at the torn-up paper window high above. Just below it were three-foot-high ceramic pots the Koreans used to store large white radishes preserved in mustard. Lam eased up on top of the large barrel-like pot and stood. He looked through the torn-up window, then quickly jumped down and waved Rafii back. Fifty feet from the house he used the radio.

"Trouble here, LC. I saw at least two army guards inside and a civilian. They have a man stripped naked and tied to a chair. He's got knife slices all over his body and his face is mashed up."

"Pull back. We need to get them outside. Come back at least forty, then throw a fragger at that side door."

"Roger that."

Two minutes later, Lam threw the grenade at the door. It fell short and shredded the boards with shrapnel. The second grenade hit just below the door and blew it off its hinges. Submachine gun fire blasted through the opening, but missed Lam and Rafii.

Murdock put his thermal imager on the open door. He saw a white figure inside the house, then it vanished only to show again a moment later as the person crawled on his hands and knees out the front door. Murdock used a silenced MP-5 and took him out with two rounds. They waited. Nothing else happened.

"Rafii, can you get a flash-bang inside that door?"

"I was an outfielder, not a pitcher, but I'll give it a try." His second flash-bang went inside the building. He and

Lam rushed inside as soon as the last piercing sounds faded.

"Left," Lam said. He went through the outside door into a small room, then through another door into the main room. Two North Korean soldiers rolled on the floor holding their ears. Lam shot one and Rafii drilled the second. A civilian held a pistol and tried to point it at the intruders but he couldn't see. Rafii shot him twice.

"LC, you better get in here fast. This Kimchee looks about well done to me."

Five minutes later they knew the story. They had put the man's clothes back on and bound up his worst wounds. The slices on his body were the start of the death of a thousand cuts, where the victim eventually bleeds out from countless wounds, none that alone are fatal. Kimchee spoke English.

"My wife and daughters are all dead. Bastards made me watch as they killed them." Tears splashed down the Korean's cheeks. He slashed them away with his hand. "I didn't talk. Can we get away?"

Ten minutes later they were halfway to the beach when Lam put them down in the dirt and weeds.

"I've got a foot patrol. Looks like eight men in a line moving toward us. They're five yards apart and look serious. They must have found the wasted Jeep patrol."

"Lam," Murdock said. "With your silenced weapon, try picking off the men at one end of the line. We're double-timing up to you. How far to the bandits?

"Moon came out, that helps. I'd say about seventy-five."

"Hold until they are at fifty yards, then open with your M-4 on single. We're moving."

Lam lay on the edge of a rice paddy. The berm that held the water in the paddy was over two feet high here. He rested the M-4A1 CAR 15 Colt Commando on the edge of the dirt and waited. The Korean patrol moved cautiously, checking out any cover that might hide an enemy. Lam felt the wet cammies in the dirt and figured he picked up two pounds of Korean soil. The line moved closer. Lam sighted in on the near end of the skirmishers and pushed the lever to single shot. He took three deep breaths, held the last, and refined his sight.

His finger squeezed the trigger so slowly he was never sure just when the weapon would fire. His sight remained centered on the nearest North Korean soldier's chest. The weapon fired with a soft *chug*. The Korean stumbled and silently went down. His buddy next in line didn't notice. Lam moved his sights to the next soldier and fired just before Murdock slid into the paddy beside him. The second North Korean soldier dropped into the dirt screaming in terror and agony.

The rest of the North Koreans hit the dirt and lay still. Sixteen weapons opened up on them, cutting up the dirt and rice stubble of the paddy, and jolting into half of the Koreans. Two lifted up and tried to run to the rear. Both went down hard with hot SEAL lead in their bodies.

Wade switched to the 20mm mode and put one contact round in the center of the Korean zone. The blast echoed down the road and to the ocean.

"How far to the wet?" Murdock asked.

Lam lifted up and stared toward the smell of salt air. "Half a mile, if we're lucky. We going back south for the boat?"

"Not a chance. We don't need it now. If Kimchee can't swim, we tow him."

The SEALs had stopped firing at the North Koreans. Murdock figured that if any of them were alive they would be crawling away. "Okay, platoon, let's lift up and jog for the beach to your right. Should be about half a mile, Lam tells me. Alpha out front in a diamond. Let's move. Lam out two hundred. Now."

"Kimchee, can you swim?" J.G. Gardner asked.

He nodded. "Like a fish," the Korean CIA spy said.

They jogged to the coast, checked for patrols, then waded

into the surf with their weapons tied over their backs and swam on the surface for half a mile. Murdock keyed his radio.

"C.B., we're ready for our close-up," Murdock said.

There were three anxious minutes.

"Gloria, we'll be right there. From the weak signal, I'd say you have us by four to five miles. You have light sticks?"

"Roger that, light sticks. We're about half a mile out and two miles north of where you dropped us."

The Navy boat Pegasus, which could do forty-five knots on a calm sea, drove forward and honed in on them five minutes later. Helping hands pulled the SEALs and Kimchee onboard, and the speedy boat darted out ten miles to where a destroyer waited for them. Within five minutes after boarding the destroyer, Kimchee rested in sickbay, getting patched up by a medic and at the same time getting debriefed by a CIA man.

2

Lieutenant Commander Blake Murdock swam along behind the new guy in the platoon, Robert Doyle, Gunner's Mate Second Class, as he led the Third Platoon of SEAL Team Seven through the calm Pacific Ocean fifteen feet down. They were headed the six miles from the Kill House on the strand north to their headquarters and the BUD/S training area in Coronado. The kid could swim. He held the directional board in both hands and kicked his swim fins in powerful strokes.

Both Murdock and Bravo Squad leader (J.G.) Gardner had liked the man the first time they interviewed him. He joined the squad to replace Wade Claymore, who was a KIA on their last mission. He burned to death in a RPG hit on a bus they were riding in near the Mexican side of the international border in Tijuana. Claymore would be missed.

Doyle spoke Arabic and had been to the Navy Language School, which was a big plus. Murdock liked his attitude, even though he was an opera buff.

Murdock spoke into his underwater safe personal Motorola radio. "Let's take a sneak peek and see where we are. Topside, but faces only."

The sixteen men slanted up to the surface, broke the water just beyond the surfline, and checked the shore. "We're about halfway and our time is good," Murdock said. "Tate, take over on the con and move us the rest of the way on the surface. Go."

They swam a steady sidestroke on the surface until they came to the BUD/S grinder. They walked in, dripped their way to their platoon section, and checked in equipment and weapons. Then they changed out of their wet cammies into civvies. Murdock watched the men. They were ready again. The layoff had been good for them, training-wise and to heal wounds. Today they had worked the Close Combat House with live rounds for score, then charged into the surf and did covert landings six times, catching one of the four-foot waves and bodysurfing in as far as possible. They let the big water wash them in like soaked logs, pushing them up on the wet sand where they lay without moving for two minutes, before they rose up and stormed the beach with dry assault fire.

Gardner came in the small office of the Third Platoon and dropped in the second chair.

"So, how is Doyle fitting in?" Murdock asked.

"Good. He's working in nicely. He swims great, is a natural athlete. He's a keeper."

Out in the squad area, George Canzoneri, Torpedo-man's Mate First Class, dressed as quickly as he could and headed over to the Quarter Deck just after 1630. They were through for the day and he was tired, but more worried than tired. Phyllis had not gone to work today at the upscale jewelry store where she was a top salesperson. That wasn't like her. And he had been disturbed by the high, wild sound of her voice when he phoned her that afternoon.

He spun the rear tires on his Honda getting out of the SEAL parking lot in front of the Quarter Deck and slammed into traffic, cutting in front of three cars with a few feet to spare getting on the highway. They lived a mile and four-tenths from the base in Coronado and he could get there in twelve minutes even hitting red lights. Today he made it in ten.

He ran up to the ground floor condo they were buying and pushed open the unlocked front door. He told her always to keep it locked when she was home alone.

"Hey, Phil, I'm home." She wasn't in the living room. They had been married for six years, had no kids, and one dog. "Phil?" Canzoneri hurried into the kitchen, then to the bedroom. Phyllis lay on the bed in a tangled robe. She looked up, tears streaming down her face. She wiped away the wetness and sat up, her head down, looking up at him quickly, then down again.

"Damn it to hell, Can, I don't know why. I just did."

He frowned. "Did, did what?"

"You know . . ." She looked away. "I . . . I was feeling so low. I missed my weekly sales quota at the store, and Mrs. Parmley was upset and didn't exactly say she might fire me, but there was that feeling in the air yesterday. I just couldn't face that witch today. I . . . I called Barney."

Canzoneri frowned. "Barney who?"

"You know, Barney. Three years ago."

"God no, that dealer? The one I punched out because he almost got you hooked on coke?" He knew she had experimented with cocaine years ago, but together they had worked out of it.

"Yeah, he's still dealing."

"He came by?"

She nodded. Tears flowed again. Her shoulder shook and she held her face with both hands. He slid onto the bed beside her and put both arms around her slender body, pulling her head against him.

"How much?"

"Two papers. All the cash I had. He doesn't take checks. I . . . I did them one right after another before the downside came. Then when that wore off I wanted to die. I threw up three times and made a mess and . . . and . . ." She broke down crying again.

He held her until she stopped. He guessed it was over

five minutes later when she brushed away the tears and looked up, her jaw set.

"I swear to God I don't know why I did it. He said he'd be back tomorrow. I told him not to come. He laughed and said I'd be begging to see him before noon. What can I do?"

"I'll be here when he shows and have a surprise for him. Now you have a shower and get dressed. We're going out to dinner."

"I . . . I don't know if I can eat anything."

"Doesn't matter, we're going out for dinner and then you're going to buy that new dress you've been wanting. You said you needed a basic black. Go."

She worked out of his arms, kissed his cheek, and started for the bathroom. Phyllis turned and stared at him a minute. "How did I ever get so lucky that you married me?"

Canzoneri pointed. "Go," he said softly with a huge grin urging her on.

They ate at Coco's. Had steak and lobster and a huge double chocolate cake sundae.

"Hey, I can eat after all."

"I had to elbow you out of the way to get even half of that sundae." Canzoneri dug into his wallet and pulled out three dollar bills. He always left a three-dollar tip no matter what the bill was.

Back home they watched TV for an hour, and then they went to bed. Phyllis rolled toward him and kissed his lips.

"Just one more thing would make this mostly-the-worst-day-of-my-life get turned around into the best afternoon and evening."

"Do I get to guess what that one more thing is?"

"No, just get naked and we'll figure out something." A thin smile crowded on her face and it gave Canzoneri a glimmer of hope that maybe they had whipped the cocaine beast again. The next morning at 0700, Canzoneri phoned Master Chief Gordon MacKenzie on the Quarter Deck at the SEAL compound.

"Master Chief, Canzoneri here. I've got a problem."

Three minutes later, Canzoneri hung up. He had a two-day family problem leave. Now all he had to do was figure out what to do if Barney did come by. Break his legs, yeah, that would be a good start. Then put two in the back of his head to be sure.

Canzoneri shook his head to get back to reality. First coffee, then he'd think it through. He heard a noise behind him and spun around, his combat mode briefly taking over. Phyllis in her robe reached out and put her arms round him.

"Sweetheart, I'm so sorry. It . . . it just happened. I knew it would be hard . . ."

He kissed her gently. "I told them I needed two days of my accumulated leave time, so, I'm not going in today."

"Good. Coffee?"

"Always."

They sat at the small kitchen counter and watched each other.

"Look Can, I'm so sorry I don't know how to start. The group told me there would be times, but I thought I could kick them. Yeah, big kick. I get to thinking about you and the danger you're in at least half the time, and it gets to me. Then I'm feeling sorry for myself and I called Barney . . ." She let it trail off and looked up at him from big brown eyes.

"You know that's the only reason I married you, woman. Those eyes of yours. So damn big they look like they belong to a young fawn. So deep brown like I could drop in and never stop sinking."

He reached over and kissed her forehead, then her nose, then her lips. "Hey, if Barney comes back today, I'll have a man-to-man talk with him. I'll suggest strongly that he never come around here again or phone you."

"Can?" She looked up, caution, then fear, flooding her face. "Just don't hurt him. He'd sue you in an instant. He's won four assault and battery civil suits in two years."

Canzoneri grinned. "Oh, yeah, I won't hurt him for long. Once a guy is dead, he don't hurt none at all." He watched her.

Phyllis nodded. "A little SEAL humor, I know that by now. First time I heard you say that I nearly wet my pants. But really, don't touch him. He might have somebody with a hidden camera somewhere."

"If he shows up, we'll invite him inside, then his camera won't help him. Six will get you ten he won't come. Now breakfast. Cereal, eggs, and hash browns, toast, more coffee, and some just-squeezed orange juice. You ready?"

By nine-thirty, Barney had not arrived, so they took a walk. Canzoneri had looked hard at his hideout .32 and decided to leave it in the drawer. He wouldn't need it in Coronado in broad daylight. He scowled. What would narrow daylight be?

They walked along the golf course on Glorietta Boulevard. Not a cloud in the sky—65 degrees and warming. Just a nice Coronado winter day. They went up past the tennis courts and then south again. A block from their condo they saw a small man get out of a Lexus and stand by the fender waiting for them.

"Barney?" Canzoneri asked.

"Yes. Let's not even stop."

They walked up to the car and went right on past. The man laughed and followed them. "Don't want to be seen talking to me, right? Happens. I'm only here because the little woman there asked me to come back."

Canzoneri turned so quickly Barney bumped into him.

"Hey, watch it."

"Barney, listen carefully. Right now I'm so mad that I could kill you and brush you off like a swatted fly. Or I could hurt you in a dozen places without leaving a mark. You want to go through the rest of your miserable life as a hunch-backed cripple with one good nut and no way to get it up?"

"Easy, friend. Easy. I know you're a big tough SEAL. The jury would love that. Your whole body is a lethal weapon. You're a trained killer with much blood on your hands. Go ahead, hit me just once."

Canzoneri spun on his heel and went back to the new, black Lexus. He knelt by the front tire and looked it over. A three-inch knife slid into his hand and he jammed it hard into the sidewall then slid it out followed by a gush of air. The knife folded and slid back into his pocket so quickly not even a long-lens camera could have seen it.

He stood and shook his head. "Well, look at that, Barney. You have developed a flat tire. Hope you didn't have a tight schedule. So stay out of my way, little man. Maybe the next time I see you my little blade might find its way deep into your black heart."

Barney nodded. "Figures, you'd have to have an outlet for your anger. I got off lucky. But then so did you. No good pictures, but my lawyer is going to celebrate when he hears the threats you made against my health and welfare." He pulled a lapel button with a thin wire attached off his jacket. "Don't worry, this microphone always gets the goods, even a whisper. That bit about your blade in my heart will be priceless."

Canzoneri barked in fury and took a step toward the dealer. The small man shook his head, patting the bulge under his left arm.

"You're fast, Canzoneri, but nothing is faster than a .38 slug. You want to play a game of chicken?"

Canzoneri stopped, shook his head, and turned back to where Phyllis stood. She hugged both arms around herself and he could see her shiver.

"Another day, Barney. Stay away, or you and I'll have another day."

The drug dealer laughed. "Oh, yeah, what a capper for my tape, Canzoneri. You did real good. Now I need to call triple A and get this tire changed. You have a terrible day now, ya'll hear?"

By the time they had walked the two blocks back to their condo, Canzoneri had cooled off. He couldn't believe what he'd said in the heat of anger. It was a threat plain and simple to kill the drug dealer. Now he had to hope that the little man stayed in the best of health from now on and didn't so much as scrape an arm or tear a fingernail. If he did, the cops would come storming down the pike to talk with one George Canzoneri, prime suspect with an attitude.

"What was that about a microphone?" Phyllis asked.

"He was just bluffing. Don't worry about it. You mentioned a new movie you wanted to see. How about we catch the matinee?"

3

Lieutenant Commander Blake Murdock lay the letter written on official Navy stationery on the master chief's desk in front of him and stabbed it with a roughened finger.

"Master Chief, just what the fuck does this mean?"

"I wondered when you'd be in for a talk. It came late yesterday, but I figured a good night's sleep might help you decipher the codes built into the letter." Master Chief MacKenzie looked up at the seasoned officer and smiled. "Yes, I figured you might have some trouble with this one. Oh, I have your new orders that came through channels this morning. I can't say that Commander Masciareli is pleased."

"Can the CNO do this? Can he just jerk me out of here and paste me back there in DC without even a persuasive phone call?"

"Lad, lad, lad. He's the Chief of Naval Operations. Admiral Hagerson can do anything he damn well pleases. He's your boss, lad."

"Yeah, Mac, but DC? And he's ripping me right out of the teams in a way that I can't ever come back for field duty."

"That part you might negotiate."

"The promotion?"

"Aye. You're not even eligible for three years yet."

"But he could do it."

"Anything he wants to, including making you a lowly ensign again."

Murdock picked up the letter from the Chief of Naval Operations. He went right to the important part.

" 'You are hereby relieved of your duties as commanding officer of Third Platoon, SEAL Team Seven. You will report within seven calendar days to my office in the Pentagon to fill a newly created task-area of Coordinating Officer of Navy and Marine Corps Special Warfare Teams and Quick Strike Forces. Effective today, your permanent rank is full Commander. With the world situation in its present state, and the probability that it will worsen, your special talents are needed here. You have argued against coming into my office before. This is not the time to waffle or to argue. Phone me if you wish.' "

Murdock dropped the letter on the master chief's desk and slumped in the visitor's chair.

MacKenzie rubbed his jaw and twisted his mouth in what Murdock had come to know was his thinking mode. "Lad, has the admiral ever asked you to come with him before?"

"Yes."

"But did he order you to come?"

"No. He left it open just enough so I could squeak out."

"But not this time, lad. So, I'd say you're out of here. You still have that one argument."

"About getting the promotion delayed for a year or so. Then if it works out right, I can come back with the teams."

"Right. Nobody over the rank of Lieutenant Commander gets into the field under fire. Long standing policy I'm sure our very own SEAL Admiral Kenner would make no exceptions for."

"True. We've talked about it before. What time is it at the Pentagon?"

"It's oh eight hundred here, so it's eleven hundred in DC."

"Call him. I want you on an extension so you can listen in. Damn it but things can change around here in the crashing of a millisecond. Call him."

Murdock settled in and grabbed the master chief's

phone as the grinning man went into the outer office and picked up a phone and dialed. The phone rang twice before a calmly efficient woman's voice answered.

"This is the office of the Chief of Naval Operations. How may I help you?"

"Ma'am, this is Lieutenant Commander Blake Murdock."

"Yes, the admiral said you would be calling. Can you hold for just a moment?"

Before Murdock could answer, there was a click then a short buzz, then the familiar, thin voice of Admiral Hagerson came on the wire.

"Well, Murdock. I expected your call fifteen minutes ago. I hope you've had a good talk with MacKenzie. Now, you have any questions I might answer?"

"Yes sir, Admiral. Is there any wiggle room this time? Any way I can slip out of the clutches of the Beltline?"

"Not unless you've got a better lawyer than I have. This is the first time I've actually cut orders on you Murdock. Lord knows I wanted to three or four times. So this is it. You're roasted turkey and on my desk in seven days."

"Yes, sir. After ten minutes of staring at your letter I'm beginning to realize that it's going to happen. I have one request, nothing huge but vitally important to me."

"I didn't think I left any wiggle room."

"You didn't sir, this is in the form of a delay. No full commander can go out with the SEALs in field operations. I'm asking that you postpone my promotion for at least a year. Then it might work out that I could still serve in a platoon for some special mission we both agree on."

The line was silent. Murdock frowned and cleared his throat.

"Yes, Murdock, I'm still here. You hit the one wiggle I hadn't really considered. Every man I've offered an ahead-of-time promotion has jumped at it. Yes, I can see your thinking. How long have you been getting shot at with the teams, Murdock?"

"A little over six years."

"How many wounds and bullet holes, broken bones, etcetera?"

"Eight is my magic number, I think. About average for our platoon, sir."

Murdock scowled at the black phone as it went silent again.

"Murdock, you've done it again. I'll keep your permanent rank as Lieutenant Commander. However, I've got so damn much brass plowing up the waters around my office here in the Pentagon that some of them won't take a light commander seriously. So I'm giving you the temporary rank of Captain. You'll wear the brass and the braid. Now clean up your affairs there and report to that hotel in your orders in four days. Understand you and Ardith just bought a condo."

"That's right, sir."

"Don't worry, she'll wait for you. Met her once when she was with her father. That's it. See you in a week."

Murdock still had his phone to his ear when MacKenzie came back into his office. "He's gone, lad. He hung up. You can put the receiver back in place." Murdock hung up the handset.

"Your situation creates a problem for me. Who is going to take over Third Platoon, SEAL Team Seven?"

Murdock stood shaking his head gently, trying to get everything sorted out. "Third Platoon Seven? I figured you had that already figured out, Chief. Only one man for the job: Ed DeWitt. He has the experience getting shot at, and with these men no less. No one else will do. Sweet talk Masciareli into moving him, today."

"Aye, Captain Murdock. Good choice. I'm on it." The master chief laughed softly. "Yes sir, Captain. You're going to have to get used to that title, at least for a while. Congratulations."

Murdock nodded and strode out of the office, the letter

and his travel orders in his hands. This changed everything. The condo. Ardith had just come to San Diego for a new job. Ardith had been the only lady in his life for the past four years. How would she react? How long would this last with the admiral? Could the master chief get Ed DeWitt moved back to Third Platoon? Would Ed want to come? Most important of all, how would Ardith react to this surprise? He had no idea what her take on it would be. Maybe she'd quit and come with him? He hoped so. Maybe she'd get a job in Washington. Lots of places would hire her well up in the governmental pecking order. He didn't know if she'd do that. Hell, the fact was he had no clue what she would do or say when he told her.

There was no doubt that he had to go. He was Navy, he obeyed the orders of his superior officers. There was only one man superior to the admiral, and that was the president. He slowed on his walk back to the shack office of Third Platoon, Seventh. It had become so routine, so familiar. He could walk these areas blindfolded. He slowed more and stared at everything as if seeing it for the first time.

When he came into the Third Platoon office, J.G. Gardner had the duty board down and was working on the training sched for the day.

"Hey, you sleep in?"

"Nope. Got shanghaighed." He told Gardner his new orders, and that Ed DeWitt would probably take over the platoon.

"Sonofabitch. Just when everything is coming together, they rat you out on me. I needed to learn from you, Murdock."

"You can learn it all from DeWitt. Let's go tell the men. You've got the con here until my replacement comes, whoever the hell he is."

In the Platoon Room the men were suiting up for the day's training.

"Fall in, squad formation," Gardner barked at the men.

"What the hell?" Jaybird asked.

"Change of plans, J.G.?" Lam asked.

"Hell yes, a big change of plans. Everyone here?" The junior grade lieutenant checked to see seven men in each line. "Okay, at ease, and listen up."

"Fuck, this is just like the black shoe Navy," Bradford said.

Murdock marched down the length of the line of men, did a perfect turn to the rear, marched, and went back to his center position in front of his men, his platoon.

"We're in the chickenshit U.S. Navy, right?"

"Hooooohah!" fourteen men roared.

"We get told what to do every other day and we do it, right?"

"Hooooohah!"

"I got orders this morning. As of right now, Lieutenant Gardner has the con on the Third Platoon, Seventh."

"No way!" Ching bellowed.

"Yes, way. A huge way. And we all follow our orders, right?"

"Hooooohah!"

"A week from today I report to the Pentagon, where I will fill a new slot called Coordinating Officer of Navy and Marine Corps Special Warfare Teams and Quick Strike Forces."

A cheer went up from the men.

"About damn time somebody got you promoted," somebody yelled.

"Yeah, get you out of the damn field where you've been taking too many rounds," Neal bellowed. "Could get yourself absolutely dead that way . . . sir!"

"Damn. Now, Commander Masciareli will be taking orders from you," Bradford yelped. A dozen voices cheered the idea.

"Nothing I could do. Admiral Hagerson has requested

that I come to his office before, but this time it was an order, all cut and certified and transmitted."

"We still have our special hook-up with the CIA and Don Stroh?" Gardner asked.

"I'll make sure of it. No reflection on you, Mr. Gardner, but I've requested that Ed DeWitt return to the Third Platoon as its CO. Can you live with that?"

"Be more than happy to have him here," Gardner said.

"I've got a desk to clean out. I want my locker and my gear to remain intact and kept updated. I turned down a promotion to Commander, so I can still sneak back and take on missions with you guys."

"Hoooohah!"

"Now, you guys are about due for another mission, so get sharp and train up to a fine point of excellence. Pour it on them, Gardner. Next, I've got to see a lady named Ardith and find out what she thinks about this coast-to-coast hop."

Back in his broom closet–sized office, he called Ardith at work. She sounded surprised.

"You never call me here. What's happened?"

"Lots. Take the day off, we've got to talk, right now. I'll see you at the condo in a half hour."

"I'll be there. Not even a hint about the big secret?"

"Not a one. Oh, no worry about me physically and probably mentally. No sweat there, so we can deal with this. See you in about half an hour."

Commander Masciareli came into the Quarter Deck as Murdock started to leave. The tall, thin boss of SEAL Team Seven was not smiling.

"Congratulations, Captain Murdock. You finally outrank me. Think the man would have had the courtesy to call me first. Not the way that Hagerson does things. You'll find out."

"Guess I will. First, I have a big problem, Commander. I have to break the news to Ardith Manchester. I better run or I'll be late."

To Murdock's surprise, Commander Masciareli came

stiffly to attention and saluted. Murdock returned the salute and hurried out to his car.

Ardith's car was in their parking spot when he arrived at the condo. He parked in the visitor's lot and hurried inside. She had just taken a beer out of the refrigerator and was about to pop the top when he came into the kitchen.

He stopped a dozen feet from her and stared. Long blond hair, a svelte in-shape body, with a face so beautiful he couldn't believe it. Now she was curious and afraid and it showed in her eyes.

"I'm Navy, and I go where they send me. I just got transferred to the Pentagon in DC."

She opened the beer and took a swallow. He liked the way she let the bottle top rest on her upper lip not sucked up inside her mouth.

"Sailor, is that all? I thought maybe this was some really, really important announcement." She laughed at the surprise showing on his face. "Old habits, darling. I called Dad the Senator just after you called me. The authorization to form the new department went through his senate committee last week."

"But . . ."

"Of course I'll go with you. We can sell the condo for five or six thousand more than we paid for it. Dad did some nosing around for me. He says the Pentagon section of JAG is looking for a civilian lawyer with lots of congressional experience to handle some JAG cases that involve Congress. He put my name in for the job this morning."

Murdock grabbed her and nearly squeezed the life out of her with a bear hug. When the kissing was over she leaned back in his arms.

"You were expecting maybe that I wouldn't want to get back to Washington? Remember, I was raised there and have had full exposure to the Beltway experience. I love it back there. The seat of our government. Everything is so exciting and alive. We're making history every day." She smiled broadly at him. "Have you had lunch yet? No? Good, let's eat out and celebrate with lobster, steak, and shrimp."

The lunch-dinner was delicious. When they got back to the condo, they decided to enjoy the luxury of the king-sized bed while they could.

"We can clean out our desks tomorrow and put the place up for sale," Murdock said. "Glad now we didn't buy all of that new furniture we've been looking at."

"Don't worry yourself about that furniture money. I'll spend it all and more on furniture when we hit Washington. This is so exciting! I get to get back to Washington in government and you'll be there in the Navy and still with Special Warfare. I wonder if I'll get the job at JAG?"

"With your dad pushing, I'd say it's as sure as anything ever is in Washington."

4

Arlington, Virginia
Captain Blake Murdock sat on the couch in the Suites
Grand Hotel five miles from the Pentagon in Arlington and
patted the spot beside him.

"Little lady, you look weary right to the bone," Murdock said.

"At least. I had three interviews today for that job at
JAG. During the last one I felt like I was being grilled on
the witness stand by three Supreme Court Justices. The last
person asked me why I'd take a pay cut from a hundred and
fifty thousand a year to a hundred. I gave him my best closing argument, which lasted almost five minutes and had
him checking his watch to be sure it was still running."

She leaned against Murdock and his arm went around
her. Ardith looked up and built a half smile. "So, Captain
Murdock, how did your third day on the job go?"

"Good for a paper-pushing billet. I sent a new order to
Little Creek, Virginia, where I'm to get one of my staffers.
I told them I wanted a highly experienced, field-tested,
First-Class Petty Officer, not a commissioned man. I'm
getting an army Ranger/Delta Forces captain and a Gun-
nery Staff sergeant from the Marines Quick Strike/Recon
outfit. They all should report within three days. In the office, I have two Navy women, a lieutenant (J.G.) lawyer as
my executive assistant, and a second-class yeoman as our
secretary and researcher. A huge staff."

"Sounds like your kind of mix. You like the input of the enlisted guys. Any hot spots showing up in your daily briefings?"

"Not so far. How did you know about the briefings?"

"I'm a lawyer, I figured it out. Extrapolation. We eating out or ordering in?"

"Not hungry."

"You email Master Chief MacKenzie and I'll order."

"How did you know that I . . ." He paused and chuckled. "Yeah, you're a lawyer and you've been messing with my laptop. He said yesterday Masciareli finally broke down and let Ed DeWitt take over the Third Platoon of the Seventh. I'll be using them whenever I can."

"Tomorrow is Saturday. Neither of us works, so let's go house hunting."

"My assistant, Lieutenant Harriet Engle, suggested some sections of Arlington or out a little farther that we might like. We can start with them in the morning."

"We have two weeks here in the hotel with maid service before the Navy kicks us out?"

"Right, and they pick up the tab for moving our furniture."

"I still can't believe you gave your car away."

"It was eight years old, worth maybe two thousand. Anyway I sold it. I flew in here and you drove your little Plymouth PT Cruiser. It's a strange-looking little car, by the way."

"Yeah, you sold your Honda to the master chief for ten dollar. Big sale!" She slid a smile over her pseudo scowl and headed for the phone. She nodded to herself. "Yes, I think Italian tonight. Then you can have the phone."

Two weeks later they had moved into an older single-family home in Fairfax County out near Linconia. They were near the off-ramp to the Henry G. Smiley Memorial Highway and about a half hour from the huge Pentagon parking lot. Murdock had worked out a routine at the office. He had his own daily briefing by his eyes and ears and had assigned each man to a section of the globe where things could go wrong. Then he and Sergeant Warnick of the Marines went in to the briefing with the CNO. It took them a week to select Ardith for the new position at JAG and then they hired her on, gave her a secretary and an office. She had a month to observe, become familiar with the military approach to the law and the various military checks and balances. She was as happy as a green frog floating on a brown lily pad in a sky-blue pool.

Over Angola, East Africa
Cruising at 43,000 feet
Mrs. Eleanor Hardesty, wife of the president of the United States, settled back in her private quarters onboard Air Force Two, the look-alike jet liner usually reserved for the vice president and visiting dignitaries. Mrs. Hardesty considered herself a working First Lady. This was her third world tour of countries where the president and the State Department thought that she could do the nation some service by visiting, listening to problems, bringing financial aid and service, and generally being a goodwill ambassador for the president.

So far, the First Lady, her husband, and State had been pleased by her work. She looked around the big plane. It was larger than the first two houses she lived it. It had over 4,000 square feet of living/working space and looked more like an executive office than an aircraft. She had her own private quarters with a bedroom bath, workout room, and office area. Her newly appointed chief of staff, Tracy Arneson, 28, watched the First Lady.

"Is there anything I can get for you, Mrs. Hardesty?"

"No, dear. We just left Luanda, and you said it was about seven hundred miles on to this new nation of New Namibia. When will we be arriving?"

"Shortly after one P.M., Mrs. Hardesty. That's local

time. Do you want to have your lunch before we land? There is only a small reception planned before you go to the Presidential Mansion."

"I'll do ten minutes on the treadmill before lunch, Tracy."

"Yes, ma'am. I'll get it ready."

"This small, new nation. I understand it split off from Namibia two years ago. Is that right?"

"Yes. They're struggling to come up with a democratic form of government. The people don't really understand yet that they can be part of the governing process. It's the far northern part of the old country."

"I can certainly speak to the people about how they can have a part in the process of government."

The president's wife was a large woman, standing five feet, eleven inches, and had broad shoulders. Some in the press had called her "horsy." Eleanor Roosevelt was her hero. She had read everything the former First Lady had written and the biographies and many books about her when she was the First Lady of the nation for almost twelve years. Eleanor came from a working-class family in Iowa, worked her way through college, and was awarded a full scholarship to Harvard for an advanced degree in political science. It was an unheard of major for a woman in those years. She met her husband at Harvard and they were married a year after both graduated.

She was most proud of her three sons, all grown now, one in politics in Iowa, one into electronics, and the other a medical doctor. After her sons went away to school she took on community service projects as her husband worked his way from state Senator to the House of Representatives and then to the governorship of Iowa. She worked mostly with underprivileged children. Lost causes, her husband had often called them in private. Now that she was fifty-two years old, she had expanded her agenda to helping these small lost nations. Everyone agreed that she was quite good at doing it. She had even received congressional support. It was often said that her popularity was somewhat greater than that of the president.

A little under an hour later, the big jet came in for a landing at the marginal airport at New Namibia's largest city and capital, Natabi. The Air Force general flying the plane touched down at the very start of the runway and rolled the plane out less than a hundred yards from the end of the hard surface. He turned the plane and taxied toward the pair of new hangars on the north side of the field where the tower had instructed him to go.

Air Force Two was thirty yards from the hangars when automatic gunfire erupted.

"Code Red, Code Red," Secret Service lead man Funister shouted. Every speaker in the plane brought the message. "We're being attacked by ground forces. All security measures in place and activated."

General Wilson, the pilot, struggled with the plane but realized quickly that at least half of the tires on the big craft had been shot out. He was riding on the rims. He cut all power and the plane ground to a slow and rough stop.

"Everyone remain in place," the speakers said. "Security is in charge now. No one, *no one* is to move without our orders. Under no circumstances are any of the outer doors to be opened."

Mrs. Hardesty looked at her aide, who sat frozen in her big chair, seemingly unable to move. "Tracy, this sounds serious. I thought they told us that New Namibia was a friendly country."

Tracy came unfrozen. "Yes, ma'am. That's what they told us. I'll try to find out what's going on."

On the third level of the big craft, in the state-of-the-art communications center, Secret Service agent Lon Henry punched up the frequency to the agency's headquarters in the White House. All transmissions were encrypted for security reasons.

"Major Bowes, this is Flying Lady One. We have been fired on upon landing at New Namibia. No apparent damage that I can see. We stopped abruptly, so the tires may have been shot out. No casualties. Standing by for instructions."

"Roger Flying Lady. Is this a terrorist hit and run, or are the nation's small military forces involved?"

"Don't know. I'll check with the tower. Hold."

He keyed another radio and heard chatter from the speaker. He broke in. "Tower at Natabi. This is First Lady One. We have been attacked. Do you see the attackers? Who are they?"

A heavy British accent came back: "We know nothing of the attackers. We see that your craft is now surrounded by forty to fifty men with uniforms and weapons. Our army commander is in the tower and he has no idea who the men are. Suggest you keep buttoned up while we try to handle the situation."

Lon went back on the satellite radio. "Major Bowes. The tower knows of no army involvement. He said we're surrounded by a large group in uniform, though. It may be a dissident group. The tower guards are trying to handle the situation."

More ground fire erupted. Lon heard several rounds hit the plane's skin and evidently ricochet off.

Lon checked out a window and could see some of the attackers. They were prone, the big plane in their sights. From the tower, a Jeep raced forward with five or six soldiers in it. When it came within two hundred yards of the men surrounding the First Lady's plane, ground fire blasted the oncoming rig with deadly rounds. The Jeep spun and turned over and all but one of the men riding in it were thrown free and cut down by a new barrage of firing. Lon reported this to Washington.

"Sir, we aren't equipped to fight a whole army. I just don't know what the hell to do."

"Get all of your security men with weapons primed and

cover all three access doors. The insurgents will probably try to force open a door. Meet them with deadly force. Good luck."

On the third deck of the Boeing 747, two men desperately worked the radios trying to make contact.

"No sir, we have had no communications with whoever attacked your aircraft," the commander in the tower said. "First we noticed them was when your tires were shot out, then they streamed across the runways and surrounded your plane."

Head Secret Service officer Major Roland Funister worked an international hailing frequency.

"This is United States Air Force Two aircraft calling those men who have attacked our plane. Tell us what you want. There is no reason for any more violence. Please respond on this international hailing frequency." Major Funister checked his watch. After two minutes he repeated the message, and again had no response. He went back to the tower frequency.

"Who is in charge there?" he asked.

"I am, Lieutenant Luscow," came the response from the tower.

"Lieutenant, order a company of your army out here at once to drive these attackers away from our plane. Do it at once! This is an international incident we can't tolerate."

"Sir, I have only two men left in the airport with weapons, and they don't have any ammunition. Our army is small and not well-equipped."

"Then you come out here with your own forty-five caliber pistol and start kicking ass, Lieutenant. We can't put up with this kind of attack on our nation and the president's wife. You know she's on board?"

"Yes sir, we know. There is little I can do."

Major Funister slammed the handset down and stared out the window. He could see the men crawling slowly forward.

He switched to the public address speakers that reached every section of the huge aircraft.

"This is Major Funister. We're in a worsening situation. There are no ground forces here to repel these attackers. Do not, I repeat, *do not* open any of the three outer doors. If we can keep them outside, we are relatively safe. Do not open any of the outside access doors."

On the second deck, just below the cockpit and communications center, Mrs. Hardesty stayed in the center of the office section and as far away from the windows as possible. Two Secret Service men had arrived moments after the plane stopped and now stood with their Ingram submachine guns drawn and facing the stairs that led to the third level.

"Mrs. Hardesty," one of the agents said. "This looks like some minor local rebel group staging a dangerous power play to get some publicity. I'm sure we'll have everything resolved quickly."

"But we can't move the aircraft, can we?" Mrs. Hardesty asked.

"No, but we have our embassy people working on that."

A burst of machine gun fire slammed into the windows, and the rounds glanced off the inch-thick safety glass. Tracy huddled low in one of the cushioned chairs. She shivered and the First Lady put her hand on the girl's shoulders.

"It will be all right, Tracy. Everything will work out. No one in his right mind attacks one of the planes of the president of the United States. You'll see."

In an armored personnel carrier parked on the taxi strip a hundred yards from the stalled presidential aircraft, Colonel Ahmed Badri watched his men move closer and closer to the big aircraft. He had no idea if the plane had external firing weapons or not. He had told his men to take no chances. He had heard the appeal from the major on the hailing frequency, and he held a radio in his hands but made no move to answer the call. Let them sweat it out a few more minutes. They might do something stupid.

Five minutes later he gave a curt hand signal and two of his own men lifted off the tarmac and ran a zig-zag course to the wing of the big craft and paused underneath it. One took a lightweight ladder from his back and snapped open the two-foot sections until the ladder stretched out twenty feet. Quickly the man moved the ladder to the space in front of the wing and up to the main entrance door. One man held the ladder, the other walked up the rungs until he was beside the latch on the large doorway. He took a crowbar from his back and tried to force the door open. After half a dozen tries, he smashed the rounded part of the bar into the mechanism, but it didn't bulge. The man held up one open hand and waved it back and forth.

On the army truck, Colonel Badri saw the signal. He stood, held up both hands, and waved them back and forth.

The man on the ladder nodded, took two packages from his back pack, and pressed them hard, sticking them against the center and bottom of the door. Then he inserted timer/detonators in the two $1/8^{th}$ pounds of plastic explosives. He set the timers for four minutes, punched them into the "on" position, then scrambled down the ladder and pulled it back out of the way under the wing.

Three minutes later, twin explosions took the people inside the plane by surprise.

"Main entrance," Major Funister shouted into his personal radio. The eight Secret Service men ran to their assigned positions. Four men covered the main door with their Ingrams. Two stayed with the First Lady, and the last two covered the rear entrance on the lower third level.

Major Funister stepped out from the First Lady's private suite and past the medical center so he could see the main entrance door. The big door had rolled back into its normal open position. Evidently, the explosions had triggered the safety devices on the door that opened it in case of any collision. He crept up to the very edge of the door and looked out at the ground fifteen feet below. A moment later he saw a ladder pushed against the plane. The major leaned out and sent a six-round burst of 9mm Parabellum into the head and shoulders of a man climbing the ladder. The climber jolted off the ladder and hit the pavement hard and didn't move.

Another figure surged out from under the wing, and before the major could track him, he threw something at the open door. The major hosed down the area with rounds, killing the attacker, but he saw the flight of the hand bomb as it sailed toward the big doorway. He jumped in front of the opening and slashed at the grenade with his stubby Ingram like he would a slow curve, but he missed. A moment later the grenade hit just inside the door and exploded.

Smoke, whining shrapnel, and fire filled the entranceway to the plane before the wind whipped in and sucked out most of it. Major Funister lay on his side on the beige carpet where the bomb had smashed him. For a minute he thought he was dead. Then he knew he wasn't. He hurt too bad. Must be the armored vest. But he couldn't move his legs. Strong hands caught his arms and pulled him back from the doorway and aft down the aisle that led past the galley. Then they left him and rushed back to the main entrance.

Already two attackers had scaled the ladder and stepped inside the plane. They shot and killed both surprised Secret Service men who confronted them in the main entrance. They waved their submachine guns. The sounds of the gunfire in the closed space echoed and slammed through the plane, making it twice as loud as it really was. One of the attackers, dressed in a green-and-black jungle fatigue uniform, rushed up the steps to the communications room. He seemed to know exactly here he was going.

"Yes, Mr. President," Agent Lon Henry said on the satellite radio. "The main entrance door has been blown off and . . ."

Two shots from the raider's .45 caliber pistol jolted Henry off his chair and dumped him to the floor. The first round hit him in the shoulder, the second just below his nose slanting upward into his brain.

The only Secret Service man in the First Lady's suite had bolted the door leading into the office section that faced the hallway near the main entrance. He had his Ingram trained on the metal door. The First Lady and Tracy were in the bedroom section at the nose of the plane just past the bathroom.

The door exploded inward when someone outside jumped and kicked it with both booted feet. The kicker went to the floor and was gunned down by the Secret Service man. He didn't see the second attacker, though, who drilled six rounds into Mrs. Smith's son from Waterloo, Iowa, killing him in an instant.

Three more attackers charged into the presidential office, then one went through the bathroom and nodded at the First Lady, who sat on one of the beds and held her arms around Tracy.

"Mrs. Hardesty, you are to come with us," Colonel Badri said in precise, perfectly pronounced English.

5

Natabi, New Namibia Airport

Mrs. Hardesty stood and stared at the man in military clothing who carried a submachine gun. Her back stiffened and her chin came up.

"Surely, young man, you're not speaking to me. I'm the wife of the president of the United States here on a diplomatic mission. What's your name?"

"I'm Ahmed Badri, not that it matters. Come, out of the plane, or I'll be forced to bring in some men to carry you."

"You're serious?"

"There are several dead men in the plane and on the ground who will assure you that I'm extremely serious. Now come, we have far to go before nightfall."

Mrs. Hardesty nodded once, patted Tracy on the shoulder. The young woman was still shivering and had kept her eyes tightly closed. "Don't worry, Tracy, I'll be fine. This man can't risk the might of the United States coming down on his head. I'll see you again soon."

She stepped forward, past the bathroom and into the presidential office. There Badri stopped her. He opened a drawer in the desk and took out a radio about four inches square and sixteen inches tall.

"Yes, the SATCOM radio," Badri said. "Right where it's supposed to be. The backup of the backup. With this I can talk to your husband." He looped the carrying strap over his shoulder and led the First Lady out to the main entrance.

They had to step over three bodies sprawled in death on the pristine carpet. The emergency slide had been triggered, stretching out to the ground. Badri pointed to one of his men and said something in a foreign tongue.

"Do what this man does," Badri said to Mrs. Hardesty. "Simply sit down and slide down to the bottom."

"I'm not an idiot, Mr. Badri." She watched the man slide down, then stepped forward, dropped on the soft plastic on her bottom, and slid to the ground where two men helped her stand. Badri came right behind her. He caught her forearm and walked her forward.

"We have ground transportation. Not the presidential stretch limo, but it will serve." He signaled and the armored personnel carrier drove up beside them and stopped. The rear of the rig opened and Badri walked the First Lady into the machine. Benchlike storage compartments lined both sides.

"Sit down and hold on. This won't be a pleasure ride."

Inside the wounded jet liner, the third in command of the Secret Service took stock. As soon as the last of the attackers had left the plane, John Ludbezian checked the SATCOM in the communications room. It was working and still tuned to the White House office and turned on. He took it from the dead man's hands and pushed the handset.

"This is John, do you copy?"

"Yes. This is Martin in Washington. What's the status of the First Lady?"

"She's been kidnapped, sir. Taken away under guns. We've lost four of our agents including the major. It was a clean, swift, precision, military attack. They knew exactly where to go and what to get. They were in the plane no more than three minutes."

"Any other casualties?"

"Not that I know of. The First Lady was last seen getting into an armored personnel carrier and heading off the airport. An airport Jeep tried to follow them, but was turned back after taking several rounds from the machine gun mounted on top of the military vehicle."

"They deploy the plane's emergency exit chute?"

"Yes, sir."

"Put someone on the radio to the tower and get stairs out there as soon as possible. Then get everyone to the embassy or into hotels. I want you to follow that personnel carrier. Get a car or a truck and tail them. *Don't let them get away.* We've got to know where they're taking the First Lady. She's your responsibility now. How much of a head start do they have?

"About four minutes, sir."

"Get moving. Call the tower for transport. Take the long guns out of the locker and your short guns. Move it, John, now!"

An airport Jeep with a large checkered flag on it stormed across the taxi strip and stopped near the emergency chute. John Ludbezian ran up to it and looked down at the airport security policeman.

"English?" he asked.

"Some."

"I need to take your Jeep to follow the First Lady's kidnappers. You drive. They went out the south gate. We've got to rush."

"My superior told me—"

"Never mind that, we need to move now. Your superior is in deep shit right now. Don't make it any worse." With that, he slid down the emergency chute.

John stepped into the Jeep and the airport policeman spun the rig around and slanted toward the south gate. Before they went through the gate, John saw a small tractor pulling a rolling stairway toward the wounded airliner, followed by three buses.

Just outside the gate, the driver turned the rig south. "Not much north, he would go south to hide."

The battle-green armored rig was nowhere in sight. A

pair of small stores and a petrol station showed on the left. Three men lounged near the pumps. The driver pulled in and chattered with them in Afrikaans a moment, then waved and pulled out.

"They say the army machine drove down this way, going fast, with three pickups and a sedan in a convoy."

"You speak good English."

"English is our first official language. More British than American."

"What's your name?"

"Botsua, Willy Botsua."

"Okay, Willy. Let's find out where these bastards went. They have more firepower than we do, so we play it slow and safe. Right?"

"Right."

They stopped three more times and asked about the convoy before they went into the countryside well south of the capital city. Roads and trails and one highway sprouted off in six different directions. John checked the hard surface of three of the dirt roads and ruled them out. It still left three directions.

"What's down this way?" John asked.

"Some farms, some lumber mills. One small diamond mine, but most of the good digging is to the north of the capital."

"Diamonds?"

"Yes, alluvial. We strip-mine the dirt and rocks and process tons and tons of it to find a few diamonds."

A few miles down the road they saw a group of men waving them to stop. Willy started to slow the vehicle.

"Do you think that was your army that captured the First Lady?

"Not *the* army, but I think those men were *part* of the army. We have only two of those personnel carriers."

"Great. If I don't rescue the First Lady, I'll probably be an airport cop myself back in Washington." He checked the pickup at the side of the road, then told Willy to pull over and talk to the men.

Badri sat beside the driver and urged him to go faster. He knew someone would follow. He had planned on it. They plowed through the edge of Natabi, then took the road south. At the first intersection he dropped off one of the pickups to watch for anyone chasing them. They had radios good for nearly ten miles. His first report came ten minutes later. One airport Jeep with two men in it was tracking them. Badri told the pickup to return to town. His next pickup stopped off five miles farther along. The driver gathered some local men around him and flagged down the airport Jeep when it raced up.

"Hey, guys. You see that military truck driving down this way?" John tried this time.

"Yeah, you betcha," one of the men said. "She turned herself off on that side road over there and went like a bat out of hell."

"Thanks," John said and they drove toward the turnoff. Then John shook his head. "No way. The rest of those guys looked at this one guy, the spokesman, like they didn't know him. Must be a plant. We go straight ahead, not on that side road."

Badri got the bad news that the ruse didn't work, and he put out one more pickup with orders to shoot out the tires on the Jeep if it didn't go the way suggested. Fifteen minutes later the radio came on in Badri's rig. This time the trackers in the airport Jeep took the bait and went down the wrong road. It would dead end twenty miles deeper into the countryside.

Badri pulled his little convoy to a stop and talked to the men in the rig behind him. He had brought only his ten Iranian special troops with him from the airport. The forty others at the plane had been ordered back to their regular barracks. They were part of the Namibia army he was reforming and would do whatever he told them to do. His job in Namibia was to work up a plan for their small army. But that's only what the officials here thought he was doing. The soldiers from the airport would return to the barracks with orders to tell no one where they had been or what they did.

Now with eight of the ten non-coms he had brought with him from Iran, he rolled forward. Within an hour he came to the big gate across the road and got out of the armored carrier. A guard came out of a concealed shack and spoke with Badri for a moment, then nodded and opened the gate.

"Welcome to the plantation of Alexi Gastrod Edwards," Badri said to the First Lady. "He's a rich and important farmer down here, and he runs half the country. Way back in his lineage he had a British father, thus the name Edwards. He's neither black nor white. We call him a half-and-half man. He's rich and powerful, but my men with their submachine guns are much more powerful."

Washington, DC
The Situation Room

"So what more can you tell us?" President Hardesty asked his chief of staff.

"Mr. President, we have tapes of the broadcasts from the plane. The first one was interrupted when the operator was shot and killed. Our timeline on that is fifteen-oh-three, or approximately seven minutes ago. We had a second transmission from a Secret Service man at fifteen-oh-seven reporting the kidnapping. Our fourth man with the Secret Service came back on after the kidnapping. He called it a precise, quick, military strike. They were inside the plane no more than three minutes."

"What assets do we have in the area?" the president asked.

"Almost nothing," the Secretary of Defense said. "I don't see how this could have happened."

"It's a small, new country with almost no army," the Secretary of State said. "A single man with ten or twelve dedicated terrorists could have done it."

"So what assets do we have in that area?" President Hardesty asked again.

"Our embassy there has only twelve marines," the man from State said.

"There is no Navy presence anywhere near the south west coast of Africa," the secretary of the Navy said. "Nothing below Portugal. Ships can't travel that far that fast. Our planes would have to find land bases partway down for refueling."

"Our closest land-based aircraft is at Riyadh in Saudi Arabia," the chairman of the Joint Chiefs of Staff said. "That's about four thousand miles across to Africa's southwest coast. We could fly in a company of marines there within twelve hours."

The president looked at his chief of staff, then at the other military men around the situation room table. Most nodded.

"All right. Alert them now and get that company moving. State, get approval from the New Namibia government for our landing troops there. Are our Delta Forces in Qatar on standby alert?"

"Yes, Mr. President. We always have one company on a two-hour alert." The president turned to Don Stroh next.

"Good. Don, in what condition is the Third Platoon?"

"Mr. President, they have had two months since their last mission. They are healed and rested. Their former platoon leader, Commander Murdock, is now with the CNO's office, though."

"Who has the Third?"

"Lieutenant Ed DeWitt. He worked with Murdock for three years."

"All right. I want you to send the Third Platoon to New Namibia as quickly as possible. I want Murdock detached from the CNO and leading the group. The Delta platoon should establish a base camp in the capital of New Namibia and protect the aircraft and U.S. citizens. Have them contain the kidnappers, but not try to negotiate with them or attack. The SEALs will do that on arrival."

The president stood. Every man in the room stood at once.

"Thank you, Mr. President," the ranking man in the group, the chief of staff, said, and the president walked out.

Chief of Naval Operations Admiral Alonzo Hagerson turned to Stroh. "You heard the man. Get the SEALs moving. It's duty hours there so give them a four-hour alert to be on North Island Air Station and ready to take off in the Gulfstream by fifteen-thirty Pacific Coast time. We want the most direct route to southwest Africa. I'll alert Murdock to get on his horse and meet the platoon in Florida."

"It's still going to take twenty-four hours to get the SEALs there. I hope the kidnapper can be stalled for a while."

The CNO scowled. "I hope so, too."

Natabi, North Namibia

By the time Badri and his two vehicles had rolled up the half-mile-long lane leading to the plantation's mansion, the owner and his six bodyguards were standing on a terrace in front of the big house waiting for them. The bodyguards all held Uzi submachine guns and waited for the visitors. Alexi Edwards had learned from years of experience that governments come and go, but the land and wealth endure—as long as you had the guns to protect your property. He waved as the armored personnel carrier came to a stop thirty feet from him in the parking lot. The engine shut down but no doors opened. The bodyguards lifted their weapons and aimed at the vehicle. Before they could get off a shot, submachine guns opened up from the back of the truck. All five of the bodyguards went down. One moved and was drilled with six more rounds.

The doors opened and Badri came out, his own weapon still hot in his hands. Alexi watched him a moment, then shrugged. "If you shoot me, I'm dead. So I don't try to run. Why have you killed my men? They were not going to hurt you."

"Anybody who waves a gun at me better be ready to use it," Badri said. "Old Iranian saying. I bring you a guest, the wife of the president of the United States, Mrs. Eleanor Hardesty."

Two of the soldiers pushed her out of the vehicle. She glared at them, then turned toward the civilian.

"This is your home, I understand. I hope you have some decency left. These animals are not to be considered as humans. Right now I'm in serious need of a bathroom. Would you show me the way, please?"

Alexi nodded, held out his hand, and led the First Lady up a gravel path past an extensive formal English garden and toward the house. Badri ran ahead of them, opened the front door, and looked inside.

"I know you have only the five bodyguards, but some of your staff might try to be heroic. Warn them to go about their duties as usual, or I will shoot them."

Alexi ignored the order. "The bath is the third door on the left down the hall, Mr. Hardesty."

"So kind of you. Be careful with him." She went down the hall and into the room.

Badri prodded Alexi with the muzzle of his weapon. "Yes, be careful. I could have killed you as well. You may be useful to me. What do you know about the diamond mines to the north?"

"So, you are here for the stones. The mine itself is not yet proved, and it is not yet in full production. They are making test runs to see where the best overburden is that might be the most productive. That's all I know about them. I'm not a mining engineer."

"Too bad," Badri said. "I am." He looked around the

expensively furnished main room. It was thirty feet long with a ten-foot ceiling and the walls glowed with original oil paintings and tapestries. Badri was impressed. "Hey, old man. I could sell all this junk in here and raise enough money to start my own army."

"Looks like you have. You're the Iranian officer in town to organize our nation's army with your non-com officers, aren't you? How did you get sidetracked into kidnapping?"

"None of your business." He hurried down the hall and knocked on the bathroom door. It opened and Mrs. Hardesty came out. Her hair was combed and her face washed. She frowned at him.

"Now that we're here, don't you make some ransom demands or some threats? You brought the SATCOM radio with you, so you can talk directly with my husband."

"Let him stew and fret for a while. I'm in no rush."

"Good. Over dinner you'll have to tell me about yourself. I'm always interested in violent transcultural personalities. I try to figure out why they do what they do."

"Transcultural? What a good word. But the word and the idea are meaningless. Why should I tell you anything about myself?"

"An even trade. I'll tell you anything you want to know about me."

They walked into the main room and this time Mrs. Hardesty looked around. "Mr. Edwards, what a magnificent room."

"Thank you, Mrs. Hardesty. I would have fixed it up more if I'd had any notice about a state visit."

"Oh, this is unofficial. No protocol. Mr. Badri took care of that."

One of the Iranian soldiers walked into the room with his submachine gun at the ready. Badri turned to Edwards and Mrs. Hardesty.

"You two stay here. I need to talk to the president about this package of his I have. It won't take long."

Badri left the house and went to the personnel carrier. He took out the SATCOM, turned it on, and dialed in the same frequency that was on the radio in the aircraft. Then he folded out the antenna and set it so it would pick up a satellite. A moment later the set beeped. It had locked on to the satellite.

"I'm calling the president of the United States. I have your wife as my house guest. Let's talk."

There was an immediate response. "This is Wally Covington, director of the CIA. What do you want?"

"It's not what I want, Director, it's what you want, which is the return of Mrs. Hardesty. How shall we handle that?"

"The long-standing policy of the United States is that we do not negotiate with terrorists."

"Of course, and I respect that. But we are not negotiating, we're talking about some way we can reach a mutual agreement. That's much different than negotiating. Why don't you put together a package of mutual benefits and call me tomorrow about this time. Don't worry. We're in a safe place with plenty of luxury items and are looking forward to a marvelous dinner. We'll talk tomorrow."

Before there could be a reply, Badri switched off the SATCOM. Remarkable piece of equipment. He knew about it, but had never seen one. Encrypted messages were shot out in a hundredth of a second so nobody could triangulate the signal unless they were tremendously lucky at three different positions at once. He headed back for the house. He stopped and looked around. This was a beautiful country. So green, so moist. Not at all like most of Iran. He laughed softly. The little nation could keep its green, he'd rather take their diamonds. As a sideline, of course. He and his ten top non-coms from the Iranian army had arrived two months ago awaiting the right time to attack. They had come in peace to restructure and energize the New Namibian Army. It would be a big job.

As they worked at it slowly, they waited for the signal from Tehran that the time was getting close. Then the long-delayed announcement was made that the American First Lady would be visiting New Namibia, giving the date and time and arrival runway. Made to order.

This morning he had taken forty of the Namibian army men out on a field exercise. He said they would be protecting the airport from an invading force. None of the New Namibian soldiers had any rounds in their rifles, and all of the Iranian soldiers had live rounds and spare magazines for their submachine guns. They had shot out the tires on the big plane, then the fifty troopers surrounded it, and then the Iranians had blasted open the plane's main entrance door.

Yes, it had all gone as scheduled. Now, the entire forces of the United States would be concentrating on one project—recovering the First Lady, unharmed, unsullied, in good spirits, and happy. Badri would do everything in his power to keep her for as long as possible, thereby fulfilling his official mission. He thought of the colonel's silver oak leaves he had on his uniform. When he returned to Iran he would be promoted at once to bird colonel, and perhaps get his own brigade to lead in the war.

Yes, the war. War was still man's grandest and most outrageous game. A murderer who killed for sport and the challenge of the chase was playing a game. But for small stakes, his own life. On the other hand a general, a president, a dictator, played with hundreds of thousands of men's lives, sometimes of millions of civilian lives, and to win was the only satisfactory outcome. In this war, he was sure that Iran would win.

While he was here, he would visit the diamond mines and do what he could to steal as many of the uncut diamonds they had produced as he and his men could carry. He wasn't greedy. If he could scoop up twenty million dollars' worth, he would be happy. Yes, this whole operation was moving on track and on schedule. He hurried into the house where he would find the best standard band radio that the old man owned. There should be some war news soon from Iran. Maybe it would happen first thing in the morning.

6

Murdock put down the phone at his desk in the chief of Naval Operations office, his smile lighting up the room. He called his assistant.

"Get Commander Masciareli on the phone. He's in Coronado at NAVSPECWARGRUP-ONE."

"Yes, sir."

Twenty seconds later the call went through.

"Commander Masciareli, this is Murdock with the CNO. Admiral Hagerson just asked me to call you and alert Third Platoon, SEAL Team Seven, for deployment in six hours. They'll fly from North Island as usual. Tell Lieutenant DeWitt to bring all of my gear out of my locker. Go in jungle cammies, all weapons and ammo. Be ready for a long flight."

"Where to, Commander?"

"Miami is the first stop. That's all the CNO said I could tell you. This is on the direct orders of the president. Tell the men I'll meet them in Miami International at the transient aircraft section."

"That's it?"

"All we can say right now. I've got to get moving. Thanks, Commander. Take care." Murdock hung up grinning. Masciareli would be eaten up with curiosity. A moment later Don Stroh called.

"We're off again, old buddy. We fly out of Andrews, so I'll meet you at the flight line. We've got an hour and thirty minutes to get onboard. So rattle your bustle."

"Left it at home. See you then."

They made it just on time and settled into the first-class luxury of a Navy UC-11, a Gulfstream III executive business jet reconfigured for the military. It was top of the line for fast movement of important people. Now, Stroh and Murdock and a Navy vice admiral who needed to get to Miami fast were the only passengers. At just over five hundred miles an hour, it would be a quick flight to Miami. Murdock didn't even want to figure how long it would take. Instead, he had a nap, interrupted by a hot lunch served on china and with real silverware and linen napkins.

At Miami they waited for the SEALs to arrive in their Gulfstream II. It was slightly smaller than the jet Murdock came down in, and a little less plush, but it carried seats for five more passengers than the larger jet. Murdock and Stroh climbed onboard as the plane idled its jets. They buttoned it up immediately and it taxied out and was given top priority to take off.

"Some damn hurry we're in," Jaybird cracked.

"One big hell of a rush," Murdock said. "We're heading for the southwest coast of Africa, to the new little country of New Namibia."

"Why the hell we going down there?" DeWitt asked.

"To rescue a damsel in distress," Stroh said. "Seems the president's wife, the First Lady herself, has gone and got herself kidnapped, and we've been elected to go in and bring her out."

"Jesus H. Kereist, Stroh," Senior Chief Elmer Neal said. "When the hell are you going to get us an easy one? Just snatch back the First Lady! Sounds like a fucking walk in the park."

"That's what you get for being the best damn platoon in the whole U.S. military establishment," Stroh said. "Now listen up and I'll tell you everything that the CIA and the president himself knows about this situation."

Over the muffled purring of the two big Rolls-Royce RB163-25 Spey Mark 511 turbofan engines, Stroh laid out the problem, the situation, and that there would be a platoon of Delta Force soldiers on site to try to contain the bad guys and clear the way for the SEALs to go in and rescue the First Lady.

"We heading over the Atlantic?" Hospital Corpsman First Class Jack Mahanani asked.

"How else can you get to Africa?" Radioman Second Class Derek Prescott jibed. "Of course we're going across. My question is can this aluminum bucket make it in one jump?"

Half the men looked at Jaybird. "Hell yes, and with barrels of petrol to spare. This bird will do over forty-two hundred miles before it needs a drink."

"We're scheduled to make a quick stop in Senegal, then go south across the Gulf of Guinea to land in Natabi, the capital of New Namibia," Stroh said, looking at some papers. "The Delta platoon came in from Qatar and should be on site ten hours before we get there. The Delta guys will bring a plane-load of ammo for us and them. Everything except our special fused twenty millimeter rounds. Any questions?"

"Yeah, Stroh," a voice called out. "When do we eat?"

"You ate an hour out of Miami. So I'd guess in another three hours or so you might expect a snack."

Murdock sat beside Ed DeWitt. "Hey old buddy, how are you doing? But more important, how is Milly?"

"She's good. We're not sure, but there may be something to announce soon, family-wise."

"Fantastic. Don't forget the cigars. And give my best to Milly and my condolences for having to put up with you. Now, are you getting your boys slapped into shape?"

"You left them in shape. Lots of new faces. You do get your troops in harm's way from time to time."

"Yeah, it happens. We don't know who we have to deal with down there in Africa. One renegade with some troops, or somebody else. The place has about a fifty-man army and not much more firepower. We could be in for a lot of trouble."

"From fifty troops?"

"Not really."

"How can he hope to hold out against even the fifty local troops? And they must have more than that."

"Yeah, about twelve hundred soldiers, but they're friendly. Delta might have found the culprits before we get there."

New Namibia Countryside

Back in the plantation mansion, Badri found a pair of rooms where the First Lady could stay. She would have her own bath and he could lock both doors from the outside. Alexi Edwards fussed around so much it made Badri angry.

"Old man, settle down or go outside and dig your own grave. Take your choice. I'm sick of your harping and jumping and being in awe of the woman. She's just another woman. She'll be here until I decide to move. Now get some food ready for us. Tell your staff to go about its usual duties, or they too might join the corpses in the front parking lot."

Edwards scooted out of the room looking over his shoulder at the invader of his house. His face showed anger, but it held fear as well. Badri nodded. He would be no trouble. The bodyguards were dead, he was free and clear until the people from the airport figured out which way he went and where he might be. He had plans where he would move, but not yet. He sat in a big chair and looked out across a five-mile swath of green trees, fields, and a few buildings. He had uncovered a box filled with good cigars and worked on one as he considered his situation. A radio. He needed a standard band radio to watch the world situation. It couldn't be long now. The whole plan was based on what the president's woman did. Now they knew in Tehran. Maybe it would come tomorrow morning. He dreamed of being there, of getting back to his tank company and leading it. But he was a soldier, and for the past five years a top Iranian Secret Service agent. He followed orders. Right now the First Lady of the United States was his project. A vital one. The trigger that would detonate the whole attack.

He found a radio in the next room near a large television set. He tuned the radio until he found a station with news in English. He was glad he had studied languages in his military training. The news was mostly local, coming from the capital of Natabi. Then a news story came on about Iran. He listened closely.

"Iraqi officials said they have proof that Iran is massing men and material along their common border. Iran has reported it is nothing more than a military exercise, to determine the mobility of the Iranian armed forces. They say they reserve the right to move their own troops and materiel around in their own nation whenever and wherever they wish to."

Badri grinned as he heard the news story. Good, they were getting ready. It couldn't be long now. They had the First Lady the stage was set. He'd bet by tomorrow morning the tanks would be rolling. How he wished he could be with them.

Just after an early dinner, Mrs. Hardesty walked up to Badri and stared at him.

"You are an intelligent man, Mr. Badri. Why are you doing this? Surely you know that your eight or ten men can't hold out long against even the small army that New Namibia must have. When the Marines land, or the special forces, you won't stand a ghost of a chance in a haunted house."

"Very good, Mrs. Hardesty, excellent. You grasp the situation precisely. If I can't hold out, then what will I and you do?"

"You'll run, of course. This is not a spur of the moment action. I didn't even know I was coming to New Namibia until a week ago. Your intelligence service must have been working overtime. You're not a New Namibian. What's your home country?"

"Not important. The vital element is that I have you. I control you, and the president will jump through hoops to get you back. It's all quite simple. How could a lowly soldier like me get twenty million dollars any easier than this?"

"Twenty million? Is that all I'm worth on the open market? I'm embarrassed. I figured it would be at least a billion and a half or some such figure. Only twenty million?"

"Actually, since your country won't negotiate for hostages, I probably will never get the money."

"Then why don't you radio the president that it's all over and you're leaving me here and fading into the woods and jungle and we won't chase you? You know that's a much better option than having the special forces chase you and fill you full of holes. Then how will you spend any of that money? You need to think through your options again, Mr. Badri. You haven't considered them all, and I'm sure that when you do, you'll realize that you're in a no-win situation."

"Unless there is some other reason for your abduction that you don't know about."

"Another reason? Money seems to be your reason."

"Good try, Mrs. Hardesty, but no prize. I have a mission to accomplish for my country, and it doesn't include letting you go free." He hesitated then motioned. "Come out here on the patio with me. I'm going to call your husband and tell him my ransom demands for you. You might find it interesting."

He had the SATCOM radio set up on a table with the fold-out antenna already in place. He picked up the handset, turned on a switch, and began.

"Mr. President. This is Ahmed Badri calling."

The response was immediate. "Yes, Mr. Badri. This is the president's chief of staff. Are you aware of what time it is?"

"I will talk to no one but the president."

"He's not here at the moment."

"Tell him he has five minutes to get on your SATCOM set or I'll cut off one of the First Lady's ears and send it to him by Air Express. You have five minutes."

"He'll be here. Wait. Don't do anything rash. Wait just a moment."

Mrs. Hardesty shook her head. "Mr. Badri, you know my husband will never negotiate with you."

"Of course not. I will make demands and he'll meet them. No negotiations involved. It's amazing how cooperative people can be when you make a proposition that they can't refuse. Absolutely remarkable."

The SATCOM speaker sounded.

"Mr. Badri. This is President Hardesty."

"How was your lunch?"

"Nothing to write home about. How is Eleanor?"

"Actually she's in quite good spirits. Trying to argue with me and talk international politics. Amazing woman. You can have her back by meeting a few requirements."

"We don't negotiate."

"No, this isn't that. I simply tell you what to do, and you do it. No negotiations required. Understood?"

"What are your conditions?"

"First, send by wire twenty million dollars to my Swiss bank account. Do this within an hour after our talk. The number is SA-46297-BA. That's all that's needed for a deposit. Second, you have seven standby cargo ships in ports around the world. Each ship holds military supplies, food, ammunition, hardware, vehicles, clothing, even a post office, and a complete field hospital. There is enough goods and material there in each ship to supply a fighting regiment of seventy-five hundred men for a month. Those ships are to weigh anchor within two hours and move toward Iran. Once there in the gulf, they are to tie up three ships at the Iranian port of Bandar-e-Bushehr, and the other four at Bandar-e-Abbas.

"The ships and their cargo become the property of Iran, to do with as the government pleases. The United States will also send by ship to those same two ports a hundred million tons of food for the Iranian people. Those are my only conditions for the release of Mrs. Hardesty.

"I am not making these demands for Iran alone, but for all Muslins all over the world who the United States has swindled, cheated, threatened, and made war against during the past fifty years. The United States will not threaten or harm New Namibia. Their officials have no knowledge or any part in the detention of the American First Lady. If the U.S. does not start shipment of these items within a week, the First Lady will remain as the guest of Allah's Dagger until the goods and ships arrive. Each week the ships don't arrive, I will cut off one finger of the First Lady and send it to you. I will contact you again after twelve hours. At that time I expect to have total acceptance of my demands."

He snapped off the set before the president could reply.

"Now, Mrs. First Lady, we will see how much the president of the United States cares for you—or find out if you are just another political toy that he manipulates."

7

General Tariz Majid eased into a soft chair in his temporary headquarters and watched a television set. It was tuned to Abu Dhabi, the Arabic-language network.

"Our reporters continue to monitor the massive buildup of forces along the Iraq/Iran border. Sources say more than fifty thousand troops and at least three hundred tanks and armored personnel carriers are in the immediate area. Iran says that they are in the middle of an extended military exercise to test mobility and that it has the inherent right to move its troops and equipment anywhere in its own country that it wishes."

He snapped off the set. It had been a long struggle, mostly political, but now the hour was at hand. He had been a loyal soldier for almost thirty years. Now was the time for him to make his statement. He moved his right hand and winced. Was it physical or still mostly mental? He had no idea. The pain was real enough. It had started the night he had been wounded in the Iran/Iraq war twenty years ago.

Those nights and days of terror and death still haunted him as nothing else could. The glory of the drive into Iraq, then the blistering, drenching, inhuman attacks with poison gas on his men—he watched his brigade wither and die in front of his eyes. No more than two hundred out of twelve thousand remained alive after it was over. At least that's the way he remembered it. He rubbed his face with his left hand and closed his eyes. Those visions would never leave his mind. He could see the men now gasping and dying. His own driver died and the car ran off the road. He had to drive himself the last fifty miles, fleeing as fast as he could to get back across the border into Iran.

His two sons, both captains in the tank division, died in that monstrous attack, and the army lost hundreds of its brightest, most able officers and men. Now was the time for revenge. He took out his wallet and removed the pictures of his family. His two sons, and his wife and two daughters. Both were married with families of their own. He would gladly die to protect them. Now he might die avenging the deaths of his sons. If so, it would be worth it.

Two weeks ago he had carried out the final tests. It had been in a remote section. He had driven into the far desert with just one man and the materials he needed. The first test was on a pen holding twenty goats. They were closely quartered so they couldn't run away. He placed a container in the enclosure and pulled back a half mile before detonating the package with a small charge. The billowing white powder burst from the container and spread over the goats, coating them in a white blanket, then filtered to the ground like snow. He watched using a twenty-power spotter scope.

At first there was little reaction by the goats to the powder. Then one stumbled. Another went down on its chest.

"They are reacting, General," the driver said.

General Majid nodded grimly. He had seen men die of poison gas. This would be different. Slower. The dose less massive than this. He watched more of the goats stumble, bleat, and fall. Three hours later all of the goats were down, not moving, and he considered them dead. He put the scope away and motioned to the car. The driver opened the air conditioned car's rear door, closed it when the general stepped inside, then hurried around to the driver's side.

Two weeks later the general and the same driver had gone to the same area of desert, only this time they had two political prisoners in the rear seat tied and gagged. At the test site the two convicts were taken from the car and pushed to the ground. They remained tied and gagged but not blindfolded. General Majid didn't talk with them. He placed the small airtight container near them and upwind, then retreated with the car a half mile and watched. The driver pushed an electric button that set off a small charge on the container and white powder sprayed from the container and drifted over the two convicts. The men coughed and blinked then tried to crawl away from the powder. They couldn't.

General Majid watched the men struggle against the powder for half an hour, then they seemed to give up, to sag where they sat. The smaller one toppled over and lay on the ground. Two hours later one of the men stopped moving and Tariz knew he was dead. The stronger, larger man held out for another two hours before his coughing and convulsions ended. Tariz checked his watch, then motioned to the driver. Ten miles from the test site, General Majid told the driver to pull over.

"Check the tires. I think the left rear one is low on air. We may have to slow down. Check them all, now."

The driver left the black Mercedes-Benz sedan to look at the tires. General Majid eased out of the car and met the driver at the rear of the vehicle. He had his pistol out and shot the driver three times in the heart, then two more in his head where he lay on the ground. He didn't bother moving the body. The first good sandstorm would cover it up and it would never be found. If for any reason the attack did not go as planned, no one could now tie him to this execution of the two political prisoners in the desert test.

General Majid had powered the big car back toward the city. He was ready now. All of the tests were completed, the pieces of the game would soon be in place. He would notify the ruling council when the exact date of the invasion would take place. Allah be praised! Long live the Glory of Islam!

Back in the army camp eighty miles from the Iraq border, in his armored motor home, General Majid remembered the tests with the anthrax powder and nodded. It was a bold move, and he would catch the Iraqi soldiers and generals off balance and in the end defeat them. He should be in Baghdad in two days.

His second in command came into the living area of the forty-foot motor home and saluted.

"General Majid, sir. We have heard from our man in New Namibia. The United States president's wife has been abducted and is being held. The ransom message has gone out to the Americans. They must be scrambling all of their powers to concentrate on southwest Africa."

"Good, good. That's our signal to start to work. Give the men ten minutes to get ready, then start the general movement toward the border. We have eighty miles to cover before dawn. The lead elements of tank companies will form our Lightning probe, followed by the armored troop carriers. Alert the air command, for air support. I want them overhead at daylight."

General Majid smiled. He took out the pictures of his two dead sons and kissed them. Before another day is over, I will avenge your deaths. I will make you once again heroes of Iran. Tears welled up in his eyes and ran down his cheeks. He didn't notice them. All he could think about were his two sons he had lost in the humiliating defeat by the Iraqi forces.

Natabi, New Namibia

The sleek business jet swept into the small airport at Natabi and landed, then angled toward the taxi strip and a hangar at the north end of the field. When Murdock stepped out of the plane, John Ludbezian met him.

"Sir, I'm the senior Secret Service man on site. We know only that nine or ten men kidnapped the First Lady and took her off the airport and headed south. I chased them in an airport Jeep but they had a twenty minute lead and we never caught them. We found out from men along the route about where they went, then we lost them. Apparently there's this huge mansion a few miles up in the direction they went. Figured maybe they'd head that way."

"Where are the Delta forces?"

"Half of them went to the point where we lost the trail. The rest are protecting Air Force Two."

"We'll need transportation, Ludbezian."

"Yes, sir. I have two vans for your use beside the hangar."

"We flew over so many time zones I have no idea what time it is here."

"It's slightly after two P.M., sir."

"Thanks." Murdock motioned to the door of the plane and Lieutenant DeWitt sent the men out. They formed in front of the plane in two squads.

"Ludbezian, you'll come with us and guide us up to the farthest point in your chase." Murdock signaled DeWitt and pointed to the two vans and the SEALs double-timed over to the transportation and climbed inside.

Twenty minutes later the vans pulled up at a fork in the road. The road had petered out into a one-lane dirt trail through the heavy vegetation. An unoccupied van had been parked at the side of the road. Murdock and his men got out and looked around.

"They look friendly," a voice called out of the jungle.

"Yeah, but they don't look like no Frogs I ever saw," another voice answered.

"Let's spray the far side of the road with about twenty rounds of HE," Murdock bellowed. The SEALs lifted their weapons and aimed them that way but didn't fire.

"Hold it, goddamn it, we're just kidding," a new voice with a parade ground bellow called out of the brush. "Hey, we're on your side." A dozen men stood up from perfectly camouflaged positions on both sides of the road and walked in. One man, who was six-feet four-inches with powerful shoulders, strode forward and saluted Murdock.

"Captain Murdock, I'm Captain Engle. I hear we're supposed to babysit you guys."

Murdock returned the salute. "Actually we'll take all the help we can get. You sent out any probes?"

"Just arrived here at twelve hundred. We've got a scout out about five hundred watching and waiting."

"Which road?"

"The left-hand one. The other one fades out about a half-mile out and heads toward the coast."

"We're sure the personnel carrier went up this road?" Murdock asked.

"Affirmative, Captain."

"You work with squads?"

"That's a roger."

"Let's move out and catch up to your scout. What kind of commo do you have?"

The captain showed Murdock the personal radios. They weren't Motorolas. "No way we can communicate with each other on them. I'll get you one of ours so you can keep in touch with us." He turned to the SEALs. "Let's move out. Lam out two hundred. You should find a Delta scout out five. Join him and stay three hundred ahead of us. Five yard intervals. Alpha leads off, then the Delta men and DeWitt and Bravo Squad bring up the rear." He turned to the civilian. "Ludbezian, take one of the van's back to town and take care of the other folks there. Men, let's move out."

Lam pushed out fast and silently through the slowly fading semblance of a road. Before he got to the five hundred yard mark, the road was no more. Now it was a grassy and weedy trail just wide enough for a vehicle. He saw where branches had been snapped off recently. Lam spotted the Delta scout, while fifty yards behind him moved up silently. He slid in beside the soldier and tapped him on the shoulder.

"Bang, bang, Delta, you're dead."

"Huh, what! Oh God, don't scare me that way. Where the hell did you come from?"

"Didn't your captain tell you I was on my way?"

"Yeah, but I didn't hear you. I mean my job is to watch out front."

"Which the two of us are going to do. But as silently as possible. We stay three hundred ahead of the troops. Let's go."

Lam used his Motorola. "Contact here, Cap. We'll stay at three. This trail is still showing signs of recent travel by a big rig. We're starting to climb. Can't see anything ahead."

"That's a roger."

Murdock moved to the rear of Alpha squad and watched the Delta men. Yes. They were good. Pros at what they were doing. They didn't jangle, they didn't talk, smoke, or make jokes. They were on the job. Each man had his personal long or automatic weapon and a sidearm. All wore combat vests loaded with goodies much the same as the SEALs.

Murdock edged back into the Delta formation until he found Captain Engle.

"Your platoon been on missions like this before?"

"Only two," Engle said. "We can't stack up against your platoon's rep. We know about you and your special connection with the president. Heard you lost a man on your last mission."

"That's the hard part. I've written fourteen letters like that in the past six years."

"Too damn many, Captain. Hey, a Navy captain is the same as an Army light colonel. What you doing out in the field?"

"The Captain rate is temporary, I'm permanent at Lieutenant Commander."

"Yeah, like an Army major. Looks like we'll have to take care of you."

"Nobody has rank on a mission. I'm glad your men don't have any showing on their sleeves or collars."

"Damn right. In combat that's a good way to get picked off by a sniper."

"I'm going back up front. Give me a call on the Motorola just to see that it's working right."

Ten minutes later, Murdock's Motorola earpiece spoke to him.

"Cap, you best come up and take a look. Might want to hold the troops where you are."

Murdock worked his way up the three hundred yards and found Lam and the Delta scout flat on the side of the road. Murdock bellied down between them and watched where Lam pointed. A newly dug line showed across the trail. It was no more than a foot wide and appeared to be fairly straight.

"A row of land mines?" the Delta man suggested.

"They couldn't carry that many," Lam said.

"Might have had them stashed in the personnel carrier," Murdock said.

"Look just beyond the dug-up place," Murdock said. "See those two four-inch trees bent almost double? Any idea what did that?"

"Trip-wire triggers," Lam said. "While we're worrying about the dummy ditch, we flounder around and set off the trip wires with old-fashioned Vietnam-type punji swinging logs with dozens of sharpened sticks ready to impale a soft body."

"So we go around the whole thing," Murdock said.

"Track back twenty yards and we'll go both ways," Lam said. "Straight off from the trail for thirty yards, then up the trail for fifty before we come back to it."

"That's a roger," the Delta man said. "Hey, sir, I'm Jamison, Sergeant First Class Jamison, from Kentucky."

Murdock shook his hand. "I'm Murdock. Pick your side, Jamison. You go one way, Lam, and I'll go the other way."

"Hell, I'm to the right," Jamison said. They backtracked for twenty yards, then Jamison went right and the other two to the left off the trail and into the brush. Lam watched the foliage closely as they moved. He saw Jamison go off the road to the right and checked his own path again.

Ten seconds later a grenade blasted the quiet New Namibia countryside on Jamison's side of the road. Murdock and Lam backtracked to the road and looked where Jamison had gone.

"Captain Engle," Murdock called on the Motorola. "Get up here. We have a problem."

8

By the time Captain Engle ran to the front of the patrol, Lam had spotted and removed two trip wires and the grenades rigged to them. Jamison lay where he had fallen when the deadly shrapnel ripped through him.

"He died instantly," Murdock said. "The grenade wasn't three feet from him when it went off."

Engle scowled. "You cleared the area?"

"Safe enough now, sir," Lam said. "I found two more trip wires and grenades."

"Why to the right and not the left?" Engle asked.

"Over ninety percent of people are right-handed. When a choice comes up right or left, most right-handers automatically will go to the right. These terrorists just played the odds."

Lam vanished to the left of the trail and Captain Engle called up two of his men to take Jamison back to the transport.

"We've got to keep moving," Murdock said. "Lam is scouting out the bypass on the left. He'll be checking everything from now on."

The rest of the men came up and filed past the body and then went to the left around the punji trap. Ten minutes later all the men were around and moving up the tracks the personnel carrier had made along an old trail.

"If there's a house up here, this can't be the main road

in," Ed DeWitt said. "There must be another entrance for cars and trucks to get in and out."

They moved almost a mile up the trail before Lam stopped them again. "Trip wires all over the place, Cap," Lam said over the Motorola. "I can see one Claymore aimed right down the trail at me. I'm getting behind a tree and setting it off. None of the two hundred steel balls inside the mine should get back to you. There may be more. This mine might set off some of the others by breaking the wires. Here goes."

Murdock heard the Claymore go off with its distinctive roar. Then all was silent. "Lam, you okay up there?" Murdock asked on the Motorola.

"Yeah, I'm fine. Two more Claymore's went off. They set them up in a crossfire. Would have taken down the whole patrol. Let's spend a half-hour and go around this spot. There could be some more bombs here I haven't found."

"That's a roger, Lam. We're on our way. Hold there for us."

A half-hour later, after a cautious advance, Lam reported that he could see buildings ahead.

"Yeah, big spread. Large house, two wings, out buildings, two cars in a paved parking lot below the house. I don't see any people."

"Any smoke, destruction, broken out windows?" Ed De-Witt asked on the radio.

"Negative. Nothing. Looks dead or vacant."

"Take a closer look, but be careful," Murdock said. "You want a backup scout?"

"Negative. Give me ten."

Murdock sat the patrol down in place ten yards apart and waited for Lam to make his recon. He reported back in seven.

"Okay. I made contact. There are people there. They told me the raiders have moved on, taking the lady with them."

"Roger that," Murdock said. "We're moving in. See if you can find whoever owns the place."

"Wilco," Lam said. "Bet it's been a while since you heard that term. It was used by the Air Force mostly in WW II. Means simply Will Comply. That's what I'm doing."

Murdock brought his men up cautiously, even though Lam said the place was clear. He found a man in his sixties waiting outside for him. Lam had radioed Murdock that the man's name was Alexi Edwards. Murdock checked him out as he walked up. He was five-six, ramrod straight, white hair, a slender body slightly sunken in the chest, with a tanned face and wide, white eyebrows. He stood stiffly at attention and saluted when Murdock stood before him.

"Colonel Edwards at your service, sir!" he shouted in the best English tradition.

"Captain Murdock, sir." Murdock replied returning the salute. "I'm told the invaders have left with the First Lady."

"That is correct, Captain Murdock. They took my two Land Rovers and went up the north trail early this morning. They also murdered five of my men. The leader is a true monster, a civil, educated, amoral, sadistic murderer."

"How is the First Lady?"

"She is a wonder. Calm, collected, arguing with this Ahmed Badri at every turn. She's educated and charming, but with a steel-solid core of grit and determination."

"She hasn't been harmed?"

"No, he threatened to cut off an ear and send it to the president, but he didn't. He has a radio he can talk directly with Washington, DC, on. They left heading north toward the diamond mine. It seems the man is also a common thief."

"How many?"

"The leader has eight men left. Two others were apparently killed at the airport."

"How far to the diamond mine?"

"About twenty kilometers over an old trail. I have only

one other vehicle that can make the trip, a flatbed truck with stake sides. How many men do you have, twenty or so?"

"Twenty-two. How long to drive to the mine?"

"Three hours. It's up and down hills and a terribly rutted and gullied-out trail."

"How long to darkness?"

"Another hour and a half. Not time to get to the mines. You may stay here tonight if you wish. I have a dormitory with twenty cots. This used to be a working plantation. The rest of you can sleep in the bedrooms."

Murdock talked with Captain Engle and DeWitt then came back to Edwards.

"Yes, too late to do any good today. We'll stay here tonight and leave at first light."

"Good. The cooks will be delighted. Give them an hour and they will provide you with a feast."

"That's not necessary."

"Correct, but it will be my pleasure. Gulba will show you to the dormitory. Dinner will be served at six P.M."

A young black man came from behind Edwards and waved at the men. "This way," he said, leading them up the steps to the main level and past the mansion to a long, low building with stone exterior and six chimneys.

Inside, the building had two large rooms, with ten metal cots in each one. The rolled mattresses made it look like a military barracks, Murdock decided. Moments later three men arrived with armloads of blankets and sheets. The SEALs and Delta men made up the beds in quick fashion. Then the locals brought in two more cots. Murdock, DeWitt, and Captain Engle talked.

"Sorry about Jamison," Murdock said. "It could just as well have been Lam or me."

"Luck of the draw," Engle said sadly. "He was a good man, and he'll be missed. He's the first casualty we've had in three years. Which means we haven't been on many shooting missions. We hear now and then about some of the covert ops you go on. Fascinating stuff."

"It can get downright dirty, as well. I've lost fourteen men in the past six years."

The Delta captain shook his head. "I don't know if I could take that many losses. How do you handle it?"

"Poorly sometimes. I've been known to rant and yell and go on a five-mile run. Then when I come back I sit down and write the letter to the man's parents or wife. Maybe those fourteen are why they kicked me up to the CNO's office. But I'm fighting that, too."

Ed DeWitt grinned. "Hell, Murdock, you might be up there, but you're here with us. Never get rid of you in the teams, that's my judgment."

"Let's hope so," Murdock said, punching DeWitt on the shoulder.

They went up to the main house and talked to Edwards about the road to the mine. They asked what state the mine was in and if the terrorists could do any damage up there.

"The mine is just starting its operation," Edwards said. "I don't think they've made many big finds. This kind of open-pit diamond mining is more like an earth-moving project. They have a crew, but not much security. Badri and his men would overwhelm them."

"Let's say they get in and out of there with what they came for. Where can he go from there if he decides to run?" Engle asked.

"There's a good road to the mine from the coast up the other side of the mountain. He could get petrol at the mine pumps and drive out that way. If you had long-range radios you could put a blocking force along the road somewhere."

Murdock looked at Engle. "Mr. Edwards. You must have radio contact with the capitol. Can you advise them what's happening and ask the army to put out a blocking force along that road before it branches off into the countryside?"

Edwards frowned. "I'm not on splendid terms with the

government, or the army." He took a deep breath. "There is a friend in the army I can call. He has enough rank that he might be able to convince his superiors. It's just a chance."

"We live or die on chances, Mr. Edwards," Murdock said. "The quicker you can get that move started the better. Badri must be at the mine by now, scouring it for raw diamonds. Which means he'll probably be there during the night. He'll have a twenty kilometer start on us if he moves out at daylight."

"And he has the good road," DeWitt tossed in.

"True."

Edwards pushed himself up from the big soft chair and nodded slowly. "All right, I'll take a chance and call my friend. It's just a try."

Dinner proved to be a huge stew with big chunks of beef and pork and more kinds of vegetables than the men could ever remember seeing. They identified the potatoes, carrots, and onions, but there were at least a dozen kinds they couldn't figure out.

Murdock sent the men to their bunks early and promised them a breakfast an hour before daylight. Edwards had assured Murdock that he would have a typical American breakfast for the men.

The next morning they pushed off in the two-year-old stake-bed truck just before 0600. Murdock checked the engine and found it in good shape. He even looked at the oil and water levels, and then they moved. Luke Howard was the platoon's top driver, so he took the wheel. The first two miles were fairly flat along the side of the valley, then the trail turned upward toward a pass they could see in the mountains ahead.

The grade increased as fast as the ruts in the road, and soon they were crawling up the side of a hill at barely five miles an hour. When they got to the top of the ridge, there was another ridge ahead of them.

Howard looked at the odometer. "We've come almost ten kilometers," he said. "Halfway there and it isn't even noon yet."

"It's just past 0800, which means were only moving at five kilos an hour," Murdock said. "Maybe we can make time going down the other side."

An hour later they realized there wasn't another side. The ridge they were on blended into another ridge that rose toward the long-viewed pass.

Just before 1000 they spotted smoke ahead. Then they came around a bend in the trail and spotted a huge gash in the side of the mountain—the mining area. Below the raw earth were a dozen wood-frame buildings, most unpainted and newly constructed. The truck was a half-mile away from the buildings when they heard rifle shots and everyone ducked.

"He's in that building at the edge of the place," Lam said. "Over eight hundred yards."

"Rear guard?" Engle asked.

Murdock agreed. "DeWitt, put a twenty just in front of that building. We don't want to ruin anything up here if we don't have to."

Ed grinned. "You testing my marksmanship, Cap?"

"No, I already know you're the best shot in the platoon. Go."

Ed sighted his Bull Pup over the cab of the stopped truck. He checked the wind and sighted in again and fired. The round hit ten yards from the wooden building, exploded with a roar, and sprayed the structure with shrapnel. There were no more rifle shots from the area.

"Let's motor," Murdock said. The truck ground forward down a slight incline toward the mine structures.

At two hundred yards they heard rifle fire, and a round slanted off the left front fender.

"Bail out!" Murdock bellowed. "Alpha to the right.

Bravo to the left. Delta, take your pick. Take cover and watch for movement."

The men jumped off the truck and raced to cover on both sides of the road behind rocks and trees. Just before they were all set, a machine gun chattered from the mine. Half a dozen rounds splattered into the truck. Murdock scowled as the radiator gushed steam.

"Okay guys, we've got a situation here," Murdock bellowed. "We need to get down to that mine layout as fast as we can without getting our heads blown off. Anyone have any suggestions?"

9

Three or four voices talked at once on the Motorola, then Jaybird's message came through.

"Cap, we've got a gully over here twenty yards to the right and some cover between us and it. Say we lay down some covering fire and move over to the gully. Take us right down to the edge of that first building."

"Yeah, I see it. Ed, you have anything on that side?"

"About the same setup. We're on this flat little ridge that gullies out on our side, as well. We've got the Delta folks over here."

"Captain Engle, what do you think?"

"Good cover, let's do it."

"Single-shot long guns on that first building we took fire from," Murdock said. "Two rounds each as we bug out for that gully. Now!"

The weapons sounded and the men moved. Murdock dove into the gully and rolled and came to his feet. He had complete cover from the buildings.

"Lam out front by fifteen, let's choggie."

The men moved down the gully at a trot, weapons at port arms ready for any surprises. At the edge of the building they spread out. Murdock frowned. No machinery running. No activity. Where was everyone? A shot sounded from a second-story window in the second building, but missed the SEALs. In reply the room took a dozen answering shots.

Rear guard? Holding action? Murdock was undecided. House-to-damn-house fighting. Not exactly his favorite activity. He motioned to Bradford and Ching.

"Get over to that second building and check it out. We'll give you some cover. Go on my firing." Murdock pulled up his Bull Pup and hit the same window with three rounds. The others in the squad fired for fifteen seconds until the two men had scurried across the thirty yards to the back door of the building.

"We've taken some fire over here," Captain Engle said. "We think it's from a third building. I've sent two men over there. Let's not shoot each other."

"Copy that, Ching?"

"That's a roger. Nobody on the first floor. Some kind of a sorting room. Listening for movement upstairs." Ching looked at Bradford and motioned toward the stairs showing at the end of the room. Both began a silent approach. They were halfway there when a hand grenade bounced down the wooden steps.

"Cover!" Ching brayed, and both men dove to the floor and rolled toward opposite walls. The hand bomb went off with a roar inside the big room. Ching felt a jolt to his left arm. He looked down and saw a three-inch gash on the upper sleeve of his cammies and felt warm blood flowing down his arm.

He rolled and fired a six-round burst up the steps, then ran toward them, pulling a grenade out as he moved. He jerked out the pin and held down the arming lever until he was at the side of the steps. He tossed the grenade underhanded up the opening, lofting it just over the rail at the top so it would fall into the room.

The small bomb hit the top of the rail, slowed, then rolled over and dropped inside. It went off before it hit the floor. The men heard a scream from the second floor and both charged up the stairs.

"I'm right," Bradford said.

"I've got left."

They paused when they were eye level with the second floor. They saw cots and foot lockers—maybe a barrack. Just beyond the second bunk a man lay on the floor moaning, his hands holding his chest. A rifle lay near his legs. Bradford rushed up, kicked away the weapon, and checked the man. Blood pooled on his chest, seeping between his fingers, running down his side to stain the wooden floor dark red. The shooter looked at Bradford, said something in a foreign language, then gave a small cry as his head rolled to the side. Bradford touched his carotid artery at his throat. There was no heartbeat.

The two men cleared the rest of the room and then reported to Murdock.

"What can you see out the front windows?"

They went to the windows and checked. "Not much, Cap," Bradford said. "Half a dozen more buildings, all one story. Big open pit behind two of them. Huge building in the middle of it all. Must have a generating plant up here somewhere. Don't see any people. Where are the workers?"

"Maybe Badri rounded them all up. Hold there. We're moving into the ground floor. Engle, what's with your side?"

"My two men cleared the third building. Nobody there, but they found some brass. We've got at least one more hostile in the area."

"Roger. Take the building and hold until we know what we have ahead of us."

Murdock went to the second story and found Bradford wrapping up Ching's left arm.

"Just a scratch," Ching said.

"Hopefully. Now, what do we have out front?" Murdock checked out the window. The complex was laid out like a large "U" with low buildings around the edges and a large building in the center with huge doors on the near end. Outside the doors he saw four large self-propelled earth-moving machines. All four stood waiting, heaped with dirt and small rocks. There was no activity. He watched carefully, sectioning the area, but no men showed, no work was being done. The place looked closed down.

"If he's here with the First Lady he's lying low," Murdock said. "Which means we have to clear each of these buildings as we move around the outside. We're at the end of the U. We've got a lot of ground to cover. Ed and Engle, you see the layout?" Murdock asked on the Motorola.

"See it, don't like it," Ed said.

"Yeah, Captain," the Delta man said. "Big layout. What's in most of these buildings?"

"We're going to have to find out. You guys move to the bottom of the U and work the other way. We'll come from this end around to the base. It's damned house-to-house, so be cautious. Ching got nicked. We don't want any more casualties. Let's go."

In the fifth building in the U, they found one area that had a large locked room. Lam pounded on the door and was surprised to hear pounding reply from the inside. He called Murdock over.

"Anyone inside speak English?" Murdock bellowed.

"Yes, English. Let us out."

Murdock nodded and Lam opened the doors and ten men came bursting out. None had weapons.

"Thank you, thank you," one man cried. "They came yesterday with guns. Shot one of us and put most of us in here. Who are they?"

"Robbers," Murdock said to keep it simple. "How many of them?"

"Eight or nine. They made us stop the machinery, close down the work. They wanted the diamonds we have found."

"Did they get them?"

"Some, most we had hidden."

"Did any of them leave in a truck or their Land Rovers?"

The man shrugged. "We have been in here for many hours."

"Murdock. Some news."

He recognized Ed DeWitt's voice over the Motorola. "We found one hostile. He got away, but we wounded him. We're about halfway done on these buildings. We think we've chased the guy up to the end place."

"We need one alive, if possible."

"We'll try."

Murdock turned back to the spokesman of the group. "Is the big building where you process the ore?"

"Yes, sir. Tons and tons of it to find a few stones. But evidently it is a paying proposition. The government runs this mine."

"Trouble," Bradford said from the window. Murdock looked out. Four men, with arms bound behind them and paper sacks over their heads and tied together, had been led out by a man in green cammies carrying a submachine gun. He lifted a bull horn.

"Attention, attention. These four men are about to die, unless whoever is shooting at us lays down their arms and surrenders. You have five minutes to come out and line up and put down your weapons. At the end of five minutes the first man will be shot in the head. Your choice."

Murdock broke out the window. "We hear you. Give yourself up, you don't have a chance. Badri left you here as cannon fodder. You'll never get out alive if you fight us. We have fifty men. You're down to two or three.

The man with the submachine gun lifted it and shot the first man with a three round burst in the back. He fell and went still.

"No joke. You have five minutes."

Murdock hooded his eyes. His lips quivered. "Any sniper have a clean shot at him?" he asked on the radio.

Three answers in the negative came back. The killer had

moved in close against the backs of the hostages. Even a clean shot from behind could go right through the man and kill one of the hostages.

"Ed?" Murdock asked.

"We could shoot low, trying for his legs. At least we wouldn't kill any of the hostages."

"Captain Engle?"

"I can work two men around for more of a side shot at him. Tricky and dangerous, but it may be all we have."

"Send them, but hold on the order to fire." Murdock saw something below a moment ago that caught his eye. What was it? He scanned the area in front of the big building again, then he saw it: a bulldozer, maybe a Cat D-8 or D-10. None of his men could run one. He looked at the civilian workers from the plant. He motioned to the spokesman.

"Who can drive that bulldozer down there?"

"I can."

"Do you want to save the lives of those hostages?"

"Yes, they are friends."

"Will you help me? It could be dangerous."

"Yes, help. Anything."

Murdock grabbed the man and they ran down the steps to the ground, around several buildings until they were directly across from the bulldozer. The hostages were thirty yards away, closer to the smaller buildings. Murdock was still forty yards away from the big tractor.

"We get to the dozer and I raise the blade to protect us, then we drive it toward the killer?" the civilian asked.

"Yes. What's your name?"

"Altoba. I am assistant manager here."

"Good, I'm Murdock." They shook hands.

Murdock used the radio to tell the troops what he was going to try. "If he comes away from the hostages and anyone gets a clean shot, take it. Any questions?"

"You want any covering fire around the guy?" DeWitt asked.

"Yes. As soon as we start running across the open spot, send him ten or twelve rounds, spaced out."

He looked at Altoba. They stood at the side of one of the buildings. "Ready?"

The black man nodded and they surged into the open and across the unprotected no-man's land. Murdock carried his Bull Pup at port arms ready to use it if he had to. Sounds of firing came from two sources, and in one quick look, Murdock saw the gunman with the hostages step between them for cover.

Murdock realized he hadn't breathed since the start of the run, when they slid to a stop behind the dozer. Altoba climbed on board and patted a place on the seat beside him. Murdock sat down. Both ducked down as low as possible. They could see the gunman and hostages. Altoba started the engine and Murdock saw the gunman turn and look at them. He lifted his submachine gun but didn't fire.

His delay was a mistake. As soon as the engine roared to life, Altoba hit the hydraulics and lifted the blade, blotting the hostages out of sight. Only then did the man fire, and Murdock heard half a dozen slugs hit the front of the big steel blade and whine off into the distance.

Murdock slapped the driver on the back. "Let's go get him," Murdock said. Altoba hit the levers and the big dozer clattered forward on its treads. He turned slightly and angled directly at the gunman and his hostages.

Murdock lifted up so he could see over the blade. A round slammed past his head only inches away. He saw what he wanted to: The gunman was still between the hostages. If he shot them down his protection would be gone. If he waited, Murdock would run right up to him and put a carefully placed single round in his heart.

The big dozer clanked forward. They were twenty yards apart when Murdock lifted up again, this time two feet to the right of where he had looked before.

"No clean shot yet," DeWitt said in Murdock's earpiece.

Murdock sneaked a peak and dropped down. The gunman had closed the remaining three hostages around him to protect him. There would be no clean shot.

"He's trying to move the group toward that building on his right," Jaybird said. "It's about twenty yards, but the dead man is tied to the others and they have to drag him. It's slow going, but there's not a fucking thing we can do to stop him."

Murdock took another quick look. The killer was fifteen yards from the building. He dropped down.

"He's getting away," Murdock said to Altoba. "Only one thing we can do to stop him. Go faster, pull up right behind him, and drop the blade on the dead man."

"No, I can't. I know him."

"If you don't, the other three will die. Do it! It'll jerk the other three hostages down and I can shoot the gunman. Do it!"

The man looked up with tears in his eyes, then he nodded and gunned the motor and the dozer surged ahead. Altoba lifted the blade a little more: just enough so they could see under it, but the gunman would still have no shot. The clanking roaring machine bore down on the five men. At the last moment the gunman saw the danger and tried to drag the dead man out of the way, but the big blade came down solidly on the corpse's legs and the three hostages stumbled and fell. For just a fraction of a second the gunman stood alone. Murdock was ready, and his Bull Pup chattered three rounds, hitting the Iranian in the chest and driving him backward away from the hostages.

Altoba lifted the blade, then killed the engine and rushed forward to help his countrymen. He lifted off the paper sack hoods and untied the men.

Murdock jogged over to the closest building. "Ed, what's our status?"

"We've been clearing the rest of the buildings. My guess is that this was the last rear guard. We have only two more buildings to check, then we're done."

"Our next job is to find a truck that will haul us and get on the road after Badri. He's got a bigger lead now. He bought time with two of his men's lives. Hard telling where he is by now. We've got to get out there and find the First Lady."

10

Near Bahktaran, Iran
On the Iran/Iraq Border

General Majid stood in front of his armored motor home on a slight hill overlooking the border. In front of him were his Lightning Units. They consisted of a spearhead probing recon group of sixteen T-55 tanks, older Soviet models that still packed a punch with their 105mm cannons and fifty rounds in each unit. They would slash through the border defenses and roam ahead at twenty miles an hour shooting up everything that moved.

Directly behind them came the armored troop carrier fighting machines, with a 40mm cannon and twin .50 caliber machine guns that could fire 360 degrees from the turret. They were called the Panthers and held eight combat troops equipped with automatic rifles and armored vests. They would slash in behind the tanks, engaging any pockets of resistance or by-passed troops and take them out.

The general watched the dawn coming. They would push off precisely at daylight. His field commanders had their orders and would launch one massive drive with the probing tanks and the surprise weapon. He rubbed his hands together in anticipation. Any minute now the tanks would fire at the close-in border defenses, then charge forward. They would present a six-tank front with the vehicles two hundred yards apart as they swept forward.

He stood on the step of the motor home to see the attack

better. A twenty-power scope hung around his neck on a cord. He wanted to see it all.

It started. Well behind the border, Iranian artillery fired twenty rounds into the border fortifications. The thundering roar of the 155mm rounds exploding on the ground less than half a mile in front of him brought tears to the general's eyes. He wiped them away and studied the area through the single-lens scope. *Yes!* He saw a shell burst five hundred yards away. The explosion showered a circle of white powder for fifty yards in every direction. *Yes!*

He ducked into his motor home and checked through the heavy glass viewing ports. As he did an assistant bundled him into a biological warfare suit and gas mask. He saw the powders raining down on the area. Saw men running from it. The Iraq soldiers had no protection from the anthrax.

Five minutes after the artillery struck, the tanks charged ahead, firing at anything that got in their way. They dodged around the anthrax pockets where they could see men gagging and going down. They hit roads and a small village. The village had been hit with the anthrax as well. Now and then the big guns on the tanks thundered away at Iraqi tanks in the distance.

General Majid had discounted reports that Iraq had over five hundred Soviet T-72 tanks with their bigger guns. His spies had seen many of the tanks in storage areas where they were slowly falling apart in the desert environment. Most had no tracks and no weapons on them. They were in a huge graveyard of over 200 tanks rusting into scrap metal.

His radio bristled with reports from the lead elements. Yes, in ten minutes the tank spearhead had penetrated over five miles into Iraq. The fighting personnel carrier Panthers had followed quickly, mopping up the shellshocked troops. They circled around the anthrax-saturated areas, letting the poison do its job.

He heard chatter from the pilots in the sleek jet fighters overhead. They had temporary control of the skies. The F-84s and the F-86s dove into Iraq defensive ground forces far in advance of the tanks. They also worked tank-killer missiles, taking out the occasional Iraqi tank they spotted.

So far he had heard of no fighter aircraft from Iraq. He knew there were reports that Iraq had over three hundred fifty aircraft, including the old Mig 21s but also the Mig 29s and the Mirage F-1. Where were they? Had they also suffered in the desert without adequate maintenance and care, changing from fighting machines to piles of metal and useless armament? He wondered.

A half-hour into the attack he knew. The Iraqi air power had finally shown over the battle field and the air war was engaged. General Majid counted on his better trained and more experienced pilots to win the day for him in the air.

He went back to the situation map that three men with radios were monitoring. They had gone over the border near Khanaqin, Iraq, and their tanks had consolidated and moved rapidly in single file down the road that led southwest—directly into Baghdad, only eighty miles to the center of the huge city of over five million people. Without any resistance they could be there by nightfall. Where was the vaunted Iraqi army, the Volunteer Divisions that had reportedly intense and complete training? Where were the one thousand tanks that Iraq was supposed to have?

General Majid checked the big situational map display of Iraq again. His lead spearheading tanks were at the twenty-mile mark down the highway and had stopped to let the Panther fighting armored vehicles catch up with them. They had been delayed by small firefights along the way and at four army posts that had been blasted by the tanks but not completely overwhelmed.

At every military target, the lead tanks had fired the anthrax rounds, then circled around the contaminated area. The tankers wore the biological suits to protect themselves.

Half of the men in the Panther fighting machines did as well.

General Majid stared at the display. What if a strong force came at his spearhead from the side? Had he allotted enough men and machines to protect his flanks? He wasn't sure. His generals had suggested that more tanks might be dropped off on the run southwest to work as a protective barrier along the corridor. He wasn't sure now how he had reacted.

"General, sir," a colonel wearing a radio headset said. Majid looked up. "We have reports from the lead elements, the recon tanks, that they have been resupplied and are on the move again. The Panthers are dropping off men along the route to act as security for the corridor. They are asking for more men to replace those, and to build up the protection along the flanks."

"Colonel, pick the units and send them in. We have the trucks. Get the men there fast, at least a battalion. Move them quickly."

"Yes, sir. I'm on it at once."

For the rest of the morning, General Majid watched the battle unfold on the map. His men were pounding the fragile Iraqi forces. The anthrax had put the fear of death into them all. Some of the forces in fixed positions had deserted when they learned of the anthrax shells hitting areas to the east.

The thundering of the big guns kept going as the tanks spearheaded forward. The air war intensified. More Iraqi planes showed up.

"General, sir. I have a report from the spearheading tanks. The commander of that company says that he has lost three of his sixteen tanks. They have been blasted by enemy air. He implores the airmen to intensify their efforts to clear the skies of the Iraq fighters. Evidently some of the Iraqi planes now have laser-guided missiles they are shooting at our tanks."

"Order up the last squadron and the reserve squadron to get into the air," the general said. "We can't afford to lose our lead elements. Throw all of our air power at them now. We can't wait."

A major worked another radio and gave the orders. The general paced the small area, looking now and then at the large scale map flat on a table in the center of the room.

"What's happening at the border? Those first units we hit with the powder?"

Another colonel looked up from a clipboard. "General Majid. Our last report came in ten minutes ago from a man on the ground skirting the contaminated areas. He said there are men lying all over the place. Some are still crawling around. The whole complex is shut down, the roadway is open."

General Majid remembered the research his scientists had done on anthrax. Everyone within the area would be infected whether asleep or awake. The powder would blow around, contaminating everyone. First the guards on duty would go down with upsets from the massive dose. The others would get sick shortly with a fever, a cough, severe respiratory distress with dyspnea, diaphoresis, stridor, and cyanosis. He didn't know what those words meant, but his doctor advisors said they were quickly fatal.

Many of the men would die within four hours. Most would be dead in twelve hours. The anthrax would contaminate the area for years.

"The road is open, yes, yes. Good. Get me a company of Rangers as an escort. I'm moving up toward the front. We'll go around the powder area. Tell the Rangers to shoot anything that moves. Get this rig ready to roll. I want the usual single tank out in front of us. Let's go."

Five minutes later the general and his armored twenty-four-foot motor home crossed the border, angled around the white powder area, and then turned back to the highway leading directly to Baghdad. He would have his victory, he would have his revenge. He would put up two statues in the capital plaza in Tehran honoring his hero sons as soldiers of victory.

He heard the machine guns on the tank ahead clearing out some pocket of resistance. The little caravan halted for five minutes, then moved on.

Ten miles inside Iraq they came to a killed Iranian tank. Two of the crew were still near the tank trying to fix it so they could fight again. General Majid stopped the convoy and went out to talk to the men. They both braced at attention and saluted when he walked up. He returned the salutes and asked their names. They told him, and one was from near his hometown.

"You men are heroes of Iran," Majid said. "Your heroic efforts will not be forgotten." He pointed to a major behind him who took down the names and ranks of the two men and their unit. He asked what the trouble was with the tank.

"A rocket-propelled grenade blew the track off on the left side, sir," the captain and tank commander said. "If we can get some quick repair we could be back in action, but the maintenance unit has raced ahead with the rest of the battalion."

"New orders, Captain. Stay here and turn your guns to the flank. You'll be in charge of defending the flank in this area. Blast any Iraqi unit you see moving out there."

"Yes, sir, we can do that."

The general moved back to his command vehicle and the convoy ground ahead. By the time they reached the twenty-mile mark inside Iraq, the Lightning Force lead elements had penetrated another ten miles and were pausing for the Panthers to cleanse the area just behind them and catch up. Now Majid could see that trucks had deposited squads of infantry every mile along the corridor to act as security and cover. He nodded. His plan couldn't fail. With the anthrax obliterating the strong points, and the probing, deadly tanks racing ahead to knock out any other resistance, he was confident that his troops could be in the outskirts of Baghdad before dark. He shivered just thinking about it. He would turn the city into a huge fireball, a cinder that the Iraqis would remember for generations. Those who lived to remember. It was so close he could almost feel the heat of the flames and smell the smoke.

He had the driver move their convoy up a mile beyond any of the white powder and stepped outside to savor his charge into this hated nation. His top field commander came up with a frown clouding his usually happy face.

"My General, we have a problem. The tank commanders report from the front elements of the Lightning Force that they are completely out of the anthrax shells."

"Not possible," Majid thundered. "General Hoseini told me he had over fifty rounds in each lead tank battalion. How could they run out? Ask the tank commanders how many rounds they have used."

The colonel went back in the mobile tactic center and talked on the radio. He came back shaking his head. "General Majid, sir. The commanders tell me they had only twenty of the blue-painted fused rounds in each tank. They were the biologicals. The rest of the rounds are standard HE."

Majid's face flamed red and he stormed into the headquarters motor home and pounded his fist into his hand. When he turned to the colonel, he was in control again. •

"Tell General Hoseini I need to see him here at once."

The colonel nodded and spoke softly into the headset mike.

"He's on his way, sir. He is in the field and says it will take him only five minutes to get here."

Majid stared at the colonel, then turned. "Order up the Third Battalion of T-55s. They should proceed with all speed to reinforce the lead elements. We're down to conventional weapons now, and it will be a fight. Also alert the trucks. We want to shuttle five thousand ground troops to the thirty-mile point as soon as possible. We should have two hundred trucks in reserve. Call them up now. I want them at the thirty-mile point before nightfall."

The colonel bent to his task.

Other men around the large map moved small elements representing Iraqi forces closer to the thirty-mile front. One marker showed a battalion of Iraqi tanks that was only ten miles to the south of the Lightning Forces penetration and moving steadily up the road toward the front lines.

"Get our air power on those enemy tanks," General Majid said. "I don't want any of them reaching our forward probe."

General Hoseini came into the room and it fell silent. General Majid motioned outside and he and the junior general walked well away from the others.

"Hoseini, you told me we had our full order of the bio rounds ready to go."

"Yes, sir. We made four hundred, and I figured that would be enough. I didn't know for sure if we would ever use them."

"How many did I tell you to make?"

"Eight hundred. Enough for fifty rounds for each of the Lightning Force lead tanks."

"You ran out of material?"

"No, sir."

"You didn't have time to make up the rounds?"

"Plenty of time, sir."

"You reported the entire budget was used, remember that?"

"Yes, sir."

"You stole the rest of the money, about a hundred million rial?"

Hoseini looked away. "Perhaps I made an error, my General."

"Perhaps you did. How can you make it up to me? You single-handedly have ruined our attack, you have stalled our swift capture of Baghdad."

"I don't know how I can make it up to you, General Majid." He looked away.

"I do," Majid said. He lifted the Makarov 9mm pistol. "Look at me, General Hoseini." When Hoseini turned to look at Majid, the commander of all Iranian troops shot Hoseini in the forehead. He pivoted away, landing on his back, dead in an instant. Majid stepped up and fired the last seven rounds from his pistol into the dead general's chest.

He turned, holstered his empty weapon, and walked back to the command vehicle. He saw a major just outside. "Major, write up a report that General Hoseini has been killed in action as he heroically led a charge against the hated Iraqi. Send a copy of it to his widow."

11

Fifteen Miles Inside Iraq

Captain Tariz Aziz felt his heart race as the word came down. They were moving forward. His company of twelve T-55 battle tanks was going on the attack with full combat loads of ammunition. He would see action at last. After the months of intense training and the years in the tank corps, he would at last get to fight for the honor and glory of his country.

"Start the engine," he barked.

The driver below started the diesel engine and let it warm up as was the usual procedure. One minute later the order came through Captain Aziz's headphones in his helmet. It was from the battalion commander.

"All tanks move out. Company A through D in order. Single file down the road to Baghdad." There was a note of triumph in the commander's voice and Aziz felt the same elation. Now the hated Iraqis would taste the bite of the Iranian tankers, the elite of the army, the leaders in the battles.

"Move out, in order. We follow Company A. Their last tank will have an orange triangle on the back. Follow that tank. We'll be in single file, and my guess is we're heading for the front at our best speed. On the road we should be able to maintain at least forty miles an hour. It could be a short trip. Last I had heard the lead elements of our Lightning Units were thirty miles down the road toward Baghdad."

A cheer went up from the other three men in the tank. He had a driver, a loader, and a gunner for his 105mm cannon.

He did not stand in the open hatch. They had been told to button up for all runs into Iraq. There would be snipers around, since they were doing a dash into the capital, not staging a slow rooting out of every pocket of opposition. He had also been warned to go around any white substance he found on military installations or other important targets. He wasn't told exactly why, but the word was out that the white substance was anthrax, a biological substance that was deadly. So far they had stayed well to the side of any such areas.

Now, fifteen miles inside Iraq, they would have only fifteen more to get to the front elements. They would serve as backup and to widen the corridor. The orders would come as they slashed ahead. Aziz thought of his wife and three sons at home. They lived in Qom, a medium-sized town near Camp Lightning Thrust, the home of his Third Tank Battalion. It was sixty miles southwest of Tehran, with excellent terrain for his tanks to train and work out military problems and maneuvers. The thought of his three boys brought tears to his eyes. He hadn't seen them for almost a month now. He had been on extended maneuvers near the border, but he realized now that had only been an excuse to bring all of the country's firepower into the area where they would attack Iraq. His boys at home were four, six, and eight. The oldest already has said he intended to be a soldier and to try to get in the tank regiment. Aziz could think of no prouder moment. He watched out the view port as they came to the edge of a village. The tank ahead of him did a sudden left turn and skirted around a bunker that had been blasted with a tank round. The whole area was awash with the white powder.

"Around it, around it," he said into the intercom. "The damn white powder again. Stay well away from it." They all wore their bio-suits to protect themselves from the powder, but no one knew just how safe they were. A sniper opened up with an automatic rifle and Aziz could hear the rounds bouncing off the tank's armor. The rifle fire was no problem, but neither was there any time to root out the shooter. They were past in a pair of minutes. What he didn't want to see was anyone at the side of the road with a rocket-propelled grenade launcher on his shoulder. One of those rounds could knock the tracks off his tank and leave him a sitting duck.

Aziz came from an influential family. He knew it was partly due to his father's confidential talks with some generals that he made it into the Tank Brigade Academy. From there it was a straight shot into the tank regiments. He had done well at the academy, graduating second in his class, and had been promoted to Captain and given command of a company of twelve tanks. Long, long months of training followed, from individual tank movements, to company-sized problems, and then to a mock attack by all forty-eight tanks in a week-long exercise in the desert. He loved the monsters and the damage they could do with their big gun and fifty rounds of cannon fire. The strategy, the movement, the ploys, the moves and counter moves were what he lived for.

The column came to an open stretch and the big machines moved faster. He saw trucks whipping past them all loaded with infantrymen. There must be a big push coming. Thirty miles into Iraq meant only another fifty miles into Baghdad. What a thrill it would be to charge down the Iraqi capital streets to the very center of the city. He reveled in the idea until his radio came on.

"To all commanders. We're now about two miles from the front lines. The Lightning Units have stalled. They are out of the anthrax rounds and now must slug it out with the Iraqi tanks. There we have no advantage. Their best tanks are the same Soviet model that we drive. So we will overpower them with numbers. Company A and B are to swing to the left. A Jeep with a red flag will lead you through some villages and up to the point of attack. Here our corridor will be slightly wider. We will push forward at twenty miles an hour. Ground troops will follow us. Be on the lookout for enemy tanks dug in at every possible point. We'll use counter fire whenever we can. Company C and D will follow the same pattern, only they break to the right following a Jeep with a green flag. Good luck to all of you. This is our day to race into Baghdad!"

The crew cheered and Aziz saw the last tank in A Company do a hard left turn and roar away at a 45-degree angle.

"B Company," Aziz said. "We'll drift back to a hundred-yard interval between tanks. As in our exercises, A Company will take the left flank and we'll be in the center with C on our right flank and D on his flank. Let's keep our eyes open. We will be in enemy territory in about five minutes."

They rolled. He saw the last A Company tank swing farther left and come on line with that company. As he watched the tank with the orange triangle on the back, it suddenly exploded with a roar he could hear inside his tank. The body of the tank shattered into a hundred pieces as the rounds inside evidently detonated all at once.

"Steady, keep us straight ahead," Aziz barked at his driver.

"Yes, sir. Did you see that explosion?"

"I did. No tank round could do that. It must be air. A laser-guided missile maybe. I thought we had control of the air."

His headset spoke again. "Commanders, we have just lost two tanks to enemy air. We no longer have total air superiority. Suggest you make a zig-zag approach to the line. We're moving up to it now. Maintain your position and drive ahead at twenty with the movements. We will overcome!"

"I have a partly dug-in enemy tank dead ahead," the gunner shouted. "He's at about a thousand yards."

"Acquire target and fire," Aziz said.

Moments later, the tank shuddered as the big round left the barrel and the empty shell clattered out of the gun and hit the floor. The loader rammed a new round in place and the gunner scanned the target.

"Hit on the edge of the bunker," the driver said. "Might have damaged the tank. No, he's moving."

"I have him," the gunner said. "Acquired and firing."

The big gun spoke again and this time the driver cheered. "Direct hit, Astar, it's burning."

"Good shooting, Astar. Now we have enemy air, so let's stagger back fifty from the tank on our left. Slow down just a little. Good."

"Enemy tank ahead, firing," the driver bellowed. "A hard right, I'm making a hard right." A second later the round slammed into the ground and exploded thirty feet to their right.

"Back left, left," Aziz shouted.

Four thousand feet above the tank battle, two American F-18s slammed onto the scene.

"Rocket One, you see them ducks?"

"Roger, Rocket Two. The bad guys are pointing toward Baghdad."

"We have guns free on targets of opportunity. Let's make a run. I get the one in the middle of the line."

They swung around in a circle and came back at the minimum altitude of 2,000 feet, slanting down at the line of tanks with Maverick missiles up for firing. The laser-guided 495-pound missile carried a 300-pound warhead of high explosives.

"I have target acquisition and firing," Rocket Two said.

"That's a ditto for me, little buddy, one away."

The two missiles streaked for the ground at mach 1.5 and hit the tanks just as the jets slammed over the top of them.

"Splash two tanks," Rocket Two said. "Seconds anyone?"

• • •

Below, the men in two of the advancing line of Iranian tanks had no idea they had just fired their last rounds. The Mavericks hit them squarely on the turret of one and the front plates of the other, detonating the high explosive rounds in the tanks and splattering them over a quarter-mile radius.

One after another the tanks in the line exploded or were knocked out of action by near misses, as the American planes answered the desperate calls for aid from the Iraqi military. More than half of the Iraq fighter aircraft had been lost to the better trained Iranian pilots. In two hours, sixteen American aircraft killed forty-two of the advancing tanks. They had previously reduced the Lightning Strike force of tanks to a third of their original strength. The entire advance stalled, even as the five thousand Iranian foot soldiers jumped off trucks and dug in a defensive line just behind the tanks.

In his command post armored motor home twenty miles into Iraq, General Majid stared at the situation board and pounded it with his fist. The colored markers jumped, and aides quickly put them back in place.

"General Majid, sir. You asked for a report on our air situation," General Ubaidi said. He was second in command of the whole invasion force. "General Khalifa reports that we have suffered almost sixty percent loss of our fighter aircraft. We no longer have air superiority. The American pilots have riddled our planes and destroyed many of our tanks."

Majid looked up, his eyes hard black diamonds. "How many tanks do we have left for the push into Baghdad?"

"Not certain, sir. The third battalion we sent up has lost twenty-two of its forty-eight. They are regrouping and reorganizing. The lead elements are worse off. Our Lightning Force has reported a loss of all but three of its larger tanks. It can't carry out its assigned task."

"Then our advance is stalled?" Majid asked.

"At this time there is no forward movement."

Majid looked at the map again. Only fifty miles from Baghdad. The resistance would stiffen, he knew that. The Iraqi military had apparently learned a lot since the second Iraq war with the Coalition Forces back in '03. But he would not let go of his dream of conquering Baghdad. "How long to darkness? Can't we move after dark?"

"It's almost three hours to full dark," General Ubaidi said. "I'm afraid that won't help much, General Majid. The American planes have some new capability of night vision, or night radar. They can find our tanks and trucks at night as easily as they can during the day."

Majid looked around at his top field staff. "So, gentlemen, what are your recommendations?"

General Musuli was a short, rotund tank expert who had developed the Lightning Force for Iran. His usually happy face was now drawn and scowling. "The Iraqis said they would never ask for help from the Americans. They did, and that changed everything. We have lost half of our engaged tank force, most of it to American air. We do not have the capability of driving our Lightning Attack forward. It is my suggestion that we regroup our forces and work out a strategic withdrawal, conserving what we have left of our men and materiel."

Majid nodded and looked at the next man. "General Kadri, your evaluation of our situation."

Kadri stood almost six-feet two-inches and was clean shaven with a close-cropped haircut. He had been a soldier for over forty years, and it was starting to show. He wiped one hand across his weathered face and sighed.

"There is no option, my General. We must withdraw. Even now we're having trouble maintaining our corridor to the border. If we extend it even twenty more miles, our forces along the flanks of the corridor will be stretched so thin a camel attack could penetrate it and disrupt our supply lines. Withdraw, yes, quickly, efficiently, conserving as many men and machines as we can."

Majid nodded and looked at the last general at the table, a man with a pointer and a determined look. He was General Ubaidi. His shoulders showed four stars.

"General Majid. With all respect for your dream of sacking Baghdad, it doesn't look like this is the time. We are outgunned in the air. We have lost half of our tanks, including most of our Lightning Force. It is time to do a strategic withdrawal."

General Majid turned and walked into his private section of the motor home, stood looking at the wall for a moment, then turned and strode back with quick steps.

"All right, it is decided. We will regroup. The Third Battalion will take the place of the Lightning Force and we will push forward in exactly two hours. Make your arrangements with your troops. Call on all of the air support we can find. We move out in two hours, and we are not stopping until I ride a tank into the central square in Baghdad!"

12

Alluvial Diamond Mine
New Namibia, Africa

Alluvial Diamond Mine
New Namibia, Africa

Lieutenant Commander Blake Murdock looked around the mine. Slowly, men began coming out of hiding places. One man ran up to Murdock.

"You okay, guy? We hear shooting. We hide. Bad guys all gone?"

"We think so. Did they have a woman with them?"

"Yes, woman."

"We need a truck to follow them. Can you loan us one?"

"Ask boss." The worker pointed to an older man with a crisply trimmed beard and a straw hat. He marched across the compound and stared at Murdock.

"You U.S. Marines?"

"No, we're U.S. Navy SEALs. We need a truck. Those men who were here are kidnappers. We're chasing them. Can you loan us some transport?"

The man frowned and rubbed his chin. "You won't get it shot up, or wreck it?"

"Not planning on it. We need to chase those guys who just left here."

"Left an hour ago. In no hurry. Tried to find our diamonds. No luck." The man frowned again. "Okay. You use big truck. Flatbed. You all climb on it."

Ten minutes later the SEALs and Delta men crawled on

the twenty-foot stake truck and headed down the well-graded gravel road.

"How far to town?" Jaybird asked.

"Who knows, at least we're moving." Mahanani said.

The road wound downslope sharply, but the grade was gradual enough and the bends well worked out. A mile down the road, the truck came around a curve and slowed to go up a slight slope.

Two rifle rounds slammed into the side of the engine and Bradford brought the rig to a stop.

"Bail out," Murdock shouted. Men scrambled off the truck and into the heavy growth on the far side of the road away from the gunman.

"Who in hell?" Senior Chief Neal asked.

"Why in hell?" Jaybird cracked.

"Anybody see anything?" Murdock asked.

"Some brush moving up the slope to the left about two hundred," Lam said. Murdock tossed him the Bull Pup.

"Put a Twenty on his ass," Murdock said.

The round slammed out of the tube and exploded in the air over the spot Lam had guessed the gunner would be by then. They heard nothing but the echoing of the shot through the valley below them.

Bradford checked the engine. "Looks like the round got through the sheet metal but didn't do any damage inside the hood. We can travel."

"Load up, and keep a watch," Murdock said.

A half-mile later, around another curve, a rifle round zipped over the top of the men sitting on the truck bed. They piled out of the truck and waited, but no more shots came and no one saw any movement.

Murdock was ready to drive again when Lam held up his hand.

"Cap, we've got a chopper warming up. Not too far down the hill. It'll be taking off in two or three, I'd guess."

"Let's drive on down, maybe there's time to stop it," J.G. Gardner said.

"Not a prayer, Lieutenant," Lam said. "Looks like she's lifting off right now."

Soon they could hear the roar and thump of the rotors as a chopper appeared from behind the next hill, turned, and angled toward the coast.

"Six-place job," Engle said. "Means they left some rear guard for us to handle before we get to the coast."

"Right," Murdock said. "Everyone back on the truck. All weapons aimed to the port side and safeties off. Let's roll until we're stopped, Bradford. Now." Murdock used the Motorola again. "Don Stroh, do you read me? How far are we from you? Come in if you can hear." He shook his head. They had to be farther than the six miles range of the radios from the airport. He'd have to try again when they were closer.

They went a half-mile when a volley of shots from the left sent the men into a flurry of return fire before they dove off the truck to the right and took cover. To the left they saw a small valley with a flat area large enough for a chopper to land. There was an old pickup there and a barrel that could hold fuel.

"The damn kidnappers planned ahead," Murdock said. "Gardner, take your squad across the road and through the brush and try to flush them out. We'll put Twenties anywhere we see muzzle flashes with rounds coming your way. Go."

They crossed the road in a rush, all at once, so there would be no picking them off one by one as they ran over the open area. It must have surprised the gunners because only one shot came, and it missed. Then the SEALs vanished into the brush and trees.

"Who you have for your scout?" Murdock asked on the Motorola.

"Rafii," the report came back.

Murdock moved the rest of the SEALs and Delta men down the far side of the road in the brush until they were directly opposite the pickup truck. They were less than fifty yards from it. There was no movement, and evidently no shooters there.

Murdock handed his Bull Pup to Captain Engle. "Put a contact round Twenty on that barrel, Captain. Let's see if there's any more fuel in it."

Engle grinned and took the weapon. Murdock showed him the selector for the Twenty and the sights. Engle nodded and aimed at the barrel with the weapon braced over a fallen log. He fired. The round seemed to hit at almost the same time the report came from the rifle. It exploded on target, with a gushing roar as the barrel went up in one huge fireball engulfing the pickup truck and singing the brush thirty feet away.

"Yep, guess there was some petrol left in there after all," Captain Engle said.

They heard gunfire from the left and across the road. At the same time, shots sounded in front of them thirty yards down from the burning truck and hot lead sang through the brush and trees that hid Murdock and his men.

"Return fire," Murdock barked. "Find cover and return." The men scattered farther, stepping behind trees or dropping behind fallen logs, and began firing at the suspect area.

Murdock put two 20mm rounds into the spot and watched for any movement.

"Gardner," Murdock said on the Motorola.

"Bit busy right now, Commander. We've got two or three hostiles who don't like us a bit. We dispatched one, and one is running deep into the brush, but the other one is totally antisocial."

"We've hit some here as well. Finish off your party there and come down the far side of the road under cover to find us. You'll see a burning truck down about two hundred yards."

"Roger that."

"Cease fire, Alpha and Delta," Murdock said on the radio. The weapons went silent and he watched the suspect area and listened.

"Lam, you hear anything?"

"Too far, Cap. Want me to go take a look?"

"Yeah, but carefully. Let's have some scattered rounds to cover Lam scooting across the open road. When you're ready, Lampedusa."

Lam sprayed the brush across the way with his MP-5 as he darted across the open roadway and dove into the concealing brush on the far side. A dozen weapons fired into the suspect area to cover Lam, then quieted when he was safely across.

"Check your ammo," Murdock said. "Might be a good time to put in full magazines."

They heard more firing from Gardner's squad.

"That wraps us up from here," Gardner said. "Two down, one running for his life."

"Bring the truck with you. Let it coast downhill. Lam is out on a hunt to see where our little friends are down here. We need to get into town and see where that chopper landed and what the madman did with the First Lady. Maybe he's running, too."

Five minutes later the truck rolled down the hill. Gardner stopped it just out of sight of the burned pickup and he and his men joined Murdock.

Lam checked in. "Skipper, I found the brass where they had been. At least five of them. Not sure where they went but they are gone, vamoosed, out of here. I'd say the area is clear, unless they try to hit us again down the road."

"Come home my son, all is forgiven," Murdock said.

Captain Engle looked at Murdock with a surprised grin. Murdock waved and told the men to get on the truck. "We're a little more relaxed in our outfit," he said to Engle. "Out here, every man relies on every other man. Rank or rate don't mean shit."

Engle nodded. "Way it has to be," he said. "We're working on it in Delta, but we're not quite there yet."

The truck rolled forward. Bradford climbed in the cab and found the last shot had not damaged the rig. He fired up the engine and Lam ran to jump onboard and they charged down the narrow but well-maintained road.

The men were prone on the bed of the truck with weapons aimed at the brush on both sides of the road. Bradford rammed the truck down the road as fast as the turns permitted and opened it up when the landscape flattened and they could see the buildings of the capital ahead and to the left.

"Get us to the airport," Murdock said. He tried the Motorola again. "Don Stroh, on the Motorola. Can you read me?"

Murdock waited two minutes and tried again. This time a faint reply came through.

"Murdock, get some of . . . transmission."

"Package is in chopper. May be at the airport now. Copy?"

"Murdock. Package in chopper. Will check airport." As the truck rolled forward, the reception improved.

"Yes, a six-place chopper with the First Lady. Check landings."

"Read you better now. Checking tower for landings and takeoffs."

"We had a few problems, should be there in twenty minutes." Murdock turned to Bradford. "Can't you get any more speed out of this machine? That devil Badri may already be chartering a plane."

"You think he'll try to fly out?"

"What would you do in a similar situation? It's what I'd do. Get away from here and try for another country. He must have the cash to go where he wants to."

It took then twenty-five minutes to get to the airport and for Murdock to find Stroh in the manager's office. The CIA man was haggard and scowling when Murdock met him.

"Bad news?" Murdock asked.

"Damn bad. Badri's chopper had landed well before your call came. The tower reported that he set down and the four passengers transferred at once to an old F-35 Beechcraft Bonanza that had been chartered yesterday. The pilot had already filed a flight plan for Namibia and took off at once. That was a little over an hour ago."

"Did they head for Namibia?"

"Evidently. No sign that's where they'll wind up. I checked. The plane has a range of a little over eight hundred miles."

"How far is it to the Namibia capital?" Murdock asked.

"The tower operator says it's only four hundred and fifty miles."

"Our jet still here?"

"Yes."

"Crank it up, we're out of here as soon as we can get loaded and cleared for takeoff. How fast is that Bonanza?"

"Not sure, maybe a hundred and eighty miles an hour, maybe up to two hundred."

"We should be able to beat them there," Murdock said. "This is sounding more and more like an orchestrated event, and we're playing the fools. Let's get out of here."

Murdock growled as it took them twenty-five minutes to get airborne. He put all the SEALs onboard, said goodbye to Captain Engle and his men, and tried to figure the times.

"Jaybird, the Bonanza should take almost two and a quarter hours to get to Windhoek, the capital down in Namibia. According to the tower, they left at thirteen-twenty. They should arrive at fifteen thirty-five. We left at fourteen forty-five. When do we hit the capital?"

"Less than an hour flight time, including takeoff and let-down. Say fifty minutes total. This biz jet rolls at five hundred miles an hour. Puts us in Windhoek at fifteen thirty-five. The same time they should land."

"If we're lucky," Murdock said. "If we don't run into a headwind of fifty knots."

"One problem, Commander," Jaybird said, shifting in his seat. "We don't have any firm speed on that Beechcraft Bonanza. It's the older model, and I don't remember any specs on it. If it can get, say, two hundred and ten mph out of that mill, they'll beat us there by ten minutes."

"Thanks, Jaybird. I really needed that. You may take one giant step out the forward hatch."

"Yes, sir. Thank you sir!" Jaybird said grinning. But he knew enough when to shut up.

Murdock went forward to see if they could go to maximum cruise speed at 25,000 feet instead of 40,000 and get another eighty miles an hour out of the plane. The Coast Guard lieutenant flying the plane shook his head.

"Not without special written instructions from my superior," the pilot said.

Murdock argued with him a minute, playing his CNO and presidential cards, but the pilot wouldn't budge.

"Hey, Captain, this is just a routine mission for me. I didn't get any notice of special circumstances that would let me go to max cruise speed."

Windhoek, Namibia Airport

They landed precisely at fifteen-forty.

Murdock hurried up to the cabin to call the tower and ask them if the Beechcraft Bonanza had landed yet.

Jaybird stood right behind him.

Murdock shook his head. "Jaybird, we'll know soon if the First Lady has landed. You realize that if she has, I'll have you shot."

"Yes, sir. Thank you, sir!" Jaybird said, his grin growing with every second.

"Yes, U.S. Military Gulfstream Four," the tower voice said over the radio. "That's an affirmative. The craft you inquire about landed here twelve minutes ago. Requested refueling and immediate takeoff. They filed a flight plan by radio for Botswana. That's to the east of us. However, air traffic controllers report the plane took off four minutes ago and turned directly south."

"Where could he land down that way?" Murdock asked.

"Not a lot of airports. About eight hundred miles south is Cape Town, South Africa. But that craft could reach Cape Town without refueling."

"So can we, tower. I'd like to ask for an immediate take-off. That plane that left is carrying a kidnap victim we're attempting to retrieve."

"Put your pilot on to file a radio flight plan and you're on your way."

Murdock gave the mike to the pilot and went back to the cabin with Jaybird. Murdock pointed his index finger at Jaybird like the barrell of a gun. He cocked his thumb.

"Bang, bang, Jaybird," he said. He told the crew what had happened.

"I hope to hell the galley is well stocked," Rafii said. "I could eat a horse."

It was, and Murdock saw that they ate as soon as they reached their altitude of 40,000 feet.

Murdock finished off the airline package dinner tray and talked to the men. "This time we should have him. If he flies into Cape Town, we should beat him there by well over two hours. Then we'll see what happens on the ground."

13

Command Motor Home
Twenty Miles Inside Iraq

General Majid looked around the table at his top command generals. He saw some disbelief, some shock, one angry face.

"Is there anyone who disagrees with my orders? Are there any of you who will not comply *immediately*?"

All but one of the men shook their heads and looked down at the situation map. Only General Musuli stared hard at General Majid.

"Sir, as your top commander of tanks, it is my duty to caution you about this thrust. We stand to lose ninety percent of our tanks with such an attack without at least artillery preparation."

"Then Musuli, you refuse my order?"

Before the general could say a word, General Majid drew his pistol and from six feet away fired two rounds into the tank man's chest. Musuli staggered backwards and then collapsed on the floor. The men remaining in the motor home blanched with shock, but at once moved out the door and began shouting orders. The last two men had to step over the body.

Majid strode to the door. "I want every plane we have that can fly in the air and bombing the advancing Iraqis. Concentrate on the Iraqi tanks, those big ones. Knock out every tank your flyers can. You hear me? Go after the damn tanks. Destroy every damn one of them. All the tanks. Bring up another ten thousand men. We'll swarm over them with mass charges if nothing else. We move ahead, or, gentlemen, we die where we stand."

The generals had stopped, listened, and now ran to their respective command vehicles to give the orders.

Ten miles ahead in the narrow corridor, four Iranian tanks had positioned themselves on the reverse slope of a small hill, concealing themselves from the enemy out front. At twenty-minute intervals, one tank would charge up so the gunner could see over the lip of the hill. He would look for targets, and whether he found one or not, he would fire a round at the best possible enemy truck or squad of men or an Iraqi tank if he was lucky, then give the order to race back down the hill and out of sight.

A mile away, a dozen T-62 Iraqi tanks were dug in on the reverse slope of a hill with only their long barrel and the hatch area exposed. They were camouflaged, and from a quarter of a mile away were practically invisible. The commander of the twelve heavy, Russian-built tanks had been watching the Iranian tanks playing run and shoot. Iraqi Captain Sabaawi had seen three tanks rush up, fire and, roll back. This time he was ready. He had designated three of his tank gunners to pick a spot along the top of the ridge, forty yards apart, and zero in the big guns on them. Wherever the next Iranian tank rolled up to shoot, there would be a 105mm gun aimed close by. The gunner would have to make only a minor adjustment in his sighting and then fire. One of his tanks should kill whichever enemy lifted up its turret.

Captain Sabaawi waited and watched. He hoped his own gunner would get the shot. The last enemy tank had shown up on the far right. It would be the far left or the center this time. He had the center responsibility.

Faster than he thought possible, an enemy tank rolled

up so its long gun cleared the hill. It had come too far. Center. His gunner adjusted his aim slightly and fired. Well before the Iranian tank fired, it took the heavy HE round that penetrated the front armor and exploded inside the tank.

Sabaawi used his battalion radio. "Major, we just killed one of the Iranian tanks."

"Good, Sabaawi, because our forward air observers report that there are forty more coming down the road toward us. They are five miles from the Iranian front lines. Our air is working, but we won't be able to stop all of them. We'll have to be ready to take them on. Hold your position. When the tanks come into the open, make every round count."

"Yes sir, Major. It will be done. Why are they pushing so hard now?"

"We don't know. They are bringing up foot troops as well. Watch for enemy air, it's increasing."

"Yes sir, Major. We're ready." He switched to his company radio and told his men about the new attack. He swallowed. Men would die out here today, lots of them. Some of his best friends might be dead already. He thought of home and his wife and the life he had chosen for him and his family. His sons were strong, they would keep the family together if anything happened. He shook his head. Now was not the time for this. He picked up his company mike. "We must pick them off as fast as we can. If you see a tank with a long whip antenna, shoot at that one first. It will be a company or section commander. Get ready, we may not have much time."

"Sir," one of the tank commanders said. "How many tanks do we have in this sector?"

"We have twelve, all dug in like we are. And there are three more lines of twelve tanks behind us all dug in and camouflaged. We control this area—about a half-mile wide. The thrust of the Iranians is a little more than three-quarters of a mile. We hold them off or they eat breakfast at your favorite Baghdad restaurant."

"We have backup?"

"The tanks behind us, and we have U.S. air support. If we can't stop them here, we go to our fall-back positions just in back of them. It's a defensive setup that's worked since El Alamein."

"Where?" a voice asked on the radio.

"World War Two, British victory over the Germans in the town of that name in Egypt near Alexandria. A classic," Captain Sabaawi said. "You should know about it."

He could hear an aircraft overhead then even through the buttoned-up tank cover. He wanted to pop up and take a look, but he had given the order to keep the hatches closed and locked. Ahead, out the view port, he could see the hill that hid the Iranian tanks. Now he had a quick look as two jet fighters swept in and fired missiles at the enemy tanks. He heard one explosion, then a sympathetic roar as the rest of the tank's rounds must have "cooked off" in the flaming mass of the missile explosion. Good, two fewer enemy tanks to worry about.

"Commanders, the enemy tank force is now crossing the line," his battalion CO said. "They are less than two miles from our front tank row. This is the hard thrust we were expecting. A final try, a suicide venture if we have anything to say about it. They'll be in range in another ten minutes. Good shooting, gentlemen."

Less than a mile from the known positions of the Iraqi tanks, Captain Tariz Aziz stared at the scarred, rutted countryside. He awaited orders from his colonel. They hadn't come. He knew the last battalion of tanks was rushing forward to replace the burned-out Lightning Thrust tanks. But when did he and his company move? He had six out of twelve tanks left. There's no rearview mirror on a tank. When were his friends coming up and roaring past him? He would wait, and when they passed he would move out and follow them.

Without any other orders, those were the best he could figure. A moment later he heard the clank and grinding of a tank moving past him on the right. He hit his company radio.

"All right, this is our time. As soon as the tanks now passing us are all ahead, we will pull out and follow them. We'll fill in any gaps in their line. Everyone report in."

He listened as the five tank commanders gave their check-in call signs.

"Good, it should be shortly. We'll close up to a hundred yards of the line ahead and follow. Let's stay fifty yards apart and in a good line until we see where we fill in any gaps. There is still enemy air. We can't do a damn thing about it, so we will charge ahead."

Suddenly one of the T-52s ahead lunged forward and vanished.

"Tank trap dead ahead. All stop." He watched another tank plunge into the hole. It must be a giant ditch for just this purpose. Must be a way around it. Then he heard them coming. Dozens maybe hundreds of artillery shells. The enemy tankers had test fired on those positions and set up concentrations before. If the tanks came they would stop at the barrier and move right or left. While they stopped and moved, the artillery would slam into the area, with a fire-for-effect bombardment, hoping that many of the rounds hit the tanks.

"Company, angle left, we'll go around it. Left full speed, let's get away from those artillery rounds." Just as his tank turned, Aziz saw two of the front-line monsters blow up as artillery or enemy tankers hit them with rounds. He found a ravine and raced his driver into it. It led around to the left, the correct way. If only it went far enough. After a quarter of a mile it angled back south again, toward the tank trap. Only the ditch didn't come this far.

He checked ahead and saw that he had flanked the other line of friendly tanks. He was in the outback by himself and his five tanks.

"Let's go south and see what we can find," he said on his company net. The six tanks angled out of the gully, which had flattened out and they saw nothing ahead but artillery smoke and the ranks of Iraqi tanks firing at the Iranian armor that charged around both ways to escape from the artillery and the tank trap.

They were far enough on the flank so he could spot the end of three rows of enemy tanks dug in on the hills. "See those Iraq T-62s to the right? Target them and fire when ready."

Moments later he felt his own tank fire. He watched the targets and saw the enemy tank in the first row spout flames with a direct hit. It tried to back out of the revetment, but couldn't move.

"Take a left turn go fifty, now," he barked at his driver. He expected return battery fire at any second. When he looked he saw the second Iraq tank spouting flames, then rounds came at him and his tank jolted one way then another to escape the fire. One of his commanders yelled that he'd been hit and couldn't move. Aziz turned and saw three men jump out of the tank and right into the middle of a high-explosive round that blew them into pieces.

"Back to the gully," he shouted into the company radio net, and his tank turned and slammed back toward the protection of the gully. Two minutes later only three of the six tanks left in the company had reached safety. He thought of edging over the lip of the gully to see where the fight was, but he knew there would be six or eight Iraqi gunners just waiting for him to pop his rig over the top. Instead he opened the hatch.

"I'm going to do some recon," he yelled at his men. "Just stay here and stay quiet. Be right back."

He jumped off the tank and scrambled up the side of the ravine. He barely lifted his eyes over the lumps of dirt and rock and peered past a scraggly bush. Smoke everywhere.

On the three hills he could spot where the enemy tanks had dug in near the crests. He counted eleven tanks along one ridge alone. Three or four ridges. All protected but the very end ones. In front of him he also saw a dozen or more burning Iranian tanks. He wondered how many men he knew and had trained with were now dead or dying. The Iranian tanks kept moving forward toward the ridges at fifteen or twenty miles an hour. He ducked as an aircraft screamed out of the sky, fired a missile, and zoomed upward as the round hit an Iranian tank and blew it into a thousand pieces. He now counted sixteen tanks on the main line that were burning. He saw his own three tanks a hundred yards ahead. One had exploded with almost nothing left. The other two had been hit and stopped. He saw two of his crews working slowly to the rear, going from one small bit of cover to the next. The Iraqi tankers would not fire a big round at a pair of men.

He watched in fascination as the twenty Iranian tanks remaining charged across the half-mile at twenty miles an hour toward the enemy tank positions. If they weren't hit they would overrun the enemy in five minutes. Another one in the line blew up. Down the line, a tank round tore off the tread on another T-54 and put it down for good, useless, its main gun angled to the rear.

Aziz felt the tears streaming down his face as he scrambled back down the bank and raced for his tank. He had to get back in the fight. He jumped up on the tank and slid into the hatch and closed and locked it in place.

Aziz grabbed his headset. "Company, the three of us are going to charge the flank of those Iraqis. Not sure how far we'll get, but at least we'll go down fighting. Are you with me?"

He heard the cheers over the radio.

Aziz took out the photo of his family and stared at it. Then he kissed the picture and put it back inside his helmet.

"All right, let's charge out of this protection a hundred yards apart, then we'll swing to the south more and angle at those bluffs. Hold fire until my first round goes off. I want to get close to those bastards who are killing all of our friends. Ready. Usual formation. Let's roll."

14

Twenty Iranian trucks had dropped off four hundred infantry troops less than a mile behind where the front line had been twenty minutes ago. The men formed up into platoons and strode forward on a quick march heading for the tankers ahead. Not even the commander of the battalion knew why they were there or what their objective was. He was told to take his men to the front lines and march forward until fired upon, then to go to ground, return fire, and move ahead, killing any of the enemy he saw.

Sergeant Jaafar Saadi kept his squad of eight men in the line of march, a spread-out assault formation that stretched over a hundred yards. He wasn't sure what they were doing, or why. Lieutenant Rabbo, his platoon leader, said he wasn't given a specific objective. They would sweep ahead and eliminate any enemy troops or tank crews that they found. Saadi wanted to ask what they did if they got ahead of the friendly tanks, but he didn't have the nerve. He was afraid of Lieutenant Rabbo, and rightly so. He had seen the officer beat a corporal and send him to the hospital. Nobody knew exactly why the officer had flown into the rage.

Now they charged across this destroyed land with tanks shooting at each other somewhere in front. They could be as little as two miles ahead. He scowled, wondering what would happen. He didn't think the major would let his men be run over by their own tanks. He wasn't so sure about his lieutenant.

It wasn't like this in the military academy. Everything done was accomplished because an order was given. A project, a study, a field exercise, physical training, learning to swim. Every move he made for four years in the school had been aimed at instilling discipline and respect for the authority of his officers.

He knew that combat would be hectic and unsure, and that there would be wild moments, sometimes lasting for hours. Strange duty and unusual tasks and danger, and that he might even face death today. Now in this total confusion, he didn't know if they were winning or losing. He had no idea how many tanks they had or if they were better than those that Iraq used. Aircraft left him totally at a loss.

Just then he heard a jet fighter screaming overhead at less than two thousand feet. He didn't know if it was one of his or an enemy. He did know that in a war there was a chance for quick advancement in rank. Especially in combat, where men ahead of you might get wounded or killed and the next man in line had to step up. He had a chance to lead his own platoon if everything worked out right. Not that he would shoot Lieutenant Rabbo, but he knew it had happened in wars before this one. He looked ahead and saw a small house. What should they do? Did they stop and clear it? Did they work around it and leave it? Maybe they should burn it down so no one could hide in it. He looked at Lieutenant Rabbo and motioned at the house.

"Burn it," his platoon leader said.

Sergeant Saadi pointed to two of his men and they ran forward. He pulled a white phosphorous grenade from his combat webbing and the three of them flattened themselves against the front wall. He motioned for one man to open the door. As soon as it was open, Saadi popped the handle on the grenade and let it arm, then he threw it inside the door. All three charged away from the structure and caught up with their unit. The grenade went off, showering the inside of the building with burning phosphorous, setting it on fire in an instant and burning through everything that it stuck to.

He got back in the assault formation and motioned for two of his men to move forward to keep the line straight. Ahead he saw nothing but small bushes not a foot off the ground, and lots of sand and rocks. The land right here wasn't even good for grazing goats. Maybe after a few good rains. He heard the shells exploding ahead. How far was he now from friendly tanks? They could roll ahead twenty to thirty miles an hour. Where were the enemy tanks?

He looked at his lieutenant walking forward in line with the rest of them. No. He wasn't the kind of officer an enlisted man asked questions of. Wait and see. Wait and die. No, he would not die. His mother would never forgive him. He was the fourth generation in his family to serve in the military. He would not be the last. He must survive and maintain the line.

They came over a small rise and could see the tanks ahead. The Iranian tankers were scattered, charging around, not going forward anymore. He saw smoke and burning tanks everywhere. He could smell the oil burning and the terrible stench of scorched human flesh. Lots of Iranians had died here today. He would not be one of them.

Something screamed down out of the sky and exploded fifty feet in front of them. One man bellowed in fear and pain and fell, shrapnel from the tank round shredding both his legs just above the knee. A medic dropped out of line and stayed with the man as the rest of the troops moved forward.

"A stray round," someone shouted. "They aren't shooting at us."

Maybe. But for a stray it came damn close to wiping out twenty of them. An order came and the men moved apart, putting ten yards between men. This way a lucky round wouldn't kill thirty of them.

Now and then he could see aircraft in the bright blue sky

above. Two angled toward each other high overhead. Another one swept in from the south and sent a long spear at one of the tanks nearest him. The tanker turned sharply, but the missile turned with him and daggered into the side of the machine, penetrated inside, and exploded. Secondary explosions rocked the whole landscape for a moment and the sound battered his ears. The tank blew into a thousand pieces. Some sailed near the advancing troops two hundred yards away.

They found tank crews now hiding in shell holes, huddled behind burned-out tanks, waving at them for water, for medical help. The infantrymen marched stoically ahead. Following orders. The men were just doing what their officers told them to do. Saadi's job: do what Lieutenant Rabbo ordered him to do. Now that was to march forward and into whatever danger was out there. Hell, probably.

The Iranian tanks slowly organized what was left of their battalion and moved forward again. This time at top speed—thirty miles an hour, Saadi figured. They rammed right up to the front of the range of hills and fired point blank at the tanks. The Iraqi armor now had guns too high to depress enough to hit them. Five, six, then seven of the Iraqi tanks in the first row died in flames.

Saadi checked again. Only seven Iranian tanks had made it through the gauntlet to the hill. Now they jolted around each end of the line and tried to gun the Iraqi tanks positioned higher on the slope. One tried to race up the side of the first slope, but was quickly hit by a tank round and exploded on the spot. The other tanks retreated to just below the bluff and waited.

Why were they waiting, Saadi wondered? Were they waiting for the infantry to come save them? For the infantry to charge up the hill and blow up the tanks? Impossible. As he wondered, he heard the sound of machine guns puncturing the air. Then the .50 caliber rounds started slashing into the troops in the assault line.

"Down, down, everyone hit the dirt!" the lieutenants up and down the long battalion line bellowed. Saadi dove to the ground, hoping for a small depression or shell hole, but there was nothing there but the flat ground. He wondered where the artillery was. Why wasn't it there blasting that collection of tanks? They could score dozens of hits the way the tanks were grouped together. He realized he hadn't seen any artillery for the past eight or ten miles as they rode forward in the trucks. Did they run out of ammunition, or what? Where were the damn long guns?

The enemy machine guns kept pounding. Alternate squads lifted up and ran forward to spread out the men even more. Then the whole battalion stood and ran forward. The lines wavered and broke as some men charged quicker than others and many fell behind. The deadly machine guns kept cutting down whole squads of men at a time. The survivors dashed across the last four hundred yards, panting and swearing and firing their weapons at the tanks above on the hill. The machine guns kept firing even though they were out of targets. Sergeant Saadi had no idea how many of the Iranian infantry never made it to the shelter of the hill. His stomach lurched and he almost threw up. So many had died!

Jaafar Saadi lay in the dirt checking his body. Nowhere did he find blood or broken bones. Allah had smiled on him today. He was safe for the moment, but what now? The enemy tanks couched less than fifty yards up the hill waiting for the chance to kill them. A few Iranian tanks below the depression range of the Iraqi tank guns were little protection.

A stalemate.

The enemy tanks couldn't take the safe routes to come down the slopes and turn and head south. Neither could the Iranian tanks turn and head north toward their homeland without being targeted.

Lieutenant Rabbo ran up to Sergeant Saadi and nodded.

"Get two good men and crawl up the slope and see if you can blow the tread off the first tank you come to. Chances are they have no men outside the tanks. Stay out of sight as long as you can. Tape three grenades together and force them between the tread and the driving wheels. Then tape a fourth grenade on the outside of the other three, holding down the arming spoon. When it's secure, let the spoon pop off and sprint down the hill to get away from the explosion. Then creep back up and see if it blew the tread off the rollers."

"If anyone comes out of the hatch, we'll shoot him," Saadi said. The officer nodded, gave him two more grenades for his web vest, and pointed them up the hill.

Saadi went first, cradling the AK-47 across his arms as he crawled up through some light brush. It was slow work. Twenty feet from the tank he stopped and looked up at the monster. The gunners couldn't see down here. He nodded to himself and crawled forward. He was almost to the tank when he heard a scraping noise and lifted up to look. The hatch on top of the tank moved, lifted up six inches, and then went back down.

Saadi had held his breath, now he took a big gulp of air and crawled up to the tank tread. It was bigger than he had guessed. Yes, a spot to put the grenades. They had been taped together by the lieutenant. He pushed them into the slack place between the tread and the driving roller. Then the second man gave him another grenade and the sticky tape. He pulled the pin on the grenade and loosened the arming handle just enough to slip the tape under it, then bound it tightly to the other grenades. He motioned the other two men back, let go of the arming handle, and knew he had four seconds to get away. He dove down the slope and rolled twenty feet, and then hugged the rocky dirt.

The explosion was louder than he figured. It jolted into the afternoon that had turned quiet now that the machine guns and the big guns on the tanks on both sides had quieted. He heard shrapnel from the grenades singing over his head, but none hit him.

He moved upward again to see the damage. Just as he was within ten feet of the tank, the scraping noise came again and the hatch pivoted back and a man heaved up until he was halfway out. Saadi shot him twice in the chest with his AK-47 and the man fell forward, blocking the exit from the machine.

Sergeant Saadi surged ahead, saw that the track was blown off the rollers. The tank was dead in the water until a repair rig fixed the tread. He rolled down the slope, took the other two men with him, and reported the success to his lieutenant.

Down the line they heard three more grenade explosions. Then all was quiet again. Saadi stared in amazement when he saw that the sun was almost down. It would be dark in an hour.

Lieutenant Rabbo passed the word: They had lost contact with their commanding officer. They were on their own. As soon as it was dark enough to move, the tanks would pull out and head north toward the old main line they had established. The infantry would make a retrogressive movement as well, making all kinds of speed to get back out of the range of the deadly .50 caliber tank machine guns. They probably would fire, but it would be hit or miss and at random. They would kill a few of the retreating infantrymen, but Saadi knew he would not be one of them; Allah had smiled at him this day.

Darkness at last settled in, and the infantry leaders had talked the tankers into letting the walkers go first so they could be safe from the machine guns above. They reluctantly gave the infantry an hour. They could be five miles away by that time.

They pulled out a half-hour after dark. Saadi had lost two men to the machine guns on the charge to the bluffs. They marched fast at rout step and made a little over four miles before they heard the tanks behind them start to move. Then came the faint sound of machine gun fire as well.

By midnight they arrived back at the spot where the trucks had dropped them off that morning. They were tired and hungry but there was no field kitchen there to feed them. A major beside his Jeep said the army generals had pulled back an hour ago. The trucks that brought them here had been sent back as well. If they marched all night they should be well out of harm's way come dawn.

"Oh, be sure your men go around any of the white powder areas you will find. It's not hard to see. You have no biologic protection suits, so don't go near it."

The long night's march began.

It was nearly four A.M. when they detoured around another anthrax-laden area. They had just stepped off the road when the man in front of Sergeant Jaafar Saadi stepped on an Iraqi-planted land mine. It exploded, cutting down seven men and wounding a dozen more.

Saadi was blasted a dozen feet away and lay sprawled in the dirt. He touched his chest and felt a mass of blood. It hurt so horrendously he wanted to scream, but he couldn't. He shook his head where he lay in the Iraqi dirt and rocks. This couldn't be happening. They were almost out of danger. Besides, Allah had smiled on him twice already today. He couldn't die. The last thing Saadi remembered was the smile on Allah's face fade away. Then Saadi died.

15

Lieutenant Commander Blake Murdock, Don Stroh, Lieutenant (J.G.) Chris Gardner, and Lieutenant Ed DeWitt sat in the Cape Town airport manager's office waiting. The rest of the platoon had stayed with the plane. The top man at the airport, Jeffrey Smith-Warner, was in constant contact with the tower.

"They should have landed ten minutes ago," Murdock said. He had been growing more worried as the flight time for the Beechcraft stretched out. The surprising efficiency of the local officials had been welcomed at first, but now he was doubting them.

"Could the tower have missed him somehow? Maybe he came in under the radar and landed at that far-off runway?"

"Not a chance, Commander. Nothing moves around here in the air that we don't know about."

Murdock stood and walked to the window wall and looked out at the airport and the tower in the distance. How in hell had he done it? Where was he? Murdock checked his watch.

"Fifteen minutes past his maximum flight fuel supply. Which means he either landed somewhere else or ran out of gas and crashed."

"What about small airports?" DeWitt asked. "Aren't

there some around here that don't have towers or controls where transient aircraft can land?"

"Yes. Several. Five at least. Yes, he could have landed at one of them and we wouldn't even have him on our radar. He wouldn't have a transponder on that ship or he could turn it off and we probably wouldn't know he was coming."

"Could your secretary give us a list of those airports and their telephone numbers?" Don Stroh asked.

"Take her about three minutes." The manager picked up the phone and relayed the request.

The Americans stood. "Thanks for your help," Stroh said. "We'll catch this guy eventually." The four went out to the secretary and took the sheet of paper she handed them.

Five minutes later in the airport terminal, the men had made four calls. Gardner looked up from the telephone and motioned to Murdock.

"I've got him. Beechcraft Bonanza landed about twenty minutes ago. Little grass strip north of town ten miles called Niles's AirField."

Murdock put down his phone. "Let's go," he said, and they headed for the taxi stands at the front of the terminal.

A half-hour later the taxi driver found the right road and rolled into the airfield. It was small, one grassed strip about five hundred yards long, one T-hangar, a small office, and a repair shop also in the form of a T to accommodate the wings and still give room to work on the engine or body. One beat-up Plymouth sat in the space next to the office. To the far side just beyond the T-hangar sat a Beechcraft Bonanza.

Stroh told the cabbie to wait for them and they went toward the office. A small black man with grey hair and a left-footed limp came out to meet them. His back was broom-handle straight and he grinned when he saw the cammies that the two SEALs wore. There had to be some military time in his background. His face was pock marked and there were only a few teeth left around the front of his mouth. He nodded and Murdock saw that the older man almost saluted.

"You must be the gentleman who called me. Can't tell you much more than I did on the phone. They came sailing in about an hour ago. Told me the plane was rented and I should notify the home field listed on the papers. I called a cab for them and the four of them got in and it drove away."

"Were they Arabs?" Murdock asked.

"Could be. I'm not much on foreigners. Could be. The guy who did the talking was dark and had a black moustache and black hair. The woman was taller than he was but they kept her far away from me and I had the idea that she wasn't happy and didn't want to go with the men. She was white, and tall, brown hair. An American I figured."

"What cab company came to pick them up?" Gardner asked.

The black man pointed at the waiting taxi. "Same one you have there. They have a sub-office out this way. Your driver can take you there." He hesitated. "You Americans, right. And you two must be military. Special forces?"

"Yes, we're military," Murdock said. "U.S. Navy. About all I can tell you."

"Classified. Yes. Navy, so you could be SEALs. Heard about you rattlers. You're damn good."

Stroh took a hundred dollar bill from his wallet and held it so the black man could see it. "Could you disable the plane so it won't fly without some minor fix? Then if the same people come back to fly it, tell them you can fix it in two hours, and give me a call at the number on the back of my card."

The owner of the small airport eyed the money and nodded. "Yes, I can do that. They would never guess."

Stroh handed the man the card and the bill.

"If you don't hear from them in twenty-four hours, give me a call and tell me."

They said goodbye and ran for the taxi.

"You've got a regional office out here?" Stroh asked the cabby as soon as the doors closed.

"Yeah, sure, about five miles away."

"See how fast you can take us there," Stroh said.

When the taxi carrying Badri and the other three came into downtown Cape Town, Badri ordered the cabby to take them to a computer store where they could get on-line access to the Internet.

"Sure, no problem," the young cab driver said. "Most let you do that for free. Some charge by the hour. Here's one." He pulled to the curb.

"You charge us waiting time. And stay here. I'll be back in ten minutes."

Inside, he got the clerk and access to the computer and stroked in a remembered Web site: www.playgroundaccess .org. It came up a moment later and Badri began entering coded words. When he navigated to Cape Town he smiled. Then he entered "Active Playground" and found three listings. He wrote down the addresses and phone numbers and hurried back to the cab. The first one on the list was always the best cell. He gave an address near where he wanted to go. There couldn't be any loose ends for the chasers to find.

On the sidewalk moments later, they walked down three blocks and over one and Badri found the address he wanted. He left the three on the sidewalk and knocked on the door of a stand-alone building in a mixed residential/business neighborhood. The place had been a business once, but had been cut up into four large apartments.

The man who answered the door at B-1 was dark with a moustache. Badri spoke rapidly in Arabic and the man grinned then kissed Badri on both cheeks and invited him inside. A few minutes later he came out and brought in the other three.

The First Lady was pushed into the room and stood to

one side. She wasn't tied, but she might as well have been. Six or seven times Badri had told her he would never give her up with no gain for himself. He said he'd kill her first. She looked into his brown eyes and believed him. It still didn't keep her from arguing with him about everything she could think of. But for now she would play it safe and not try to get away. She could trade a few more days of captivity for the rest of her life.

She watched the Arab man Badri had found on the Internet. It had to be al Qaeda. The network. It must still be working. The three men spoke in Arabic. Twice the resident looked up at her and smiled. She wasn't sure how to read him.

Badri still had the SATCOM over his shoulder on the strap. He was seldom without it. He was careful never to let her near it.

Mrs. Hardesty knew when the topic switched to money. The tones hardened between the Arabs in the foreign tongue, and the sentences became shorter. The exchange was sharp for a moment, then the South African Arab moderated and at last nodded. Bills exchanged hands. She could see only that they were $100 U.S. banknotes.

The living room looked comfortable and lived-in to the First Lady. She was no stranger to plain living. She had grown up in Iowa on a farm and often there wasn't enough money for the usual trip to town on Saturday night. Her mother canned lots of the food that they raised in the garden. They ate what they needed, and froze and canned the rest. Her roots were planted deep in the good black Iowa soil.

Badri motioned to her. "Sit here. My friend is fixing a secure room for you. He said his wife will have food for us in a half-hour."

"You mean I get to eat at an Arab table like a real person? Not like a veiled woman, slave, baby maker, washer of clothes, and receptacle for the famous two-inch Arab penis?"

Badri stiffened. She watched him fighting to control his temper. At last he took a deep breath and scowled at her. "No wonder American men are so two-faced. They have to learn to deal with women like you who think they are intelligent, who believe that they are something more than chattel, yet who are so stupid in the ways of the world that they are laughable."

"Mr. Badri, you must know that in Iraq there are women lawyers, women doctors, women who own stores and businesses. One thing that Saddam Hussein did right was not let the fundamentalist Muslims run the country. He allowed women almost as much freedom as women have in the Western world. And it worked. Women brought a great deal to the Iraqi culture and economy. Iran isn't like that. You enslave your women, you keep them pregnant, veiled, barefoot, and in the kitchen. You should be ashamed of yourselves."

"Women have their place in Islamic society. I have a wife and two daughters and a son."

"And your two daughters will not go to school, will barely learn to read and write, and will be married to men not of their choosing by the time they are sixteen. I know the ritual. Again, you should be ashamed of yourself."

Badri stood and scowled at her. "You are a sassy-talking female who should be disciplined. You should be stripped naked and left that way for two months with only bread and water to eat. You should be made to do all of the most menial tasks. You should not be allowed to speak. You should be shut up in a windowless room for every daylight hour, and then staked out in the backyard during the night so you could howl at the moon."

"You, sir, are no gentleman. You should be stripped naked, castrated, made to eat your own balls, and then a sack put over your head and paraded through a national convention of the NOW organization. That's the National Organization for Women. They are devoted feminists who believe women are just as good as men. You should be made to sit and listen to the work of the group and how they are striving to get equal pay for equal work for women. How they are fighting the glass ceiling in business firms. How they are making women's rights the law of the land. No, on second thought, you should be placed on the stage without the sack over your head but still naked so the women could associate a face with your pathetic naked form."

She watched Badri. He sat there seething. He could no longer contain himself and rushed from the room. She laughed as he left, her voice clanging in his ears, then she slumped in the chair. She did not like verbal fights. She would rather use logic and reason, but sometimes the nasty, insulting, and castrating words were all that could get through the armor of the listener. This man was such a dastardly, black character. She had no idea what his long-range reaction would be. They had argued repeatedly over the past two days. Had it only been two days since she landed in New Namibia? It had. This was the second day and it was about over. It was nearly dark when they had come inside.

The radio? No, he had taken it with him. She thought about the Arab that Badri had found. He had to be part of an al Qaeda cell. How much of the network was left? She'd throw that at him next. There was nothing else that she could do. The three men came back into the room. The other two Arabs who traveled with Badri had never spoken to her. She didn't think they knew any English. One of them motioned and they all went into another room where a table had been set. A short, fat, long-haired Arab woman wearing a veil had just put food on the table, family style. She left quickly. The man they had seen first, who evidently owned the house, came in and told them all to sit down. He used both English and Arabic.

They sat down, and, before anything was passed, Mrs. Hardesty cleared her throat. "Gentlemen, just before I left Washington, I saw a top-secret message that proved that

Osama bin Laden is dead. DNA on record of him matches with those samples taken from a body discovered in one of the bombed-out caves in the mountains of Afghanistan. This is absolute proof that he is dead. That must really have torn apart the whole al Qaeda network."

She watched as the host translated for the other two Arabs. One leaped to his feet and ripped off a dozen words in Arabic.

Badri caught the man's hand and pulled him down to his chair. Badri turned to the First Lady.

"My friend here is emotional. He had been trained in Afghanistan and knew Osama while he was there. But I'm not as gullible as my friend. You are playing another of your disruptive cards hoping to somehow get free. But it won't work. Osama bin Laden is alive and well and guiding his worldwide network of cells and action platoons."

"Then why is this cell of his so strapped for money? Why isn't he supplying them with men and cash? You obviously got this address from some secret word game on the Internet. Just how isn't important. The state of this house and a one-man cell is more important. This man must be simply trying to stay alive. He must have a job and a family and is leaving the terrorism until the time the cell is healthy again with men and money."

Badri laughed. "You are a comedian, Mrs. First Lady. You should be in show business. There is no cell here. This is a friend of long standing I knew in Tehran. He moved here years ago and we are friends. That's all."

"So he keeps his address coded on the Internet just for the convenience of a visitor every ten years? Not even a good try at lying, Mr. Badri. Make another stab at it."

"I don't need to explain anything to you. You are but a woman, chattel, a slave as you say. I should cut off your ear and send it to your husband. Then he would send me the money."

"I thought you had twenty-five million dollars in a bank in Switzerland." Didn't the government send it?

Badri grew angrier as he passed up the food. He pushed his chair back. "We did, it was deposited. But at once the Swiss government seized the money and froze the account until I can prove that I are not an international kidnapper and terrorist."

"So, you're broke again. I remember how that was in my early years in Iowa."

The talk trailed off then as they ate. The food was good, but she was not sure what it was. Some kind of meat, and a bread and mixed fruit. After the meal the two of them went back into the living room. She could hear a hammer pounding at the back of the house.

"Mr. Badri, you talk about the United States as the Great Evil. Interesting choice of words. Remember when your country was fighting against Iraq and the United States sent you money and weapons and aircraft and rockets? The United States gave your country more than twelve billion dollars in assistance and asked for nothing in return. Remember when Kuwait was invaded by Iraq and again the United States led the coalition of forces that battered back the Iraqi in a short war, but one that cost my country two hundred and ninety-eight lives and more than twenty billion dollars in spent hard cash. Again we asked Kuwait for nothing. Did not ask her to repay us what it had cost us.

"Then ten years later we again went into the Gulf with a coalition of forces to overthrow Saddam Hussein and his murderous regime that kept the Iraqi people flat on their backs. On that one we spent more than sixty billion dollars, and we liberated Iraq, let her chose her own form of government in free elections, ripped off the sanctions, and got her oil production going again. Sounds like the Great Evil is the Great Good Guy who has bailed out Arab nations lately to the tune of more than a hundred billion dollars. What has the

Arab world done for the United States lately? Or ever?"

Badri began pacing as she talked. At last he threw up his hands and rushed around the room, his face a mask of fury, his hands doubling up into fists and then opening and doubling up again. At the door, he sent her a horrendous look and stormed out. She was alone.

Mrs. Hardesty had seen him lay down the SATCOM when they entered the room after the dinner. Now she rushed to it, folded out the antenna the way she had seen him do and angled it through a window at the sky. Then she moved it until she caught a satellite. She turned on the set and, using the same channel he had it set for, began talking.

"This is Mrs. Eleanor Hardesty, wife of the president of the United States. I've been kidnapped and am at a house in Cape Town, South Africa, on Wander Street. The house number is one four, three, six. That's fourteen thirty-six. If anyone can hear me, please notify the president at once. I've got to go." She turned off the set, moved the antenna back and folded it and left the SATCOM exactly the way it had been. She went across the room and sat on the sofa, waiting to see what happened. Her fondest hope was that someone in Washington had heard and could act quickly.

Less than two minutes later, Badri rushed back in the room, looked for the SATCOM, saw it, and grabbed it and hurried out of the room with only a look of pure hatred directed at the president's wife.

16

The taxi cab company's branch office north of Cape Town was a one-room affair with one cab waiting outside and a telephone answering machine inside. The cabby told Murdock and Stroh what they wanted to know. They called the cab company's main office, explained that they were working with the police and needed the drop-off point on the cab driven by Charles Majors when he took four persons from the AirField airport north of town, back into Cape Town.

It took several minutes of persuasion and working through two pencil pushers before they got the address. Moments later their cab raced into town and to the spot designated. It was a partly business, partly residential street. They had no building number, just a street. They worried about it for ten minutes, then Murdock called it off.

"Badri knew we would track him, so he came out of the cab here and then walked or took another cab to his destination. This is a dry hole."

Stroh reluctantly agreed. "Back to the airport where the rest of the platoon waited in the aircraft. The Army liaison I contacted has arranged for us to use a pair of vans and has set up a temporary barracks for us in one of the vacant hangars. He didn't want us traipsing into one of the hotels with our cammies on and packing our weapons. I can understand that."

The taxi took them back to the airport and to the hangar.

"Sure you don't want to go somewhere else?" the cabby

asked. He was young, a student at the university, he had
told them. "You the best customers I've had all day."

Murdock gave him a five-rand tip and he grinned and
drove away.

In the big hangar, they had set up twenty cots and two
tables with chairs. Stroh contacted a catering service that
would bring in meals twice a day, the first one at five that
afternoon. Murdock, Gardner, and Stroh sat at one of the
tables with pads of papers and pens trying to figure their
next move.

"We've alerted the airports to let us know if three Arabs
and a white woman try to buy commercial air tickets,"
Stroh said. "We've talked to half a dozen of the best aircraft rental firms about not renting a plane to the same
group. We don't even know how many such outfits are in
the area. There are over three million people in this little
town, and lots of private planes."

"Maybe he's contacted Washington again," DeWitt said.

Murdock set up Stroh's SATCOM and handed him the
mike. Stroh had immediate response to his call.

"What's happening down there?" Wally Covington, the
CIA director himself, asked on the first transmission.

Stroh filled him in on the lack of progress.

"We transferred the twenty-five million to his account in
Switzerland. The director said the government there froze
all assets of that account the moment the transfer was complete. We're waiting to hear from the kidnapper again.
Sounds like you're stymied there with no leads."

"About the size of it, Mr. Director. Any suggestions?"

"You might listen in on the set on this channel. He's due
to contact us in about two hours. We don't have a clue what
he's going to say."

"Best idea yet, sir. We'll keep the channel open. Maybe
something will turn up to help us. This town is so crowded
it's like Hong Kong. Well almost. Good luck with your
next call."

The evening meal came. Sixteen-ounce slabs of roast beef that melted between the molars. Stroh winced at the price, but he paid it in cash. After all, they were saving on the hotel bill.

Murdock called his brain trust in after the meal and put them down at the table.

"Okay, you brain whuppers, come up with some ideas about what we can do. I don't like this dead time. The First Lady could be in real trouble and we can't help her."

"If he's worked with al Qaeda before, he will again," Jaybird said. "We could raid any al Qaeda cells the local cops know about."

"Possible. Stroh?"

"Let me call my new police friends downtown." He left the group and headed for a telephone.

"What else?"

"We should cover the small airports better," J.G. Gardner said. "He could cut and run again and we'd know nothing about it."

"Take two men and start phoning," Murdock said.

The SATCOM came to life.

"This is Mrs. Eleanor Hardesty, wife of the president of the United States. I've been kidnapped and am at a house in Cape Town, South Africa, on Wander Street. The house number is one four, three, six. That's fourteen thirty-six. If anyone can hear me, please notify the president at once. I've got to go." The transmission stopped.

At once the set spoke again, the voice high with emotion and excitement. "Stroh, did you hear that?" the CIA director said. "Get moving on that right now. She got hold of the SATCOM somehow. Move it, Stroh. Murdock, get cranking. You should be halfway out the door by now."

Murdock waved and the SEALs ran for their equipment.

"Find Stroh," Murdock yelled at Fernandez, the nearest SEAL. "Get him back here. Saddle up you guys, we're moving."

A moment later Stroh came charging up, panting, his face red.

"True? A transmission from her?"

"Yes, we're on it."

"I better contact the local police so we don't get in trouble if there's any shooting. I'll do that and catch up with you." He ran back to the phone at the edge of the big hangar.

Three minutes later, the sixteen SEALs loaded for combat, piled into the two vans and raced away from the hangar. They stopped at the airport gate and picked up a guard to guide them to the right street. Stroh caught them there and climbed in the van.

"I got the watch commander on duty. He said he knew the street. He would dispatch a car there to help us."

The guide gave them the quickest way to the street. It was on the far side of town and with stop lights and one wrong turn, it took them just over twenty-five minutes to get to the right address.

It was a four unit. Each had a separate number. Fourteen thirty-six was on the ground floor left. They covered the front, and the back. Then Murdock went to the door and knocked. No answer. He knocked again.

"Anyone around at the back door?" he asked on the Motorola.

"Negative," Lam answered.

Murdock tried the door knob. It was unlocked. He twisted it inward and waited. The inside of the house was dark. Murdock waited ten seconds, then charged in, dove to the right, and came up with his weapon ready. Nothing moved. No one made a sound. Jaybird reached around the door and found a light switch and snapped it on.

They quickly cleared the five rooms.

"Nobody," Jaybird said.

"Someone was here a short time ago," Murdock said. He pointed to a cigarette still burning in an ashtray. There were dirty dishes in the kitchen sink and pots and pans still on the stove.

"Somebody left damn fast." They searched the place, but found nothing that would indicate that the kidnappers or al Qaeda had ever been in the house. Murdock motioned the men outside and turned off the lights and shut the door. He barged up to Stroh, who had stayed with the vans.

"Nobody knew we were coming except the Cape Town police. Somebody in their outfit called ahead and warned these people."

"Looks that way," Stroh said. "Next time we don't trust anybody, anywhere, at anytime. The damn patrol car didn't even get here."

Less than a mile away, Badri, the First Lady, and Badri's two Arab men sat in the al Qaeda cell man's rusting 1978 Volkswagen van and stared into the darkness.

"How did they know to come to that address?" Badri brayed. "Who could have told them?" He turned and stared at the First Lady. "Shit! I left you alone with the SATCOM for maybe three or four minutes. You used it, didn't you? You transmitted with it and told someone where you were."

"Well, Mr. Badri, thank you for the compliment. But I'm not mechanical or science minded. I can't even work a computer. How in the world could I get that funny radio to work? You give me more credit than I'm due."

"It had to be you, fancy-talking woman." He took a deep breath. Never had he felt so frustrated, so unsure of what to do next. He was doing his job. Keeping the First Lady away from the United States agents for as long as humanly possible. But had his string run out? No. He would fly out again. Only to where? He could take off in a small plane at night. He had trained to and had done that many times, but where would there be a lighted runway for him to land? There wouldn't be, not until the next big town, and he had no idea where that would be.

He found a spot where they could spend the night. It was in an industrial area with a few street lights and only a few other cars. He parked and tied the First Lady's ankles together, then her wrists. He had sat her on the wide rear seat.

"Don't roll around and you won't fall off. You'll be fine until morning. Then we figure out what to do. No way am I going to let the damn Americans find you."

"So you tie me up like a slave, like an animal. Don't you think you three big strong Arab men can keep me in this van? You must be remarkably unsure of yourself. Is this what they taught you in Afghanistan at al Qaeda training school?"

"I never went to Afghanistan. And yes, we could keep you safe in here, but then one of us would have to stay awake all night. Tying you up is easier, simpler, and we all sleep. Now be quiet and go to sleep."

"You really believe that Arab propaganda about the United States wanting to hurt the Arab countries? Or are you just spouting it so you can pocket a few million dollars by kidnapping me? You'll never get away with it."

"It's not propaganda. It's the truth. The United States is hated by every nation in the Arab League. We know what you are and how you undermine us and cut us short and keep us at the Third World level."

"So why did we spend a hundred billion dollars in three wars to save your countries and to free the Iraqi people?"

"Protecting your oil interests in our countries. It's all about oil. It always will be all about oil until your country discovers more oil of its own, or makes practical dual-power cars—gasoline and electricity. Or maybe the fuel cell if you're really lucky, because we all have all the hydrogen that we need in the atmosphere. Now, shut up, Mrs. President, and let me get some sleep, too. We will have a hard day tomorrow."

"You don't know how to treat women who stand up to you, do you, Badri? I wonder what your wife is like. Probably younger than you, and you let her get fat, and don't let her take care of herself, so she's not as attractive as she was at sixteen and her beauty won't be a threat to you. Tell me, did you marry her when she was fourteen or fifteen?"

"Shut up, or I'll put a gag in your mouth."

"Yes, a typical Arab man's reaction to a logical argument from, of all people, a woman. Good night badass Badri." She grinned. She had been wanting to say that for three days now. It was worth it just to see the fury on Badri's face.

Badri held his tongue. He knew he was no match for her in these verbal fights, but he had to do his best. He bit his lip and stewed about it for a minute. Then thought about the problem at hand. His first job was to find a small airport. For that he needed some help from a local. A good map of the country would help as well. Tomorrow.

Two men slept sitting on the front seats and the third used the floor. They didn't complain.

The First Lady smiled into the darkness. So her message on the radio had been heard. Someone must have called Badri at the house, and at once they rushed out of the place, into the van, and sped away. She had no idea if that's how Badri knew that the Americans were coming, but that would be the only reason for them to leave so quickly. She smiled again. One small victory for her side. Now, what was she going to do next to complicate this kidnapper's existence?

Just after daylight, she felt the van moving. One of the men untied her hands and feet and she sat up.

"Where are we going?" she asked.

Badri ignored her question. Twenty minutes later they stopped at a small store and Badri went inside. He came back with a sack of fruit and pastry and a map of South Africa in a strange accordion-type fold.

One of the Arabs asked him a question and he nodded.

"Yes, I found a small airport out this way. Maybe fifteen miles. We drive there and see if they have any planes to rent. Money will buy anything in this country."

They gave her a banana, a reddish fruit that looked like a pear, and two rolls that could be first cousins to a Danish. The trip took a half-hour and it was not quite nine A.M. by her watch when Mrs. Hardesty saw the small airstrip with a blacktopped runway. They drove in and stopped in front of a building that proudly proclaimed with a small sign that it was the office.

Badri went inside. He had been studying the map and asked for a plane that they could fly to Durban, seven hundred and fifty miles away. He showed them his international pilots license in a false name.

"You coming back?"

"Day after tomorrow. Business trip."

"You one of them Arabs?"

"Yes."

"You going to blow up anything?"

"No. I'm a businessman."

"Credit card?"

"American MasterCard."

"Best. That and eight hundred dollars will get you up there. You'll have to make a gas stop in Port Elizabeth. There's a fueling area there you can use."

"I can do that."

Five minutes later they left the van and walked toward the plane. Badri had no idea what kind it was, but it had range enough to get to the next big town across the bottom of South Africa. It would put them that much farther away from the Americans. As they walked toward the plane, the First Lady saw a chance and she bolted away from the trio of men and ran toward the small office. One of Arab soldiers caught her after six steps and turned her around. Once they got in the plane the man slapped her hard across the face.

Badri yelled in Arabic at the man.

"You're defending me?" Eleanor asked.

"No. I told him when someone messes up your pretty face, it will be me."

Ten minutes later they were in the air.

17

Ten Miles Inside Iraq

Lieutenant Yasser Rabbo paused over the silent form of Sergeant Saadi and shook his head as the last dying gush of air came from his lungs. Saadi was his second sergeant who had been killed so far on this devil's mission. How many more men would he lose? He keyed the battalion radio hanging over his shoulder on a strap. Only static came back, then even that stopped a moment later and he looked at the set in the faint moonlight. A piece of shrapnel from the exploding land mine had torn a deep gash in the back of the case. The set was useless. On the positive side, the radio had probably saved his life.

He urged his men forward. So far he had lost nearly half of his platoon. He looked around for the rest of the battalion; none were in sight. He sent runners ahead and behind to try to contact them, but the men returned empty handed. Push on north, Rabbo decided. Those had been his original orders. He moved to the head of the column, reduced now from thirty-five fighting men to eighteen.

They skirted another anthrax death zone without hitting any more Iraqi mines and hurried back to the highway. The tanks began passing them, grinding along the highway, not even pausing as the men scattered into the ditches as the fighting machines rolled by. Rabbo counted them as they clattered past. Fourteen. Out of two tank battalions. He wasn't sure how many tanks to a battalion, but he thought it was forty-eight. Ninety-six tanks went into Iraq, and only fourteen of these two battalions were coming out.

Before a week had passed there would be executions, and a whole new general staff of the army and air force would take over command of what was left of Iran's fighting forces. Heads would roll. Lowly lieutenants would not be affected. He shook his head and kept walking. The men were tired, they needed pushing, but tonight he didn't feel like pushing them. He knew he was lucky to be alive.

Without warning, a machine gun opened fire from a collapsed house a hundred yards off the highway. Bullets slammed into his platoon and men crumpled onto the road. Others dove to the ground and rolled toward the shallow ditch on the far side of the highway.

At the head of the column, Rabbo was not immediately targeted, so he sprinted for the ditch and dove in. Even in the darkness he could make out forms lying on the hard-surfaced road.

"Return fire," he bellowed. Half a dozen AK-47s fired at the structure where the machine gun kept chattering out death. The weapon had angled its rounds on down the road now and Rabbo and his men poured full magazines of rounds into the smashed-up house. Lt. Rabbo tried to evaluate the enemy. Perhaps one or two men who had been by-passed in the rush forward. Probably not more than three of them, and the gun was firing only fifty yards down the road. He motioned to the two men nearest him.

"Follow me. Get full magazines and bring four grenades each." He saw their medic moving out to the wounded on the highway. Rabbo lifted to his feet and sprinted across the highway, then into the field on the far side. The two soldiers followed him. There was little cover between them and the house. They ran forward toward what Rabbo thought looked like a ditch less than fifty yards from the house. They made it, panting hard, and rolled into its protection.

For a moment they rested. "Get out your grenades,"

Rabbo told his men. "We'll go singly from here. We split up and go at the house from three points. One of us should get through close enough to throw grenades. Throw all you have, then we'll charge back to the platoon." The two men nodded. Both were seasoned veterans, one of them a corporal.

When they left, they crawled through weeds and some short shrubs moving toward the house twenty yards apart. The machine gun chattered now and then, took rifle fire from troops down the road, and evidently the gunners were not hit.

They crawled forward until they were twenty yards from the chattering gun. Lieutenant Rabbo took a grenade and held it high so the other men could see. Then he pulled the pin and threw the hand bomb as far as he could toward the house. The round hit short and rolled forward, detonating with a roar ten feet outside the building.

His two men threw as well. One grenade went through a broken window, another bounced through a smashed-in doorway and both went off with resounding roars. The three men threw the rest of their grenades even after the machine gun stopped firing. Then the lieutenant waved and the men came to their feet and ran back to the highway.

The column moved two dead members off the highway into the ditch so the tanks wouldn't run over them and then marched on north toward their own country. He was down to sixteen men, and six of them had wounds. For just a moment he wished that he could be one of those in the firing squad that would end the lives of the generals who planned this disastrous invasion.

By four A.M. they were exhausted. He called his men to the side of the road for a break. Other units straggled by. None of them were from his battalion. He had no idea where the battalion was, ahead of him perhaps.

Rabbo checked his men. Two were seriously wounded. A third could not walk. They would have to leave him. Fifteen. He shuddered.

After a twenty-minute break, Rabbo moved his platoon again. They walked for another hour and finally came to a cluster of vehicles. Just off the road he saw the command motor home, well known to all of the troops. It was where General Tariz Majid lived, where the top commanders met to decide the fate of the men under their orders, to plan strategy and tactics, and to manage the war from this field headquarters.

The motor home was so laden with armor plate that the word was that it could travel at no more than fifteen miles an hour. Both dual rear tires had been shot out and the rig tilted toward the back. Three trucks and two Jeeps also were parked nearby. Loud voices came out of the motor home as they came toward it. Two soldiers ran into the highway and stopped Rabbo's men. No questions were asked, and no explanations given.

A moment later four army officers exited the motor home and were marched toward a covered six-by-six truck. The men were hoisted into it, and one of the officers directing them hurried to the road guard. The sergeant in charge shook his head.

"My orders are to protect this sector, Captain. I can't leave it."

The captain turned to Rabbo. "You, Lieutenant. Pick out six of your men and come with me."

Without questioning the superior officer's orders, Rabbo pointed at the first six men in line and jerked his thumb. "On me," he said, leading them behind the captain, who went back to the big army truck. He stopped them at the tailgate.

"You men are guards of important military prisoners. All four are generals, and all four have been found guilty of treason and are being rushed back to Iran. Do not let any of them escape or you will be executed on the spot. Into the truck now, quickly."

The seven men jumped up into the truck and stared into

the darkness. They saw four men at the front, but couldn't identify them or see their rank. All generals, the captain had said. Rabbo wondered if General Majid was one of them. The truck engine started, and soon the rig blasted down the highway, honking its horn to move retreating soldiers off the roadway as it sped past.

As his eyes widened to accommodate the low light, Lt. Rabbo saw that the two generals next to the cab were handcuffed. One was four-star general Majid. He didn't know the other three. He looked at the captain who had brought them along. He had a submachine gun pointed at two of the generals.

Rabbo touched the captain's sleeve and he looked around. "Where—"

The captain cut him off with a shake of his head.

The truck lurched ahead. Moments later it took some enemy sniper fire that slammed through the top canvas of the truck's roof. Everyone crouched down, but they were past before any more shots came. A small radio that Rabbo hadn't seen before on the captain's chest spoke.

"Five miles from the border. The colonel says to get ready, we may have some trouble with the home guards."

"Right," the captain said into the radio. Then all was quiet.

"Do you fully realize, Captain . . ." General Majid said it, and before he could continue, the captain shot him once in the leg with the submachine gun. The sound inside the truck was deafening.

General Majid growled with the pain but didn't say anything more.

"You were warned not to speak," the captain said.

A few minutes later they heard shouts and cheers, then they were past the border and the speed of the truck increased. Before long the truck slowed and turned off into a rough road that Rabbo figured was dirt or gravel. The truck geared down and went up a slope and around sharp corners, then leveled out only to climb again. Rabbo could see nothing out the rear of the truck. The canvas drape had been pulled down; it kept some of the dust out of the truck now on the dirt road.

Ten minutes later the rig stopped. The captain pulled up the canvas and ordered the infantrymen out. Then he brought out the generals one at a time. In the dark, Lt. Rabbo knew which one was General Majid because he limped with his shot-up leg.

Rabbo had never been in this part of Iran. They were on a hill with a few trees and some sharp bluffs. They had parked the truck below one of these bluffs. For a moment it reminded him of a firing range.

The generals were led to the face of the bluff and turned toward the truck. Two colonels stepped down from the truck and brought flashlights. They went to the generals.

"Lieutenant, bring your men to this point," one of the colonels said. Rabbo led them to a spot ten yards from where the generals stood. Lt. Rabbo felt his body go cold. His head ached and he saw the scene plainly. It was a firing range, and it was an execution setting. His six men were a firing squad. He looked at the two colonels who now stood before the four generals. One read from a white paper.

The colonel read off the four men's names and rank. All were generals. Rabbo recognized only Majid. The colonel continued. "Seeing that you have been found guilty of treason and high misdemeanors by a legally convened military court, you are hereby sentenced to death by firing squad. Sentence to be carried out with all due speed."

The colonel turned. "Captain, is the firing squad ready?"

"A moment for instructions, Colonel."

The six infantrymen stood with rifles slung. They still didn't understand their part in this drama.

"Detail, unsling rifles, port arms, charge one round into the chamber, safety off." He watched and listened as the men obeyed. When all were ready he continued. "Rifles up, and aim at the first man on the left."

Lieutenant Rabbo turned and saluted the colonel. "Colonel, sir. The firing squad is ready."

"First man on the left, ready, aim . . . fire." The six AK-47s fired and five slugs ripped into the chest of General Majid. He slammed backwards into the dirt and didn't move.

The colonel waited a moment. "Aim at the next man. Ready, aim . . . fire." Again the rifles barked one round and the second man pivoted and spun to the ground. He groaned and tried to crawl, then he gave a cry and died.

When the four generals were all dead, the colonels returned to the cab of the truck, the captain put the firing squad back in the truck, and it turned and drove down to the main road. There the six infantrymen were ordered out of the truck and it continued north toward its home base.

Lt. Rabbo put his six men under a tree and sat down with them. Nobody said a word. It was up to him. He tried to figure out what to say, but nothing surfaced. At last he just began.

"Men, we've been part of history here, tonight. We shot four men who undoubtedly deserved to be executed. It was not our choice. We were following the orders of our superior officers. Whether the executions were legal and proper, only the historians and legal experts will decide. Right now, we're still in the army. When our battalion comes by, we'll join it. I'll report to our major, if he's still alive, and try to find the rest of our platoon. Until then, get some sleep. It's been a long day and night. For us, the war is over. I don't see how we could possibly continue the war unless it's to defend ourselves against an attack by Iraq on us. They may very well do that, but I wouldn't think for some time so they can recover and reform their troops and fighting machines. So rest, I'm on guard duty."

Lt. Rabbo went closer to the road and sat down. He knew he could stay awake, although it had been a totally exhausting day. The fighting, the long march. The firing squad duty had been so unnerving that he wondered how he got through it.

He nodded and snapped up his head. The second time he nodded off he slumped to the ground and didn't wake up for nearly three hours. By then a pathetic parade of wounded and defeated soldiers struggled by. It was daylight. Lt. Rabbo sat up, rubbed his eyes, leaped to his feet, and ran to the closest man.

"Third Battalion, what's left of us?" the soldier said.

"You know where the First Battalion is?"

"Don't know if any of them survived. If they did they should be behind us."

An hour later he found the Third Battalion. At the end of the line the nine men from his platoon limped along. He joined them with his men from under the trees. No one asked any questions. By that time it had been grapevined through the survivors that the four top generals had been executed. They marched toward home. Lt. Rabbo was sure now the war was over. It would be many years before Iran tried to invade another country again, especially Iraq. He didn't question his position now in the battalion. The major had been shot through the head and left on the battlefield. A captain was in charge, and two of the company commanders had been killed. There was plenty of room for advancement. He found his one remaining sergeant and left him in charge and moved up through the ranks, looking for the captain now commanding the First Battalion. The war was over. It was time to start working on plans for his own advancement, his own career in the army, for that's where he would stay.

18

Cape Town, South Africa

Back in the hangar at the airport, Murdock and his platoon checked over weapons and equipment. Then Murdock called his idea men around a table and they began working through various scenarios that Badri could be following.

"He's running, but to where?" Jaybird asked.

"In town or out of town?" DeWitt asked. "This is a big country."

"Should we cover the airports, the smaller ones?" Lam asked.

"Wouldn't hurt," Murdock said. "He used small ones before. We'll get Stroh on that. What else?"

"The city cops told me that the address we hit is on their watch list for al Qaeda activity," Gardner said. "So he must be connected with them somehow. How does he find them once he gets close?"

Nobody knew. They sat there looking at each other.

"We've got no rope to throw at him," Senior Chief Neal said. "Nothing to get our teeth into."

Don Stroh had been on the phone at the side of the hangar. He hung up and hurried over.

"I just checked with the cops. They have an airport manager at a small strip outside town who just reported that a guy rented a plane with a stolen credit card. He was Arab and had a woman with him who looked English or American. Said he was a businessman."

"Flight plan?" Jaybird asked.

"Manager said he wouldn't file one. He finally did when the manager told him he couldn't rent the plane without one. Said he was going to Durban, but would have to stop at Port Elizabeth for gas."

"How far is that?" Murdock asked. "Durban."

"About four hundred and fifty miles. Cops said the manager said the guy took off about an hour ago. It took the manager that long to find out the credit card had been stolen."

"Say it takes Badri two hours to get there," Jaybird said. "We can make it in less than an hour."

"Sure, but which airport?" Lam asked. "He can get refueled at any little strip."

"Move it," Murdock said. "Jaybird, run out to the plane and get the guys to warm her up for take off. We'll check by radio when we're in the air to see how many places a small plane can land."

"On your feet, you guys," Senior Chief Neal barked at the rest of the SEALs. "Take off in five. Bring all your gear. No telling where we'll end up."

In the air they checked with the Port Elizabeth airport. There were four modest air strips where small planes could land near the city. They had the identification number and the make of the plane they were hunting. Halfway to Port Elizabeth they began to radio the four small landing fields. Three of them responded and said they would watch for the suspect plane and delay any departure if possible. The fourth airstrip didn't answer its radio call.

"Guess which one he's gonna land at," Lam said. "No advance notice and we get fucked again."

Ten minutes before they landed at the main airport, they had word from one of the small landing fields. The plane had landed, and when the manager tried to stall the Arab, he pulled a gun, tied up the manager, and stole his car and roared off down the road. They were in town, somewhere. Murdock growled. He knew the cops would find the stolen car empty and the Arabs and the First Lady nowhere around.

An hour later Murdock and Stroh talked to the Port Elizabeth police. They had found the stolen car, empty. It was downtown near a taxi stand.

Most of the SEALs stayed with the plane at the airport. Murdock took Jaybird, Lam, and Rafii and caught a taxi to the address where the stolen car had been found. They got out and looked around. Murdock asked Lam and Jaybird to stay in the taxi.

"What's the first thing you'd do in a strange city?" Murdock asked Rafii.

The slender Arab rubbed his jaw and frowned. "First I'd look for some friends, in this case other Arabs. I'd call every Arab Friendship Center in the city."

"Why wouldn't he try for another al Qaeda cell?" Lam asked.

"Probably thinks this is too small a town to have one," Rafii said. "They are centered in larger metropolitan centers where they are easier to hide."

"So where would he call from?" Murdock asked.

Rafii looked around and pointed to a medium-sized hotel across the street. The SEALs were still in their cammies, but had left their long guns and combat vests in the plane. Murdock and Rafii caused a stir when they went into the hotel. It was smaller than it looked, with one desk clerk and no bellhops.

"Yes sir, a room for the night?" the clerk asked.

"No, but we do need some help. Did an Arab man make some phone calls from your phones over there less than an hour ago?"

"Yes, actually he did. He came to me twice for more change. I asked if I could help him locate someone but he ignored me and went back to call."

Murdock and Rafii went outside, where the commander

tried his Motorola. He couldn't raise the airport. They took the cab back to the transient aircraft hangar. Stroh had been busy talking with the Port Elizabeth police by phone. They said they would cooperate any way they could.

"Call them and see how fast they can get the record of calls made from the second phone from the end on the phone bank at the Lawton Hotel. The quicker the better."

The phone company cooperated fully and less than an hour later the police faxed the list of numbers and length of calls along with the names and addresses to Stroh at the airport manager's office. Twelve calls. Six of them were less than a minute long.

"Those could be calls where he used an al Qaeda code word that the person on the other end did not recognize and hung up," Rafii said. "Many Arabs are curt and impolite on the phone."

"What about these two that are for almost five minutes each?" Stroh asked.

Rafii checked the times and names. "Both are Arab Friendship Leagues. Usually these are men-only clubs where Arabs get together in non-Arabic cities and talk in Arabic and shoot the breeze."

"Let's hit them both, right now," Murdock said. Four men each in two taxis. Take side arms and hidden MP-5s. DeWitt, pick three men and take the first address. I'll get the second one with Bradford, Ching, and Van Dyke. Let's move."

DeWitt's team found the Arab Friendship League on its second run down the street. The sign over the door was small—in English and below it in Arabic. They went inside with their weapons covered by the floppy cammie shirts worn outside. A bearded man hurried up to them just inside the door. He asked in Arabic if he could help them.

Rafii answered in the same tongue.

"Yes, we're looking for our friends. Three Arab men and a white woman came here less than an hour ago. Are they still here?"

"Members or newcomers?"

"Newcomers."

"No, no such men came. And as you can see, we are men only. You must have the wrong club. There is another one on Water Street."

Rafii told DeWitt what the man said. They looked around. It was a small club, with tables for games and a small snack bar, but no rooms for guests, and no other facilities. Gardner nodded at the spokesman and they left. He used the Motorola, got Murdock, and told him they struck out.

"Our cab driver must be on his first day on the job," Murdock replied. "We went by our place three times before he found it. We're just about ready to go in. Wish we had Rafii. My Arabic is rusty, but will have to do."

The sign over the door said "Arab Friendship Circle." Murdock took Ching with him and left the other two in the taxi to hold it. Inside was a small lobby with a man sitting behind a desk. He stood when the SEALs came in, frowning at their uniforms.

"What may I do for you?" he asked in accented English.

"We're looking for friends of ours, three men and a woman who came in here this morning."

The Arab frowned and shook his head. "Nobody came in I didn't know. Were these new to town?"

"New, yes."

Murdock moved swiftly, grabbing the man's shirt front with his hand and twisting it until the collar dug into the shorter man's throat and he struggled to breathe.

"No more lies. We know they came here, three Arab men and an American woman. Where did you put them?"

The man waved his arms and Murdock relaxed his grip.

"Yes, they came, but no woman had ever come in the door before and we were horrified. We turned them out at once. I don't know where they went."

"You lie again. You have facilities here. To the left there

are steps that go up to hotel rooms. What rooms are they in? Tell me or I'll cut off your air and you'll die like a fish on the shore." Murdock began to tighten his grip on the man's shirt.

"Okay, okay, stop." He took several deep breaths after Murdock released his shirt.

"Show us," Murdock commanded. Murdock let the tail of his cammie shirt flip back so the guy could see the .45 automatic pushed into his waistband. The clerk got more nervous, stumbled getting the key.

"He's stalling," Ching said.

Murdock stepped toward him and the man jerked a key off the desk and almost ran to the stairs. Murdock and Ching were right behind him. On the third floor he paused in front of a room.

"This it?" Ching asked.

The Arab nodded and knocked. Murdock grabbed the key, opened the lock, and slammed the door inward. A minute later they saw there was no one in the double room. One blue man's sock strayed halfway out from under the bed as if it were trying to get into a suitcase.

"I thought they were still here," the clerk yelped.

Ching snorted. "He stalled just long enough. Must be another stairway down, in back probably. Now I remember. Somebody walked up those stairs just after we came in the front door and before we said a word. Somebody tipped off Badri."

The First Lady tried to settle down in the strange room that Badri had brought them to. She knew it was sometime Monday, afternoon maybe.

An hour later, Badri swore when the messenger said there were two men in army cammies downstairs. He rousted his two men and the First Lady and went down the back stairs into the alley and out the far way to the street. They walked to the next cross street, which carried a lot of traffic. Badri hailed four cabs before one stopped. He leaned in the front open window.

"Four of us, can I sit in front?"

"How far?" the cabby asked.

"About forty miles up the coast highway. I'll give you a hundred rand note now to show I will pay you."

"Sounds good. I need a long run. I'll tell my dispatcher I'm off the air for about two hours."

The driver didn't say another word for a half hour. Then he pointed to a sign.

"We're about twenty miles from Brahamstown. You sure this is the way you want to go?"

"Right, this is the way," Badri said. He suddenly held his stomach. "Uh-oh. I'm getting car sick. You better pull over up here at that wide spot, quick!"

The driver pulled off the road. There was little traffic. Once the cab stopped. Badri took out his pistol and motioned to the driver.

"Out of the cab," he said. The driver stared at him in surprise.

"You said forty miles."

"Out or your widow collects your insurance."

The driver got out and Badri moved over to the driver's seat and slid out. He marched the driver into the woods near the road. A short time later they heard a shot.

Mrs. Hardesty blanched. She touched a handkerchief to her forehead and her eyes hooded. Badri ran back to the car, got in, and drove back to the road.

"You didn't have to kill him," the First Lady said. "You could have tied him up."

"Shut up."

"You're really afraid of me, aren't you, Mr. Badri? You're frightened of intelligent women who speak their minds, stand up for what is right, and hate the men who constantly batter us down."

"I said shut up, woman."

"Oh, is that like talking to a dog? You tell the dog to be quiet, and if it doesn't stop barking you shoot him, right? Well I'm not going to shut up. I'll talk your ear off. Do you remember that England had a woman as Prime Minister? Also Israel had a woman who was the head of the government. A few years back we had a woman run for vice president. She didn't get the job, but at least she ran. One of these days he United States will have a woman president."

"Then you will be simple to defeat in war and have terrorism blanketing your whole nation."

"Terrorism! How, with your beloved al Qaeda network virtually non-existent? With no Osama bin Laden to funnel money to the cells, they are dropping by the wayside one by one. Soon, the network of al Qaeda will be nothing but a memory. You saw it yourself at that last place. They were practically starving. With Osama dead and the money tree in Saudi Arabia dried up, your network is finished."

Badri slanted the car off the road to a gravel spot and skidded to a stop. He waved his pistol at the First Lady, his face deep red and his eyes bulging. His screaming tapered off and he pushed the weapon within inches of Mrs. Hardesty's face.

"Bitchy fucking woman! Shut up! Shut up this instant or I'll shoot you right between the eyes and dump your body on the road. You hear me, shut up!"

The First Lady eased back in the seat and folded her arms. She nodded. Badri stared at her a moment more, let the hammer down on the .45 slowly, and turned back to face front. He sat there breathing heavily for two or three minutes. Then he coughed, took a deep breath, and started the car, driving on north along the coast highway that often was six or eight miles inland from the ocean.

The two Arab soldiers in the back seat leaned against the doors and went to sleep. When they got in the car they had put handcuffs around the First Lady's ankles. She sat there, knowing there was nothing more she could do. She had to trade this treatment for the chance to stay alive. Right now that was what mattered most. She could give up chiding Badri about the Arab treatment of women. Stay alive, dummy, she told herself, concentrate now on staying alive.

They finished the one hundred and fifty mile drive to East London. Badri checked the accommodations and picked a motel near the highway that was not the best of the lot. They took two rooms and Badri took the ankle cuffs off her before they walked into the room, then he put them back on. There was one single bed. He looked at it and grinned.

"So, famous First Lady, you want to get naked and sleep with me on the bed? Or would you rather keep your clothes on and sleep on the floor?"

She ignored him. It was Monday night and she was exhausted. She'd sleep in her clothes again, but she would take off her shoes. It would be a long night. Badri would sleep on the floor.

19

Port Elizabeth

Monday afternoon, Murdock and his men rode back to the airport in the taxi where he met with Gardner, DeWitt, and the rest of the SEALs. Don Stroh had been working with the local police. He set up a reward with them to be publicized to all law enforcement agencies in the nation. The United States government offered five million dollars for the safe return of the wife of the president of the United States. The announcement went out at once.

"At least we're covered with a reward," Stroh said. "That much cash could make a lot of people change their minds about how loyal they are to whoever is running this operation."

"They just may fly out again," Murdock said. "Can we get the local LEAs to notify all airports and small airstrips about the dangers of this group, and how we want them to hold anyone of this description who tries to rent a plane?"

"Did that just after you left," Stroh said. "We've got that angle covered as well. Let's hope we get some response."

"So what else can we do?" Gardner asked.

"Not a damn thing," Ching said.

"They could be driving back toward Cape Town, or going the other way," Jaybird said. "No good airfields that way. They could steal a car and be gone and we'd never know it."

"Roads go north, south, and inland," DeWitt said. "If they go by car, we're fucked."

"So we sit on our combat packs and wait," Murdock said. "Stroh, you have any of that catered food coming? We could use some chow about now."

"It will be here at five o'clock sharp," Stroh said. "I've got no limit on my expense account on this one. Not with the First Lady involved. So I figured we should be ready for some medium-rare prime rib. I ordered twenty sixteen-ounce dinners. Hope to hell you guys are hungry."

The food came. They ate. They waited. They were frustrated. J.G. Gardner pulled out a four-inch square traveling chessboard with stick figures. He set it up and looked for some competition. Robert Doyle moved over and watched. Gardner looked up.

"You play?"

"Some."

"That means you're an expert. Let's give it a go."

Before it grew dark. They hit their bunks. Like in combat they slept whenever they could. Stroh kept his SAT-COM set on RECEIVE whenever they settled down to one location. He had heard nothing from his boss or the White House.

"So we wait," Murdock said. "Get some sleep, you never know when we'll get time to snooze again if this guy is still running."

East London, South Africa

Tuesday morning the First Lady woke up where she had slept on the floor in all of her clothes. She had taken off her shoes. She had found two blankets and two extra pillows in the bottom drawer of the dresser. Still her bones ached from the hardness. She grinned. Who would believe that she had slept in the same clothes three nights in a row and hadn't had a shower for four days?

Badri lay on the bed, covered up and still snoring. He had taken command of the bed and pushed her off last night. Right now, she thought of bashing him over the head with a convenient lamp, but she saw that the lamp was fastened tightly to the table. Nothing else looked solid enough to make a dent in his Arab brow.

She sat up, combed back her hair with her fingers, and stood to go to the bathroom. Badri woke up, the .45 in his hand pointing at her.

"The bathroom, all right?"

"Uh, yeah." He lowered the weapon.

She shook her head. "You are weird, Arab man. You treat your own women like dirt, but you haven't touched me."

"You are not a woman, you are a valuable commodity who I can bargain with your husband for a great price. If you are damaged then you are worthless. I'm a realist. I know that to get my money, I must be careful with you. Otherwise I would have shot you yesterday when I stopped the taxi."

"Won't the police be looking for the taxi by now?"

"Probably. One of my men drove it a mile away and set it on fire. It won't be a problem."

"Why didn't you get your twenty-five million dollars? I never did figure that out."

"I told you once. Your husband sent the money, but also asked the Swiss government to put a freeze on it, so I couldn't withdraw any, not a dollar of it. Worthless to me. The Swiss will wait a proper amount of time, then wire the money back to the U.S. government."

"You had figured on that."

"No."

"So, here we are over a hundred miles from Port Elizabeth. The chasers can't have any idea where we are, right? So we sit here and wait for another time to make demands on my husband?"

"No, I want to get to Durban. There's a good cell there, men I can trust. I used to know one of them in Iran. To do that we will fly."

"Another small airport and a puddle jumper?"

"Right, the only way to fly." He took out the telephone book and looked at the ads. There were three small airports listed. He picked the one with no ad, just a listing. He called them and asked where it was and how to find it. The man at the airport told him.

They took a taxi. The bill was a hundred and forty-eight rand. The rand was about eight to a dollar. Badri gave the driver two hundred rand and he left happy. The airport was small, with one blacktop runway, three small hangars, and two T-hangars. One building had an "office" sign. They went inside.

The room looked like a museum for the early days of flying. Two wooden propellers adorned the back wall. The counter was on top of an old wood-and-fabric aircraft body. All the walls were pinned with black-and-white and color pictures of planes, flyers, and some stunt flyers with smoke trailing out of their planes. The man behind the counter wore an English aviator's jacket and cap with a white scarf around his neck like the pilots wore in the open cockpit days. He grinned as they looked around.

"So, what do you think of my own little aviation museum?" the man behind the counter asked.

"Interesting," Badri said. "We need a plane, a four-placer to rent today. Bring it back tomorrow. How much?"

"Hey, sorry. Only have two planes I rent and both are out. Should have one back tomorrow."

"Won't do, I need one right now."

"Sorry, only plane I have is my private sweetheart. She's a Robin H4-100 made in France. She's a bit old, but I never fly in anything else."

"We'll take her. How much for two days?"

"Not a chance, mister. I told you, I don't rent her out. Robin is probably the last plane I'll ever own. Love that little ship. She's got a low wing, seats four and a range of over twelve hundred miles. Suits me fine."

"I'll give you five hundred U.S. dollars for two days

rent. That's over four thousand rand for two days. How can you turn that down?" He watched the older man shake his head. Badri put out six one hundred dollar bills on the counter. The aviator started to reach for them, then took his hand back.

"No, sir. I just can't do it. Don't want anything bad happening to my Robin. You haven't even shown me your pilot's license."

The First Lady tensed. She had to warn him. "Sir, you better do what Badri here asks. He's not a man to push around or deny something that he wants."

"Shut up, woman," Badri said. "You didn't ask me about a license. Those the keys?" Badri indicated a key ring on the counter top.

The aviator reached for them, but Badri got there first and swept them up with his left land. His right hand brought out his Spanish-made Star automatic and he shot the airport manager twice in the chest. He staggered backwards and fell on his face on the floor. One hand tried to push him up, but it collapsed, and a long gush of his last breath powered out of the man's lungs.

"Let's go," Badri said. The two men hurried out of the office and Badri dragged the First Lady by one arm. They saw the plane in one of the T-hangars and walked over to it. Badri looked around but didn't see anyone else at the small airfield. The Robin aircraft sat nose out in the hangar. The three men rolled it out to the taxi strip and they all got inside. Badri looked at the controls for a moment, then figured out which key on the ring would start the craft and cranked it over. It started on the second try and Badri grinned.

"They told us with our training we should be able to fly any plane made in the world today, except the huge ones." He taxied to the end of the strip and turned.

"Mrs. Hardesty. No comment about the demise of the aviation museum owner?"

"No. I expected it. You're a ruthless killer. What else would you do?"

"You're becoming more logical about your position in this situation, Mrs. First Lady. Now buckle on your seat belts, we are going for a ride."

Mrs. Hardesty hung on as the little plane gained speed and took off. She always felt a small thrill as the ground faded away. Here it was so much more evident and exciting than on a huge jet liner. She felt as if she were flying all by herself without the help of the airplane. The country was so green, trees everywhere, but fewer and fewer towns and villages as they flew north. The plane stayed near the coast line and worked toward Durban. She could see the white of the breakers far below and wondered just how long this kidnapping would last. She didn't know of any contact that Badri had made with her husband in the last two days. Was he giving up, or just not sure how he could get a big amount of money for her exchange?

She wanted to rail at the man about a great many things, but she was more cautious now. She had just seen him kill a man with absolutely no regret or shame. And he had killed the taxi cab driver. He could kill her the same way, except that she was worth a lot to him. At least he still thought he could collect. As long as he thought that, he would keep her alive.

It took them three and a half hours to fly the three hundred miles to Durban. The town was larger than Badri expected, maybe fifty or sixty thousand. He found a small airport just north of town and landed. He had avoided using the radio and now taxied up near a hangar. The four got out of the plane. He signaled to a waiting cab at a stand. The driver wheeled up to them with a cheery smile.

"Right, governor. Where can I be taking you?"

"A mid-sized hotel with a restaurant and room service. Your choice."

"Right, governor. I've got just the spot for you. About a twenty minute ride. You can sit in front with me."

Later, Badri registered for two nights while the other three waited in the lobby. He got two rooms, one with a balcony, and they were shown up. He and the First Lady were in the room with the balcony. He locked the door and put a chair under the handle so no one could get in, and getting out would be slower. Then he took out his SATCOM, set up the antenna on the patio, and got it aligned correctly with the satellite.

"Let's talk to your husband, Mrs. Hardesty. I want you to tell him how well I'm treating you. Any miscues or telling where we are will get you cut off quickly. Understand?"

She nodded furiously, trying to remember the code words the CIA had taught her once on a lark. Some didn't matter. They knew she was captured and being held. Others: treatment? She couldn't remember a one. Location? They would know nearly where she was. She gave up. Nothing came to mind. She watched him turn on the set and get a beep from the antenna, then he pushed the send button.

"Mr. President."

The president came on the air, "Yes, I'm here. Go ahead."

"We haven't spoken since you double-crossed me and had that twenty-five million frozen in Switzerland. You owe me one for that. Now, to the future. This is what you will do. First, you will call off your dogs. Some military group is tracking us. Make them stop or I'll send the First Lady's little finger neatly preserved to the closest police station. An expert there can send a copy of her fingerprint to you to confirm that it's hers.

"Second, you will package five million dollars in two suitcases that I can X-ray and send them to me at a location I will tell you when the packages are ready. Five million in each suitcase. Ship them by UPS Air. Don't try to follow them since they will be forwarded to several different locations once they hit the first destination here in South Africa.

"Third, you will release all al Qaeda prisoners you have at Guantanamo Bay in Cuba and fly them at once to Pakistan.

"Now here is your lovely wife to say a few words." He handed the mike to the First Lady.

"Yes, Milton, I'm fine. Mr. Badri is afraid to touch me. He's a poor debater as well. He's determined to get some money in return for me. Of course he said nothing about returning me, did he? Oh, well . . ."

Badri grabbed the mike and took it away from her. "So, President Hardesty, you see that your wife is alive and well and still has a sharp tongue. I'll expect to hear from you on this channel within four hours that you have the cash package ready to ship. I don't care what time it is in Washington. Get it done."

Badri snapped off the set so he would not receive any transmissions.

"So, now, glib-talking woman. We will wait and see just how much this president values his First Lady. If he stalls or does not do as I say more than once, you could lose three or four fingers in the process."

20

Port Elizabeth, South Africa

Tuesday morning the SEALs had chow with the soldiers at the South African army base and then went back to their barracks. They checked their equipment and waited.

Murdock, Ed Dewitt, and J.G. Gardner stared at each other over a small table. Another day on the chase and not a thing they could do.

Don Stroh set up the SATCOM and turned it on to RE-CEIVE. He'd had it on and receiving almost every hour since they hit South Africa. He had turned it off to put in a new battery to be sure it didn't go out on him.

He sat at the table working on the report he sent to his boss in Washington every day, noting progress or failure, or no progress and stalemate. It was depressing. He worked on it all morning as the SEALs slept and played cards and chess. Murdock stewed and worried.

Just after noon a soldier came in with a portable phone for Don Stroh. He took it, listened, and gave the phone back to the soldier. Stroh motioned to Murdock.

"Local law people say a taxi cab here in town has a rig missing. One of their drivers said yesterday morning that he had a fare going up the coast a hundred miles or so, so he'd be off the air for three hours. He never reported back, and the cab is still unaccounted for."

"Could be Badri grabbing some convenient transport," Murdock said. "Since the cabby hasn't reported back, the odds on him being alive after meeting Badri aren't good."

"What town is up north?" Lam asked.

"That would be East London," Jaybird said. "About a hundred and fifty miles or so north on the coast."

"So maybe our bird flew that direction," DeWitt said. "It's the best clue we have so far."

It was a half hour later when Stroh heard a faint click and looked at the SATCOM sitting next to the window.

"Mr. President," the SATCOM's speaker blared. Stroh and half the platoon ran to the window where the radio sat.

"Yes, this is President Hardesty."

"We haven't spoken since you double-crossed me and had that twenty-five million frozen in Switzerland. . . ."

When the transmission was over, the SEALs all began talking at once.

"How can the president call us off?" Jaybird asked. "No way he'll do that. He can't."

"Agreed," Stroh said. "I'll give the brass a half-hour to decide what to do before I call them. I don't think we've ever had a First Lady before this with one finger missing."

"He'll do it?" Luke Howard asked.

"I'd bet the farm on it," Stroh said. "The question is, how do we follow that ransom money so we can nail this guy?"

A soldier came in asking for Don Stroh. He held out a portable phone and Stroh answered it.

"This is Don Stroh."

He listened, nodded, and then gave the phone back to the South African soldier.

"That was the local police. They had a report an hour ago that a small-airport manager in East London was shot and killed and an airplane stolen from his airfield. One witness said it was three dark-complexioned men and a white woman. They took off this morning, but the man didn't know about the killing until later. The East London police have no idea where the plane was flown to."

"East London is about a hundred and fifty miles or so

north," Jaybird said. "If that's them, then they did drive up there yesterday."

"From there they could fly on to Durban, or come back here or go on to Cape Town," Murdock said.

Don Stroh went to the SATCOM and switched it to a different channel than the one that Badri had used to talk to Washington. He used the hand mike.

"Calling Director Covington."

The answer came at once. "Stroh, make it fast."

"We heard the demands. We will follow the package of money when it is delivered, wherever it is delivered. Hopefully we can grab whoever picks it up."

"We'll tell Badri that we're taking you off the case, that the military unit is being withdrawn. A lie. Do you know where he is?"

"He's been moving by car and plane, but we're not sure. We'll break into units to cover the places we think he might tell you to send the money."

"Good. Be damn sure to keep him covered. That finger-cutting threat really made the president angry."

"We'll stay in touch."

"So how do we split up?" DeWitt asked.

Senior Chief Neal pointed at the map Jaybird had spread out on the nearby table. "We can forget about small towns. He'll want a town with a major airport for his UPS Air delivery. So we leave two men here in Port Elizabeth. Durban is a good bet, and so are Cape Town, Pretoria, and Bloemfontein."

"I agree," Murdock said. "The three capitals of the country. Bloemfontein is closest to Durban, only three hundred miles away. Then there is Pretoria, about three hundred and fifty miles away. Four prime locations."

"He wouldn't go back to Cape Town," Mahanani said. "Too far."

"Stroh?" Murdock asked.

"My guess is the two capitals to the north and Durban.

He might mess with us and come back to Port Elizabeth. So we cover those four spots. The jet can drop off teams. We'll have to establish telephone setup so we can stay in contact without a SATCOM."

"We need civvies," Jaybird said. "With our cammies anyone at the drop site can spot us a mile away."

Murdock looked at Stroh. The CIA man shrugged. "Give me your pants and shirt sizes. Jaybird you gather the sizes. I'll find a store somewhere and buy them out. Who goes where, Murdock?"

Jaybird began writing down each man's sizes.

"J.G., you take three men and get out to Pretoria as soon as you get your new pants. DeWitt, you grab three men and the jet will drop you off at Bloemfontein on the way to Pretoria. The jet comes back to the coast to Durban where I'll have Jaybird, Lam, and Howard. Stroh, you get command of Port Elizabeth. Everyone choose up sides."

"We're skins," Jaybird said.

Howard punched him on the shoulder and Jaybird fell down wailing in pseudo pain. Nobody laughed.

Don Stroh took the sizes and hurried out the door.

"Weapons?" Gardner asked.

"Handguns, one MP-5 per team. Keep it concealed in a box or a bag. I've got a hunch we'll do a hell of a lot more running and watching than shooting. Let's get this operation in motion."

Durban, South Africa

Eleanor Hardesty sat in the hotel room watching TV. The reception wasn't the best, but Hollywood Western from the sixties was coming through. She had the sound turned down so low she couldn't hear part of the conversations. Badri sat at the small desk working with a pen and pad of paper. He had scrapped half a dozen sheets so far.

Tuesday evening. She wondered what was going on at the White House tonight. Something was always happening.

She didn't have to go to every event, thank goodness. She knew that Badri was working out the arrangements to pick up the two suitcases stuffed with five million dollars each. How to pick them up and vanish without getting caught was his big problem.

For just a moment she thought about *The Ransom of Red Chief.* She forgot who wrote it. About a little devil of a twelve-year-old boy some ne'er-do-wells kidnapped. The kid gave the kidnappers such a bad time that they kept lowering the ransom. At last they agreed that if the father would come and grab the boy and hold him until the kidnappers could get away, they would give the father $20.

Maybe she could be a Red Chief to Badri? She decided it wouldn't work. He'd just shoot her and end the game.

She had noticed at once that this room had twin beds. She wouldn't have to sleep on the floor. She went into the bathroom, locked the door, and had a shower. It was worth it even if she did have to put the same clothes back on. She felt better when she came out.

"You still working on your delivery plan?"

Badri looked up. "You want to help me?"

"Oh, no, you're so much better at being sneaky and underhanded than I am."

He scowled at her and went back to his writing. She looked at her watch. "Incidentally, your four hours are up and Washington hasn't called you."

"Good. I'm not ready for them."

"You'll never be ready for them. You realize you're taking on the whole might of the United States of America? That's over three hundred million people, all who are mad at you right now. Your puny little country must not have fifty million. We could swallow you up and not even burp. I saw on the news about the Iran-Iraq war, the new one that started last week, about the time you kidnapped me. Any connection, buster? You don't seem like you're trying very hard to get that ransom. More like a stall. Are you trying to divert attention from your country's use of anthrax in your invasion of Iraq? You know the close ties the U.S. has had with Iraq since we liberated that country from Saddam Hussein. Close. Close enough so that we used our jet fighter–bombers to wreck about a thousand of your tanks. It's all on the news. Haven't you been watching any of the news?"

"Shut up, you pig! Shut up, you slut with ears. Just shut your mouth and let me think. I've got to get this just right, then I'll live anywhere I want to with more money than I'll ever need. Don't you get it yet? I don't care about the damn war. I just want the money!" He was panting when he finished. His face was red again and she was afraid he was going to reach for his gun. He didn't. At last he turned to the small desk and his pad of paper.

She looked back to the TV. She shouldn't antagonize him, she told herself. He was so easy to get all furious and red-faced. No, she had to maintain and overcome and stay alive. Her big job, to stay alive. Badri kept working and throwing away papers. The First Lady dozed. When she woke up the ten o'clock news was over. Badri stood and grinned.

"Done," he said. "I'm calling Washington."

He got a response on his first try.

"Washington, good to hear from you. Is the package ready?"

"It is, ten million in one hundred dollar bills packed into two canvas bags tied together. Going with an armed guard on UPS Air with a pickup in an hour and a half at six P.M. local time."

"Good. Send it to the Three Star Hotel in Pretoria, South Africa. It's on Easterside Street. Take it to the office, where the office manager will give the delivery man new directions. That's all you get to know right now."

"When will you release Mrs. Hardesty? As soon as you get the money?"

"That will depend if you've called off your military

detachment that's been tracking me. Get rid of them, or get a First Lady finger." He switched the set off immediately.

Mrs. Hardesty frowned. "Badri, that doesn't sound very sneaky to me."

"We're just getting started, Mrs. President. Just the first little hint of what's to come."

Port Elizabeth, South Africa

It was nearly 2330 when the SATCOM came on. Stroh had been waiting for it and sat up on his bunk. When the transmission by Badri finished, he frowned. Deliver it to a hotel in Pretoria. Only not deliver it, there they would give more delivery instructions. Would there be a new delivery site for UPS to handle?

Three hours before, Stroh had seen the other SEALs board the Coast Guard jet and take off. All had on civvies, mostly khaki or blue pants and shirts. He had grabbed them quickly. Now he checked the phone network they had set up. He had two phones in the barracks. He called J.G. Gardner in Pretoria, who had been dropped off second. He had set up in a small hotel and established the phone number and called Stroh.

"Yeah, they're coming here first," J.G. said. "But you said it's just a forwarding location? That the UPS guys are going to take the cash somewhere else?"

"That's what it sounded like. Check out that hotel and see what they know about it. We figure it could take twenty-four to thirty-six hours to get there."

"We'll be waiting."

Stroh tried to call DeWitt in Bloemfontein. He had been dropped off first but evidently hadn't set up in a hotel yet. He was supposed to call in with a hot number as soon as he was situated. No rush. The cash couldn't get there for some time.

Just after 0030, Stroh's phone rang in the barracks. He had drifted off.

"Murdock here in Durban. We're set." He gave Stroh the phone number. "I also have a SATCOM. So far nothing on the DC channel. We can talk on some other channel if you want."

"For now the phone sounds safer."

"Nobody said how long it would take to get the goods there," Murdock said. "Any idea?"

"Could be twenty-four to thirty-six hours, but that could be off by a day or two. It's watch and wait. How are the new duds?"

"Hey, you did good. They almost fit. Talk to you tomorrow."

21

Don Stroh hung up the phone. What time was it in DC? They were seven hours behind South African time. Just after midnight here, that would make it after five P.M. in Washington. Might catch the boss in. He flipped the SATCOM to the CIA channel and called.

"This is South Africa calling. Anyone home?"

There was some dead air. Then the word came back.

"Just about out the door, Stroh. You have your men set up?"

"Right. We're in four major cities where he might forward the package. Any idea when delivery might be?"

"We have a small change in plans. UPS wouldn't take the package. Too much liability in case of loss. So we're sending a pair of F-15s to Pretoria on a Friendship Fly-in. We've already cleared it with State and they have talked to the embassy down there and it's a go. Makes a difference time-wise. The planes will be taking off in about a half hour. They move quickly, over sixteen hundred miles an hour at altitude. Can jump over two thousand miles without a drink. We're plotting their route now out of Andrews. My planners tell me it's about a sixteen-thousand-mile jaunt. So with two midair refuelings, the run should take about twelve hours to Pretoria."

"It's midnight here now, so that would get them into Pretoria about noon tomorrow. Sounds good. Have you told Badri yet?"

"About to do that. Listen in on that channel. This is one we can't fail on, Stroh. That's the First Lady we're trying to save out there."

"We're all too aware of that Mr. Director. We'll do everything we can, and we will get her free and catch this maniac."

"Oh, and save the ten million if you can. I'm out of here."

Stroh changed channels to get on the number four that Badri used to talk to Washington. The set spoke three minutes later.

"Badri, I hope you're listening. We've had a change in delivery plans."

There was no response. Stroh stared at the SATCOM willing it to bring word from Badri. The director made the call twice more, then waited. Stroh tried to figure out what the next step would be from Pretoria, but he had no idea. The two packages could be sent anywhere by air, or rail, or even a Volkswagen bus.

Five minutes later the SATCOM spoke again, with the director's call to Badri. This time he responded.

"CIfuckingA. What do you mean a change in delivery plans? I spelled it out. No changes possible."

"You didn't check with UPS first, Badri. They don't transport cash, diamonds, or bearer bonds. Too much of a risk factor. So, we're flying the packages out today. It's about 5:30 P.M. here. Two Air Force F-15 fighters will arrive in Pretoria about twelve hours later and hire a taxi to make the delivery to the hotel. Best we can do."

There was dead air space.

"Badri, do you copy?"

"Yes, I got it. That will work for me. They should be at the hotel with the items at one P.M. tomorrow. Have you pulled back your military hit men yet?"

"They have orders to disengage and return to the States."

"Sounds good, if true. Just get the damn money here on

time. When I have it, and your military is long gone, then we talk about releasing the First Lady. I'm through here."

Stroh left the set on RECEIVE and used the telephone to call J.G. Gardner in Pretoria. He laid out the new delivery schedule.

"We'll be ready. We have two rooms at the hotel. We'll have it covered front, back, and all the windows. Wherever that cash goes from here, we'll be astraddle it but not holding it back. Hope we can call you with the where as soon as we find out."

"The hotel manager know why you're there?"

"Yes, and he's cooperating. Someone there has to know the new directions before the package arrives. We hope that he'll tell us so we can get a jump on the next leg of the delivery."

"Sounds good. I've got to tell the others about the new schedule. Keep up the good work."

Stroh alerted the other two elements about the changes, then tried to get Murdock in Durban. He said he'd heard the word on the SATCOM. Stroh told him to get some sleep. The CIA man lay there on his bunk near the four SEALs. He usually didn't get this involved in the field, but he was glad he was here. He could help. He could pave the way, coordinate, and hopefully bring this mission to a successful conclusion. The more he thought about it the more he realized that this was his life. What else did he have? No family. One failed marriage fifteen years ago that still gave him pains. One son somewhere. Phil would be almost eighteen now. Maybe Phil would join the Navy. Stroh turned over but it didn't help. Sleep was the last thing his body was willing to allow right then.

Fifteen years with the Company. Yeah, he'd done all right, but not spectacular. He wasn't even a section head yet. That would mean giving up the SEALs and the CNO and the president. No way. He would stay right where he was as long as he could get out with the SEALs. As long as nobody was shooting at him. He'd been in a few shootouts with the troops. No fun. Well, yes, it was a kind of gut-pumping terror/thrill that he'd seldom had. The idea that either you killed the bastards out there or they would kill you could have startling, mind-wrenching effects, especially on a desk jockey like him.

He went over the problem again. How to nail this Badri and at the same time keep the First Lady from any harm. If Badri saw that he was cornered or that he was wounded and couldn't win, Stroh knew for certain that the Arab would kill the First Lady. That was a given. They had to take him out clean or capture him when the First Lady was not near him. Either one would be a hell of a tough job. Tomorrow? Was there anything else that he could do to make tomorrow a winning day for them? He went over it again and again. There was only one person who could know what would happen after they went to the hotel in Pretoria. And that one person, Badri, wasn't about to tell them a thing.

Durban, South Africa

Far up the coast from Stroh at Durban, Murdock was restless, too. He and the men took two hotel rooms near the tourist/hotel area and then waited. There was nothing more they could do right then except be ready. Murdock rented a car and put it in the hotel garage where he could get to it quickly. He'd be on standby with the rest of his men, waiting for any talk on the SATCOM. They had heard the exchange between Badri and the CIA in Washington. The advanced schedule was good. So the Air Force pilots would fly into Pretoria about noon tomorrow and taxi into the city to deliver the goods. Would they be transported to the next drop or would someone else show up to make the run?

Murdock had a gut feeling about Durban. It was large enough to have an al Qaeda cell here, if any of them were still functioning. Such a group could be a big help to Badri. He could go to ground here in the Arab community and be

nearly impossible to find. Murdock sighed. He hated waiting. He was good at it, but still didn't enjoy it. Several
times he had to stretch out in a swamp for four hours and
never move a muscle. It had paid off. He just hoped that
this waiting would pay off tomorrow.

Less than two miles from where Murdock tried to sleep,
Badri shifted on the bed, knowing he needed the sleep so
he would be sharp tomorrow. He could take a pill. No, he
decided not to. He would command himself to sleep. The
woman in the other bed with all her clothes on had been
sleeping now for two hours. He didn't understand how she
remained so calm, so self-assured. In her place he would
be screaming and throwing fits.

Tomorrow would be a great day. He would have the
money, and he would still have the valuable package. Then
he would decide what to do with her. He could milk the
cow for more money, or he could let her go at some other
hotel. Or he could simply put a bullet in her head and dump
her body along the road somewhere. He would decide tomorrow, after he had the ten million U.S. dollars in his hot
little hands.

He had listened to the news tonight. As Mrs. Hardesty
had told him, the war in Iran was going badly. He heard
that General Tariz Majid had been executed by a firing
squad. A council of colonels had taken over the country, so
his power base with the old regime was shattered, nonexis-
tent. There was no reason for him to even return to Iran. He
might be caught up in a dragnet by the council and blamed
for the ruinous war and be jailed or even shot. No, he
would not be going back to Iran. So, he needed all the cash
he could gather. He still had his money belt and a good
supply there. But he needed to think in terms of twenty
years or more. Ten million dollars would help a lot. So tomorrow had quickly become vital to his own best interests.
Damn the nation he had been working for. It was now him
and his two men on their own.

Pretoria, South Africa

Captain Lonnie "Loony" Chambers caught sight of the
two blips on his screen as he and his wingman came
across South Africa heading for Pretoria, less than thirty
miles away.

"Closing fast," Captain Browning "Brownie" Phillips
said on the radio.

"They passed us off from that pair we met at the coast
about a half-hour ago," Loony said. "They will be friendly."

The international channel chirped at them and the
voice came across. "Yanks, we have you on our screens.
Two F-l5s if we hear right. We're on your radar by now as
well. Your welcoming party of two Mirage Fl-AZs at your
service."

"Roger that, Mirage. Let them know at Pretoria that
we're friendly. I have a set down in about six minutes."

"Right, Yanks, glad to escort you in. You might pick up
on frequency four to get our base tower. Our military air
force base is about ten miles north of town so we don't
scare the locals."

·The two American planes landed side by side on the
wide north/south runway and turned onto the taxi strip
where a Jeep with a large green flag led them to a transient
military hangar.

Captain Chambers stepped down from his aircraft and
met Phillips and they supervised the transfer of the two
canvas packages from their planes to an armored car that
had been waiting for them.

"Gentlemen, you are requested to accompany the car to
our destination where you will sign off on the items," the
armed guard said. "Do you know what you brought here?"

"No, sir," Brownie said.

"Just as well. Get on board, we're about ten minutes
late."

They drove quickly from the military airport and toward
Durban. There was no small talk. The pilots heard the

driver and his guard radio that they were on their way.

Thirty-four minutes later they wheeled in at the Three Star Hotel on Easterside Street.

The driver turned to the pilots. "Gentlemen, standard procedure here. I go in and check to be sure this is the right address and that they are ready to receive the goods. Then I come back and transport it inside, you go in and the receiver signs off on it and all is well. I'll be less than two or three minutes." He left the armored car by the front driver's door and the second guard watched the two pilots, his right hand never far from the big .45 automatic on his right hip.

Lieutenant (J.G.) Gardner felt the sweat popping out on his forehead. He wasn't used to this type of pressure. He'd rather have somebody shooting at him. The very fact that ten million dollars would soon roll into the hotel parking lot and the life of the First Lady hung in the balance as well, were almost too much to bear. He and Canzoneri, Fernandez, and Rafii had talked to the hotel manager just at noon. The manager said he was not authorized to tell anyone anything about the shipment coming in or what further instructions he might have for whoever delivered it. Gardner told him who he was and the manager was impressed, but said he still couldn't reveal the instructions. He had been handsomely paid to do this small task and he would do it. Gardner told him he would be nearby in case of any trouble.

After that, Gardner had spotted his men in the best defensive/offensive locations around the front of the hotel. He had the MP-5 and sat at a small table just outside of the office where he played solitaire. The MP-5 was well out of sight.

He almost lurched out of his chair when the armored car arrived. It stopped in a no-parking area ten feet from the front door. He watched one uniformed guard get out of the truck and go inside. Gardner used the Motorola with the concealed mike. "Okay, it's probably here. Stay cool. If the armored truck leaves the goods here, we watch and wait. If it leaves with the canvas packages, Rafii, you bring up the car and we get in casually and follow it. Everyone cool?"

They checked in and waited.

The driver left the hotel after a few minutes in the office and went back to the armored car. The truck's headlights blinked three times. A junker car parked halfway down the lot with three doors of different colors and serious body damage on the passengers side drove up to the armored car. The side door opened and the guards pulled out the canvas packages. The trunk lid popped open electrically and the guards dropped the ten million dollars in the trunk and one of them slammed it shut.

"Go, Rafii," Gardner said. He saw Rafii quickly walk twenty feet to a two-year-old Chevrolet, get in, and back out. He rolled forward just as the junker that was mostly blue, eased away from the armored car and headed for the street. The SEALs stepped into the Chevy and Rafii was five car lengths behind when he pulled into Easterside Street.

"Stay three cars behind him," Gardner said.

"He's in no rush, just cruising along," Rafii said.

"Stay with him," J.G. said. "I bet he's going to lead us to the First Lady, wherever she is by now. He's heading toward the outskirts of town" he said, pointing.

Five miles later the junker car pulled into a line of two cars waiting at a car wash.

"He's getting that bucket of bolts washed?" Rafii blurted. "What in hell for?"

"That's what worries me," Gardner said. "Canzoneri, you get out here and watch him to be sure he goes into the wash. Use your radio if he suddenly backs out and heads the other way. We'll go up near the outlet to be ready if he comes there. As soon as he hits the water, come up and get back in the car."

Canzoneri dropped out of the car and found some shade to sit in as he watched the junker move up in the line.

Gardner noted it was a new-type car wash where the car went into a plastic booth and was enveloped in steam for a few seconds. They drove near the outlet and stopped. Gardner got out and took a walk back to the carwash and watched it. He could see the booth. There was a driveway on the far side of it not connected with the car wash.

"Canzoneri," Gardner said on his Motorola.

"Right."

"Make sure that the trunk of that car doesn't move for any reason."

"Roger that."

The cars edged forward.

"I've got the junker in the booth, steam, water, suds, but the trunk lid hasn't budged."

"Good. Keep on it all the way through. We'll pick you up."

Gardner noticed a black car drive up near the side of the wash booth and stop. Curious. A moment later the side of the plastic tent opened next to the black Porsche. Steam gushed out and with it came a man in a yellow slicker with a hood. He carried both bags of money. He threw them in the back seat of the Porsche, climbed in, and the car sped toward the exit and the street.

"Canzoneri, on me to the car, they switched cars. They're in a black Porsche."

Gardner and Canzoneri got to their car at the same time and dove inside. Already Rafii had it starting forward. They slammed the doors.

"He's ahead of me half a block," Rafii said. "No cars between us. Will he know we're following him?"

"He will unless he's an idiot," Fernandez said. "No sense being clandestine now. He's made us. He'll try to outgun us. And with that big engine of his, he can."

As Fernandez said it, the black car ahead charged away. It slid through a yellow and Rafii gunned after him, hitting about half of the red light as it changed. Rafii rammed down the gas pedal and caught up a little when the Porsche hit a red light. Then they were in more open country heading south and the Porsche vanished over a hill on the four-lane road.

Rafii gunned the Chevy to its top speed and came over the hill quickly. Far ahead they could see the black car slamming down the roadway.

"Keep going, we might get lucky," Gardner said. They drove for five miles, then Rafii pointed ahead.

"Some trouble. Looks like a wreck."

Gardner saw at once that it was. Two cars were smashed up, blocking both lanes going south. "A wreck. This might have held up our runner," Rafii said.

Rafii stopped the car twenty feet from the mangled cars. One of them was a black Porsche.

"It has to be our boy. Try and find him. No, two of them."

That's when they heard tires squealing and a woman screaming. The four men ran around the wreck to where cars had stopped on the other side.

The woman kept screaming. Gardner tried to calm her down.

"They stole my car. Two of them looked like damn Arabs. Stole my car and drove away. They just took my car and drove away!"

"What kind of a car?" Gardner asked. Rafii sprinted back to the Chevy and began working it through the shallow ditch and around the wreck.

"Car, what kind of a car is it?"

"A brand new red Ford."

"We'll get it back for you," Gardner said. He rushed to the side of the road where Rafii had stopped the Chevy. Gardner jumped in the front seat and Rafii spit gravel from the rear wheels until he got back on the blacktopped road.

"Red Ford," Gardner said. Rafii turned the lights on to

bright and tore down the road. The lights were a warning that he was coming. A minute later the speedometer showed 160 kilometers per hour.

"That's a hundred miles an hour," Gardner said. "What is this a freeway?"

"Close enough," Rafii said. "My guess it's the route to Johannesburg. Some curves coming up, I better slow down."

"There it is," Gardner said. "Red car ahead, we're gaining on him."

"We better be. He must be doing only eighty-five."

"No, he's slowing down, turning off," Rafii said. "Divided road up there."

The car slowed and took the turnoff. A second later the red Ford burst out from a side road and charged back down the highway the way they had just come. Rafii swore, did a quick braking, and spun the car around and slammed through a natural divider between the lanes of traffic and headed north back toward Pretoria.

"Will someone tell me what's going on?" Canzoneri asked. "If the dumb ass didn't want to come this way, why did he wait until he got all the way out here to turn around?"

Nobody answered him. Rafii caught the red Ford ten miles from Pretoria, and it didn't seem in any rush to lose them.

"What's he doing now?" Gardner asked.

"Maybe leading us away from the money," Fernandez said. "He could have stashed it back up there where he turned around."

"Leave ten million in the bushes?" Rafii said. "No chance. He's got something else in mind."

"Whatever happens, remember, we follow the money and we find the First Lady."

They drove behind the red car until they came to the airport. The car took the first off-ramp and to the departing passenger's ramp. The red Ford stopped in a no-parking zone. The two men got out and walked into the airport each with one of the canvas bags. Rafii parked right behind them, waved away a parking-enforcement man, and the four SEALs ran into the airport. The two Arabs dressed in grey shirts and pants stood in a ticket line. Rafii moved up near them to find out where they bought tickets for.

He came back a few minutes later. "They're going to Durban. Flight 204 leaves in half an hour. We'll have time to make it."

Gardner had the money, over five thousand rand. He went through the line, bought four tickets, and they ran for the boarding area. Their flight was loading. They saw the two Arabs and their canvas bags they would use as carryons. At the plane door the flight attendant looked at the bags and shook her head. One of the Arabs folded some bills in his hand and shook hands with her. The bags went in the special compartment in front of first class.

A few minutes later the four SEALs got on the plane singly and sat apart. Gardner looked out the window and shook his head. Follow the money. They were on the trail of the cash. He didn't know what would happen once they hit the next airport. There was no way and no time to contact Murdock in Durban. He'd have to wait and hope his Motorola would reach out to wherever Murdock was waiting in Durban. It was a chance. It was his only chance.

22

Durban, South Africa

J.G. Gardner tried to call Murdock on the Motorola from the commercial jet aircraft just after it set down. To his surprise he got a response.

"Yeah, J.G., that you coming in?"

"Right, and we have the two Arabs and their two canvas bags of cash. They're wearing gray civilian clothing. We'll let them get off first and follow them. Where are you?"

"At the airport reception area. They'll have to come right past me. I'll follow them to the outside, the taxi stand, I'd guess."

"Good guess. We'll be right behind you."

Murdock picked out the two Arabs the moment they came out of the landing ramp. They each carried one of the canvas bags, which were gray with a heavy plastic covering. Handles had been strapped to the bags. They walked to the main lobby, checked the signs, and went directly to the taxi stands. Murdock looked behind and saw Gardner and his team following closely.

Outside there was no line waiting for cabs. It looked like a free-for-all, with drivers shouting fees and waving. Murdock signaled for Lam, Howard, and Jaybird to join him and he grabbed the first taxi he saw and he and his men piled in. They watched the two Arabs getting into a cab three cars ahead.

"Follow that Blue and White cab, but not too closely,"

Murdock told the driver. The cab had "Blue and White" stenciled across its flanks. "There's a hundred rand tip for you if you don't let him spot you."

"Yes, sir," the driver said with a British accent. The accent still surprised Murdock after all the years that the Brits had been out of South Africa. He looked back and saw J.G. get into a cab with his men. The driver jerked his cab into the traffic and Murdock saw the Blue and White cab still three cars ahead.

"Yes, stay three cars back."

The trip into town was smooth, uneventful, and quick. Then the Blue and White cab driver seemed to have trouble making up his mind where to go. The taxi made quick turns, backtracked, and ran into a dead-end street. Murdock's driver avoided the no-outlet street and waited for the Blue and White to emerge.

After another five minutes of playing tag, the Blue and White cab pulled into a large parking lot with at least twenty-five cabs with identical paint jobs.

"I can't go in there," Murdock's cabby said. "That's the Blue and White Cab Company parking lot."

Murdock threw some bills at him, told him to wait, and climbed out of the cab as the other cab full of SEALs stopped behind them. J.G. Gardner came up behind him. "Jaybird, Lam, take a run around the right side and back of the lot. They might go over the fence. J.G., send two men around the other way. We'll play cop here and see if they drive out."

Five minutes later Murdock and the rest of the driveway SEALs were still waiting.

"Nothing," Murdock said. "Where the hell did they go?"

"Got them," Lam said on his Motorola. "They came out from between the cabs on this side, dragging the cash. Then they went over a six-foot fence and are shagging ass up the street. I'm on them like a coon dog on a possum."

"Coon dogs chase raccoons," Prescott said. "I used to have one."

"Jaybird, see if you can find Lam and stick with him. We'll use the cabs we kept here and follow."

J.G.'s two men came back from the other side of the lot and they got back in their cabs and eased around the lot. Murdock saw Lam a block ahead, moving slowly.

"Damn, they split up," the Motorola said. "I didn't hook up with Jaybird and I can only follow one. I'm on him."

Murdock found Jaybird sitting on the curb in the next block and picked him up. Murdock had no idea where Lam was.

Ten minutes later the SEALs in the two parked cabs caught Lam's disgust.

"Yeah, big tracker. The damn Arab went into this alley with some business backed up to it. About a dozen doors down there. I thought he went in the second one. Wrong. It was some kind of a women's wear store and they threw me out. I'm fucked. Corner of Tenth and Trent if you want to pick me up."

Before they got there the Motorola came on again. "Hot shit, I've got them again. Both of them, so they hooked back up. Must have holed up in one of those stores for a time. I'm not gonna let them see me this time. All smoke and shadows. Here we go. Keep back. Don't spook them. Looks like they're getting tired each carrying five million dollars."

"Stay with them, Lampedusa," Murdock said. "We'll pick you up when they go to tree."

"What in hell?"

"Fox-hunting term, I think," Murdock said. "When the varmint gets tired of running and climbs up a tree so the dogs can't tear him into bit and pieces."

"Gotcha." Lam eased from behind a ten-year-old sedan and kept his gaze on the two men moving slowly up the street. A cab went by and they waved at it frantically, but it sped on past. "So tired they couldn't piss straight if they tried," Lam said softly. He grinned, glad he wasn't packing about sixty or seventy pounds of one hundred dollar bills.

Lam saw the men look behind several times. Each time he was out of sight behind some cover. They tried for another cab and then a third, but this was a through-traffic street, not a pickup street.

After just over a half-hour of walking, the men were now dragging the canvas bags. They eased across a main street and into a small hotel. Lam got close enough to see them registering and then they vanished up some steps, still dragging the ten million dollars between them.

"Right, Cap. Looks like they registered and are here for a while. Place probably has a back or side door. I could use some help watching the rest of the place."

"Can do. Tell me where you are and you'll have company." It was Third Street and St. James. A holdover name from the Brits for sure.

Five minutes later Jaybird and Howard eased up beside Lam and he jumped.

"What the hell, you guys aren't supposed to slip up on the scout. No respect." He grinned. "Jaybird, you get the back. There is a back door over there into the alley. Just this one in front. We'll trade off. The boss say how long we were to stay here?"

"Not a peep. Long as it takes. If they move, we tell Murdock and move with them."

"Unless they take a cab or get a car."

"Murdock is stashed about two blocks over for just such a trick."

"Right, so we watch and wait," Howard said.

In a small hotel less than two miles away, Badri picked up the ringing phone. Only two men knew he was in this hotel.

"Yes?"

"Colonel, it's Imran. We still have the two packages. Haven't looked inside to see if it's really money. Should we?"

"Absolutely, Sergeant. Cut a small hole so you can see inside, but not big enough to interfere with moving it. Do it now." He waited while the soldier did as ordered. When the man came back on the phone, Badri could hear the excitement in his voice.

"Sir, you wouldn't believe it. It's real. Stacks and stacks of plastic-wrapped bundles of bills. All hundreds, right out of the mint. So beautiful."

"Good. You checked both bags?"

"Yes. One other thing, Colonel. We were trailed and tracked and chased by at least six or eight men. All were young and had close cropped haircuts like they were military. But they wore civilian clothes. I didn't see any weapons."

"Damn those Americans. They didn't pull the military trackers off our trail. They are still there. That means we're going to have a little party with the First Lady."

"Her little finger?"

"Exactly. Did the Americans follow you to the hotel?"

"I don't think so. We watched behind, and we never saw anyone."

"Good. Just to be sure, wait until dark. Then buy a hat and pay a woman from the bar to walk out the front door with you and get a cab. Call one to pick you up. Buy or steal a different shirt, so if anyone is watching they won't know it's you. Should be dark in an hour or so. I need you here. Oh, stop by at a store and buy a small cleaver."

"Yes, sir."

Lam and Howard had moved up to be just across the street from the hotel. They sat behind some shrubs that shielded them from the front door. Just after dark they saw a man in a baseball cap and tan shirt and a woman with a short skirt come out the hotel door and get into a cab.

"Couldn't be," Howard said.

They kept watching.

Twenty minutes later, across town, Imran knocked on

the hotel room door, and Badri let him inside. He handed a small paper package to the terrorist, who grinned when he felt the weight.

Mrs. Hardesty looked up at them from where she had been watching an old movie on television. She frowned. She had been surprised earlier when she found that she was alone with Badri. The two other men had vanished yesterday. Now one of them was back.

Badri sat down across from the First Lady. "Now, Mrs. President, this would be a good time for you to lecture me that the Arab world is fifty years behind the Western world in science, in business, in medicine, in morality, and in our treatment of women. Now would be an excellent time to make me just furious."

She frowned. "What on earth are you talking about? I never said you were fifty years behind the times. Maybe twenty, not fifty. Of course Iraq is closer to women's rights than any other Moslem nation. Do you know there are women doctors and lawyers in Baghdad? There are women who run their own business firms, and they are required to go to school, and they can drive a car, and go on the streets without a male escort from their immediate family." She smiled. "Of course you know that. You've done a lot of traveling. Seen the world. But have you ever been to the United States? Have you viewed the Great Evil up close and personal? Have you seen how so many Arabs have prospered and developed and become highly thought of in the United States? No, of course you haven't. That would shatter all of your prejudices, would sink the arguments that you have convinced yourself are right even though you have no logical or practical reasons to justify them."

"Whatever you say, Mrs. President. That's a beautiful heavy wooden armrest on that easy chair. Solid."

She frowned. "Yes, and it's also varnished and polished."

"Good. Kindly put your left hand on the armrest."

"Why?"

"Because if you don't, I'll shoot you through the head. Reason enough?"

In spite of herself, Mrs. Hardesty shivered. "Yes, all right."

"Now make a fist but leave your little finger stretched out straight."

"Like this. I really don't see . . ." The other Arab grabbed her hand and held it rigidly in place. She couldn't budge it. She never saw the blade descending. The cleaver jolted through flesh and bone and her little finger lay there on the arm of the chair completely detached from her hand.

Eleanor Hardesty gave a small groan and then fainted into the overstuffed chair with the solid wood arms.

She came back to consciousness less than five minutes later. She groaned and looked up, wide-eyed, then stared down at the arm rest on the chair and saw the cut in the smooth surface and the trace of something dark. For just moment she wanted to scream. It rose in her throat and almost made it to freedom but she clamped her mouth tightly closed and squeezed her eyes shut and felt a tremor slant through her body. Then she took a deep breath and looked down at her left hand. The small finger was gone, only a bloody tissue covered what must be a stump. She shivered again.

Then the pain came, a throbbing, burning, searing that tore through her body like a whirlwind. It passed and she gasped, then looked up at Badri.

"Yes, Mrs. President, you have just sacrificed the small finger on your left hand for your country. I don't know if it will convince your husband that I am serious, but I hope it does. If he doesn't do as I tell him, you will suffer the consequences. Be sure to remind him of that fact when you talk with him again.

"Now, to business. Your amputation has been cleaned

and disinfected and bandaged by my man who also is a
medic in the army. So don't worry about infection. Your finger is even now being sent to the police so they can take
your fingerprint and send it by email to your husband for
verification."

Mrs. Hardesty sat there listening, feeling her finger throb
now. She wanted to scream at him, to yell, to cry, to wail,
and whimper. Mostly she wanted to talk, but she wasn't
sure that she could without breaking down. She would not
cry. No. She would have to talk sooner or later. She held her
bandaged hand in the palm of her right hand and looked
away from Badri. This nightmare had to end soon. It had to
be over. She wasn't sure how much longer she could fight
this madman.

Murdock gave up on his stakeout with the car. He radioed
Lam and his helpers.

"Looks like a wrap for tonight. You men hold the fort
there until midnight and we'll have replacements for you.
Just make certain that the money doesn't leave the hotel.
There's no underground driveway or even a side drive. If
anyone loads anything large into a car or pickup, you may
have to check it out in person to make sure it isn't the
money bags."

"That's a roger, sir," Lam said. "No action here. I think
they have settled in for the night."

"I'm going back to our hotel. The car that brings your
replacements will take you to our hotel. You'll have to
drive. Keep alert. I'm checking in with Stroh. He's in town
somewhere."

Back in his hotel, Murdock opened up the SATCOM
and set it up to SEND. He used the frequency Stroh often
used and tried two calls. On the third one, the CIA agent
answered.

"Yeah, Murdock, wanted to get to you. The president is
kicking holes in the walls of the oval office. About a half-

hour ago they got an email picture from Durban showing a fingerprint. It's of the First Lady's small finger on her left hand. The Durban police have the digit in formaldehyde."

"Did Badri say why he cut it off?"

"Because we told him we would call off you SEALs. Of course we never figured to do that."

Murdock filled in Stroh on the day's jaunt. "So we know where the money is, but we don't know where the First Lady is. We hope they will join up tomorrow. If they do, we still won't be able to rescue her until we are absolutely sure we can do so without any chance of wounding or injuring her. We need a stable situation, preferably a hotel room where we can do the job quickly, neatly, and without firing a shot."

"Agreed. Until then we follow the money. You have a watch on all that cash?"

"We do. Changing the guard at midnight. Now, all I need to do is find Gardner and get two of his men to take the second watch. What hotel is he at?"

"I don't have a clue."

Murdock frowned. "Damn it, neither do I, which means I'll be the one standing the second watch tonight at midnight at the hotel with the money."

23

At midnight, Murdock went back to the hotel where the money was to relieve his three men.

"Who else is with you?" Lam asked.

"Just me, I couldn't locate Gardner. He got lost in the hassle of following these guys."

"Not a one man job here," Lam said. "I'll stay with you and we can take two-hour watches."

"Thanks, buddy. I can use the help."

They sent Jaybird and Howard back to the other hotel.

It was a long night. Nothing moved around the hotel after two A.M. Lam was on the four-to-six shift when he called Murdock on the Motorola.

"Hey, Cap. We've got some action. Side door. Civilian car with three people inside. One got out and went in the side door. Could be a pickup of the cash."

"I've got them. Go get the car up this way so it'll be close if we need it. Must be Badri picking up the money. Maybe he has the First Lady with him."

"Too much to hope for."

"Still, we can't take them down yet. If she is in the car, we can't shoot. Even if they shoot at us, we have to hold fire. We need a nice contained room we can work with."

"Roger that, Cap. Uh-oh. Here comes somebody. Same guy who went inside. He's packing something. Yep, the money, half of it at least."

"I've got another body right behind the first with another

money bag. They put the cash in the trunk and locked it. Now what?"

"Half-block to the car, Cap," Lam said. "I'm running. Watch which way they go."

The black sedan that picked up the money and the man had left before Lam skidded the rental Chevy to a stop and Murdock climbed inside.

"Straight ahead, they're a block up there. Don't let them know we're back here."

"Right, I don't have the headlights on. Should help us. Not much traffic, so it'll be harder, though. Nobody to hide behind."

They drove through the light downtown traffic for two or three miles, keeping close enough to tail the other car. Then it suddenly sped away, made a sharp turn, and tried to lose them.

"Now he knows we're here, it's a car chase," Lam said. He switched on his lights and followed. He came up to within six car lengths of the other car as the night faded into dawn. Soon they were in a suburb, and then there were fewer and fewer houses and they were in the country.

The speed slowed down as the road worsened. Twice when Lam closed up the distance between them, came shots from the car ahead as someone leaned out the window and fired at them.

"Pistol," Lam said. "Be a miracle if the rounds come within fifty feet of us." A moment later one round hit the passenger's side windshield but didn't penetrate. It left a long jagged crack in the safety glass.

Just ahead, in a small hamlet, Lam held back as he saw a police car swing in and follow Badri's car. Its lights flashed and the siren roared as the policeman pulled the black sedan over. Lam eased to the side of the road and waited. The cop went up to the car and said something. A second later someone inside the car shot the policeman twice in the chest and he jolted backwards and fell. The people in the car rushed out of the sedan and jumped in the police vehicles.

"Land Rover," Lam said. "Four-wheel drive. Thing can go anywhere. And there's no way we can stop them from taking it."

They saw the three men push the First Lady into the rig and throw in the bags of money, then it drove away. Lam was right behind it.

"Why didn't we bring at least one long gun?" Murdock said. "We could have ended it right there and taken them out one by one."

"Next time," Lam said.

The route got tougher. Whoever drove the Land Rover now cut off the streets of the small town into the countryside and off road, rolling through a pasture that had few fences and lots of trees.

Twice Lam thought the Chevy was hung up on the rough ground, but each time he gunned the motor and worked out of it.

A mile later the four-wheel-drive rig splashed across a small creek and up a slope and vanished. Lam drove up to the creek and eyed it. He nodded.

"Yep, we can get across." He eased the car into the foot-deep water, hit the accelerator just right, and surged across the water and up the slope on the far side. It was a sharp ridge and the front wheels went across then came down without any land under them. The rear wheels tried to drive the rig forward, but it hung there high, centered, and not able to move.

Lam watched the SUV in the distance break through a fence, gain a blacktopped road, and speed off to the south and back toward town.

They got out and tried to push the Chevy forward, but it was stuck.

Lam shrugged and looked toward the road. "Wonder if

they know about hitchhiking in South Africa?" he asked.

As it twined out, the locals understood about asking or a ride, but it still took the SEALs almost three hours to get back to where they could hire a taxi to take them to their hotel. There they found the rest of the SEALs, including Stroh, waiting for them.

"So what's our boy Badri going to do now?" Stroh asked.

Everyone had gathered in Murdock's room and they looked at him.

"With the money he has, he can go wherever he wants to and do whatever he wants to do," Murdock said. "If he's smart he'll drop the First Lady off at some street corner, give her coins for the phone to call the police, and fade away into the night never to be heard from again."

"But you don't think he will, do you?" Gardner asked.

"Nope. He's greedy. He'll look for another pay day with the First Lady again as the bait."

"The president is furious. I've seen him mad before. They have to hold him down sometimes, but this is really putting him over the edge. He did raise the reward for the return of the First Lady to ten million. The local press and TV will have it on today."

"That might scare some action out of the woodwork, but we can't count on it," Gardner said.

Stroh used the phone and talked to the police. He came away with a grin.

"Could be something. A report from an airline saying that they just sold tickets to an Arab man and a white woman who had a scarf over her face and looked like a "reluctant" passenger. They boarded a flight to Maputo, Mozambique."

"Easy enough to check," Lam said.

"I'll call our embassy in Maputo and get them on it. Flight should take about two hours. We'll see what shows up then."

"In the meantime . . ." Murdock said.

"We watch and wait," Stroh said. "Maybe we'll get lucky and that disguised white woman is actually the First Lady with Badri and we snag them both at the same time."

"Fat chance of that happening," Dexter Tate said. "Great big fat chance."

Badri had driven the police car on the chase. He kept looking for a hazard that would stop the Chevy. Then the creek came into play and the sharp ridge behind it. He had to struggle to get the four-wheel-drive Land Rover over it and figured the Chevy wouldn't have a chance. It didn't

"Now you see the superior planning of the Arab World over that of the Great Evil Western World," Badri said, looking quickly at the First Lady in the back seat. "Superior planning and execution does it every time for the Arab nations."

"Execution is the right word," Eleanor Hardesty said. She held her left hand in her right as she had been doing since she woke up.

"Murderer is a better word. How many men have you killed so far on this little escapade of yours, Badri? Two, four, are you up to six or eight by now? How can you live with yourself? You're nothing but a killer with the morals of a rattlesnake."

Badri smiled. "Go ahead, try to get me angry. How can I be unhappy? I have ten million dollars, and a key hostage who should be worth even more.

"Ten million dollars should be plenty for a cheap crook like you. You wouldn't know how to live with ten million. What would you do, buy a house and servants and a big car and fly to Monte Carlo to gamble away your loot? What an asshole you are, Badri. You're the bottom of the food chain. You'll eat anything and anyone to get what you want. Men like you should be locked up and starved to death to prevent any contamination of the honest people in the world."

"Okay, stop. That's too much. I told you I'm in a good mood, but I can change. You saw me kill two men, that's all. Now shut up your face before I do you a favor and put a bullet in your thick skull and dump you along the roadside so the wolves and jackals and other assorted wild animals can tear your body apart as they have a square meal."

They drove in silence then. Shortly they returned to the large town, and Badri parked the marked police car and the four walked away from it for two blocks to a highly traveled street. The first taxi they saw stopped and picked them up. The money went in the trunk and the four people filled up the cab.

Back at the hotel, Badri ordered steak dinners and two bottles of wine for all of them from room service. He cut open one of the bags of money and took out a square package sealed in plastic wrap. Inside were neat stacks of wrapped bundles of $100 bills. He slit the plastic and stacked the Federal Reserve wrapped bundles of bills on the small desk. There were eight of the bundles in each package.

"Look at this. Eight of these stacks and hundreds in each one. That's ten thousand dollars in each of these inch-high bunches. In this one package, that's eighty thousand dollars."

"Enjoy it while you can, Badri," the First Lady said. "You'll never live to spend much of it. My prediction."

The big .45 caliber pistol came out of his belt in one swift motion, and Badri pushed the cold muzzle hard in the soft tissue under the First Lady's chin, jamming her head upward to relive the pressure.

"I could blow your fucking brains out right now, Mrs. President. You know that? Why are you so nasty all the time?"

"I've learned a great deal from you lately, Badri. Nasty is just one of those attributes."

Badri snorted, and then laughed. "I have to give it to you, Mrs. President, you never stop. You're a fighter." He pulled the pistol down and slapped her sharply on the face. "If you give me any more trouble, I'm going to tape your mouth shut, so I don't have to listen to your caterwauling. Do I make myself perfectly clear?"

She nodded.

"Good." He walked up and down in the room, waving a stack of ten thousand dollars. "Now, what's next? I might just call off any more moves and fade into the distance, never to be heard from again." He did a little dance and looked out the hotel window. Then he checked his watch.

"Where's the big radio?" One of his men brought the SATCOM to him. He set it up with the small dish antenna aimed out the window. He had left it set to the correct frequency and pushed the send button on the hand mike.

"President Hardesty. You better get on this radio. You have five minutes to get here. I don't want some lackey; I will speak only with you. Get back to me quickly."

He let up on the send button and listened. Less than a minute later the set came on.

"Badri, that must be you. It's five A.M. here in Washington. The president is sleeping. I'll get him up. It will take ten minutes. Then he'll talk."

Badri smiled. At least he was messing up the old man's sleep. That amused him. He worked over his plan as he waited. When the set came on he was ready.

"Mr. Badri. This is President Hardesty."

"My next demand is going to have a consequence. If you do not comply with my demand, the next package that goes to the police here in Durban will be Eleanor Hardesty's right hand. Do I make myself clear?"

"Absolutely clear, Mr. Badri."

"Good. Now listen carefully. I assume you're recording this message. You can play it over a dozen times, it will still say the same thing. You will put fifty million dollars in one hundred dollar bills in a business jet aircraft that can fly five hundred miles an hour, and send it to the airport here at Durban. There will be no armed guards, no military personnel, no police or CIA members on the plane. Just the fifty million and the two pilots and a crew chief if required. These may be military pilots. You will tell me the flight plan of the plane, when it takes off from Washington, where it lands to refuel, what countries it flies to, and when it is due to arrive in Durban. There will be no advance notice to the Durban police or to any South African army, or its air force. It will be a secret flight. Once on the ground, the plane will remain with me as part of the demands. The pilots and crew will be free to take commercial air home after staying incognito for three days in a hotel of my choosing. At that time the First Lady will be freed unharmed.

"If you don't follow these instructions to the letter, the First Lady loses her right hand. There are only so many body parts that I can deliver to you without endangering the lady's health.

"Have you heard my demands?"

"I have heard them, Mr. Badri. I'll consult with my advisors to see how they can be implemented. It will take at least twenty four hours for us to evaluate and prepare for a flight like this. Goodbye."

The transmission stopped and Badri turned off the set.

In the hotel where Murdock was quartered, he had his SATCOM tuned to the CIA channel that Badri had been using, as usual. Don Stroh, who had gone to his room after they had lunch, came hurtling through the door into Murdock's room.

He looked at the SATCOM set.

"You heard?" Stroh asked.

Murdock nodded. "We've got to stop this bastard and do it within twenty-four hours."

24

Murdock scowled at Stroh and then wiped his face with both hands. "It's just after fourteen hundred, that's two P.M. to you, Stroh. We have to get done before two A.M. What? How? When? Where? Why can't we locate this guy?"

"Over two hundred hotels, big and small, in this town. We can't check them all."

"Maybe we should try. We have seventeen men. If each one took ten hotels, we might just find him."

"Might? I can't risk the First Lady's life on a maybe."

"What else? What's his pattern? New town. Contacts?"

"We know he used al Qaeda once, maybe twice," Stroh said. "I'll check with the local law and see what they know about the bunch. This place is big enough. There could be a local cell."

Murdock nodded and used his Motorola. "All hands report to my cabin, right now," Murdock said.

The fifteen men hurried in. Jaybird was the last one.

"The kid was climbing the outside of the hotel naked, so he had to crawl inside and get dressed before he could come," Senior Chief Neal said. A bunch of hoo-oooh agreed.

"Badri made another money demand, accompanied with a threat, if he doesn't get confirmation within twenty-four hours, that he'll chop off the First Lady's right hand," Murdock said. "We've got to find this bastard. He must be in a hotel. DeWitt and Gardner, take the men and split up the hotel section of the telephone directory and start canvassing them. Dig into everyone you can find and ask about three Arabs and a white woman. Hopefully, they'll stand out and be remembered. Go."

The men filed out into DeWitt's room, and began to work. Murdock looked at Stroh, who was on the phone.

"Three? Why haven't you done something about them?" Stroh listened and grunted twice. "Give me the names and the addresses. We're facing a serious disaster unless we find these people in a rush." He wrote on a scratch pad on the telephone table. "Yes, I understand. We'll be making a survey, a peaceful inquiry of some kind. If we need you, we'll give you a call."

Stroh put down the phone and looked at Murdock. "He said the cop I should talk to is on holiday. They got the names of al Qaeda members here a couple of weeks ago from a computer search of an international roster. Sloppy of al Qaeda. Some LEA put it together in Britain."

"So why are the cells just sitting here and not doing anything? Can't the cops take them down?"

"This police captain said the Arabs involved haven't done anything illegal. It's not against the law to belong to al Qaeda or any other organization."

"Let's go pay them a visit." Murdock went to the door and looked in the hall. Two SEALs in their tan civilian clothes were heading for the stairs.

"Mahanani, Tate. On me. You've got a new assignment. Both of you have your Glocks?" the men nodded. He took the sheet of paper Stroh had worked on. "We're going visiting, trying to make new people in town feel welcome."

"You got addresses?" Mahanani asked.

"Three. If we're lucky somebody might be home." He looked at the CIA man. "Stroh, you with us?"

"Why not? You look short-handed."

"We can always call in the reserves. You have any teeth?"

Stroh patted his waist. "Nice little .32 with an eight-round bite. When do we leave?"

They took the new rental Murdock had arranged. It was smaller and four people filled it. The first address was a business firm halfway across town. They found it after a fifteen-minute search along one of the main shopping streets. It was a curio and antique shop featuring art, glass, and metal products from Asian and Arab countries. Murdock took Tate into the store and left the other two in the car.

Murdock and Tate both wore civilian floppy hats to conceal their white side give-away haircuts. Murdock approached a clerk.

"I'd like to talk to the manager."

"What about?" the male in his thirties and all Arab, asked. "Maybe I can help you."

"No, this involves a rather large purchase. I need to see the owner or manager." Murdock saw there were no other customers in the small store.

The Arab frowned. "I really shouldn't disturb him."

"Take me to him and I'm sure he'll be glad you did."

The clerk took a deep breath. "Follow me," he said.

Murdock waved to Tate. "Lock the front door," he whispered. Tate nodded.

Murdock followed the clerk to a back storage room, then to a small office. One man sat inside at a desk. Murdock pushed the clerk inside and drew his automatic.

The manager looked up in alarm. He had been working on a computer, which he tried to shut down.

"Don't touch it," Murdock said. "Move over to the wall." He looked at the screen. It was filled with Arabic writing.

The two Arabs scowled at Murdock and whispered to each other.

"No talking," Murdock snapped. "We know you're a cell for al Qaeda. Your shop is understocked and the goods overpriced. How many members do you have?"

"I am a merchant. I try to make a living. I don't know what this al Qaeda is."

"You're lying," Murdock said. He looked at Tate, who had now joined them. "Keep them here. I'll look around the rest of the operation."

He did, but found only two more rooms. One was outfitted as an apartment and it was evidently where the men lived. Murdock went back to the office. Tate had tied the hands and feet of the two Arabs, who now sat on the floor. He was checking out a filing cabinet and the desk. He shook his head.

"I can't find anything that looks like al Qaeda material. No list of targets, members, anything like that."

"Maybe they're inactive. Keep them here for eight hours. If you don't hear from me on their telephone, let them go and get back to the hotel by taxi. I don't want them to warn any other Arabs in town that a search is underway."

Outside, Murdock shook his head and walked back to the car. He turned to the back seat. "Now, mister CIA big shot. Where is the next possible al Qaeda address on your list?"

Badri paced up and down the hotel room. He glanced at Mrs. Hardesty now and then, but didn't say anything. She was watching a ballet on television. He snorted. Ballet was a pile of nonsense. Bad acting, ridiculous convoluted dancing, and music that was strident and not even pleasing to listen to.

He jerked his thumb at his two men. "Pack up, we're getting out of here. We've stayed in this hotel too long. They could be checking."

"Where to?" one of the soldiers asked.

"I have an old friend in Durban. I looked him up before we left home. He's still here and I have his address. He's the leader of the only real active al Qaeda cell in town. Mrs. President and I and the money will go in our rented car. You wait a half-hour then you two come in a cab. I'll give you the address. It should be interesting, talking to a man I haven't seen or worked with in almost ten years."

"What if I won't go with you?" Eleanor Hardesty asked.

"Simple. I'll knock you out, tie you up in a sheet, and take you out the side door and into the car. No one will notice. You want that?"

The First Lady felt a wave of anger and fear. He would do just what he said he would. "No, I think I can manage to walk to the car." She stared at him hard. "You really mean that about cutting off my right hand, or was that a bluff?"

"Did I bluff about your finger?"

"But a whole hand. I couldn't write or type or use the computer except with one hand. I would have a hard time dressing myself. How would I cut up a nice juicy steak?"

"Yes, so many problems. I'm sure the president will think of all those things when he decides to send the money. Don't worry, he'll send it and you'll save your precious hand. Now get up, we're moving. I'll carry both the bags. You try to run or contact anyone and I'll drop one bag and shoot you dead before you move two steps. Do you fully understand how precarious your life is right now?"

"I understand."

It took Badri a half-hour to drive to the outskirts of town and then find the quiet street with the stand-alone house. He had put the two bags of money in the car's trunk and locked it. He paused at the curb and watched the house. It was supposed to be the real power in most of South Africa for al Qaeda. He hoped it was still active and could help protect him. For the past hour he had felt strange, like something bad was going to happen. He had tried to shake it off, but it kept coming back. The move to this house, where he would be among friends and countrymen, should help. He took Mrs. Hardesty's arm and guided her up the walk to the front door. His knock brought a slow opening of the door an inch and a dark eye that stared out at them.

"I've come to see my countrymen," Badri said in Arabic.

"I don't know you, go away."

Badri put his foot against the door so it wouldn't close. "I come with good news from groups all over the world." It was the universal words that were known by all al Qaeda members everywhere. It was supposed to open doors and to make you instant friends.

"Who is the woman? She is not one of us."

"Actually she is my prisoner, and I need help controlling her. I can pay for our keep. We are in a difficult situation for the next twenty-four hours."

"You can pay?"

Badri took six of the one hundred dollar bills from his pocket and pushed them through the opening. They were grabbed immediately and pulled out of his hand. A moment later the door opened and an Arab with a full black beard and dark eyes stared at them.

"Does Fathi Alsunar still work with you?"

The man's face broke into a smile. "You know of the great Fathi? Yes, he is our leader. We do many good works for Islam. Come in, come in."

The house was South African, but had been tempered with Arabic pictures, a wall hanging, and oriental rugs on the floor. The smell of incense filled the room. Two men sat at a low table near a fireplace. One stood. The other remained seated, smoking a long-stemmed pipe that ended in a water bowl. Badri stared at the seated man. The others watched.

"Fathi?" Badri asked.

The man looked up, his eyes heavy, his movements languid. Then his face brightened. "Badri, you son of a bastard camel. What are you doing in my town?" He spoke in Arabic and Badri responded in that language.

"Working. Working for the good of Allah and Iran and the faith of Islam."

"You always were a shithead, Badri." He stared at the First Lady. "And who is your American friend?"

"Just a friend I'm keeping safe from her people. Can you help me?"

"Never let it be said that Fathi has turned away a fellow Arab in trouble or who needs help." He waved one hand and two men who had been standing near him relaxed and removed hands from under loose-fitting shirts. Probably moving hands off pistols, Badri thought.

"Sit, my friend, sit, and we will eat and drink and remember the good times in Tehran. What was it, ten years ago?"

"At least, old friend," Badri said.

"First, the payment. We need another six hundred American dollars to let you stay here."

"That's reasonable. I hope to be gone tomorrow by noon. Until then I feel the need of my own people and sanctuary." He took a roll of bills from his pocket and was peeling off six when a rough hand hit his wrist and he dropped the roll that had three thousand dollars in it. The money fell to the table where Fathi picked it up and nodded.

"Yes, just about right. We know who the American lady is. We read the paper and watch the TV news. A valuable hostage, the wife of the president of the most powerful nation in the world. We didn't know it was you who kidnapped her. Now we wonder where you have the rest of these brand new American hundred dollar bills."

A man grabbed Badri from behind and lifted the automatic pistol from his waistband. Fathi smiled.

"Now, old friend, Badri, who lied about me back home and drove me out of the country, we'll see just how good a friend you are. Where is the ransom money?"

"I radioed them this morning. They are to deliver it tomorrow at the airport. Why are you doing this?"

"You lied about me years ago." Fathi shook his head. "Now you don't even remember." He stared hard at Badri. "I promised myself I would gouge your eyes out if I ever saw you again. Now I have compassion. You aren't worth it. I'll simply have you shot and dumped in the garbage.

Your friend is another matter. She is a meal ticket. She can be a source of income for years. We can ask for ransom every month. Get fifty million a month for her. The president will pay. He's a compassionate man. We'll have the finances to work again. It's been difficult to get any money since Osama passed on. As for you, Badri, you think small. It's good that you came to us. Now all I have to do is decide which of my men will have the honor of killing you."

25

When Murdock eased into the car on the street outside the Arab store, he asked Stroh over the Motorola where the next al Qaeda cell was.

Mahanani had the answer.

"We've been kicking that around, LC. There's a close one, and one way across town. The one here is on the outskirts but closer, so we figured you'd want to go to it rather than wasting time."

"You've got the city map, tell me how to get there."

"Okay. Right down this street for about a mile, maybe more, then take Imperial Avenue."

"We're moving. That last location was a bust. Nobody knew anything and we didn't find any hint of al Qaeda. Tate is baby-sitting them so they don't warn anyone else that we might be calling."

Murdock used the Motorola.

"DeWitt, are you in range?"

"Barely, Commander, but I copy."

"Good. I'm feeling naked out here. Gather up five more men and meet us on Imperial Avenue. I'm really feeling naked. Bring along three MP-5s. We might need them. Just a hunch."

"I've got four men here. Will stop by the hotel and pick up the long ones. Out."

"How far do we go out on Imperial?" Murdock asked.

"Looks like about ten blocks," Mahanani said. "We can

stop near the end and lead DeWitt on the Motorola to where we're waiting."

Later Murdock worked it that way. The two SEALs met outside the cars and talked, then got back in and Mahanani directed Murdock to the right street. They found the address.

In the daylight the only way they could go up to the house was in the open. The house looked freshly painted. The lawn had been recently mowed and trimmed. It looked like a pleasant suburban house. Murdock looked at his helpers.

"Stroh, you get baptized on this one. You're with me. We walk up to the house and take the soft, gentle route. You at least have a suit on. That won't scare them. You know what to ask."

The two men left the car two houses down and walked up to the two-story brown and white house. Murdock knocked on the door and stepped back, leaving the talking to Stroh. After a respectable time, they heard the door open.

An Arab man about thirty-five looked out. He was clean shaven and wearing a T-shirt and blue jeans. His brow wrinkled.

"Yes?"

"Good afternoon. My name is Don Stroh, and we need to ask you a few questions."

"Why?"

"We're looking for some friends of ours. We thought you might be able to tell us if there are any Arab Friendship Groups in town."

The man closed his eyes and he took a deep breath and let it out, then opened his eyes. "Just because I'm Arab doesn't mean I know anything about other Arabs. I'm into computers and work here from my home. I've done well since my wife and daughter and I came here five years ago from Saudi Arabia."

"Fine. Do you know of any Arab groups here in Durban?"

The man looked away, sighed again. Then he looked

back. "I hate what they are doing. Despise them. They are cowards masquerading under the name of Islam. I am Moslem, but what they do has nothing to do with our religion. Yes, I can give you two names and locations. The first is an antique shop down on Bennett Street. The second is just outside of town where a man named Fathi is the leader. He's on Concord Street, 1515. I remember that address. Don't let them know that I told you about them."

"We won't. We also want to pay you for your trouble." Stroh took three one hundred dollar bills from his pocket and handed them to the man.

"No, I can't take your money. It is enough that perhaps this one small blot on the Arab community here might be destroyed. I wish you well in your search." He smiled and then closed the door.

Back in the car, Murdock slapped Stroh on the back. "Now, my fishing buddy, you have earned your wings. Damn nice work back there. You know that the address he gave us is the third one on our list. Let's go and see what this Fathi guy looks like."

It took them forty-five minutes to drive across town and out to its edge. They found the street, turned the wrong way, and doubled back to get to 1515 Concord. Murdock stopped the car four houses away and DeWitt's rented sedan stopped a house in back of Murdock.

He used the Motorola.

"We have a good ID on this place. Single house, no fences around it. House right in back of it and an alley. Small garage at the side with two cars in the long driveway. Won't be dark for an hour yet."

DeWitt broke in. "We wait for dark. Hey, wasn't there a McDonald's back there about a mile?"

Nearly an hour later the eight men left the fast food restaurant that looked identical to those in the States. With

DeWitt were Doyle, Prescott, Canzoneri, and Van Dyke. They climbed in the same cars they had come in and drove slowly back to the target house. This time they stopped six lots away. Murdock radioed for DeWitt to drive his men to the far side of the house after dropping off Van Dyke with Murdock.

"When DeWitt is in place, we move in slowly," Murdock said. "Our tan outfits might give us away, so keep under cover whenever possible. DeWitt, cover any doors on your side and the rear door. We'll take the front and this side. The house is too big to get everyone with flash-bangs. We'll get in place and wait a half hour to see if anyone exits. Then we'll play it by ear."

"You going in hard?" DeWitt asked on the radio.

"If we can determine there are two or three of them in the front room, we'll use the flash there, then dig out the rest of them wherever they are in the house. They'll be ready and shooting."

"Roger that," DeWitt said. They all had on their radios. A short time later, "We're in position," DeWitt reported.

"Moving up toward the place now," Murdock said as he eased up to the wide porch across the front of the house. He had Van Dyke beside him and Mahanani covering the side of the house with Stroh. This side had two windows that could be escape zones. Murdock held one of the MP-5 submachine guns. He checked his watch.

"Change of plans. We're going up to the door, now. Watch any windows on the sides." He motioned to Van Dyke and they stepped over a small railing to the porch and moved past heavily curtained windows to the front door. Murdock put his ear to the wood and listened. He held up three fingers, then four.

Murdock whispered: "Remember, the First Lady could very well be in there. No harm to her, if so."

Murdock took out a flash-bang grenade and pulled the

safety pin, holding down the arming spoon with his other
hand. He nodded at Van Dyke, who was on the doorknob
side of the door. He reached out and gently twisted the knob.
The door was locked. Murdock studied the door handle and
latch. It was fifty years old. He handed the flash-bang to Van
Dyke, then backed off to the edge of the eight-foot-wide
porch and surged forward, jumping and kicking out hard
with both boots right at the door lock. The door smashed inward and Van Dyke lobbed the flash-bang inside the moment the top of the panel fell.

Murdock dropped to the porch on all fours and dove side-
ways to the wall. Van Dyke hugged the other wall. Four-
point-two seconds later the flash-bang went off with six
piercing strobes of light that came in brilliant flashes guar-
anteed to temporarily blind anyone who didn't cover up the
eyes. Then the series of six extremely loud explosive sounds
blasted through the room to disable the ears.

When the last thundering sound came, Murdock and
Van Dyke stormed inside. From a doorway ahead in the
well-lit room a submachine gun chattered off six rounds.
Murdock dove to the left and Van Dyke to the right. Murdock targeted the muzzle flash with six rounds of his
own. He saw three people in the room, one of them the
president's wife. She sat on a big chair, her hands over
her ears, her eyes tight shut. One large man rolled on the
floor moaning and holding his ears. The other man was
behind a low table. He had fallen forward onto stacks of
U.S. $100 bills, moaning and shaking his head, his hands
holding his ears. He suddenly reached under the table and
came up with a pistol, but he didn't have time to fire it.
Van Dyke put two rounds in his chest and he flopped
backwards. Van Dyke then jumped to the other writhing
man on the floor and put plastic riot ties around his ankles
and wrists.

Murdock came to his feet and darted to the doorway

ahead where the gunman had fired. The man lay on his side, blood gushing from a head wound. The First Lady stirred, moved her hands, and stared blankly ahead, her eyes not working yet.

Murdock peeked around the corner of the door to find another room, a dining area with a formal table and eight chairs. He heard footsteps on the floors upstairs. How many? He wasn't sure. Two at least. There was no open stairway. A door near the wall to the left was a possible. Neither of the dead men nor the live al Qaeda was Badri. They had seen his picture. Van Dyke knelt beside the First Lady whispering to her. She smiled and nodded. He stayed near her, his Glock raised and ready.

Murdock waved at Van Dyke, getting his attention. He pointed to the First Lady, then stabbed his finger at the front door. Van Dyke nodded and whispered to Eleanor Hardesty. She nodded and stood on trembling legs. Then she steadied and took Van Dyke's arm and they walked quickly out the front door.

Murdock listened to upstairs footsteps again. The sound of breaking glass came as a surprise. Where from?

His earpiece spoke to him. "We've got someone breaking through an upstairs window," DeWitt said. "He's dropping to a shed in back. Now he's on the ground and running. Our shots missed him. I've put Prescott and Doyle on him. One Glock and one MP-5. He's heading down an alley back here."

"Anyone else hear or see any more terrs?" Murdock asked.

Nobody answered. The footsteps came again from upstairs.

Murdock moved silently to the door against the wall and opened it without a sound. Steps led upward. He listened. Feet shuffling. He reached for a flash-bang. He had already used the one he had. He grabbed a fragger and pulled the pin, then eased up the stairs. He lifted the MP-5 in his left hand and aimed it upward.

A stair tread squeaked as he stepped on it.

Sound of footfalls, then a black object came over the railing at the top of the stairs. Another flash-bang. Murdock fired at the same time the other man did. Bullets chipped the wall next to him, angled downward into the floor. Murdock fired twelve rounds before he let up on the trigger. The sound of the flash-bang in the enclosed space was deafening, literally: His ears rang and then he went deaf. He couldn't hear a thing. He looked upward. Nothing.

Slowly he moved up two steps and waited, the grenade still in his right hand.

Two more steps. Listening. Nothing.

Two more steps.

He saw a flash of something that darted across the opening above, then was gone. He went quickly up the rest of the steps and peered around the railing when his head was floor level. Light came in through four windows, with one broken out. It was one large room with three beds and two dressers. One mattress had been pulled off a bed and leaned against the wall. He watched it. No movement. Was someone there? Slowly his hearing came back.

He checked the rest of the room. One of the dressers shook just a moment, as if someone had pressed against it. The movement came again. The mattress was a ploy to get him in the open. Murdock judged the distance to the dresser. It stood two feet from the wall. He let the arming handle fly off the grenade, held it for two seconds, then lobbed it toward the dresser.

The fragmentation hand grenade exploded just as it vanished behind the dresser. Murdock ducked down the steps for the explosion, then came charging into the room, the MP-5 aimed at the dresser.

He heard a moan, then a scream of pain. Murdock

edged toward the dresser. It had been blown another foot from the wall, the top drawer pushed outward and a small headboard splintered. His hearing was normal again. He listened but heard no more sounds.

Slowly he came up to the dresser and looked around it, then he jerked his head back. A submachine gun stammered off six rounds from behind the dresser. Most were caught by the shattered wood, but two broke through and one took Murdock high in the right thigh. He pressed forward, pushed the MP-5's muzzle around the end of the dresser, and hosed down the area with twelve rounds.

A low moan seeped into the silence after the roar of the submachine gun quieted. Murdock edged forward and poked his head out to look behind the dresser. He jolted it back, then nodded and took a longer look. The terrorist lay with the submachine gun across his chest, his face a mass of blood and bullet holes. Murdock hurried down the stairs.

"Stroh, do you have the package in one of the cars?" he yelled into his Motorola.

"Yes, indeed. And everyone is resting easy."

"DeWitt, any report from your runner?"

"That's a negative, Commander. Prescott reported that the man has a submachine gun, so they are keeping tabs on him but not pushing it. Doubt if we could find them now if we tried."

"Try. Take the other car and track them. Radio contact all the time. We need that last man. I think he's Badri."

"It's done."

"Stroh, send Van Dyke back in here. We've got some cleaning up to do. There is paper all over the place. The kind that's green and has Ben Franklin's portrait on the front. There are two big bags we can use. One hasn't been opened."

"They knew we were coming," Stroh said. "The chief of police and one national security man said they would cooperate."

"Be just as well if we could be gone before they get here

anyway. Give us five minutes. If the police come, ease away with the First Lady. How is she doing?"

"She's great, but worried about you guys in there."

Van Dyke ran into the room and they stuffed the loose hundred dollar bills into the opened case, then held it together and both left the house and walked down six houses to the car, each lugging one of the bags with five million dollars in it. They had just put the cases of money in the trunk and stepped inside the car when they heard the first sirens.

Stroh drove away from the sound, circled the block, and found his way back to the main street. Stroh looked at Murdock.

"Anybody hit by all that firing?"

Murdock shook his head. "Nobody but me that I know of. I took one in my right leg. An in-and-out, so no big worry." He chuckled. "This rental car outfit is going to wonder why they have blood on their front seat."

Mahanani growled. "Pull over the car, CIA big shot, so I can take a look at the commander's leg."

It took Mahanani five minutes to find the bullet holes and patch up his commander. Murdock used his Motorola.

"DeWitt, any luck with the runner? Where are you?"

"Not sure where we are. Both our men are still on the runner. He's getting tired. May try a standoff soon. He's been shooting and lights have been coming on. Surprised the cops aren't here yet. We've come about half a mile so far."

"Stay on him. We're clear and the First Lady is safe. Now get that man you're after. It has to be Badri. None of the men I saw in the house could be him. We need to put him down and dead as soon as possible."

26

Derek Prescott peered just over a trash barrel in the alley and checked out the area ahead. Houses on both sides. Unpaved alley with a cross street two houses ahead. The terr had vanished into some boxes and stacks of lumber behind a house and Prescott couldn't see him. The man had a subgun. He'd fired at them several times.

Robert Doyle crouched just behind him. "Wish we could throw a fragger," Doyle said. They had been cautioned not to use the hand bombs in the residential area. The terr fired three rounds at them. One ricocheted off the can and the other two missed. Prescott returned fire with a three-round burst from his MP-5. They listened but heard no cries of pain.

The terr moved again. They could see his dark form slide from the boxes and race down the street. A house right behind the terr kept Prescott from shooting. Both SEALs stormed after the man. He turned and fired again, this time only two rounds and Prescott thought he could hear the weapon's receiver lock open. Was the terr out of rounds?

The man ahead ran with renewed energy, came to a small park, and darted into it and slid behind the trunk of a large tree. The SEALs approached cautiously.

"Too damn much cover in there," Prescott said. He dropped to the ground, watching the darkness ahead. Lots of trees and some brush. The terr leaned round a tree and fired six rounds at the dark blobs of his pursuers.

Prescott yelped in surprise and returned fire. He saw the shape jolt from behind the tree and crash into the brush.

"Damn close," he said. He looked over at Doyle. "Hey, man, you okay?"

"No, caught one. Right shoulder. Broke it I think. Can't move my arm."

Prescott rolled over and checked the wound in the half light. Blood all over the place. Nothing he could do. He hit his Motorola. "Doyle is hit, we need a medic in the north end of this little park."

"Roger that, Prescott," DeWitt said. "We're coming up on the park now. I'll patch him up."

"Hang in there Doyle, DeWitt is coming. I'm after this sombitch."

Prescott ran to the edge of the heavy growth and listened. He could hear someone crashing through brush ahead. He ran forward, stopped, and listened again. He changed directions, then stopped again. No sound. The runner had stopped. Now all Prescott had to do was find him.

In the brush ahead, Ahmed Badri stifled a groan. His left arm hung uselessly at his side. He'd been hit with two rounds, one in and out, the next one into his shoulder joint somewhere and it was killing him. The pain came in waves and wouldn't stop. He blinked sweat out of his eyes and lifted the submachine gun. He didn't know what kind it was. He'd jerked it out of Fathi's guard's hands when the shooting began downstairs. He'd killed the guard with two good butt strokes, then got out the window and down the roof and ran. Who were these guys chasing him? They had to be U.S. military. They were good. Flash-bang grenades. He'd heard about them but never used any.

He'd have to get some.

The damn money was gone. First Fathi had found it in the trunk of the car and then the attack. At least the gunfire downstairs had kept the guard from killing him. Now all he had to do was keep running. He had put down one of the chasers behind him. He heard the talk and the groaning. One to go. How could he kill the man quickly and then find some friends in town who could help him? He heard the stalker coming after him. Then the sounds stopped. Smart. Watch and wait. He could play that game, too.

He tried to stop the bleeding from his shoulder, but he had no bandages. When he tried to tear his shirt to make strips, the fabric wouldn't give. He rubbed his face with his hand and realized too late that it was smeared with blood. Where in hell had he gone wrong? Everything had seemed to be going his way. Now there would be no ten million, which he had once had right in the palm of his hand. He should have faded away right then and called it quits. He got greedy. He was afraid that he might, but with such a valuable hostage, who wouldn't want a little bit more? They would have paid, he was sure, if he had held out the twenty-four hours.

He looked at the weapon. He wasn't sure how many rounds he had left. It held thirty. How many had he fired? He should have brought a second magazine with him. But that was a grab-and-run time. He heard the stalker move closer but had no clue where he was. Just a general direction. The cat-and-mouse game continued. He would not move a muscle until he saw the American plainly for a good shot. He had to make every round count now. He moved the selector lever to single shot, rested the weapon on his bent-up knees, and waited with his finger on the trigger.

It had been a good run. He had won time and time again. Why hadn't he taken the ten million and got lost in the wilderness somewhere? He could surface later in Rio de Janeiro, or the south of France, or even Las Vegas. Too damn late now. His arm pounded again with pain and he felt his vision flutter for just a moment.

No, no, he would not pass out. He wouldn't make it easy

for them. No, he would kill this one and get away. Find a doctor who would help him. He still had a few thousand dollars in his money belt. The fools had forgotten to check him for that after finding all the U.S. dollars in the car. Grenades and automatic weapons: that must have been U.S. military. One of the Special Forces groups that was so damn efficient.

Not efficient enough. He had escaped. Now all he had to do was kill this one last pursuer and he would be ready to find a doctor. Just one to go.

His eyes widened, his nerves twanged and surged as he sensed someone near. In the thick brush to the left? He squinted to see better, but he could detect no motion of the brush, could hear nothing. He was aware that his heart had surged—beating, wildly. Probably pumping more blood out of his shoulder. He could feel the warm red stuff running down his arm.

There. To the right?

No, nothing there.

He felt a wave of dizziness, then it passed. He wasn't that badly shot. He'd been hit lots worse than this in the war. What the hell was happening?

Then he couldn't help but move. A groan seeped out of his tight lips and he shifted his knees down and let go of the weapon to shift his useless arm more in front of him. His fingers flexed involuntarily, as if saying that they couldn't help him.

The sudden blast of a shot came at the same time a round hit the submachine gun resting on his legs and blasted it three feet away from him. He rolled and dove to the left, away from the sound. Another round clipped him in the leg but inflicted no big damage. He found a log, dropped behind it, and panted. His left arm throbbed and dragged in the dirt as he dove.

He had lost the weapon. He had no revolver or pistol. Not even a knife.

Enough. He was a soldier. He wouldn't die groveling in the dirt of some backward African country. He would face his tormentor. Yes, that was the way to go out. Not like some sniveling coward. Like a man. Like a soldier. He pushed up with his right arm to his knees, then stood slowly.

"Come and get me, you dirty American," he bellowed. He saw brush move ahead and slightly to the left.

Badri ran straight at where he knew the American must be. It was time. He had run out the clock. The game was over. His charge was slow and ponderous, but went forward. He had lost a lot of blood, and his body showed it. He stumbled once, and then caught himself. His left arm dangled at his side.

From six feet away, the MP-5 stuttered out twelve rounds. Six of them drove deeply into Ahmed Badri's chest, stopping his forward motion. He hung there for a moment as if trying to decide what to do. Then he sank to his knees and fell forward on his face, never to move again.

Derek Prescott lowered the MP-5 and felt sweat run down his forehead. He stood from where he had been behind a foot-thick tree and went forward cautiously. He turned the body over with his boot and stared at the Arab face. It had to be Badri. He noted the area, and walked back to the edge of the park. There he called on the Motorola and asked Gardner to come and confirm the kill. After making the call he sat down on the curb and vomited.

Stroh drove the First Lady back to their hotel. He knew there were no official U.S. diplomats in Durban. He put the First Lady in a suite where she could have a shower or a bath and order some new clothes. Then he set up the SATCOM.

"Yeah, that's right. We have Mrs. Hardesty safe and well and delighted to be free. Right now she's probably taking a bath in her suite. The ambassador is in town, but I don't know where. I'm sure he'll find us. Badri is dead. Confirmed by two SEALs. The local police will take over and we're out of it. We took down an al Qaeda cell in the process. Badri was holed up there but we got a tip."

"Outstanding," the CIA voice that Stroh didn't recognize said. "I'll tell the president at once, and the director. They said to call them at any time. Do you have any casualties?"

"Two wounded. We'll get some local hospital help on that. Nobody dead. The men will take a breather for the rest of the night and tomorrow. Then I'll arrange transportation. We still have the biz jet here on standby."

"Right, let me get off here and make some calls. If we have any further instructions, we'll call. Oh, what about the ten million?"

"We have most of it. Might be ten or twenty thousand missing that Badri spent or lost. The rest of it is in-hand."

"Bring it back with you on the plane. Good work. I'm out of here."

Stroh hung up the mike but left the set on RECEIVE. He gathered up Murdock and Doyle and headed to a hospital he had seen on their travels. It had an emergency room. He phoned the chief of police to send a detective there to explain that they were special deputies of the force and the bullet wounds were okay to treat.

An hour later Murdock came out with a slight limp and a bandage on his right thigh covering the entry and exit wounds. Doyle was in worse shape. They operated to take out bullet fragments. Two rounds had hit him and one had broken a shoulder bone. It would be set in the morning after they were sure they had taken out all of the chunks of lead.

Doyle was angry when they told him. "What the hell you mean a cast? Just bandage it up so I can get back to work."

"You're on the shelf for at least two months, Doyle," Murdock told him. "More likely three. You'll be going back to the States and into Balboa Naval Hospital in San Diego as soon as we can get you there."

"So, you're washing me out of the team?"

"Absolutely not. We'll get in a temporary to replace you, but the slot is yours just as soon as you can convince the medics that you're fit for SEAL duty."

Doyle's frown faded. "Like a three-month liberty?"

"Something like that. Pretty nurses over there."

Doyle grinned. "Yeah. Okay. I guess I can take that for a while. Just remember to hold my slot."

"I just got you broken in, Doyle," DeWitt said. "You do good work, so you're a keeper. Now take it easy. We'll see you soon in one of those breezy hospital gowns."

By the time they got back to the hotel, the place was buzzing. The press had found out about the First Lady being recovered and three TV transmitter trucks and about thirty reporters immediately crowded around Stroh, who seemed to be enjoying it.

"Nothing much tonight. Yes, the wife of the president of the United States, Mrs. Eleanor Hardesty, was rescued tonight from an al Qaeda cell here in Durban. Yes, there was a gun battle and several of the terrorists were killed. Your police spokesman can fill you in on that.

"The First Lady will hold a short press conference tomorrow morning. Right now she's enjoying her privacy, and a long, hot bath. We'll see you in the morning, about ten A.M."

He ignored shouted questions and hurried into the hotel. Uniformed police guards at the door held up Murdock and DeWitt for a moment until Stroh vouched for them.

In their room, Stroh was ecstatic.

"Yes, we did it, and the First Lady has no more worries."

"And she still has both hands," Murdock said.

"What about her little finger?" Gardner asked.

"Nothing we can do about that. It's been off too long to

reattach. The police doctor is going to come in about a half hour to treat her finger and make sure there's no infection. She'll be showing off a nice new bandage to the TV cameras in the morning. After her bath, she wants to talk to her husband. I'm trying to arrange it."

The SATCOM came on.

"Stroh, are you still receiving? This is the director."

"Right, ready when you are."

"Good. Hate to step on your moment of glory here, but the CNO and our boss and the president have a new mission for First Platoon. You are to get them organized and use the biz jet to fly them up to Qatar, our military enclave on the Persian Gulf. Don't worry about equipment. They can get anything they need for the mission there. As for the First Lady, Air Force Two has been repaired and refitted and has remained at the airport in North Namibia. It will fly into Durban in a day or two, as soon as all arrangements can be made. A skeleton staff has remained with the plane, including four of the First Lady's people, so she will be well taken care of.

"With that in mind, it might be good for you, Stroh, to go with the SEALs. Oh, and send the ten million back with the First Lady."

"I can arrange that, Mr. Director. Can we leave sometime tomorrow afternoon?"

"That would be good. They said they want you up there as soon as possible."

"We'll do it. The First Lady said she wanted to talk to the president. Is he available?"

"I'm sure he is. Let me call you back."

Stroh hung up the mike and looked at Murdock.

"Get your traveling clothes on, big guy; we're heading to a serious international hot spot. The war up there is about over, but the president has another little job he wants us to take care of."

"Glad for that 'us' Stroh. I've got a parachute and an

MP-5 with your name written all over them. Oh, you'll see that Doyle gets to fly back to the States in the First Lady's big plane?"

"I'm sure that will work out."

"Good. Let me go tell the guys to get some sleep. Looks like we're going to need it quicker than we expected."

27

Al-Udeid Air Base, Qatar
Recent consolidations of U.S. military power in the gulf region had turned this air base some twenty miles from the capital city of Doha into the most formidable collection of military power anywhere outside the U.S. Murdock knew this, but coming in on the business jet into the giant base with its 15,000-foot-long hard runway made him feel extremely small.

The plane landed and taxied to a special hangar.

"Look at the size of this place," DeWitt said. "Bet they didn't have to tear down a single house to make it. We're in the middle of a humongous desert out here."

"Didn't have to go far to get sand for the concrete," Jaybird said.

A Jeep with a red flag on it met them and led them to another hangar.

"That red flag Jeep is usually for generals and admirals," Don Stroh said. "You guys are getting the fast red carpet treatment."

They had changed into their cammies in Durban. Their combat vests and weapons were carefully stowed under seats and in the small cargo area. The ship stopped and the crew chief let down the stairs. Stroh was the first out the door. He held the others up as he talked to a bird colonel who met them. A moment later a small bus rolled up and Stroh motioned for the men to come down the steps.

"First class bus transport to your quarters," he said. "You'll have fifteen minutes to get yourselves put together. Same clothes, no weapons. Then the bus will take us to a meeting. Hope to hell you guys got some sleep on the plane. There won't be any from now on for at least forty-eight. Let's move."

Murdock stopped beside Stroh. "You're sounding like a first sergeant or a major with his battalion."

Stroh grinned. "Hell, I've been listening to you for enough years that some of it has rubbed off. I don't know what's coming up, but a three-star general usually doesn't send a bird colonel as a messenger boy."

Murdock knew that the sprawling base bad been used as the main combat control center for the buildup and then the attack on Iraq and Saddam Hussein's dictatorial government several years ago. The short, successful war had convinced the U.S. military that they should concentrate their power in this small country on the Persian Gulf. They quickly pulled men, equipment, and facilities out of Kuwait, Bahrain, Oman, and Saudi Arabia and brought most of it here.

The bus traveled two or three miles, Murdock figured, before it stopped in front of new-looking two-story building. There were no unit signs on it, just one that said "Transient Barracks."

As they got off the bus, the colonel waved at them. "Enlisted in this door, officers down to the second door."

Murdock walked up to the bird colonel and saluted. "Sir, if it's all right with the colonel, the officers would prefer to bunk, eat, and train with our men. It's a SEAL tradition, and has worked out very well, especially in our combat operations."

"Permission granted. I understand you ate on the plane two hours ago. Our meeting is at fourteen hundred, that's twenty minutes from now. The bus will take you there. It's your personal transport while on base. Welcome to Qatar."

"Thank you, sir. Any hint about our mission?"

"Not a clue. Not more than three or four men on the base know about it. You might say you're top secret."

Murdock nodded and followed the last SEAL into the barracks. It had been set up with rooms to hold twenty men, ten along each side. Regular army cots, mattresses, and pillows.

"We're in heaven," Luke Howard said.

At the end of the row of bunks were showers and the head.

The bird colonel stepped into the room. Jaybird saw him first and shouted, "Ten hut!" The SEALs dropped what they were doing and jolted to their feet in a strained attention.

"At ease, as you were. Just want to talk to your commander for a minute."

Murdock walked up. "Sir, Lieutenant Commander Blake Murdock, First Platoon, SEAL Team Seven. At your service."

The colonel held out his hand. "Colonel Ben Allbright. Staff with Lieutenant General Walloused. He's the head man at this base. You'll be meeting him in twenty. Oh, he wants to see all of your men at the meet. He's never worked with SEALs directly. We understand that some of your EM take part in your planning and in setting up field tactics and operations."

"Yes, sir. More than once one of my men has pulled our platoon out of a disaster. Some of these guys are so smart and bright that it makes me keep hustling to keep up with them."

"Good. We'll see you outside in eighteen."

Murdock turned to his men. "Okay, wash up, comb your hair if you have some. Don't worry about clean uniforms, we don't have any. All sixteen of us will be going to meet with the base commander and his staff. Use your brains, and talk only if you have something brilliant to say. Let's play it by ear, gentlemen."

• • •

Twenty-seven minutes later, the bus stopped in front of the post headquarters. It held a ring of concrete barriers around it. Inside the ring sat two quad fifty machine guns mounted on halftracks. Beyond that sidewalks led to three main doors. At each one stood two marines holding MP-5s with double banana magazines. Each man was at least six-feet-five inches tall. The colonel led them into the center door. The marines snapped to attention with a weapons salute, holding the MP-5 pointing straight up and right in front of their chests. The SEALs slithered inside, all eyes as they saw a part of the military that usually was off limits to them.

The new building was massive, four stories tall, with corridors leading off all directions. Colonel Allbright led the way. They passed two more guard stations, then went through a room filled with ten desks and every one of them manned and busy. At the far side, two massive doors stood ten feet tall. Two more marines, these in dress blues, stood guard. They checked the colonel's badge, saluted him, and eyed the SEALs with curiosity.

"Sir, the meeting has been moved to E-three," one of the marines said.

"I know the way, sergeant. Thanks." The colonel gave a forward signal with his arm and the SEALs followed him down another corridor to a bank of elevators. They took up all three elevators and got off on the third floor.

The conference room was windowless, held twenty chairs and a polished oval table at the head with three padded swivel chairs behind it.

"Take the seat closest to the table," Colonel Allbright said.

Just as the last SEAL sat down, the doors behind them opened. The colonel shouted the attention command and the SEALs jolted to their feet.

Lieutenant General Wallace Walloused marched to the front of the room, his three polished silver stars gleaming on his shoulders. Three other men followed him. Two of them were also generals and the third a bird colonel. The colonel was the only one in the room wearing a side arm. He stood to the left of the big table at a stiff parade rest. The generals sat down and the three-star in the middle spoke.

"First Platoon, SEAL Team Seven, congratulations on your recent successful mission rescuing the First Lady. Our commander-in-chief is absolutely delighted with your work. He recommends you highly. What we have for you now is a little different, although we understand you have penetrated enemy homelands before on missions." He pushed a button on a control panel in front of him and a large scale map lowered from the wall behind.

"You're going into Iran. You know about the recent, and brief, war between Iran and Iraq. It's over now, and both nations are trying to rebuild and reestablish control. Their economies have been shattered. A new clique of military officers control Iran with what's left of the army. Riots and looting have taken place where we never thought they could. The nation will soon be under strict embargoes by the United Nations for starting the war, and more importantly for using anthrax as a combat weapon." The general looked to his left and nodded.

"Gentlemen, I'm Ralph Hallander. No, I'm not Dutch. I'll be your contact on the biological side. Your target is anthrax. We can't do much to clean up Iraq where the anthrax was used. The UN, with help from some American university research people, are doing that. They have developed a system of spraying a gamma-phage on contaminated areas to kill the anthrax virus outright.

"Your job is much more complicated. You will go into Iran, discover where the anthrax has been manufactured, and then you will attack and destroy the facility and any stockpiles of anthrax that may be stored there. It's a big order, but we have certain information to help you. Most of the ground work must be done by you men in Iran. Are there any questions?"

Jaybird lifted his hand. The general pointed at him.

"Sir, what kind of information? How detailed? Will we have to search all over the country?"

"We hope not," the general said. "Our agents in Iran have narrowed down the possibilities to three areas. All are remote, where mistakes or accidents would not endanger large numbers of Iranians."

General Walloused turned to the third man at the table and nodded.

"Good afternoon, gentlemen. I'm Norman Eckerson, and I'll be your base liaison for anything you need to accomplish your mission. General Walloused received a phone call yesterday from the Secretary of Defense. That doesn't happen often. The secretary told him that you men have the highest possible priority for anything on base or in our arsenal to get your job done. This includes helicopters, ships, aircraft, weapons, munitions, uniforms, the works. If it's on-base, you'll have it within an hour. If I have to get it from off-base, it might take a day. We have prepared packets for each man. Included are tips and hints about Iranian life, dress, some easy to remember phrases, maps, guides on customs and lifestyles. The more you know about Iran, the safer you'll be if you come to a point where you need to deal with some of the native population. Any questions?"

"Will you give us a language coach to help us learn Arabic?" DeWitt asked.

"One is on standby and will be available anytime you men are on-base. He is yours twenty-four hours a day. Just don't overwork him."

Rafii held up his hand and was acknowledged. "Sirs, I was born and raised in Saudi Arabia. I have been on missions like this inside Iraq and Iran before. It seems that it works best if we can do our search and find information about the location with a small party of four or five. Can we split up our platoon and search out these three possibilities?"

"Sounds like a good suggestion," General Eckerson said. "At this point we are entirely unstructured. We have some people for you to meet with at nineteen hundred. These are planners and some who know Iran. Whatever you two groups come up with as a mission plan will be evaluated and most likely approved."

A sergeant came into the room and passed out foot-square envelopes to each man.

Murdock stood and General Walloused nodded at him.

"Generals, I might be a little out of line here, but four or five times this platoon has been left high and dry deep behind enemy lines without the promised extraction transport. We made it out each time, but the casualties we took were excessive. I hope this time if we are deep into Iran that every effort will be made to complete our withdrawal, if such a procedure is called for in our mission plan."

"Commander Murdock," General Eckerson said. "I know of at least one of those missions. The one I remember was a diplomatic problem about air clearance that grounded your choppers. There will be nothing of that sort of problem here. We'll be going in covert and operating covert and coming out just as quickly and silently as we can. Nobody will be left behind."

"Thank you, sir." Murdock sat down.

"That completes the meeting," General Eckerson said. "Colonel Allbright will take charge." The generals stood. The SEALs surged to their feet as the three officers walked out of the room.

"At ease," Allbright said. "Now you've met our leaders. The bus is waiting. Your mess call is at seventeen hundred about a block from your barracks. The bus will go by it on the way back. Then it will stay at the barracks to take you to the meeting at nineteen hundred. Oh, and don't worry, we eat extremely well on this base. Let's get onboard."

●　　●　　●

The meeting at nineteen hundred was also in the headquarters building. It was on the second floor in a situation room. The walls were blank but had spots for dozens of large-scale maps. There were three sand tables that had been covered with layouts of three sections of Iraq during Operation Freedom back in 2003. They showed the progress of troops, location of hot spots, and the eventual destruction of all Iraq troops and armor.

Murdock had brought his top planners, Sadler, J.G. Gardner, Jaybird, Rafii, Lampedusa, and DeWitt. They sat at a large oval table. On the far side were seven locals. Two were captains, one a major, and four enlisted men, mostly E-7s and E-8 sergeants. To Murdock's surprise, a master sergeant led the meeting.

"Gentlemen, good evening. We could give names around the table but most of us would forget them in a few minutes. Let's concentrate our time on working out this mission. First, I want you to know that four of us here have been in Iran recently on covert missions. Whatever help that might be, we will be glad to give. Our major problem is finding the exact location of the manufacturing facility, and any off-site storage there might be."

One of the captains spoke up directing his question at Murdock. "I understand it was suggested that groups of four or five might go in and check out the three potential locations and report back by radio. Is this a practical idea, Commander?"

Murdock stirred. "Yes, it has worked before. One of our men is an Arab and speaks perfect idiomatic Farsi. We all have had some language training but need more. I'd think the three probes would be a place to start. But we need to have continuing plans in place for each one for when we hit the hot location."

The major spoke. "I know it's not military style, but let's see a show of hands for those who think the three-probe idea should be used." All the hands went up.

"Now, where are these locations?" Senior Chief Sadler asked.

One of the sergeants moved in back of the table and pulled down a large-scale wall map of Iran. It was five feet tall and eight feet wide. He used a pointer and indicated spots on the well-lighted map.

"One is here somewhere, around the port city of Bandar-e Bushehr, which is just across the gulf and north from us, no more than two hundred and fifty miles away. We think the potential location there could be in the mountains behind the port. The second suggested area of concern is the high desert near Nay Band." His pointer touched the map halfway up and well on the western side of Iran.

He let the men make notes, then moved on. "The third suspected area is near the Turkish border at the very northern part of Iran, near the small town of Khvoy. This one will be the most difficult for access and to exfiltrate."

The meeting rolled on. An hour later, Murdock saw it coming together. They would have transport in and out, tricky sometimes but possible. They would have all of the explosives and weapons they could carry. They could go in by air-drop or overland. It was quickly decided that the mid-Iranian location would have to be an air-drop. The Turkey border spot could be accessed through Turkey by land and the close one across the gulf would be water launched.

They were well into the second hour of planning when Murdock raised a question that had been bothering him.

"Gentlemen, say we find our manufacturing plant, take it down, and now we have a ton of anthrax. How do you kill the anthrax virus?"

The captains and the major looked at each other and shook their heads. One of the sergeants opened a file folder. "We've been doing some computer searches on that.

Researchers are working on that problem, have been for ten years. Best so far is the gamma-phage—a virus that attacks and kills the anthrax virus. This is in active use now and works on a small scale and will be used in Iraq in those death zones as soon as facilities can be set up.

"With a ton of anthrax you'd need a ton of gamma-phage, which isn't practical. Other researchers have been working on different methods to dispose of anthrax. It is a living organism and as such is susceptible to certain environmental dangers. They tried drowning them. Didn't work. The best method so far is heat. Tests have shown that heat of eighteen hundred to two thousand degrees Fahrenheit will destroy the virus. Such heat will burn up anything the virus was on as well, so for most applications, the heat method is not practical. Here it might be."

"How do we get anything that hot?" Lampedusa asked.

"The inside of a pottery kiln would work great," one of the captains said.

"How about a brick kiln?" Jaybird asked. "That would be big enough to load the goods into."

"A good gasoline-fed fire can generate heat up to four thousand degrees," Murdock said. "If heat will do the job, it might be our solution. We would appreciate it if the sergeant could continue his research on this problem and keep us up to date while we're here and in the field. We'll want to use the SATCOM, you have them available here?"

"We do," the sergeant said.

"Timing," Murdock said. "We need to work out who goes where, how we get there, and contingencies. We've done enough for tonight. My men have been on their feet for the past twenty-four. We'll be sharper tomorrow. Can we meet here at oh-eight-hundred?"

The master sergeant looked at his team. They nodded.

"Oh-eight-hundred it is. We'll have some transport folks here, and some other specialists. Let's call it a night."

They stood together and walked out.

"Gonna be a hot time in old Iran soon enough," Jaybird said.

"Yeah, but only if we can find the fucking anthrax," Bill Bradford said.

28

Back at their barracks, Murdock, Gardner, Jaybird, and DeWitt worked out the teams to go to each location. They balanced them for Arabic language, for weapons, skills, and experience. They kept squad members together as much as possible. The roster looked like this when they finished:

Team One: Murdock, Jaybird, Lampedusa, Bradford, and Ching.

Team Two: Gardner, Canzoneri, Rafii, Fernandez, and Prescott.

Team Three: DeWitt, Howard, Van Dyke, Mahanani, Neal, and Tate.

Murdock read over the list out loud and everyone nodded. "Okay, let's get some sack time. Chow is at oh-seven hundred, so look sharp. I've ordered new cammies for us, three pair each, so they should be here tomorrow. Showers are suggested. See you guys in the morning."

Murdock sighed as he sat down on his bunk. It had a mattress and a metal frame and was just that—a military cot. They would always be the same and feel the same. Even so, he knew after a quick shower he would be sleeping in about fifteen seconds.

At the meeting the next morning there were fifteen present. They split into teams. Murdock assigned them to their areas. He would take the interior location with the air-drop.

Gardner would have the Turkey campaign and DeWitt would investigate the south coast of Iran across from Qatar.

The planning went fast after that—transport, recovery, weapons, uniforms or civilian clothes. They opted for Iranian middle- to lower-class clothing. There was a spot on the base that could outfit them. Weapons would be restricted to side arms and to one MP-5 per team. Concealment would be the ultimate factor on weapons.

When the three teams had worked out transport with the specialists in that area, Murdock called them all together.

"Okay, say my team finds the location in mid-Iran. Do I rely on local explosives and gasoline to get the anthrax vaporized, or do we have a special flight that comes in with fuel and explosives?"

The sergeant major spoke up. "Depends, Commander. Where I was in Iran I didn't see a gas station for hundreds of miles. There was nothing out there. That probably will be the case around your back country area. Where could you get a three thousand gallon tanker filled with gasoline?"

"If we tried to air-lift in a tanker, it would be slow going with a chopper," one of the captains said. "And the Iranians do have a few jet fighters left with missiles."

"So we'll have to use what we have on the ground," Murdock said. "That might mean a side trip into some town and find a tanker and divert it to the location."

"Would a house fire, a building fire, generate enough heat to do the job?" DeWitt asked.

"Checked that last night on the computer," another sergeant said. "Wood fires can burn hot—up to two thousand degrees—but we don't know if the buildings there are stone or wood or brick. Any new construction for a factory probably would be metal, which wouldn't help us at all."

"So what it comes down to," Murdock said, "is that we have to play it by ear, using local fuel to do the job any way we can. The hot fire is the key. Oh, one more thing. We have one SATCOM with us. We'll need two more so each team can have one. We establish one frequency to use so we all can stay in touch."

"I can get two more SATCOMs," Colonel Allbright said.

"What about some anti-biological safe suits?" Gardner asked.

"We have them, but how can you infiltrate with one on?" the other captain said.

"We carry them in a suitcase," Lam said. "Would one fit in an average-sized suitcase?"

"We could make them fit. You wouldn't need all the equipment, just the biological."

"We need at least two of those suits for each team," De-Witt said.

"We're getting there," the master sergeant said. "Now what about timing? Night drop would be best for the interior team, that's Murdock. Night coastal landing also for the DeWitt team across the gulf. The walk across the border from Turkey would depend."

"Let's get moving tonight," Murdock said. "Say a nineteen hundred takeoff in a fixed wing for a night drop over central Iran for my team. We can do a HALO jump if that would help."

"We can do that," the major said.

"Let's get the teams outfitted with new clothes and money for emergencies," Murdock said. "The rial, if I remember right. About eight thousand for a U.S. dollar, so we'll have large denomination bills. We'll need six hundred dollar's worth per man. We'll turn in what we don't use. Any questions?"

"What if you get captured?" the major asked. "Won't the U.S. be identified as an aggressor?"

"No sir, Major. We don't carry any I.D. No dog tags, wallets, pictures, anything that could tie us to the U.S."

"No I.D.? How do you function in the military?"

"Oh, we have I.D. You just can't see it." Murdock said. "Your security people may know about it. Three months ago we were all implanted with microchips with our complete military and personal history, our medical updates, any injuries or allergies, rank, enlistments, almost everything in our two-oh-one files. Your security people may have a microchip reader that can detect and read the chip. Best I.D. in the world."

"Heard they were coming. Didn't know they were here. Where do they put the chip?"

"In a fleshy area in the back of your neck, just above some bones. The chip is small, about a quarter of an inch square, but loaded with information."

Murdock looked around. "Now, if there's nothing more to do here, we have equipment to get, ammo to pick up, clothes to put on, and a thousand other tasks before we go. Work with Gardner and DeWitt to set up their departures. I think we're done here."

Colonel Allbright was all over the place. He brought the SATCOMs to the barracks and arranged for the six biological suits to be delivered. All the men went to the clothing building where they were outfitted with working-class Iranian clothing. The men were issued Glock pistols and two hundred rounds of ammo. Murdock checked over his team and nodded. They had all they needed. The Iranian clothing felt strange, but they wore it now to get used to it. They stood out in the chow line.

At nineteen oh-four Murdock and his team stepped into the huge C-141 Starlifter. It was the same plane used for dropping paratroopers and could haul 155 jumpers or 200 regular soldiers. It was a four-engine jet transport that could do 556 mph on maximum cruise speed and fly up to 41,000 feet.

Murdock talked to the crew chief, an Air Force first sergeant.

"Not quite six hundred miles over there, the way we'll

go. We'll be at forty-one thousand, so no problem with missiles. How high do you want to jump from?"

"Can you come down to twenty thousand? We don't have our cold weather masks or oxygen tanks along."

"Twenty will be no problem. We'll let down once we're over the mountains and into the boonies. Got some bucket seats along the side there. We'll use the side door for you to jump from. You've done this before?"

"More than I want to remember. How long to the jump zone?"

"A little over an hour, counting our takeoff and let-down to twenty. I'll give you a heads-up at ten minutes to drop."

The sergeant looked at their civilian clothes. "Going in undercover, huh? Good luck. Not too much action out in this part of Iran, but you never can tell about these crazy Arabs." He gave Murdock a thumbs up and went back to the cabin up front.

Then the motors started and shortly the big plane taxied slowly out to the runway.

"This is a big mutha," Jaybird said. "A hundred and sixty feet wingspan and the turkey is a hundred and sixty-nine feet long. Nice kind of plane for our private use. Wonder how much she gets per gallon of JP-4?"

The motors revved then and the big craft raced down the runway and lifted into the Qatar night sky heading west over the gulf and then into Iranian air space. Murdock hoped this wasn't the time that Iranian fighters were out looking for payback for the shellacking they took during the invasion. Some estimates were that Iran used up all but ten of its jet fighters in the war. He hoped they were right.

The flight gave Murdock some time to think through his current situation. So far his promotion to the CNO's staff hadn't cramped his SEAL operations. But it wouldn't always be so. After this the CNO might not clear him to participate. Have to play it by ear. Ardith would be just as pleased if he stayed in Washington full time. After this mission, he'd reconsider. Maybe he'd been lucky not to get shot up any more than he had been. That afternoon he let the medics look at his leg. They changed the bandages and told him to stay off the leg for a week. He said sure, good idea, and got out of there quickly. The leg still hurt, but he could block it out. Any action and he wouldn't even know the bullet had ripped through there.

Don Stroh had sat in on the last meeting, and then vanished. He came back with the name of a contact in the little town Murdock was aiming for. The man's name was Salama Masud. He was a wool buyer who then shipped it to factories to the north. He was an important man in the area, and the CIA had not used him much, but he was ready.

Murdock felt good, not nervous or jittery. He had done this before. HALO, High Altitude jump, Low Opening. They would come out of the plane at twenty thousand feet and freefall for fifteen thousand feet and open their chutes at about five thousand, or lower in densely populated areas. They would keep tabs with each other with the Motorolas.

"Sir, sir." Murdock heard someone and felt a hand on his shoulder. "Sir, heads up, we'll be over the DZ in ten."

Murdock woke up and nodded. "Right, sergeant. Thanks. I guess I dozed off there."

The Air Force man chuckled. "Never saw anyone do that before, sir. You're not uptight at all about this jump. That's a good sign. I'll be back to open the door when we hit the DZ."

Murdock looked at his men. Two of the four were sleeping. He woke them up.

"Let's go, ladies. Time to check gear and chutes. Everybody on your feet. Jaybird, check me."

They were ready to go when the sergeant came back. All had on helmets, face protectors, and gloves against the cold at twenty thousand. The fall wouldn't take long. They lined up at the door with Murdock last. No ripcord to snap on the rail. They would pull the cord later.

"Ready in two," the sergeant said. Then he opened the side door and the gush of air rushing out of the plane jolted them a step forward.

"Easy, easy," the crew chief said. The green light snapped on over the door and Jaybird dove out the opening. Lam went right behind him, then Bradford and Ching. Murdock was close behind them. The quicker they got out of the plane, the closer they would land together.

Murdock felt that gut-gripping emptiness as he dove into the void. Nothing but black sky, whistling wind, and enough frigid air to freeze the balls off a brass monkey. He opened his eyes. He wasn't sure why he closed them when he dove out, but he always did. He checked around, but it was too dark to see any of the others. He spread out his arms in a swan dive and kept that attitude as he picked up speed. He checked the radio.

"Hey, team, everyone on board?"

They all checked in. "Good, my handy-dandy little wrist altimeter shows us at eighteen thousand and falling. I'll give the word to yank the rip cord at five. Everyone have that little rope in his hand?"

"Oh, yeah," Jaybird said. The other chorused in.

Below, Murdock could see only blackness. No streaming lights on a freeway. No brilliant lights in a city. Not even the lonely light of a thatched roof hut in the mountains. They should come down in the edge of some hills near a plains or a desert, he wasn't sure which. But not a lot of people.

The first faint glow of lights showed to the north. He checked his altimeter. Six thousand.

"Okay, let's pull the magic string and become butterflies," Murdock said. He pulled his ripcord and braced himself as best he could for the balls-busting jerk of the parachute crotch straps. When it came he wasn't ready. He was still diving and it jerked him backwards and upright at the same time. He looked up as the glorious brown silk blossomed above him. It was the most beautiful sight in the world every time it happened. It meant he wouldn't slam into the ground at a hundred and twenty miles an hour.

"Everyone afloat?" Murdock asked.

He heard a jumble of voices; he couldn't see any of the chutes in the dark. They had planned it that way. Brown silk is tough to see at night.

"Light sticks," Murdock said. They each had a different colored stick that would produce a soft glow.

"I've got a red to my right," Murdock said.

"Red. That's me, Lam. Anyone else see me?"

"No, but I've got a green," Bradford said.

"That's me," Murdock said. "Move my way, I'm closing in on Lam. Jaybird, where the hell are you?" Murdock waited a minute. "Jaybird, this is no joke, where the hell are you? Are you all right? Talk to me, damn it!"

29

"Jaybird, come in," Murdock pleaded on the Motorola. "If you're in trouble, blow into the mike."

They waited. Nothing.

Murdock looked down. He couldn't tell how far they were from the ground. He had moved to the side with the directional pulls on the chute until he could make out the SEAL next to him.

"How far to the ground?" he asked on the mike.

"Maybe a thousand," Lam said. "Where the hell is Jaybird? He bailed out first. He should be first one on the ground to our right. I'm swinging my chute that way to try to see him."

"Everyone keep a look-out," Murdock said. "We've got to find him."

Then the land came up fast. Murdock saw some lights a quarter of a mile away, then he saw the ground and as soon as his feet touched it he ran forward with the chute, collapsing it and keeping his feet. He shucked out of the shrouds and ran with the wind. He met Lam and they found Bradford and Ching. Nobody had seen or heard from Jaybird.

"Spread out, twenty apart, we'll sweep downwind for a quarter and then expand to both sides. Leave the chutes here, bring everything else. We don't have time to bury the silk. Let's go." Murdock had never lost a man on a jump. He didn't intend to break his record.

They walked slowly, looking all around them. They were near the end of their quarter mile when Ching sounded off at the end of the line.

"Got him. He's down, his chute opened. Oh, hell, some of the lines are tangled round his neck. Over this way, fast."

The men charged to where Ching worked on Jaybird. He had the shroud lines untangled from Jaybird's throat and had him stretched out. Jaybird had cut and scratches on his face.

"He's breathing," Ching said. "My guess is the straps cut off his wind for long enough to make him pass out. Then he hit the ground and the line loosened and he was breathing again."

Murdock knelt beside the silent form and gently slapped both his cheeks. "Come on, Jaybird. Wake up. Chow time, let's get out of here. Wake up, little buddy. We've got work to do."

The form didn't move. Murdock took his canteen and slashed some water on Jaybird's face. He snorted, then coughed and opened his eyes. Murdock saw they were glassy.

"Jaybird, you with us, buddy? You took one hell of a ride. Jaybird, look at me."

Murdock saw the eyes blink then focus more and at last settle on Murdock's face.

"Oh, damn, am I dead?" Jaybird whispered.

"Alive and kicking," Ching said. "Anything feel broken?"

"Busted? On a little jump like that?" Jaybird started to sit up, groaned, and lay back down. "Give me five, I'm a little woozy."

"You should be," Murdock said. "You had a bad case of shroud strangulitis."

"Yeah. I pass out?"

"On the way down after you pulled the ripcord. Try sitting up again."

This time he made it. Murdock gave him a drink out of his canteen.

"Let's see if you can stand up and walk," Murdock said. "We need you."

Jaybird got up by himself and stood. He looked around. "Where's my fucking MP-5?"

"If you didn't have it tied onto your pack, you dropped it when you passed out. Don't worry about it. We have two more. Can you walk?"

"Oh, yeah. My momma taught me that several years ago."

"Lam?" Murdock asked.

"Been trying to orient us. My best is that those splash of lights up there north shows from our little town. Maybe five miles. We ready to choggie?"

Murdock looked at Jaybird. "Want to take a hike?"

"What I dreamed of doing when I was passed out. Let's go."

Murdock walked beside Jaybird for the first mile, then moved apart the usual ten yards, coming behind him. Lam was out two hundred and they made good time toward the village. Best estimates were two thousand people. They had directions to the home of Salama Masud, the deep cover CIA agent. Murdock hoped he was home.

They came to the outskirts of the small town a half-hour later. Jaybird was functioning, but Murdock didn't know how well. They had hunkered down behind a low rock wall just beyond a house and waited for Lam to make his recon. He came back in ten.

"Found the street. The house must be the one at the far end. Not all of them are numbered. You said one-eleven."

"Right, it's one story, block with stucco on the outside. Supposed to be one scraggly tree in the front yard, if it hasn't died."

"Yeah, saw it. Nobody on the streets, but we'll go round and come toward the place from the back."

Ten minutes later they lay in the dirt watching the back

of the house. It had no lights. Murdock and Lam went up to the rear door and tried the knob. It wasn't locked. The door led into a closed-in porch. The door inside was locked. Murdock knocked six times on the door, rattling the hinges. There was no response. He beat on the door again with the side of his fist, hitting it a dozen times. Now a light glowed from somewhere inside and shined under the door. Murdock and Lam stood back from the panel.

A voice asked a question in Farsi. Murdock wasn't sure what it meant. He used the two words he knew for friend in Arabic, then knocked once more, this time gently. He moved close to the door. "Your uncle needs some help," Murdock said. It was a secret phrase that every CIA person in the world was supposed to know.

"A moment." The words came in English through the thin door. It opened slowly. It was now dark inside the room.

"Yes, what do you want?"

"Your uncle needs some help. We come on a mission. Can you aid us?"

"Yes, yes, come in. I had to be sure. I'm not the least bit suspected here. Of course I haven't done much yet. How many?

"Five of us. Salama Masud?"

"Yes, yes. I am. Come in. I will do all I can for you."

"You've told your contact that there was a new facility built somewhere near here that could be a place where biological weapons have been developed."

"Yes." He turned on a light, making sure the blinds were drawn tight. It was a kitchen with a table and four chairs. They sat down. "The place is not far, maybe fifteen kilometers, ten miles. Strange things going on. Big trucks came in for a while. About twenty people work there and live there in large tents."

"You have a car? We need to go there tonight and check it out."

"Tonight? It is late."

"We work best in the dark. A car?"

"No, a small pickup truck, but it will hold all five of you. I have freedom of movement since I talk to the herders about their wool. I'm a wool buyer. We can drive within two miles of the secret place before the road turns away from it. There may be a roadblock. Since the new regime took over, it's hard telling what might happen. You heard about the riots and looting in several cities."

"Yes. Strange. Can we leave now?"

"Yes, but let me get my rifle. I am permitted to carry it. Wild dogs and thieves sometimes waylay lone vehicles."

A few minutes later the five SEALs and the driver settled into an older pickup of undetermined make and drove out of the small town to the west, into a range of low foothills that escalated into a ridge of mountains.

They still had two MP-5 submachine guns. Murdock put men with both of them in the back of the pickup so they could stand up and fire straight ahead or to each side. He put Jaybird in the cab with him and Masud. Murdock worried about Jaybird. He wasn't his old self yet. He was awake and functioning, but no bright remarks or wisecracks. He would watch the man closely.

They had driven out five miles, winding into some low hills on a good paved road, when the road faded into a gravel track that had been well graded and maintained.

"Rougher from here on," Masud said. "Road doesn't go much of anywhere out here. They tried to drill for oil once, but nothing came of it. The big trucks going into this new place pounded the road hard, but they kept repairing it."

At the seven-mile mark, Masud slowed. "Up ahead, a roadblock. At least I can see one army truck off to the side."

The closer they came in the darkness, the less it looked like the place was manned. Then they were there. The truck had two flat tires and there were no soldiers in sight.

"Gave up on it," Murdock said. "Maybe the new regime hasn't got word out to the troops in this area."

The road slanted upward into the mountains. The slopes were mostly barren, with a few blushes of trees and brush along ravines that would carry runoff from any sudden desert rain. Masud had to shift into second gear to get up the next sharp incline and then he pointed.

"Up there a quarter of a mile is the turnoff into the new facility. No idea what it might be for, but it's been kept top secret around here."

"We drive in or hide your truck and walk?" Murdock asked.

"I can't drive in there. If there are still people there they would take my truck and shoot all of us. We have to hike in if we want to stay alive."

Ten minutes later they had hidden the truck in a small wash well off the road and started the walk into the buildings. Murdock watched Jaybird.

"How do you feel, tiger?"

"LC, I'm fit and ready to go. Just a little headache. Okay, so it's a whanger of a headache. But I can play hurt. Let me get at 'em. I'm ready."

Murdock grinned. That sounded more like the old Jaybird.

After a mile's hike, they stopped and Murdock opened the SATCOM and set up the antenna. He had it on the right frequency and called.

"Murdock calling Home Team Leader."

"Home Team Leader here. What's the word?"

"Don't know yet. We're down, made contact with our man, and we're about a mile from the facility we need to check. No problems so far. We'll keep in touch."

"No reports yet from the other two groups. Home Team Leader out.

Lt. Ed DeWitt stood in the cabin of the Pegasus and watched the coast of Iran come out of the shifting moonlight. The sleek insertion boat for the SEALs had throttled down from its top speed of forty-five knots to five and coasted toward shore. The boat was eighty-two feet long and only seventeen and a half feet wide. It had a range of five hundred and fifty-five miles without refueling.

The shore line was still a mile away when the SEALs slipped into the water in their Iranian costumes, without their rebreathers and only disposable swim fins. DeWitt and his five men swam on the surface with an easy side-stroke to make as little splashing as possible. The coastline here was rocky, with a quarter of a mile of lowland leaping upward into a series of low hills. Aerial recon flown that afternoon had picked the spot for them to land. It was twenty miles south of Bandar-e Bushehr, a town of around three hundred thousand persons.

This short stretch of beach was unoccupied, with the coast road going south almost twenty miles inland. There were no towns or settlements shown on their maps along this coast for a hundred miles. With nearly seventy percent of Iran's army wiped out in the charge into Iraq, there was probably no army presence in this part of Iran at all. De-Witt thought about all of this as he stroked cleanly for shore. They stayed together and landed within a few yards of their objective, a stunted pine tree that had been gnarled and twisted by the gulf winds.

The SEALs washed up on shore with the small waves like sodden driftwood, then lay in the wet sand as they scanned the land in front of them.

"Looks all clear," Van Dyke said on the Motorola.

"Clear this end," Tate said.

"Straight across the beach to dry land and see if we can find some cover," DeWitt said.

They lifted up and ran forward, across the dry sand, past some coarse salt grass growth, and then into the baked brown, dry Iranian land mass.

"Down," DeWitt said on the radio, and they stopped and took a knee, everyone alert, watching for any sign of humans, any danger. DeWitt scanned the area as far as he could see in the darkness. He could spot no lights of any kind. The soil wasn't farmed. It looked like it was a dried-up salt marsh.

"Okay, troops. Looks clear as far as we can see. We might not spot a live one until we get near the big town. Until then we have a twenty-mile hike, so let's get moving. Drop the swim fins if you haven't. We won't be needing them again."

They hiked north in a column of ducks. One man with an MP-5 led out, the other MP-5 holder brought up the rear. DeWitt wished he had Rafii in his team. They had the name of a contact in the town, but not sure how to find the address. Rafii could have sniffed it out and come back and led them in. This time they'd have to play it by ear. It was such a big city, they could easily get lost.

DeWitt checked his watch. It was only 1920. They had hit the beach a half hour after full dark, giving them lots of time to get to Bandar-e. What they did when they got there would depend on what they found, and who they could ask direction from. They would have to split up into two groups and tail each other. He hoped that the military and the civil authorities were lax in their duties after the devastating defeat in Iraq.

They took a break at 2200.

"How far have we come, Howard?"

"Two aching feet and a knee that's twanging at me. That means we're closing in on ten miles."

"I figure ten and a half, but who's counting?" Mahanani said.

"I think our team stands the best chance to find the plant," Neal said. "This area has lots going for it. Close to the port, so they can get the needed materials in easy and the goods out. Protection in the hills, and far enough away from population centers."

"No protection at all this close to the coast," Tate said.

"That's why we won't find it here. Look how easy we got onshore and in business. Nope, it's got to be farther inland."

They marched again.

By midnight DeWitt figured they had covered another eight miles, so they should be close. He could see the faint glow of lights in the distance. That could be Bandar-e. They hiked around a small point of land where the gulf had not worn down the edge of a ridgeline. Just beyond it they saw headlights coming toward them. They scattered and hit the dirt.

"They couldn't have seen us," DeWitt said on the Motorola. "Just hold your positions and don't move. Could be a tourist or a fisherman or maybe a two-man army patrol. We hold steady until we see exactly what we have to deal with."

30

Agri, Turkey

Lieutenant (J.G.) Chris Gardner flew his team into Ankara, Turkey, the same afternoon the other SEALs left for their assignments. From there they were shuttled by U.S. cargo plane to Agri, a modestly sized town in far eastern Turkey where the U.S. has a small base. They arrived just as it was getting dark and the choppers there were ready.

"We've worked it out with the local Turkish border guards and the Turkish Air Force," Gardner told his four men. "There is little military activity in the region around Khvoy, Iran. The town is larger than we expected, more than two hundred thousand. Our contact lives just outside the main town to the south, so he shouldn't be hard to find."

They were in an Army Blackhawk, the same as the Seahawk SH-60 the Navy used. Gardner came back from the flight deck of the chopper. "Just talked to the pilots. The flight from Agri to the border is about seventy-five miles. We'll slant southeast and it will take us a little over twenty-two minutes to get there. This bird travels at three-point-four-five miles a minute, or two hundred and seven miles an hour. Jaybird isn't here, so I thought I should fill you in. From the border with Iran, we fly due east for twelve minutes and we're there. We expect no Iranian air power up here, or ground fire problems, but we have one door-mounted machine gun just in case. Any questions?"

"Yeah," Fernandez said. "Is this same bird going to fly

back over the border and wait for us to call him for a pickup?"

"That's what the pilot told me. He will get a relay message from our SATCOM for the pickup. We'll give him GPS coordinates when we want a ride."

"I still feel naked without my gear," Canzoneri said. "No combat vest loaded with goodies, no long gun, no grenades."

"We'll have to get by," Gardner said. "I've never seen any military operation coordinated as slick as this one has been so far. First the flight to Ankara, then a plane waiting to fly us here, and our chopper warmed up and ready to go. Amazing. When the president orders something done, the generals and admirals jump to."

"Be more amazing if we can find the fucking anthrax factory," Rafii said. "I'm hoping."

They took off then and slanted southeast toward Iran.

"Half-hour of flight time, then we get into action," Prescott said. "Hell, I think I'll have a little nap."

They had been over Iran less than five minutes when the pilot called Gardner to the cockpit.

"Lieutenant, I'm seeing all kind of action down there. Looks like the war is still on. Lots of tracers, and what has to be artillery or rockets going off. Looks like a wavering main line of resistance down there. I haven't seen any aircraft, but I've been checking some frequencies and there's a lot of radio chatter. It sounds like it's from aircraft."

"They said there wasn't any military action going on up here," Gardner said. "Report this to your HQ and see what they know about it."

The pilot made his transmission and got a response in his headset. He looked up at Gardner.

"Okay, they say they now have reports of heavy fighting in and around the town we're heading for. Evidently there were two battalions there loyal to the old regime. They are fighting anyone from the new Council of Colonels."

"How far to the town?"

"Another four minutes."

Gardner looked at the ground. They had been hugging the landscape and were less than two hundred feet in the air. He saw tracers lancing across the ground, then a series of explosions that had to be artillery rounds walking up a ridgeline ahead. Two well-armed outfits down there were closed in intense combat.

"Turn us around, Captain," Gardner said. "We can't do our job in this kind of a situation. Get us out of here and back to Turkey."

Bandar-e Bushehr, Iran

As the headlights came closer out of the gloomy night, Ed DeWitt scowled from where he and his team lay in the wet sand. It looked like a military Jeep. Then he was sure. A high-powered light snapped on and the big beam began sweeping the beach in front of the rig.

"Take out the light," DeWitt ordered. At once, both of their MP-5s spoke on single shot and the light crashed. The driver must have cranked the wheel as the rig spun around in the sand. By then the MP-5s sounded again on automatic and lanced out three- and five-round bursts. The two men in the Jeep jolted to the side, then the rig stalled and the men flopped over the wheel, shot before they knew what had happened.

"Make sure, Tate," DeWitt said.

Tate lifted out of the sand and ran forward. He stopped at the Jeep and touched the throat of the passenger. Dead. He moved to the second Iranian soldier just as the man lifted a pistol and swung it toward Tate. Tate fired his Glock three times, two rounds hit the Iranian soldier in the head and one in chest. He sighed and slumped back onto the steering wheel.

"Down and done," Tate said. "We want transportation?"

DeWitt grinned. "Oh, yes. Wouldn't hurt to get a lift for a few miles. We can dump it when it's a liability."

The SEALs ran to the Jeep, pulled the bodies out of it, and climbed into the back section. DeWitt drove. He turned the headlights off on the rig as soon as they started. He stayed on the hard sand, which gave better traction than the dry section. Two miles ahead, DeWitt stopped. Ahead he saw what could only be an army camp. There were six or eight large tents, a parade ground layout with dozens of ghostly pup tents set up in straight rows.

"No lights," Van Dyke said. "That's strange."

"I don't see or hear any people," Sadler said. "Looks like the place has been closed down or abandoned."

DeWitt drove forward slowly. He came to the front gate. Just two poles in the ground with a tattered banner between them that was so faded he couldn't read it.

Still no people.

He went down what appeared to be the main street through the camp. To the far side they saw two six-by-six trucks. He drove faster as he decided the place had been abandoned.

"So where did the two soldiers we met come from?" Mahanani asked.

"Probably up ahead somewhere closer to town," Howard said. "From a permanent base that must still be manned."

"This is spooky, let's get out of here," Tate said.

DeWitt agreed and speeded up and slashed through the rest of the camp and out another gate onto the flat hard sand again. Less than a quarter of a mile ahead they came to a road that angled down almost to the beach. It came up from the south inland somewhere and continued to the north. Now the lights of the town were easy to see, and DeWitt was about ready to stop and examine the maps they had been given. They had a street address, so maybe they could find the place in the dark. It was supposed to be somewhere just south of the main part of town.

"This looks like a city," Sadler said. "How far in can we drive?"

"Until somebody challenges us or looks like they're going to give us trouble," DeWitt said. "Neal, see if you can read that map and find the street we need and how to get there."

"No way in the dark bouncing around on this road," Sadler said. "Pull over where we can use a flash and get ourselves oriented."

"Yeah, good idea." DeWitt turned off a short time later and halted well away from the road. They hadn't met any cars, but now he saw two or three go by, heading into the city.

While Neal worked the map, DeWitt took the SATCOM out of its waterproof pack from his back and set it up. He got the fold-out antenna set up and angled it for a satellite.

"Team Two looking for Home Team Leader."

He had to send the message twice before a response came.

"Yes, Team Two. How is it going?"

"On schedule so far. No landing problems and we're almost at the city limits, trying to find the right street. Any other news?"

"Yes, Team Three got turned around in their chopper. Intense fighting between holdouts and the new regime where they were headed. So we're relying on you two."

"How is Murdock doing?"

"Making progress. Last report he was a couple of miles away from his target."

"We'll stay in touch. Out." DeWitt hung up the handset and put the antenna away. "So how are you doing?" He asked Neal.

"It's on this side of town. Damn big place. This south road is I-40 and it comes into Bandar-e at Twentieth Street. We stay right on Twentieth for what looks like half a mile, then turn left on Date Palm Street, which is where our address is. Can we drive all the way?"

"Unless we run into some army unit," DeWitt said. "Let's get moving."

•   •   •

Nay Band, Iran

Murdock and his team had hiked halfway up the two-mile road and came to a slight rise. They stopped and looked ahead, where they could see reflected light coming over another hill.

"Must be the place," Jaybird said. The men gave small cheers, glad that Jaybird was back in form.

A mile later the six men lay in the weeds and dirt on a hill overlooking the buildings below. Murdock was surprised at the size of the facility. There were three buildings, and all looked to be made of metal, with some kind of aluminum or sheet steel siding. All were one story. In front of one, the parking lot lights revealed eight cars. The SEALs were three hundred yards from the buildings.

"Anyone see any army or armed guards down there?" Murdock asked.

"I've got one guard on each building," Lam said, looking through a scope. "They don't look army, but they have rifles, probably AK-47s."

Murdock looked at Masud. "You said there were tents?"

"Must have replaced them with the buildings."

None of the structures had windows. "Does anyone see lights on inside any of them?" Murdock asked. Nobody replied.

"Okay, my guess is one is for supplies, one for the manufacture and storage of the anthrax, and one for sleeping and eating. Trouble is, we don't know which is which."

"Watch for doors opening," Lam said. "Wouldn't be lights on in the sleeping or storage shacks."

They watched for ten minutes. Lam stood. "I'm going down. My guess is the place with the cars parked outside. Okay, LC?"

"Go. Be careful. Float like a butterfly."

"That was what Muhammad Alli said along in the1960s," Jaybird said. "'I'll float like a butterfly and sting like a bee.'"

"What a mind," Lam said.

Jaybird threw his hat at Lam as he headed down the slope at a trot.

Murdock was concerned with the lights. Six tall poles held bright combinations of bulbs that lit up the hundred square foot area around the buildings like midday.

"We take the lights out before we go in?" Jaybird asked.

"Not if we want to surprise them," Murdock said. "Depends on what Lam finds."

Ten minutes later their Motorolas spoke.

"Yeah, it's the one with cars. Got a small little peek inside. The place is mostly empty, but ten to twelve civilians are at work. I eliminated the three guards."

"No army?"

"Didn't see a single uniform. I'll check the dormitory building to be sure."

Five minutes later the Motorolas came on again.

"I've got a squad of seven soldiers and about ten more civilians sleeping."

"Good," Murdock said. "Stay there. I'll send over Ching. When the game starts, gather up all the army weapons and march the soldiers and the civilians out of the building and down the road a half mile. Then tell them to hike into town."

"I can do that."

"We're moving in. We'll take the assembly building and get the civilians outside and send them hiking to meet you." Murdock stood and waved his men down the slope. All five of them would crash into the door at the same time and cover the civilians. Ching would then go to help Lam taking the workers with him.

Murdock and company jogged to the building unnoticed. Jaybird grabbed the door handle and looked at Murdock. He nodded. The door jolted outward and Murdock and the rest of them charged into the building. Murdock fired a burst of three rounds from the MP-5 into the ceiling.

There were four low tables with vats and heating devices and dryers and a dozen other mechanisms Murdock did not understand.

"Anybody speak English?" Murdock asked.

One woman in a white jumpsuit held up her hand. He motioned her forward.

"Yes, I speak English."

"Tell them we will not hurt them. They are to leave the building at once and walk over to the bunkhouse where they will be escorted toward town."

She spoke quickly in Farsi. One or two groaned, but she shrilled at them. Moments later they all had left. Murdock kept the translator with him.

"Miss, what is your name?"

"Kanza."

"Kanza. You manufacture the anthrax here, right?"

"Yes."

"Where do you store it?"

She pointed to the far end of the building. It had a floor-to-ceiling wall with one small door.

"Have any of you taken ill?"

"Yes, about half over the past year. We have to keep replacing workers."

"Is there any finished anthrax on these tables?"

"No, just the start of a new batch."

"Then nothing is dangerous out here."

"No, we haven't reached that stage on this batch yet."

He looked around again. At the near wall and halfway to the far end stood a butane tank ten feet long and three feet in diameter.

"You use the butane to generate heat to make the anthrax?"

"Yes. This tank was filled yesterday, a thousand gallons."

"It's in liquid form, right?"

"Yes, I think so. It all goes through valves, then into special hoses that are fitted to the heating units."

"Are there extra hoses?"

"I don't know."

Murdock turned to his men. "We need to find all of the hoses that we can to use on the butane tank. Look all over this place." The men began searching. He heard some yells.

"Jackpot, LC," Jaybird shouted. "A hundred-foot-long coil, all brand new. You thinking what I'm thinking?"

"If the hose will reach the end of this building, we bore a hole the same size as the hose, get an on-off valve on the hose, and see what kind of a blowtorch we can make."

Murdock yelled at Bradford. "Take the SATCOM outside, set it up to transmit, and tell Home Team Leader to call off the other teams, we have the plant and are dealing with it."

"Roger that," Bradford said, grabbing the SATCOM and hurrying outside.

They found a valve and a nozzle that fit the hose and attached the open end to the tank of butane at one of several outlets. Murdock tested the jet in the open area of the warehouse. He used a lighter to snap at the end of the nozzle and a bright blue flame came out. He held the hose tightly and opened the valve all the way. A four-foot roaring flame jolted out the nozzle.

Murdock closed the valve and the flame disappeared.

Murdock and the rest of the SEALs checked the heavy-duty wall at the end of the building. It was solid, looked like concrete. There was one small observation window. Murdock looked in and saw mounds of white powder. The carrier for the anthrax virus. He couldn't help but shudder.

The Iranian woman watched them. "You're going to destroy the anthrax virus?"

"If we can. Are you a scientist?"

She nodded. "Without another virus that will eat up the anthrax virus, heat is the only way to destroy it."

"I hoped that was the case. Now it's good to be sure."

"Two thousand degrees should do it."

Murdock looked around. "You don't care if we ruin all of your work?"

"They made me do this. Do it or go to prison and be raped and killed. This sounded better. Please, destroy all of it."

They bored a small hole through the access window with on-site tools. Murdock turned on the valve so it produced a six-inch flame on the end of the nozzle, then he jammed the nozzle through the hole and four feet of hose inside the sealed room right up to the valve. Murdock took a deep breath and turned the valve slowly until it was fully open.

"Oh, damn, but that's hot," Jaybird yelled. "A flame six feet long in there eating up everything it touches."

"It won't have to burn it all up," Kanza said. "When the temperature in the room hits two thousand to three thousand degrees, all of the anthrax virus will be dead."

"How long will it take?" Murdock said.

"No idea, maybe an hour," Kanza said.

"Okay, we're out of here. In an hour we'll come back for a quick check. Bradford, figure out how to put two quarter pound chunks of C-5 on that butane tank. We'll blow it when the anthrax is cooked."

Outside, Lam and Ching came back grinning.

"Hooooorahed them suckers down the road at a slow trot," Ching said. "Most of them were glad to get away. The soldiers said they would be shot, but I told them better by their own people than by us. They won't be back."

"The pot inside is cooking," Jaybird said.

Murdock looked at the third building. "Lam, you check out that other structure?"

"Nope. Can do."

"Good, do."

He left and the rest of them stayed back 200 yards from the cooking building.

"You're Americans?" the Iranian woman asked.

"Yes," Murdock said. "But don't tell anyone, if your government officials ask you. We're a secret." He winked at her.

Kanza smiled. "The old government is gone. But this new one will be just as bad. I won't even admit that *I* was here."

It was just short of an hour when they heard a noise. It was a small explosion, then a larger one. The far end of the manufacturing building blew its roof off. A thirty-foot section flew into the air and they didn't see it come down.

Murdock looked at Bradford. "You rig that C-5 with a remote?"

"Did that. I didn't want to go back inside and push in a timer."

"Now would be a good time to hit the destruct button."

Bradford ginned, took out a small red plastic box from his pocket, and opened it. He pushed down a black button, then put his thumb on the red one and looked at the building. He pushed the red button.

A microsecond later the rest of the building blew up with a gigantic roar. Clouds of dust and debris shot into the sky and began falling around them.

They ducked and looked on in amazement at the total destruction of the whole building and damage to the other two standing structures.

"That's what happens when you touch off seven or eight hundred gallons of liquid petroleum," Murdock said. The stuff is better than a bomb that size. Remember that. We may need to use the idea in the future."

Salama Masud wiped dust and grit off his face, but he was grinning. "Now I'll really have something to tell my grandchildren."

"Let's see if we can find your truck and get moving out of here," Murdock said. "Oh, one small task. Bradford, the SATCOM. He reported the total destruction of the anthrax stockpile and the manufacturing plant. He told Home Team

Leader that no civilians were harmed, all were marched off
to the little town.

"Well done, Team Three. Let us know when and where
you want the chopper to drop in. It will come out of
Afghanistan. Much closer there than the other route. Give
us a call when you're ready."

They hiked up the slope and then down the hill to the
pickup. Lam went ahead but saw that it was intact—no
bombs, no apparent damage to the vehicle. They loaded
onboard, including the Iranian woman.

Masud had just put the rig into gear and turned around
when rifle fire slammed into the pickup. The SEALs bailed
out and Kanza jumped out and landed flat on the ground.

Murdock had given the MP-5 to Bradford, who now hid
behind the rear wheels and fired around them at the muzzle
flashes about three hundred yards away.

Lam gritted his teeth. "The LC has been hit. He never
left the cab. I'm going to swing around that little slope over
there and try to get behind the attackers. Keep shooting,
even though those pistols won't hit anything. They don't
know what you're using. Hold tight, people, I'll be right
back."

31

Bandar-e Bushehr, Iran

After Sadler had checked the map and figured out the general direction, DeWitt drove the Jeep back onto the road and forward. They were still in the country, but the town was coming up fast. DeWitt saw a car slam past him going too fast. He watched to the rear now as more cars came. They met few, since most of the cars and small trucks seemed to be going into the city.

A mid-sized bobtail truck swung by him, turned back into his lane, and slowed. Dewitt had to use the brakes. A car slid in beside him so he couldn't go around the truck. The truck slowed more and he had to brake again. He looked at the car to his left, a heavy sedan of an unknown make. He waved at them, but they didn't notice him. The car beside him slowed, keeping pace with him.

"A trap," DeWitt said. "Hold on tight." He jammed on the brakes, the other two rigs rolled forward. He was behind them two car lengths. He hit the gas pedal and the Jeep jumped ahead, but the car that was in the second lane didn't move and he was trapped again.

A man leaned out the rear window with a shotgun aimed at them. He motioned for them to pull over. There was little he could do. Ed growled as he pulled back into the right-hand lane and then stopped behind the truck that had stopped ahead of him. The man with the shotgun came out of the car. Another man got out of the front seat waving a pistol.

"Weapons ready, we shoot on three," DeWitt said. "One, two, three."

Four pistols and the MP-5 barked in the darkness. Both Iranians went down before they had a chance to shoot. De-Witt kicked the gearshift into reverse and roared backwards on the road, spun the wheel, turning the jeep around, and raced back the way they had come. The heavy sedan backed up and turned and came after them.

"No contest," DeWitt said. "That car will catch us in five. They want the Jeep, not us. Bandits roving the country without much law. Just around that next turn, we hit the ditch, get out and make ourselves invisible just off the road. If they want the Jeep, we let them take it."

A rifle round snarled past the open Jeep. Then a second one hit inside. Dewitt saw Tate jolt forward from where he sat in the front seat, his head hitting the windshield. De-Witt didn't have time to check the man; he had to power the Jeep around the corner, out of range, and brake hard as they rolled into a shallow ditch and stopped.

"Out, everybody out and into the brush or whatever we can find. They want the damn Jeep. Anybody hit?" DeWitt looked back at Tate. He was still slumped over against the windshield. DeWitt pushed him back to the seat. His hand came away sticky with warm blood.

DeWitt grabbed Tate and boosted him on his shoulders and ran away from the road. He saw the lights of the sedan stabbing through the night. Fifty feet off the road, he went to ground and let Tate down as gently as he could.

"Mahanani, Tate is hit. Over here," he said to his Motorola.

They watched the bandits race up, jump out of the sedan, and check the Jeep. DeWitt had pulled the ignition key out from habit as if it were his own car. The men shouted at each other, then pushed the Jeep onto the road. They tied a rope or cable to the front bumper and onto the sedan and towed the Jeep away toward the lights of the town to the north.

When the bandits left, the SEALs grouped around Mahanani and Tate. The men knelt shoulder to shoulder, shielding the light the medic used.

"LT, Tate is bad. That round must have tumbled after it went through the seat. It cut up his chest something fierce. I don't know how bad. Must have hit a lung. He's lost a lot of blood and his breathing is shallow and slow. Pulse is pretty good. If we had a chopper in here now, we might save him."

"Break out the SATCOM," DeWitt said. "First we move Tate and the rest of us a quarter of a mile off the road so we aren't sitting ducks. Careful with him."

Ten minutes later they were in a small ravine and had the SATCOM set up. It answered to DeWitt's first call.

"We've got trouble, Home Team Leader. We have a casualty and need an immediate chopper evac."

"Roger, copy. Your evac is on the way in five. Murdock's team found the factory and destroyed it. Your work there is done. Give me your GPS coordinates. Estimated flight time to you should be about two hours."

DeWitt looked at Mahanani.

"Ask for a doctor and nurse on the chopper."

"Our medic asks for a doctor and a nurse to be on the chopper. He's not sure our man can live four more hours without some serious medical attention."

"We'll try. Give me those GPS coordinates again as a double-check. The chopper will lift off in five. I'm assigning a medical team, and I'll relay the coordinates to the pilot again. Do what you can for the man."

"Will do. Rush it. Tate is critical."

The SEALs spread out in a perimeter defense facing outward with DeWitt, Mahanani, and Tate in the middle. There was nothing they could do except wait. DeWitt checked his watch. It was nearing oh-three hundred. In two hours it could be starting to get light. He had no idea when sunup was in this part of the world.

DeWitt checked Tate. "Is he still unconscious?"

"Yeah. At least he isn't hurting. He took a wicked hit. Too bad we didn't get the word to abort about an hour earlier."

"Yeah, too bad." DeWitt stared at his bloody hands. He could just make them out in the darkness. The road had more traffic now. He wondered where the Jeep was. Those had to be road bandits, blocking in a car or truck they wanted. No way around. The sudden braking had given them a chance. Blowing away two of the bandits had opened it up for them. DeWitt pinched his eyes shut and wished that he had set up a regular schedule for checking with Home Team Leader. Too damn late now. This was the part he hated, waiting for help to come and absolutely nothing he could do to hurry it. There was no way he could have prevented what happened. Totally random. Wrong place at the wrong time. The damn bullet could have been two feet over and gone through him instead. Milly would watch him and in her soft way tell him to stop feeling sorry for himself. This was the life he had chosen, live with it or dump it. Milly was a most practical wife. He watched Tate. His breathing was even but light, shallow. It would be a miracle if he lived. Ed shook his head and looked around. He had four other men to take care of. He sat up and stared at the dark landscape. They all were on guard, but it wouldn't hurt if he moved out a little and watched the road better. He didn't want the bandits coming back and trying for some vengeance for their two dead men. He moved to the top of the ravine. He could see over the dirt and check the cars moving along the highway. More of them now, and a few small trucks. He wondered just how much civil law there was left in this part of Iran. Those bandits were a bad sign.

An hour later, Tate seemed a little better. He was in and out of consciousness. He asked them where he was hit and they said just a scratch. He grinned and dropped off again.

As DeWitt watched from the top of the gully, he saw a

small army convoy go past heading south. Three six-by-sixes, two Jeeps, and a half-track with what must have been mounted machine guns. He was glad they hadn't run into that one earlier.

At oh-four-thirty he started watching the sky to the east. There were a few first hints at dawn. He couldn't tell how Tate was. He was still alive, that's about all he knew.

It was oh-five-fifteen when they heard a chopper to the east. The Blackhawk came soaring over the ground at thirty feet. They didn't have any red smoke to show an LZ. DeWitt climbed up the last few feet of the ravine and waved his arms. The bird circled once, then came down on a flat spot fifty feet from the ravine.

Neal had them moving Tate as soon as he heard the bird. Two men carried him in a chair position with another man behind him. Dust kicked up a cloud as they walked toward the bird. The door came open and DeWitt hurried them along. Inside the chopper was a folding cot that they put Tate on. A doctor and a nurse were there with a large suitcase kit of medical equipment, including a portable defibrillator in case Tate's heart stopped.

The bird was on the ground for two minutes, then DeWitt jumped in and closed the door. The doctor and nurse had the SEALs hold the cot steady as they took off and headed the six miles across Iranian land to the Persian Gulf and much safer territory.

Mahanani watched the doctor. They had hung a saline drip and detailed Mahanani to hold it. Then they began doing what they could in the unsterile situation.

DeWitt sat along the side of the chopper and covered his face with his hands. Two hours. If they had been closer, Tate would have had a much better chance of staying alive. Now the doctor looked up and told them it was a fifty-fifty chance whether Tate lived or died.

• • •

Nay Band, Iran

Jaybird watched Lam crawl up the slope to a shallow ravine that would give him cover on his route up the hill and around the attackers. He checked Kanza. She lay low to the ground in the edge of the ditch where they had taken cover. Salama Masud worked his way up to the lip of the shallow ditch so he could see the men firing. He had his rifle up and loaded.

"I can see them," he said. He sighted in and fired and Jaybird was glad for the throaty sound of the AK-47. It would give the attackers something to think about besides the pops of the handguns.

"Yes, Salama," Jaybird said. "Keep firing, but conserve your rounds. How many do you have?"

"About forty. I can do lots of damage."

Bradford and Ching were hunkered down out of sight, wishing they had better firepower.

"Save your pistol rounds," Jaybird said. "If they try to rush us, we'll need the close-in firepower."

There was a pause in firing from below. Jaybird crawled down the ditch and up to the pickup. He used one of the front tires to protect himself and lifted up so he could see inside the cab. Murdock lay sprawled on the front seat. Jaybird powered up to check him. He saw an ugly pool of blood on the floor of the cab. One arm dangled down, dripping the red stuff. Murdock's chest was a mass of red. Jaybird checked his breathing. Yes, some, light and not regular, but breath. He touched Murdock's throat to find the carotid. A good pulse. He was alive, but Jaybird didn't know for how long.

Jaybird's Motorola spoke.

"Okay, sport fans," Lam said. "The game is about to begin. I'm within fifty of them. They don't know I'm here. I want whoever is using the AK-47 to start popping in there regularly. A shot every fifteen seconds. That might get them moving around and give me more targets. There are only six of them. I spot no officer. They do have on army uniforms and a vehicle of some kind, looks like a three-quarter-ton truck. Try to nail some of them with the AK. I'll clean up. Let's go now."

Bradford was nearest Masud. He told the Iranian what to do, and he began firing. That brought some return fire, but not much. Then they heard the stutter of the MP-5. Jaybird had come out of the pickup and watched over the lip of the ditch. He saw one soldier look behind him and stand up. Just then Masud took him out with a round and he slammed to the ground.

Masud continued to fire. Lam kept up a chatter with the MP-5.

"Yeah, we got them coming and going. Four are down and the last two are playing a waiting game. Keep the AK working. I'm moving up each time you get off two or three shots."

Masud grinned and kept shooting.

There was a pause, then the MP-5 fired again, a pair of six-round bursts. Then there was a silence.

"We're clear down here," Lam said. "Did the LC get hit?"

"A really bad chest hit," Jaybird said. "I don't know if the pickup will run. We've got to get him some medical."

"I'll bring up this army rig. It's got the keys in it. Hold for me."

Five minutes later Bradford got the pickup running. The back window was shot out and one tire was low on pressure. They moved Murdock gently into the bed of the pickup and lay him on a pad, then drove down the hill and toward town. Lam left the army rig and joined them. Kanza hovered over Murdock, blotting blood, trying to stop the bleeding. Tears came quickly and she wiped at them and kept tending to Murdock.

Salama Masud had a plan. "I'm a buyer of wool from the outlying herders. Many times I run into bandits trying to kill me and steal my truck. The doctor in town is young but good. He'll believe my story that Murdock was helping me and he was hit but I fought them off. The rest of you we leave outside town and you come to my house after dark."

Jaybird held up his hand. "We are done here. We are supposed to call our home base and a helicopter will come in from Afghanistan and pick us up. I don't see how Murdock can make the flight. Can you get him to a good hospital?"

Masud stopped the pickup a half mile from town. The SEALs got off. Jaybird had the SATCOM.

"First I talk to Dr. Ghani," Masud said. "He can do a lot of minor repairs and stabilize your leader, but he doesn't have the equipment for any serious surgery."

"How far away is that kind of equipment?" Jaybird asked.

"That would be at Zahedan, big town, over five hundred thousand people and some good hospitals. It's right near the Afghanistan border. Dr. Ghani would report it if he treated a non-Iranian and then he vanished the next day amid talk in town of a helicopter coming over."

"We can't just leave Murdock here," Jaybird said.

Lam had been listening. "Actually it's the only thing we can do. We can't fly him out in his condition. We need this doctor. And if he treats him we can't fly him out. So it's this Zahedan and the big hospital until he's well enough to get across the border into Afghanistan."

Bradford and Ching agreed with Lam. They let Masud and Kanza take Murdock into town to the doctor. They vanished into the countryside until it got dark, when they would work their way to Masud's house for some food and rest. As soon as they were hidden in some brush and a gully, Jaybird set up the SATCOM and reported the situation to Home Team Leader.

"Yes, Team One. We have assets in Afghan we can use. First we'll lift you four out of there. Too late to make arrangements for tonight, but we'll be there after dark tomorrow. Can you maintain until then?"

"Affirmative Home Team Leader. You agree on leaving Murdock here?"

"Yes. We know about Zahedan. We have an agent there who can assist. Suggest you get Murdock to a good hospital as quickly as possible. We can communicate with him through our agent. Good work. Lay low for twenty-four and we'll have you out of there."

"Right, Home Team Leader. We'll talk later."

In the little town, it took almost no explanation to Dr. Ghani before Murdock was wheeled into his small operating room and he began repairing as much of the damage as he could. He hung a saline solution and an antibiotic and probed for bullet fragments. Kanza hovered around watching. At last she offered to help.

"I was a nurse in Tehran before I became a microbiologist," she said. He let her help.

An hour later Dr. Ghani was done. He washed up and gave Murdock another shot and let out a long sigh.

"I hate it when the bandits do this to you. You help so many of the herders make a living. He has to go to Zahedan as soon as possible. I'll drive him in my station wagon. It's almost an ambulance, but not quite. You said he isn't an Iranian. He's from where?"

"I think he's Russian, or perhaps from one of those other states. He's a traveler, offered to work with me a while."

"He has papers, of course."

"No, we lost them in the fight. I don't even know where to go back to look for them."

"Don't worry. I need to go to Zahedan anyway to pick up my six months worth of medical supplies. It's three hundred and sixty miles, and usually takes me all day, depending how well they repaired the roads."

He looked at Kanza. "Would you go along as my nurse to tend to him while we travel? I need somebody to watch him. It would be a big help."

She smiled. "Well, I did have a job at the factory, before the big accident. I'm unemployed. Yes, I'd like to go. Maybe I can get work in that big town."

Before they started, Salama Masud decided he should go along, too, to help get Murdock through the hospital stay and then out of the country and into Afghanistan.

Thirty hours later, the SEALs caught their ride in a special Blackhawk from Afghanistan. It was painted all black, had no markings of any kind, and flew so low over the mountains that Jaybird nearly threw up.

Four days later they limped into North Island Naval Air Station with the rest of the Third Platoon. Missing was Dexter Tate, who had died in the chopper on the way back to Qatar, and the wounded Robert Doyle. Ed DeWitt had command of the platoon again and the men had their three-day passes, then settled into the training routine to keep sharp. DeWitt and Master Chief Petty Officer Gordon MacKenzie began interviewing men to fill in for Tate and for Doyle, who had been promoted to a bed in Balboa Naval Hospital there in San Diego.

"What about Murdock?" DeWitt asked the master chief.

"We're working on it almost every day. The medics in Iran think that he will need to stay there for at least a month before he's ready to fly out. The civil government there is in a shambles. Almost no national control. Should make it easier to get him out. We're working on it."

32

The moment that the men of Third Platoon, SEAL Team Seven hit the compound they changed clothes and raced for the parking lot. They had three-day passes and a dozen plans. George Canzoneri didn't phone home. Actually he was worried about what he would find. He drove home, hitting two red lights, but still making good time. When he parked in his slot he noticed a Buick Century in the visitors area. The DeWitt's had a Century. He raced to the ground floor unit and paused before entering. He rang the bell, then opened the door.

Inside the smell hit him first, spices and cooking smells. Then the laugh that could only be Milly DeWitt. He frowned.

"Honey, I'm home," he called. Phyllis rushed out of the kitchen and grabbed him with both arms and hugged him so tight he screeched in mock pain.

"Easy, girl, don't squeeze me in half." He saw Milly come around the kitchen door.

"So, you guys finally got home. We've been waiting for you. Kind of." She pulled off a small apron. "Well, I guess it's time for me to bail out. The SEALs have landed and it looks like the ship is under control and in good hands. You've got the con, Canzoneri, as you sailors say."

She nodded as she went past.

"Give you a call tomorrow, Phyl. Maybe we can hit that matinee we talked about." Then she was gone.

"Baby, I've waited so long for you. Months and months." She hugged him again, then kissed him and pushed him against the hall wall and came away, her expression showing delight and fear and a flood of joy. "I'm so . . . I can't tell you . . . the girls have been coming over . . . I didn't know what else to do."

"Barney kept coming back?"

She nodded.

"Pack enough things for three days. We're going to a motel. Then I'm going to look up Barney. Nothing overt, nothing he can use against me. Some dirty tricks he's never even thought of."

It took them a half-hour to turn off the cooking in the kitchen, pack, and drive out to a motel in Mission Valley. He called Maria Fernandez. She said she understood, that she could come over and stay with Phyllis the rest of the afternoon and night."

"But Miguel just got home."

"Hey, he's cool and he knows what's happening. He and Linda are coming with me. He'll help you on your next mission."

She hung up before he could answer.

Later, in the motel, Fernandez grinned when they started talking about Barney. Before he left his house he had used the Internet to find Barney's telephone number. It came up with two, one in town and one in Vista. With the address to work with, they drove to the spot in Fernandez's car. They watched the stand-alone house from four lots down. About six o'clock a black Lexus convertible parked in the street in front of the house and Barney walked into the place. They scanned the area for any security and found two men outside the house. It took them fifteen minutes to slip up on the men just as it was getting dark. They put both down without hurting them, gagged them, and used plastic ties on their hands and feet.

Fernandez had an idea. "I've got this buddy who runs a small concrete outfit. He has one road mixer and sometimes he has a half a yard of concrete left in his rig at the end of the day. Let me give him a call."

His buddy, Wally, loved the idea. He had heard of Barney. "He said he'd put some cardboard over the logo on the door of his truck and splash the license plate with mud. He'll be here in half an hour."

Fernandez met the mixer at the end of the block and used the Motorola they had borrowed from their gear to call Canzoneri.

"He's here. When we get in place, make a call on your phone to Barney and keep him on the wire for two minutes. That's all we need, two minutes."

The truck rolled up and Canzoneri made the call. He pleaded with Barney to bring him some goods. "Come on man, just two papers, all I need. Just two. Promise to pay you next week. My old lady's check comes next week."

Canzoneri kept talking as the concrete mixer moved next to Barney's convertible. Fernandez swung the chute over and the drum started turning. The wet, ready-to-set concrete poured down the chute into the front floor of the Lexus convertible. When it came up to the seats, Fernandez swung the chute to put the rest in the back seat.

"Come on, Barney! Hell, I been good for it for two years with you. You can't cut me off."

"I don't know who you are. What's that noise?"

"Just some kids and their souped-up cars. Man that Dodge is hot. Come on man. I'm Jodie. You remember me. I got a party planned."

The concrete fall ended. Fernandez swung the chute around and the driver pulled away and rolled down the street.

"On second thought, drop dead, Barney. I ain't gonna

buy from you no more," Canzoneri said and turned off the cell phone. He ran up the street and met Fernandez.

"We need to move the guards. Put them in a safe place where someone will find them in the morning." The job took a half-hour, then they came back near the house.

"The electric breaker switch box is usually on the outside of these houses," Canzoneri said. "Let's find it." It was just in back of the garage, well out of the nearest street light's beams. Canzoneri pushed the master switch to the off position, shutting off all electricity in the home. Then they waited in some bushes near by.

A man with a flashlight came out the side door of the garage. He stumbled over a box and fell to the grass. That made him drop the light and he swore. The light snapped off when it hit the ground and the man groped around trying to find it. Canzoneri moved quickly, jolted a hard fist into the man's jaw, and knocked him flat on the ground. They used plastic strips on his hands and feet and a no-danger gag over his mouth.

"Barney?" Fernandez whispered to Canzoneri.

Canzoneri nodded. "Did you see that mail slot through the front door? Should be a hose around here somewhere." They found it near the garage and a faucet just down from the front door. They pushed the open end of the hose through the mail slot and forced as much of the hose into the house as they could. The other end went on the faucet. Canzoneri turned the faucet handle three full turns that gushed water into Barney's living room. Then they walked to the street and down to their car.

"I feel like a kid doing Halloween pranks," Fernandez said.

"We're just getting started," Canzoneri said. "I did some investigating three years ago when he gave us a hard time, and I found out some things about him. He's squeaky clean at his house. He keeps his stash in a small storefront downtown. Let's see if he's still operating there."

The drive took twenty minutes. They cruised past the empty-looking store twice. No lights. Nobody around. It was just after eight o'clock. They parked a block away and came back to the store. It was in a light manufacturing district and the small closed building stood alone on the corner. The front door was locked. They checked the rear. The door was old and the lock older. One solid kick on the door knob jolted the door inward. They used mini flashlights to explore the back room. Nothing much there. A door led to a middle room. They found two paper grocery sacks on a high shelf. Each was stuffed with small bills, ones, fives and tens. They set them aside. A locked storage cabinet against the wall gave them more trouble. At last they pried the hasp off the top drawer and pulled it open.

"Ten kilos of cocaine in there," Fernandez said. "Must be worth at least ten thousand a kilo. That's a hundred thousand dollars worth."

A cry came at them as a door to the front section of the place burst open and two men stormed into the room, each with a handgun waving in the air. The two SEALs attacked, slamming into both surprised men. The guns fell from hands and the SEALs had both men flat on their stomachs and plastic around their hands and ankles before they knew they were in trouble.

"Two keepers," Canzoneri said. "Barney couldn't trust just one." They checked the other drawers in the cabinet and found a variety of pills and meth and a lot of marijuana.

"How about a nice little fire?" Fernandez whispered.

"No WP."

"No, but we have newspapers and this old wooden building. I'd say it would go up in a flash. We get the two bodies out of here and then do it."

It took them twenty minutes to lug the two inside security men out the back door and half a block down where they stashed them behind two wrecked cars.

They set the fire against an inside wall. The paper

caught fire at once, and soon they saw that it had enough fuel to catch the wall, then the ceiling and was off and roaring. They watched it a few minutes more. No windows here so it wouldn't be seen for some time until it burst through the roof. They found a quart of paint and opened it and poured it on the fire. Canzoneri looked at the sacks of bills.

"Hey, no sense all this cash burning up. What do you think?"

Fernandez grabbed them. "I know just the place for this loot." He carried the sacks as they slid out the back door into the darkness and walked a block away. They got the car and parked where they could see the building. Canzoneri dug through the sack of bills. He found one banded stack of tens.

"Must be a thousand dollars there alone," he said. "My guess is over twenty thousand in these sacks. What did you mean you know just the place for the cash?"

"Father Joe Carroll's place. He has a batch of buildings and shelters and facilities for the homeless down here. We can put them outside one of the places and ring the doorbell or something."

Canzoneri nodded. "Yeah, good idea. Where is the stupid fire department?"

A moment later the fire broke through the roof and painted a red glow on the surrounding buildings.

"Now we'll get some action."

Seven minutes later two fire engines shrilled up to the scene. The men strung hoses and attacked the flames. It took them only ten minutes to put down the flames. By then the twenty-by-thirty-foot building was half burned to the ground. The roof had caved in and all of the pot probably had burned, but there would be plenty of the cocaine left for the inspectors to find.

Canzoneri grinned as they drove away. "I figure we just cost good old Barney more than a hundred and fifty thousand dollars tonight. Not counting the fifty or sixty thousand he paid for the Lexus."

"Think that he'll leave Phyllis alone now?"

"He'll have so much trouble getting his act back together that he won't even think about her. Or about me. Nothing really happened to him. He isn't dead, so my threat isn't worth much. Especially since we'll tie Barney to the half-burned building down there."

"How do we do that?"

"On the phone." Canzoneri took out his cell phone and dialed the emergency number for the San Diego Police Department.

"San Diego Police."

"Good. Glad you finally nailed old Barney Givens. You know, the drug dealer. Somebody torched his stash house down on Fourteenth and G Streets. Damn glad. He's been using that old building as his stash for years now. Get your drug busters down there in a rush."

"Yes. Who is this please?"

Canzoneri closed the phone and chuckled. "Now let's see him get out of this one. Those two inside guards will sing their heads off as soon as the cops find them."

"Is that enough?" Fernandez asked.

"Yeah, I think so. And we still have two days of leave. You still have that tent?"

"Sure."

"Let's get our stuff and tomorrow morning go camping up in the Laguna Mountains?"

"Oh, yeah. First, we put this stash of cash where the right people will find it."

They drove to one of the missions that Father Joe ran and carried the sacks up to the door. It was after-hours and the door was locked. They rang the bell. A speaker came on.

"We're closed now. It's after-hours. Please come back tomorrow."

"No, wait, we don't want to come in. We have something for you. A donation. Send out your night manager."

"A donation?"

"That's right. It's cash. Come quickly."

The men pulled down their floppy hats to conceal their faces. A moment later bolts were thrown and the door opened on a chain.

"Yes?"

Canzoneri held up the paper sack so the person inside could see the cash.

"Oh, my. Is that real money?"

"Yes."

The door closed and the chain came off. When the priest opened the door, he found only the two sacks filled with greenbacks. The two men he had seen were gone. He smiled and went back inside.

33

The second day in the Naimullah Hospital, Murdock regained full consciousness. Until then he had been wandering in and out of reality, sometimes mumbling in English. Salama Masud stayed with him. When he checked Murdock during that first day he told them his name was Rashad and he was a wanderer who had saved Salama's life in a shootout with bandits.

The doctors there were unconcerned with just who the patient was. Dr. Ghani had brought him in and that was enough. He had helped during the operations. They were worried about his wounds. They operated twice on him, first taking out the rest of the two shattered lead slugs that had struck his chest, narrowly missing his heart. They repaired his left lung, removed his spleen, and stitched him back up.

That second day, Masud told Murdock that his men had all been choppered out to Afghanistan and were safe. He didn't tell him about the dead SEAL. Dr. Ghani visited them once more, then picked up his supplies and headed back to his home town.

"Your name here is Rashad, no last name, just Rashad," Masud told Murdock. "It is enough. This hospital is famous for attracting some of the best doctors and specialist in all of Iran. Here they are not so closely watched and ordered around as in other large Iranian cities. They simply don't care about politics. The important thing is they won't release you until they are sure that you can survive a trip."

"How long?" Murdock asked.

"They say six weeks, at least."

"You can talk to your contact who can tell them in the States that I'm okay?"

"Already done. The Company man here is excellent. He has contacts on both sides of the border. When it's time, he'll be the key to getting you out of here."

For another hour, Salama Masud worked with Murdock, teaching him some basic Farsi phrases he would need. How to say "It hurts here," "bathroom," and "I'm hungry."

Murdock tried to pick up the strange words. None like he had learned before like "Hands up or I'll shoot." He felt like a horse had kicked him in the chest. Two slugs dead center and he should be dead. He didn't believe in fate. There was no all-powerful force out there guiding those bullets to spare his life. Life was what each person made it. Sure there was always chance. Sometimes events worked in ways a person had no control over. But for the most part, a person's life was exactly what he made of it. That's why he was lying there in bed recovering. He had asked to be a SEAL, but had asked for this assignment. He knew that Ardith back in DC would be worrying her heart out. He turned to the wool buyer.

"Salama, be sure that they tell Ardith in Washington that I'm okay, that I'm getting patched back together."

"Done. That was my first message. To her. The second was to my contact in DC. Now, don't worry. Uh-oh. Here comes some trouble. This town's head commissioner. Big boss. Close your eyes and be sleeping. No more English." He switched to Farsi and pretended not to notice as the tall man entered the private room.

The man cleared his throat and Masud turned and stood.

"Oh, we have company," he said in Farsi.

The visitor was six feet tall, broad shouldered, and carried himself with a military stiffness. He had a full black beard and small dark eyes that bored out of a deep set. He watched Masud for a moment and then looked at Murdock.

"This is the one they call Rashad?"

"Yes, the only name I know him by. He worked for me as a guard on my trips into the bandit country."

"And you are Salama the wool buyer? I have heard of you. But this one has no papers."

"That's right. He did, but we lost them when we were attacked. We couldn't even get back to our camp and thought it wiser to bring Rashad here for treatment than worry about getting his papers."

"How long has he worked with you?"

"Only during the buying season. We shear sheep once a year, and it takes me three months to contact all of the herders in my area."

"Probably a wise choice to get him medical attention. But a man without papers . . ."

"Perhaps I can talk with him when he's lucid again and get his family name, his history, birthplace, schooling, work history, all of that so we can do new papers for him. With your permission, of course."

"I'll consider it. Is your wool-buying season over?"

"We were on the last run when we were attacked."

The head man of the large city nodded. "Yes. I have much work to do, but I'll think about your suggestion. We have the need of every good man we can find. I'll let you know soon." The commissioner didn't say goodbye, he just turned and walked out the open door and down the hall.

Masud didn't like the way the man stared at Murdock. He was powerful and could take almost any action he wanted. Masud moved up close to Murdock. "Keep your eyes closed and listen. That was close. He could rout you out and shoot you dead any time he wishes to. There is little control over him."

"Did I see Kanza here?"

"Yes. She's working as a nurse until she can get new papers and her records from the university. She won't expose you. At least we have the medicine here that is needed. Dr. Ghani left two days ago, so we're on our own. I'll stay with you."

The days drifted by for Murdock, who was still on medications and often slept during the day as well as at night.

The third week he came out from some of the drugs and felt better. He touched Masud's hand. "Hey, I'm mending. I can breathe better now. I don't even wheeze anymore. When can I go home?"

A nurse came in, checked his chart, nodded to Masud, took Murdock's temperature and put it on the chart and left.

"Not yet. When it happens, you won't know in advance. I've talked to Kanza. She reads the charts for me and listens to the doctors. They are surprised how strong you are and how quickly you are healing. She says another week and your breathing will be close enough to normal that you can stand a helicopter flight over the mountains. But that presents us with a problem."

"Didn't the rest of the team chopper out into Afghanistan?" Murdock asked.

"They did, but not all the way to Kabul. They crossed the border and then went south into Pakistan to Karachi where they could get commercial air. The choppers my contact says that are available here now don't have that kind of range."

"So what do we do?" Murdock asked.

"We're working on it. Don't worry. Just get yourself well enough to travel. We'll be going with Kanza's help."

"Is she coming along?"

"If she wants to. We'll have to see. She may have to if she wants to stay alive."

"You have a tough act here, Salama."

"I know, and I wish it were better. Not for a while."

• • •

Three days later, just after midnight, Murdock felt a hand on his shoulder. He roused and came wide awake. Kanza was there in a white nurse's uniform. Salama Masud wore the white lab coat of a doctor. They had him sit up and put on heavy pajamas and a hospital robe, then slippers, and eased him into a wheelchair.

"Is this it?" Murdock asked.

"If it works out. Otherwise none of us will worry about retiring."

They rolled him out of the room, down a corridor, down two floors to the ground floor, and into a waiting ambulance that had a wheelchair ramp. Masud and Kanza both stayed with him. They strapped the wheelchair down and drove.

A half-hour later they stopped. When the doors opened, Murdock saw a silver business jet sitting on the airport tarmac.

"That's my new bird?" he asked Masud.

"I prefer to think of it as more of a camel. It can go a long time without a drink."

They freed the chair and rolled him to the aircraft. It had no markings other than a number on the rudder. Strong hands helped him go up the steps one at a time, then eased him into one of the first-class-style seats. Kanza and Salama Masud belted him in, made sure he was comfortable.

"Can I get you a pillow or a blanket?" Kanza asked.

"You're coming with me?" Murdock asked.

She nodded.

"Her position at the hospital was too dangerous. The head nurse said if she didn't show them her certificates by tomorrow, they would turn her over to the secret police."

The jet rolled down the runway and took off. Murdock felt a surge of satisfaction. He was on his way home. No more hiding under an Iranian name. He figured the Company would bring out Masud as well, since what he had done against Iran couldn't be covered up for long.

Murdock settled into the seat, wondering what the first thing he would do when he got home. More hospital time, he knew that. Somewhere near DC, close to home. At the first real stop he was going to make them take him to a phone where he could call Ardith, then the CNO. He grinned. The admiral would chew him out for getting shot up. Yeah, he could take it. Ardith would be a different matter. He could see the worried, agonizing, frightened look on her face. Now that would be a real problem. He wished he had Jaybird and Lam there to help him with it. He sighed. He'd just have to cope, like a real SEAL!

SEAL TALK

MILITARY GLOSSARY

Aalvin: Small U.S. two-man submarine.

Admin: Short for administration.

Aegis: Advanced Naval air defense radar system.

AH-1W Super Cobra: Has M179 undernose turret with 20mm Gatling gun.

AK-47: 7.64-round Russian Kalashnikov automatic rifle. Most widely used assault rifle in the world.

AK-74: New, improved version of the Kalashnikov. Fires the 5.45mm round. Has 30-round magazine. Rate of fire: 600 rounds per minute. Many slight variations made for many different nations.

AN/PRC-117D: Radio, also called SATCOM. Works with Milstar satellite in 22,300-mile equatorial orbit for instant worldwide radio, voice, or video communications. Size: 15 inches high, 3 inches wide, 3 inches deep. Weighs 15 pounds. Microphone and voice output. Has encrypter, capable of burst transmissions of less than a second.

AN/PUS-7: Night-vision goggles. Weighs 1.5 pounds.

ANVIS-6: Night-vision goggles on air crewmen's helmets.

APC: Armored Personnel Carrier.

ASROC: Nuclear-tipped antisubmarine rocket torpedoes launched by Navy ships.

Assault Vest: Combat vest with full loadouts of ammo, gear.

ASW: Anti-Submarine Warfare.

Attack Board: Molded plastic with two handgrips with

bubble compass on it. Also depth gauge and Cyalume chemical lights with twist knob to regulate amount of light. Used for underwater guidance on long swim.

Aurora: Air Force recon plane. Can circle at 90,000 feet. Can't be seen or heard from ground. Used for thermal imaging.

AWACS: Airborne Warning And Control System. Radar units in high-flying aircraft to scan for planes at any altitude out 200 miles. Controls air-to-air engagements with enemy forces. Planes have a mass of communication and electronic equipment.

Balaclavas: Headgear worn by some SEALs.

Bent Spear: Less serious nuclear violation of safety.

BKA, Bundeskriminant: Germany's federal investigation unit.

Black Talon: Lethal hollow-point ammunition made by Winchester. Outlawed some places.

Blivet: A collapsible fuel container. SEALs sometimes use it.

BLU-43B: Antipersonnel mine used by SEALs.

BLU-96: A fuel-air explosive bomb. It disperses a fuel oil into the air, then explodes the cloud. Many times more powerful than conventional bombs because it doesn't carry its own chemical oxidizers.

BMP-1: Soviet armored fighting vehicle (AFV), low, boxy, crew of 3 and 8 combat troops. Has tracks and a 73mm cannon. Also an AT-3 Sagger antitank missile and coaxial machine gun.

Body Armor: Far too heavy for SEAL use in the water.

Bogey: Pilots' word for an unidentified aircraft.

Boghammar Boat: Long, narrow, low dagger boat; high-speed patrol craft. Swedish make. Iran had 40 of them in 1993.

Boomer: A nuclear-powered missile submarine.

Bought It: A man has been killed. Also "bought the farm."

Bow Cat: The bow catapult on a carrier to launch jets.

Broken Arrow: Any accident with nuclear weapons, or any incident of nuclear material lost, shot down, crashed, stolen, hijacked.

Browning 9mm High Power: A Belgian 9mm pistol, 13 rounds in magazine. First made 1935.

Buddy Line: 6 feet long, ties 2 SEALs together in the water for control and help if needed.

BUD/S: Coronado, California, nickname for SEAL training facility for six months' course.

Bull Pup: Still in testing; new soldier's rifle. SEALs have a dozen of them for regular use. Army gets them in 2005. Has a 5.56 kinetic round, 30-shot clip. Also 20mm high-explosive round and 5-shot magazine. Twenties can be fused for proximity airbursts with use of video camera, laser range finder, and laser targeting. Fuses by number of turns the round needs to reach laser spot. Max range: 1200 yards. Twenty round can also detonate on contact, and has delay fuse. Weapon weighs 14 pounds. SEALs love it. Can in effect "shoot around corners" with the airburst feature.

BUPERS: BUreau of PERSonnel.

C-2A Greyhound: 2-engine turboprop cargo plane that lands on carriers. Also called COD, Carrier Onboard Delivery. Two pilots and engineer, Rear fuselage loading ramp. Cruise speed 300 mph, range 1,000 miles. Will hold 39 combat troops. Lands on CVN carriers at sea.

C-4: Plastic explosive. A claylike explosive that can be molded and shaped. It will burn. Fairly stable.

C-6 Plastique: Plastic explosive. Developed from C-4 and C-5. Is often used in bombs with radio detonator or digital timer.

C-9 Nightingale: Douglas DC-9 fitted as a medical-evacuation transport plane.

C-130 Hercules: Air Force transporter for long haul. 4 engines.

C-141 Starlifter: Airlift transport for cargo, paratroops, evac for long distances. Top speed 566 mph. Range with payload 2,935 miles. Ceiling 41,600 feet.

Caltrops: Small four-pointed spikes used to flatten tires. Used in the Crusades to disable horses.

Camel Back: Used with drinking tube for 70 ounces of water attached to vest.

Cammies: Working camouflaged wear for SEALs. Two different patterns and colors. Jungle and desert.

Cannon Fodder: Old term for soldiers in line of fire destined to die in the grand scheme of warfare.

CAP: Continuous Air Patrol.

Capped: Killed, shot, or otherwise snuffed.

CAR-15: The Colt M-4A1. Sliding-stock carbine with grenade launcher under barrel. Knight sound-suppressor. Can have AN/PAQ-4 laser aiming light under the carrying handle. .223 round. 20- or 30-round magazine. Rate of fire: 700 to 1,000 rounds per minute.

Cascade Radiation: U-235 triggers secondary radiation in other dense materials.

Castle Keep: The main tower in any castle.

Cast Off: Leave a dock, port, land. Get lost. Navy: long, then short signal of horn, whistle, or light.

Caving Ladder: Roll-up ladder that can be let down to climb.

CH-46E: Sea Knight chopper. Twin rotors, transport. Can carry 25 combat troops. Has a crew of 3. Cruise speed 154 mph. Range 420 miles.

CH-53D Sea Stallion: Big Chopper. Not used much anymore.

Chaff: A small cloud of thin pieces of metal, such as tinsel, that can be picked up by enemy radar and that can attract a radar-guided missile away from the plane to hit the chaff.

Charlie-Mike: Code words for continue the mission.

Chief to Chief: Bad conduct by EM handled by chiefs

so no record shows or is passed up the chain of command.

Chocolate Mountains: Land training center for SEALs near these mountains in the California desert.

Christians In Action: SEAL talk for not-always-friendly CIA.

CIA: Central Intelligence Agency.

CIC: Combat Information Center. The place on a ship where communications and control areas are situated to open and control combat fire.

CINC: Commander IN Chief.

CINCLANT: Navy Commander-IN-Chief, atLANTtic.

CINCPAC: Navy Commander-IN-Chief, PACific.

Class of 1978: Not a single man finished BUD/S training in this class. All-time record.

Claymore: An antipersonnel mine carried by SEALs on many of their missions.

Cluster Bombs: A canister bomb that explodes and spreads small bomblets over a great area. Used against parked aircraft, massed troops, and unarmored vehicles.

CNO: Chief of Naval Operations.

CO: Commanding Officer.

CO-2 Poisoning: During deep dives. Abort dive at once and surface.

COD: Carrier Onboard Delivery plane.

Cold Pack Rations: Food carried by SEALs to use if needed.

Combat Harness: American Body Armor nylon-mesh special-operations vest. 6 2-magazine pouches for drumfed belts, other pouches for other weapons, waterproof pouch for Motorola.

CONUS: The Continental United States.

Corfams: Dress shoes for SEALs.

Covert Action Staff: A CIA group that handles all covert action by the SEALs.

CP: Command Post.

CQB house: Close Quarters Battle house. Training facility near Nyland in the desert training area. Also called the Kill House.

CQB: Close Quarters Battle. A fight that's up close, hand-to-hand, whites-of-his-eyes, blood all over you.

CRRC Bundle: Roll it off plane, sub, boat. The assault boat for 8 SEALs. Also the IBS, Inflatable Boat Small.

Cutting Charge: Lead-sheathed explosive. Triangular strip of high-velocity explosive sheathed in metal. Point of the triangle focuses a shaped-charge effect. Cuts a pencil-line-wide hole to slice a steel girder in half.

CVN: A U.S. aircraft carrier with nuclear power. Largest that we have in fleet.

CYA: Cover Your Ass, protect yourself from friendlies or officers above you and JAG people.

Damfino: Damned if I know. SEAL talk.

DDS: Dry Dock Shelter. A clamshell unit on subs to deliver SEALs and SDVs to a mission.

DEFCON: DEFense CONdition. How serious is the threat?

Delta Forces: Army special forces, much like SEALs.

Desert Cammies: Three-color, desert tan and pale green with streaks of pink. For use on land.

DIA: Defense Intelligence Agency.

Dilos Class Patrol Boat: Greek, 29 feet long, 75 tons displacement.

Dirty Shirt Mess: Officers can eat there in flying suits on board a carrier.

DNS: Doppler Navigation System.

Drager LAR V: Rebreather that SEALs use. No bubbles.

DREC: Digitally Reconnoiterable Electronic Component. Top-secret computer chip from NSA that lets it decipher any U.S. military electronic code.

E-2C Hawkeye: Navy, carrier-based, Airborne Early Warning craft for long-range early warning and threat-assessment and fighter-direction. Has a 24-foot saucer-like rotodome over the wing. Crew 5, max speed 326 knots, ceiling 30,800 feet, radius 175 nautical miles with 4 hours on station.

E-3A Skywarrior: Old electronic intelligence craft. Replaced by the newer ES-3A.

E-4B NEACP: Called Kneecap. National Emergency Airborne Command Post. A greatly modified Boeing 747 used as a communications base for the President of the United States and other high-ranking officials in an emergency and in wartime.

E & E: SEAL talk for escape and evasion.

EA-6B Prowler: Navy plane with electronic countermeasures. Crew of 4, max speed 566 knots, ceiling 41,200 feet, range with max load 955 nautical miles.

EAR: Enhanced Acoustic Rifle. Fires not bullets, but a high-impact blast of sound that puts the target down and unconscious for up to six hours. Leaves him with almost no aftereffects. Used as a non-lethal weapon. The sound blast will bounce around inside a building, vehicle, or ship and knock out anyone who is within range. Ten shots before the weapon must be electrically charged. Range: about 400 yards.

Easy: The only easy day was yesterday. SEAL talk.

Ejection seat: The seat is powered by a CAD, a shotgun-like shell that is activated when the pilot triggers the ejection. The shell is fired into a solid rocket, sets it off and propels the whole ejection seat and pilot into the air. No electronics are involved.

ELINT: ELectronic INTelligence. Often from satellite in orbit, picture-taker, or other electronic communications.

EMP: ElectroMagnetic Pulse: The result of an E-bomb detonation. One type E-bomb is the Flux Compression Generator or FCG. Can be built for $400 and is relatively simple to make. Emits a rampaging electromagnetic pulse that destroys anything electronic in a 100 mile diameter circle. Blows out and fries all computers, telephone systems, TV broadcasts, radio, streetlights, and sends the area back into the Stone Age with no communications whatsoever. Stops all cars with electronic ignitions, drops jet planes out of the air including airliners, fighters and bombers, and stalls ships with electronic guidance and steering systems. When such a bomb is detonated the explosion is small but sounds like a giant lightning strike.

EOD: Navy experts in nuclear material and radioactivity who do Explosive Ordnance Disposal.

Equatorial Satellite Pointing Guide: To aim antenna for radio to pick up satellite signals.

ES-3A: Electronic Intelligence (ELINT) intercept craft. The platform for the battle group Passive Horizon Extension System. Stays up for long patrol periods, has comprehensive set of sensors, lands and takes off from a carrier. Has 63 antennas.

ETA: Estimated Time of Arrival. The planned time that you will arrive at a given destination.

Executive Order 12333: By President Reagan authorizing Special Warfare units such as the SEALs.

Exfil: Exfiltrate, to get out of an area.

F/A-18 Hornet: Carrier-based interceptor that can change from air-to-air to air-to-ground attack mode while in flight.

Fitrep: Fitness Report.

Flashbang Grenade: Non-lethal grenade that gives off a series of piercing explosive sounds and a series of brilliant strobe-type lights to disable an enemy.

Flotation Bag: To hold equipment, ammo, gear on a wet operation.

FO: Forward Observer. A man or unit set in an advanced area near or past friendly lines to call in artillery or mortar fire. Also used simply as the eyes of the rear echelon planners.

Fort Fumble: SEALs' name for the Pentagon.

Forty-mm Rifle Grenade: The M576 multipurpose round, contains 20 large lead balls. SEALs use on Colt M-4A1.

Four-Striper: A Navy captain.

Fox Three: In air warfare, a code phrase showing that a Navy F-14 has launched a Phoenix air-to-air missile.

FUBAR: SEAL talk. Fucked Up Beyond All Repair.

Full Helmet Masks: For high-altitude jumps. Oxygen in mask.

G-3: German-made assault rifle.

GHQ: General Headquarters.

Gloves: SEALs wear sage-green, fire-resistant Nomex flight gloves.

GMT: Greenwich Mean Time. Where it's all measured from.

GPS: Global Positioning System. A program with satellites around Earth to pinpoint precisely aircraft, ships, vehicles, and ground troops. Position information is to plus or minus ten feet. Also can give speed of a plane or ship to one quarter of a mile per hour.

GPSL: A radio antenna with floating wire that pops to the surface. Antenna picks up positioning from the closest 4 global positioning satellites and gives an exact position within 10 feet.

Green Tape: Green sticky ordnance tape that has a hundred uses for a SEAL.

GSG-9: Flashbang grenade developed by Germans. A cardboard tube filled with 5 separate charges timed to burst in rapid succession. Blinding and giving concussion to enemy, leaving targets stunned, easy to kill or capture. Usually non-lethal.

GSG9: Grenzschutzgruppe Nine. Germany's best special warfare unit, counterterrorist group.

Gulfstream II (VCII): Large executive jet used by services for transport of small groups quickly. Crew of

3 and 18 passengers. Maximum cruise speed 581 mph. Maximum range 4,275 miles.

H & K 21A1: Machine gun with 7.62 NATO round. Replaces the older, more fragile M-60 E3. Fires 900 rounds per minute. Range 1,100 meters. All types of NATO rounds, ball, incendiary, tracer.

H & K G-11: Automatic rifle, new type. 4.7mm caseless ammunition. 50-round magazine. The bullet is in a sleeve of solid propellant with a special thin plastic coating around it. Fires 600 rounds per minute. Single-shot, three-round burst, or fully automatic.

H & K MP-5SD: 9mm submachine gun with integral silenced barrel, single-shot, three-shot, or fully automatic. Rate 800 rds/min.

H & K P9S: Heckler & Koch's 9mm Parabellum double-action semiauto pistol with 9-round magazine.

H & K PSG1: 7.62 NATO round. High-precision, bolt-action, sniping rifle. 5- to 20-round magazine. Roller lock delayed blowback breech system. Fully adjustable stock. 6×42 telescopic sights. Sound suppressor.

HAHO: High Altitude jump, High Opening. From 30,000 feet, open chute for glide up to 15 miles to ground. Up to 75 minutes in glide. To enter enemy territory or enemy position unheard.

Half-Track: Military vehicle with tracked rear drive and wheels in front, usually armed and armored.

HALO: High Altitude jump, Low Opening. From 30,000 feet. Free fall in 2 minutes to 2,000 feet and open chute. Little forward movement. Get to ground quickly, silently.

Hamburgers: Often called sliders on a Navy carrier.

Handie-Talkie: Small, handheld personal radio. Short range.

HE: High Explosives.

HELO: SEAL talk for helicopter.

Herky Bird: C-130 Hercules transport. Most-flown military transport in the world. For cargo or passengers, paratroops, aerial refueling, search and rescue, communications, and as a gunship. Has flown from a Navy carrier deck without use of catapult. Four turboprop engines, max speed 325 knots, range at max payload 2,356 miles.

Hezbollah: Lebanese Shiite Moslem militia. Party of God.

HMMWV: The Humvee, U.S. light utility truck, replaced the honored jeep. Multipurpose wheeled vehicle, 4×4, automatic transmission, power steering. Engine: Detroit Diesel 150-hp diesel V-8 air-cooled. Top speed 65 mph. Range 300 miles.

Hotels: SEAL talk for hostages.

HQ: Headquarters.

Humint: Human Intelligence. Acquired on the ground; a person as opposed to satellite or photo recon.

Hydra-Shock: Lethal hollow-point ammunition made by Federal Cartridge Company. Outlawed in some areas.

Hypothermia: Danger to SEALs. A drop in body temperature that can be fatal.

IBS: Inflatable Boat Small. 12×6 feet. Carries 8 men and 1,000 pounds of weapons and gear. Hard to sink. Quiet motor. Used for silent beach, bay, lake landings.

IP: Initial Point. This can be a gathering place for a unit or force prior to going to the PD on a mission.

IR Beacon: Infrared beacon. For silent nighttime signaling.

IR Goggles: "Sees" heat instead of light.

Islamic Jihad: Arab holy war.

Isothermal layer: A colder layer of ocean water that deflects sonar rays. Submarines can hide below it, but then are also blind to what's going on above them since their sonar will not penetrate the layer.

IV Pack: Intravenous fluid that you can drink if out of water.

JAG: Judge Advocate General. The Navy's legal investigating arm that is independent of any Navy command.

JNA: Yugoslav National Army.

JP-4: Normal military jet fuel.

JSOC: Joint Special Operations Command.

JSOCCOMCENT: Joint Special Operations Command Center in the Pentagon.

KA-BAR: SEALs' combat, fighting knife.

KATN: Kick Ass and Take Names. SEAL talk, get the mission in gear.

KH-11: Spy satellite, takes pictures of ground, IR photos, etc.

KIA: Killed In Action.

KISS: Keep It Simple, Stupid. SEAL talk for streamlined operations.

Klick: A kilometer of distance. Often used as a mile. From Vietnam era, but still widely used in military.

Krytrons: Complicated, intricate timers used in making nuclear explosive detonators.

KV-57: Encoder for messages, scrambles.

Laser Pistol: The SIW pinpoint of ruby light emitted on any pistol for aiming. Usually a silenced weapon.

Left Behind: In 30 years SEALs have seldom left behind a dead comrade, never a wounded one. Never been taken prisoner.

Let's Get the Hell out of Dodge: SEAL talk for leaving a place, bugging out, hauling ass.

Liaison: Close-connection, cooperating person from one unit or service to another. Military liaison.

Light Sticks: Chemical units that make light after twisting to release chemicals that phosphoresce.

Loot & Shoot: SEAL talk for getting into action on a mission.

LT: Short for lieutenant in SEAL talk.

LZ: Landing Zone.

M1-8: Russian Chopper.

M1A1 M-14: Match rifle upgraded for SEAL snipers.

M-3 Submachine Gun: WWII grease gun, .45-caliber. Cheap. Introduced in 1942.

M-16: Automatic U.S. rifle. 5.56 round. Magazine 20 or 30, rate of fire 700 to 950 rds/min. Can attach M203 40mm grenade launcher under barrel.

M-18 Claymore: Antipersonnel mine. A slab of C-4 with 200 small ball bearings. Set off electrically or by trip wire. Can be positioned and aimed. Sprays out a cloud of balls. Kill zone 50 meters.

M60 Machine Gun: Can use 100-round ammo box snapped onto the gun's receiver. Not used much now by SEALs.

M-60E3: Lightweight handheld machine gun. Not used now by the SEALs.

M61A1: The usual 20mm cannon used on many American fighter planes.

M61(j): Machine pistol. Yugoslav make.

M662: A red flare for signaling.

M-86: Pursuit Deterrent Munitions. Various types of mines, grenades, trip-wire explosives, and other devices in anti-personnel use.

M-203: A 40mm grenade launcher fitted under an M-16 or the M-4A1 Commando. Can fire a variety of grenade types up to 200 yards.

MagSafe: Lethal ammunition that fragments in human body and does not exit. Favored by some police units to cut down on second kill from regular ammunition exiting a body.

Make a Peek: A quick look, usually out of the water, to check your position or tactical situation.

Mark 23 Mod O: Special operations offensive handgun system. Double-action, 12-round magazine. Ambidextrous safety and mag-release catches. Knight screw-on suppressor. Snap-on laser for sighting. .45-caliber. Weighs 4 pounds loaded. 9.5 inches long; with silencer, 16.5 inches long.

Mark II Knife: Navy-issue combat knife.

Mark VIII SDV: Swimmer Delivery Vehicle. A bus,

SEAL talk. 21 feet long, beam and draft 4 feet, 6 knots for 6 hours.

Master-at-Arms: Military police commander on board a ship.

MAVRIC Lance: A nuclear alert for stolen nukes or radio-active goods.

MC-130 Combat Talon: A specially equipped Hercules for covert missions in enemy or unfriendly territory.

McMillan M87R: Bolt-action sniper rifle. .50-caliber. 53 inches long. Bipod, fixed 5- or 10-round magazine. Bulbous muzzle brake on end of barrel. Deadly up to a mile. All types .50-caliber ammo.

MGS: Modified Grooming Standards. So SEALs don't all look like military, to enable them to do undercover work in mufti.

MH-53J: Chopper, updated CH053 from Nam days. 200 mph, called the Pave Low III.

MH-60K Black Hawk: Navy chopper. Forward infrared system for low-level night flight. Radar for terra follow/avoidance. Crew of 3, takes 12 troops. Top speed 225 mph. Ceiling 4,000 feet. Range radius 230 miles. Arms: two 12.7mm machine guns.

MI-15: British domestic intelligence agency.

MI-16: British foreign intelligence and espionage.

MIDEASTFOR: Middle East Force.

MiG: Russian-built fighter, many versions, used in many nations around the world.

Mike Boat: Liberty boat off a large ship.

Mike-Mike: Short for mm, millimeter, as 9 mike-mike.

Milstar: Communications satellite for pickup and bouncing from SATCOM and other radio transmitters. Used by SEALs.

Minigun: In choppers. Can fire 2,000 rounds per minute. Gatling gun-type.

Mitrajez M80: Machine gun from Yugoslavia.

MLR: The Main Line of Resistance. That imaginary line

in a battle where two forces face each other. Sometimes there are only a few yards or a few miles between them. Usually heavily fortified and manned.

Mocha: Food energy bar SEALs carry in vest pockets.

Mossberg: Pump-action, pistol-grip, 5-round magazine. SEALs use it for close-in work.

Motorola Radio: Personal radio, short range, lip mike, earpiece, belt pack.

MRE: Meals Ready to Eat. Field rations used by most of U.S. Armed Forces and the SEALs as well. Long-lasting.

MSPF: Maritime Special Purpose Force.

Mugger: MUGR, Miniature Underwater Global locator device. Sends up antenna for pickup on positioning satellites. Works under water or above. Gives location within 10 feet.

Mujahideen: A soldier of Allah in Muslim nations.

NAVAIR: NAVy AIR command.

NAVSPECWARGRUP-ONE: Naval Special Warfare Group One based on Coronado, CA. SEALs are in this command.

NAVSPECWARGRUP-TWO: Naval Special Warfare Group Two based at Little Creek, VA.

NCIS: Naval Criminal Investigative Service. A civilian operation not reporting to any Navy authority to make it more responsible and responsive. Replaces the old NIS, Naval Investigation Service, that did report to the closest admiral.

NEST: Nuclear Energy Search Team. Non-military unit that reports at once to any spill, problem, or Broken Arrow to determine the extent of the radiation problem.

NEWBIE: A new man, officer, or commander of an established military unit.

NKSF: North Korean Special Forces.

NLA: Iranian National Liberation Army. About 4,500 men in South Iraq, helped by Iraq for possible use against Iran.

Nomex: The type of material used for flight suits and hoods.

NPIC: National Photographic Interpretation Center in D.C.

NRO: National Reconnaissance Office. To run and coordinate satellite development and operations for the intelligence community.

NSA: National Security Agency.

NSC: National Security Council. Meets in Situation Room, support facility in the Executive Office Building in D.C. Main security group in the nation.

NSVHURAWN: Iranian Marines.

NUCFLASH: An alert for any nuclear problem.

NVG One Eye: Litton single-eyepiece Night-Vision Goggles. Prevents NVG blindness in both eyes if a flare goes off.

NVGs: Night-Vision Goggles. One eye or two. Give good night vision in the dark with a greenish view.

OAS: Obstacle Avoidance Sonar. Used on many low-flying attack aircraft.

OD: Officer of the Day.

OIC: Officer In Charge.

Oil Tanker: One is: 885 feet long, 140 foot beam, 121,000 tons, 13 cargo tanks that hold 35.8 million gallons of fuel, oil, or gas. 24 in the crew. This is a regular-sized tanker. Not a supertanker.

OOD: Officer Of the Deck.

OP: Outpost. A spot near the front of friendly lines or even beyond them where a man or a unit watch the enemy's movements. Can be manned by an FO from artillery.

Orion P-3: Navy's long-range patrol and antisub aircraft. Some adapted to ELINT roles. Crew of 10. Max speed loaded 473 mph. Ceiling 28,300 feet. Arms: internal weapons bay and 10 external weapons stations for a mix of torpedoes, mines, rockets, and bombs.

Passive Sonar: Listening for engine noise of a ship or sub. It doesn't give away the hunter's presence as an active sonar would.

Pave Low III: A Navy chopper.

PBR: Patrol Boat River. U.S. has many shapes, sizes, and with various types of armament.

PC-170: Patrol Coastal-Class 170-foot SEAL delivery vehicle. Powered by four 3,350 hp diesel engines, beam of 25 feet and draft of 7.8 feet. Top speed 35 knots, range 2,000 nautical miles. Fixed swimmer platform on stern. Crew of 4 officers and 24 EM, carries 8 SEALs.

PD: Point of Departure. A given position on the ground from which a unit or patrol leaves for its mission.

Plank Owners: Original men in the start-up of a new military unit.

Polycarbonate material: Bullet-proof glass.

PRF: People's Revolutionary Front. Fictional group in *NUCFLASH,* a SEAL Team Seven book.

Prowl & Growl: SEAL talk for moving into a combat mission.

Quitting Bell: In BUD/S training. Ring it and you quit the SEAL unit. Helmets of men who quit the class are lined up below the bell in Coronado. (Recently they have stopped ringing the bell. Dropouts simply place their helmet below the bell and go.)

RAF: Red Army Faction. A once-powerful German terrorist group, not so active now.

Remington 200: Sniper rifle. Not used by SEALs now.

Remington 700: Sniper rifle with Starlight Scope. Can extend night vision to 400 meters.

RIB: Rigid Inflatable Boat. 3 sizes, one 10 meters, 40 knots.

Ring Knocker: An Annapolis graduate with the ring.

RIO: Radar Intercept Officer. The officer who sits in the backseat of an F-14 Tomcat off a carrier. The job: find enemy targets in the air and on the sea.

Roger That: A yes, an affirmative, a go answer to a command or statement.

RPG: Rocket Propelled Grenade. Quick and easy, shoulder-fired. Favorite weapon of terrorists, insurgents.

S & R: Search and Rescue. Usually a helicopter.

SAS: British Special Air Service. Commandos. Special warfare men. Best that Britain has. Works with SEALs.

SATCOM: Satellite-based communications system for instant contact with anyone anywhere in the world. SEALs rely on it.

SAW: Squad's Automatic Weapon. Usually a machine gun or automatic rifle.

SBS: Special Boat Squadron. On-site Navy unit that transports SEALs to many of their missions. Located across the street from the SEALs' Coronado, California, head-quarters.

SD3: Sound-suppression system on the H & K MP5 weapon.

SDV: Swimmer Delivery Vehicle. SEALs use a variety of them.

Seahawk SH-60: Navy chopper for ASW and SAR. Top speed 180 knots, ceiling 13,800 feet, range 503 miles, arms: 2 Mark 46 torpedoes.

SEAL Headgear: Boonie hat, wool balaclava, green scarf, watch cap, bandanna roll.

Second in Command: Also 2IC for short in SEAL talk.

SERE: Survival, Evasion, Resistance, and Escape training.

Shipped for Six: Enlisted for six more years in the Navy.

Shit City: Coronado SEALs' name for Norfolk.

Show Colors: In combat put U.S. flag or other identification on back for easy identification by friendly air or ground units.

Sierra Charlie: SEAL talk for everything on schedule.

Simunition: Canadian product for training that uses paint balls instead of lead for bullets.

Sixteen-Man Platoon: Basic SEAL combat force. Up from 14 men a few years ago.

Sked: SEAL talk for schedule.

Sonobuoy: Small underwater device that detects sounds and transmits them by radio to plane or ship.

●

Space Blanket: Green foil blanket to keep troops warm. Vacuum-packed and folded to a cigarette-sized package.

SPIE: Special Purpose Insertion and Extraction rig. Essentially a long rope dangled from a chopper with hardware on it that is attached to each SEAL's chest right on his lift harness. Set up to lift six or eight men out of harm's way quickly by a chopper.

Sprayers and Prayers: Not the SEAL way. These men spray bullets all over the place hoping for hits. SEALs do more aimed firing for sure kills.

SS-19: Russian ICBM missile.

STABO: Use harness and lines under chopper to get down to the ground.

STAR: Surface To Air Recovery operation.

Starflash Round: Shotgun round that shoots out sparkling fireballs that ricochet wildly around a room, confusing and terrifying the occupants. Non-lethal.

Stasi: Old-time East German secret police.

Stick: British terminology: 2 4-man SAS teams.

Stokes: A kind of navy stretcher. Open coffin shaped of wire mesh and white canvas for emergency patient transport.

STOL: Short TakeOff and Landing. Aircraft with high-lift wings and vectored-thrust engines to produce extremely short takeoffs and landings.

Sub Gun: Submachine gun, often the suppressed H & K MP5.

Suits: Civilians, usually government officials wearing suits.

Sweat: The more SEALs sweat in peacetime, the less they bleed in war.

Sykes-Fairbairn: A commando fighting knife.

Syrette: Small syringe for field administration often filled with morphine. Can be self-administered.

Tango: SEAL talk for a terrorist.

TDY: Temporary duty assigned outside of normal job designation.

Terr: Another term for terrorist. Shorthand SEAL talk.

Tetrahedral reflectors: Show up on multi-mode radar like tiny suns.

Thermal Imager: Device to detect warmth, as a human body, at night or through light cover.

Thermal Tape: ID for night-vision-goggle user to see. Used on friendlies.

TNAZ: Trinittroaze Tidine. Explosive to replace C-4. 15% stronger than C-4 and 20% lighter.

TO&E: Table showing organization and equipment of a military unit.

Top SEAL Tribute: "You sweet motherfucker, don't you never die!"

Trailing Array: A group of antennas for sonar pickup trailed out of a submarine.

Train: For contact in smoke, no light, fog, etc. Men directly behind each other. Right hand on weapon, left hand on shoulder of man ahead. Squeeze shoulder to signal.

Trident: SEALs' emblem. An eagle with talons clutching a Revolutionary War pistol, and Neptune's trident super-imposed on the Navy's traditional anchor.

TRW: A camera's digital record that is sent by SATCOM.

TT33: Tokarev, a Russian pistol.

UAZ: A Soviet 1-ton truck.

UBA Mark XV: Underwater life support with computer to regulate the rebreather's gas mixture.

UGS: Unmanned Ground Sensors. Can be used to explode booby traps and claymore mines.

UNODIR: Unless otherwise directed. The unit will start the operation unless they are told not to.

VBSS: Orders to "visit, board, search, and seize."

Wadi: A gully or ravine, usually in a desert.

White Shirt: Man responsible for safety on carrier deck as he leads around civilians and personnel unfamiliar with the flight deck.

WIA: Wounded In Action.

WP: White Phosphorus. Can be in a grenade, 40MM round or in a 20MM round. Used as smoke and to start fires.

Zodiac: Also called an IBS, Inflatable Boat Small. 15×6 feet, weighs 265 pounds. The "rubber duck" can carry 8 fully equipped SEALs. Can do 18 knots with a range of 65 nautical miles.

Zulu: Means Greenwich Mean Time, GMT. Used in all formal military communications.

The SIXTH FLEET series
by David E. Meadows

★★★★★

The Sixth Fleet
0–425–18009–3

The Sixth Fleet #2: Seawolf
0–425–17249–X

The Sixth Fleet #3: Tomcat
0–425–18379–3

The Sixth Fleet #4: Cobra
0–425–18518–4

★★★★★

**Available wherever books are sold or at
www.penguin.com**

From the author of
Marine Sniper
CHARLES HENDERSON

The Marine Sniper's true Vietnam story continues in

SILENT WARRIOR
Available in paperback
from Berkley
0-425-18864-7

And don't miss Henderson's
GOODNIGHT SAIGON
The story of the fall of South Vietnam
and the evacuation of the last American Marines
from that country.

0-425-18846-9

DAVID ALEXANDER

MARINE FORCE ONE

*A special detachment of the Marine Corps whose prowess
in combat and specialized training sets
them apart from the average grunt. They charge where
others retreat, and succeed where others fail.
They are the best America's got.*

MARINE FORCE ONE
0-425-18152-9

As tensions continue to build between North and South Korea,
Marine Force One is sent on a recon mission that reveals North
Korea's plans to use chemical weapons against the south. But before
they can report to H.Q., they are ambushed and overwhelmed by a
relentless pursuit force.

MARINE FORCE ONE: STRIKE VECTOR
0-425-18307-6

In the deserts of Iraq, there's trouble under the blistering sun. Using
an overland black-market route that stretches from Germany to Iraq,
extremist forces have gathered materials to create a new weapon of
devastation. It's a hybrid nuclear warhead that needs no
missile—it can be fired from artillery. And it could cast a
radioactive cloud over the entire Middle East.

MARINE FORCE ONE: RECON BY FIRE
0-425-18504-4

To find the leaders of a terrorist organization, Marine Force One
heads to Yemen—but the terrorists have kidnapped an
American Air Force Officer—and getting close to
them puts his life in danger.

**Available wherever books are sold or at
www.penguin.com**